Prais

Inte face

also by Neal Stephenson and J. Frederick George

"A *Manchurian Candidate* for the computer age."
—*Seattle Weekly*

"Qualifies as the sleeper of the year, the rare kind of science-fiction thriller that evokes genuine laughter while simultaneously keeping the level of suspense cranked to the max."
—*San Diego Tribune*

"Complex, entertaining, frequently funny."
—*Publishers Weekly*

Now available wherever Bantam Books are sold.

Also by Neal Stephenson and J. Frederick George

INTERFACE

The Cobweb

Neal Stephenson and

J. Frederick George

BANTAM BOOKS

THE COBWEB
A Bantam Book

PUBLISHING HISTORY
Previously published under the pseudonym "Stephen Bury"
Bantam trade paperback edition published September 1996
Bantam mass market edition / September 1997
Bantam Spectra edition / June 2005

Published by
Bantam Dell
A Division of Random House, Inc.
New York, New York

Map design by Jeffrey L. Ward
Cover illustration © 2004 by Bruce Jensen
Cover design by Jamie S. Warren Youll

Book design by Carol Malcolm Russo

Library of Congress Catalog Card Number: 95-53187

ISBN 0-553-38344-2

Printed in the United States of America
Published simultaneously in Canada

www.bantamdell.com

BVG 10 9 8 7 6 5 4

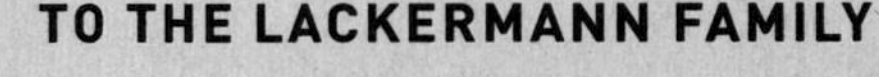

TO THE LACKERMANN FAMILY

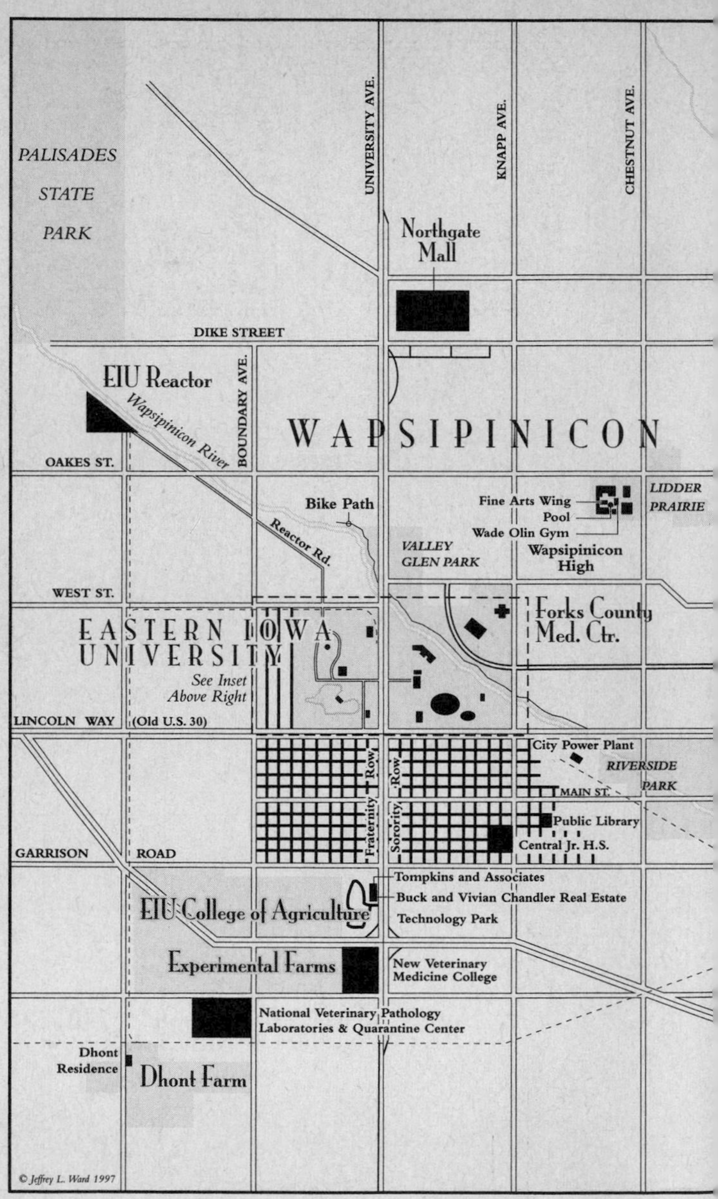
PALISADES
STATE
PARK
UNIVERSITY AVE.
KNAPP AVE.
CHESTNUT AVE.
Northgate
Mall
DIKE STREET
EIU Reactor
Wapsipinicon River
BOUNDARY AVE.
WAPSIPINICON
OAKES ST.
LIDDER
PRAIRIE
Fine Arts Wing
Pool
Wade Olin Gym
Wapsipinicon
High
Bike Path
Reactor Rd.
VALLEY
GLEN PARK
WEST ST.
Forks County
Med. Ctr.
EASTERN IOWA
UNIVERSITY
See Inset
Above Right
LINCOLN WAY
(Old U.S. 30)
City Power Plant
RIVERSIDE
PARK
MAIN ST.
Fraternity Row
Sorority Row
Public Library
Central Jr. H.S.
GARRISON
ROAD
Tompkins and Associates
Buck and Vivian Chandler Real Estate
Technology Park
EIU College of Agriculture
Experimental Farms
New Veterinary
Medicine College
National Veterinary Pathology
Laboratories & Quarantine Center
Dhont
Residence
Dhont Farm
© Jeffrey L. Ward 1997

WACKY WATERS
LAKE PLA-MOR
PHYSICAL PLANT
BELL TOWER
LIBRARY
PRESIDENT'S HOUSE
UNION
LINCOLN WAY (Old U.S. 30)
ST. JOSEPH'S HOSPITAL
Bike Path
SCHEIDELMANN AGRISCIENCE CTR.
METHODIST HOSPITAL
OLD GYM
NEW GYM
Playing Fields
Wapsipinicon River
VALLEY GLEN PARK
Indoor Practice Fac.
TWISTER STADIUM
Practice Fields
AUDITORIUM
COLISEUM
Riverview Heights
NISHNABOTNA BIBLE COLLEGE
BLUFF AVE.
IOWA RIVER
MATHESON AVE.
PECK DR.
N. 20TH ST.
SPEEDWAY RD.
NISHNABOTNA
RIVER ST.
J.H.S.
N. 10TH ST.
Lukas Meats
University Heights
Nishnabotna Police
PARK AVE.
DENVER-PLATTE-DES MOINES LINE NISHNABOTNA RAILWAY
Forks County Courthouse
City Hall
MATHESON WORKS
Albertson's
LINCOLN WAY
Nishnabotna Meat
Knightlys
RED OAK PARK
Clyde's New Apt. Bldg.
Nishnabotna High
Old Warehouse
S. 10TH ST.
Fort Stapleton S.H.I.
CENTRAL AVE.
INDUSTRIAL AVE.
Byproducts Unlimited
S. 20th ST.
INTERSTATE 45
Iowa Air National Guard Base
MAIN TERMINAL
Matheson Hangar
Private hangars/ tie-downs
New U.S. 30 (Bypass)
IOWA RIVER
United Hangar

The Cobweb

Clyde was a quiet sort who spent a lot of time thinking about things. During this period he primarily thought about Desiree. He had not spent much time outside the upper Midwest and so had not graduated to more cosmic and general issues—for example, whether it was advisable to live in a part of the country so inimical to life that buildings only a few dozen feet apart had to be connected by expensive glass tunnels.

Clyde was not the only young man staring at Desiree, but he did have a more highly developed contemplative faculty than most of the others, and so he had come up with a rationalization for why Desiree and he were a natural match for each other: neither one of them was technically from Wapsipinicon. Clyde lived on the other side of the river, just outside Nishnabotna, and should have been going to the county high school, but his grandfather and guardian, Ebenezer, who had a thing about education, wouldn't hear of this and dug up a wad of money from one of his hundreds of tiny, secret, widely dispersed bank accounts, or perhaps just dug up some gold coins from one of his many secret, widely dispersed coffee cans, and actually paid tuition to send Clyde to school in Wapsipinicon.

Desiree's family lived several miles south of town, on a farm. The farm lay adjacent to a spur on the Denver–Platte–Des Moines Railway. This particular spur ran up into the middle of the Eastern Iowa University campus, taking coal to the university power plant. When Dan Dhont, Jr., the oldest Dhont boy, had reached junior high school, the Wapsipinicon City Council had voted to annex the first few miles of the railway spur. The Wapsipinicon town line now sported a long, needle-thin, Aleutian-like isthmus running straight out to the Dhont farm. Accordingly, Dan Dhont and all the other Dhonts matriculated and, more to the point, wrestled in Wapsipinicon.

So there was sort of a connection between Clyde and Desiree from the very beginning, or so Clyde had, by dint of lengthy contemplation, led himself to believe. He had not yet figured out a way to parlay this uncanny link into an actual conversation with the girl, but he was working on it. He had run through a number of options in his head, but all of them required ten or fifteen

one

MARCH 1990

CLYDE BANKS was standing in line, in the early stages of hypothermia, when he first saw his future wife, Desiree Dhont, wrestle. At the time, both of them were juniors at Wapsipinicon High School. Its Wade Olin gym, home of the Little Twisters, was named after the greatest wrestler in the history of the world—an alumnus. It was connected to the high school proper by a glass-walled breezeway, which enabled students to pass back and forth between academics and PE, even in the middle of winter, without getting lost in whiteouts.

On the night in question the Little Twisters were about to play a basketball game against their archrivals from just across the river: the Nishnabotna Injuns. The ticket line filled the breezeway and extended into the parking lot. The early arrivals' breath condensed on the insides of the glass walls, which became steamy in the middle and frosty around the edges. The steel framework of the breezeway was growing leaves of frost.

Clyde Banks was on the outside and Desiree Dhont was on the inside, which was typical of their lives at that point. He did not mind the cold, because this arrangement enabled him to stand and stare through the frosty windows at Desiree without her being aware of it.

minutes of preliminary explanation, and he did not think this was the best way to get started.

Equally absorbed in the charms of Desiree Dhont was a Nishnabotna boy standing just behind her in line. Naturally, he was traveling with a whole group of other Nishnabotna boys. Just as naturally they egged him on, shouldering him forward playfully until he was almost rubbing up against her. After all, what was a Wapsipinicon/Nishnabotna athletic event without a few incidents of assault, battery, rape, and even attempted murder, perpetrated by Injuns against Little Twisters?

Finally the boy from Nishnabotna made the stupid but (to Clyde) wholly understandable mistake of reaching out and grabbing Desiree Dhont's left buttock.

Not in his worst nightmares did this boy imagine that Desiree might be in any way related to the Dhonts. There was no family resemblance. After bearing five consecutive male children, Mrs. Dhont had concluded, contrary to medical opinion, that she was biologically incapable of having little girls, so she and Dan, Sr., had gone out and adopted Desiree from somewhere. Then she had vindicated her decision, and flummoxed the doctors, by having another three boys.

Unlike the biological Dhonts, Desiree tanned. She tanned marvelously and perfectly. Her dark eyes were set at an outlandish and seductive angle, and her thick, glossy hair was perfectly black. So the boy from Nishnabotna could not have known he was in danger; this alluring creature was cut off from her natural ethnic group, whatever that might be, and he could have his way with her.

Everyone has a role in the cosmic story, no matter how small, dangerous, or humiliating. The roles picked out for boys from Nishnabotna tended to fit all three descriptions. This one's was to answer a question that had confounded the wisest gossips and blowhards of Wapsipinicon for at least a decade, to wit: Could Desiree Dhont wrestle?

Everyone knew that the living room of the Dhont house had a wrestling mat instead of a carpet. Everyone knew that there was another mat on the basement floor. The *Des Moines Register* had printed an aerial photo of the farmstead showing their outdoor mat in the side yard, next to a home-built weight-training set under the shade of the windbreak. Everyone knew that the Dhont boys learned how to wrestle before they learned how to walk, and that Darius Dhont, upon bursting from his mother's womb after forty-eight hours of furious labor, had gripped a nurse's lower lip in an illegal hold, his long newborn's fingernails darting four tiny crescent-shaped cuts into her mucous membranes before Dan, Sr., had spanked him loose, one, two, three, like a ref slapping a mat.

Smart money said no. The whole idea behind having Desiree was that Mrs. Dhont would have a more feminine presence around the house. Why go to all that trouble to import X chromosomes from Timbuktu and then have her rolling around the living room in bib overalls, body-slamming her muscular brothers? So Desiree had been raised to be markedly feminine in more than just her name. Clyde had attended the same junior high school as Desiree, and he could still remember sitting behind her in algebra, tracing the construction of her French braids—straight dark hair pulled in on itself, stretched to explosive tension like the strings of a piano—and getting woozy over the lace that draped around her tanned neck like a ring of Ivory soapsuds.

The mystery had deepened when they had matriculated at Wapsipinicon High School. In order to justify the expense of the indoor swimming facility, all students had to take swimming classes. The girls changed into stunning black spandex one-pieces, and all the boys were stripped down to black spandex trunks that didn't conceal things any more effectively than their own supply of pubic hair. They needed no encouragement to get into the water.

The girls' suits were cut deep in the back, and everyone knew that a fella could grasp the straps from behind and pull them apart and down and strip a girl naked to the waist like shucking an ear of corn. So all the girls pulled the laces out of their gym shoes and used them to tie the straps together between their shoulder blades. Clyde spent at least a night a week fantasizing about this unbearably erotic rite: all the girls in the locker room binding each other's straps together with dingy gray shoelaces, pulling those granny knots tight, locking their breasts away so that only the greenish water of the pool could touch them. It made the suits visually narrower, as seen from behind, which made the girls' shoulders look broader than they were.

Desiree Dhont was thus given away by her deltoids. By the end of her first swimming class everyone knew that Desiree had indeed been full-nelsoning her siblings since she had been in the cradle. They were not at all masculine, not unbecoming at all, and underneath them her armpits were as sheer and smooth as the backs of her knees. But unmistakably they were powerful and developed, death-dealing Dhont deltoids, fairer and sexier than any breast or buttock.

And on the night in question they were concealed beneath Desiree's fluffy down-filled ski jacket. The boy from Nishnabotna knew nothing of the deltoids. He only knew that Desiree was a relatively tall girl; but he was even taller, and he was a boy, and he was with his friends, tough Nishnabotna boys who worked throwing hay bales and pig corpses. He was safe. He reached out and grabbed her ass.

He blinked as Desiree's long black braid snapped across his face, whipped around by tremendous centrifugal force.

She was in violent motion; his hand was empty before the pleasing sensation had even traveled up his arm to his brain.

A moment later she was behind him and his arm had been wrenched up behind his back, bent like a hairpin. Desiree shoved him face first across the breezeway and gave his arm a final twist. He opened his mouth to holler.

The sound was muffled by a chunk of steel window frame that went directly against his tongue. The frame was not insulated. It was January. Desiree let him go but the window frame didn't. His tongue, and about fifty percent of his lips' surface area, remained flash-frozen in place, as if the window frame had been coated with Krazy Glue.

Her girlfriend held her place in line. Desiree returned, hitching her jeans back around.

"My name's Desiree," she said. Desiree had been in this country since the age of five weeks, but Clyde still imagined she spoke with a haughty crisp accent like the models in the *Sports Illustrated* swimsuit video.

"Aaah," the boy from Nishnabotna said, swiveling his eyes way around in their sockets.

"Desiree *Dhont*," she said.

"Aaaaaaaghhh!" the boy said, and began to struggle.

"Darius ain't here—*yet*. He's parking the truck."

Clyde decided not to stick around and watch the kid rip his own tongue off the window frame. He had a lot to think about now, and the Injuns–Little Twisters game was not the place to do it. Better, and much more his style, to walk around aimlessly in the blinding cold. What he had just witnessed was very important. He was going to have to do a lot of thinking about it.

He knew from that moment on that Desiree was the woman for him and that he was the man for Desiree and that one day they would get married and have a family. Actually getting introduced to her, getting her to fall in love with him, and all of that stuff were just details.

The details ended up taking about fourteen years to sort themselves out. Things got off to a false start the next year when Clyde seemed to spend about half his life wrestling Dick Dhont, younger brother of Darius. In any other municipality in the world Clyde would have been the champion of his weight class. In any other state he would have been state champion, and in any other country he would have had a fair shot at the Olympic team. At Wapsipinicon High he was a perpetual loser and object of merciless derision. The only way for him to move upward in life was to defeat Dick on the mat, which he tried to do once a week. On two occasions he actually won, only to be beaten by Dick the following week. Clyde and Dick got to know each other a lot more intimately than many married couples. Naturally he hoped that this would lead to a relationship with Desiree. It did; but the relationship was distant and platonic. Clyde was vindicated six years later when Dick won a gold medal at the Olympics, but this had done him no good during high school.

Desiree went off to nursing school. She was the only Dhont who could not obtain a full-ride wrestling scholarship to any school, and so she went the ROTC route instead. After she got her degree she spent four years in the Army, paying back her obligation, and then reupped for another couple of years. She married a guy she'd met in the Army and settled down in California. Two years later she divorced him and came back to Wapsipinicon.

Clyde worked construction for a couple of years, ostensibly to fund a future college education, but by the time he could afford it, he was no longer interested. He did not have any specific job ambitions that required a formal degree, and he had learned that he could read books in the EIU library for free and spend his money traveling.

He spent his tuition money riding a motorcycle around the United States and Canada and even did the wandering-around-Europe thing for a while. He came back to Wapsipinicon, goofed off for a year, got bored with that, and finally went to the Iowa Law Enforcement Academy in Des Moines. After he graduated, first in his class, he was able to obtain his current job as a deputy county sheriff in Forks County, which included both Wapsipinicon and Nishnabotna. Sooner or later he ran into Desiree. They discovered to their mutual surprise that they had a lot to talk about. They dated for a few months, rented a house in Wapsipinicon and moved in together, then got married a year later.

After a couple of years of relatively carefree fun, they decided to start a family. They made this decision in June of 1989. They knew other couples who had had trouble getting pregnant and who had spent years pursuing various therapies and adoption strategies, and so they felt that they should start trying as soon as possible. Desiree got pregnant within approximately forty-five minutes.

Not long afterward Clyde Banks began to think about career issues again. It was time to move up in the world or find another line of work. The only way to move up was to run for Forks County sheriff in the 1990 election. This would mean putting his boss, Kevin Mullowney, out of a job. Mullowney was a Democrat.

Clyde Banks had no choice but to grit his teeth and become a Republican. The Republican party was glad to have him, but there weren't many Republicans in the area, and the party did not have a lot of money.

So Clyde Banks had to do some serious thinking about inexpensive campaign strategies. He was thinking about them at six-thirty A.M. on the morning of March 1, 1990, as he stood in his kitchen, browning one pound of ground beef in a large black iron skillet. He had just come off the night shift and was still wearing his brown uniform. The walls were making a hissing, whining noise as hot water rushed through the pipes; Desiree was taking a shower. If he stepped away from the stove and got his head out of the column of grease vapor rising from the skillet, he could get a whiff of the peachy stuff she used on her hair.

On the counter next to the stove there was a big piece of white paper that had until recently been wrapped around the ground beef. It had MARCH 01 90 stamped on it in several places. Next to it was a stack of three other white paper bundles, each one of which contained a single sirloin steak and was also stamped MARCH 01 90.

The first thing that the Big Boss had done when she'd got out of bed that morning was gone to the freezer, which was stacked from the bottom to the top with bundles wrapped in white paper, and sifted through them until she had found the four items stamped with today's date. Clyde would never have even thought of doing this; none of their meat had expired in at least two months, and it was neither his habit nor Desiree's to go through the freezer memorizing all those little blue numbers. But Desiree, with her all-consuming Nesting Instinct, somehow knew, as if ghostly voices had been calling to her all night, that the spirit of the steer that had given up the ghost at Lukas Meats a year or so ago was haunting her to make sure he had not given up his shanks, loins, gams, or whatever, just so they could be thrown away. So now Clyde was browning this meat that had to be consumed before the stroke of midnight lest it turn green and purulent. The steaks were waiting on the counter. Desiree was going to drop them off at the neighbors' house on her way to work, shifting the moral burden onto their shoulders.

She came out of the shower with her hair wet, smelling of peaches and something sharper mixed in with it. She was wearing one of Clyde's bathrobes because none of hers would go around her big belly anymore, and even Clyde's had to be fixed with a safety pin in order to stay closed.

"You are an amazing creature," he said, turning to look at her, continuing to stir the meat with his other hand. The Big Boss just crossed her arms over her breasts, on top of her belly, and smiled at him.

"Remember we have class tonight," she said.

Clyde wanted to make a disparaging comment about the class, in which a nurse from Methodist Hospital, a woman with long gray hair parted in the middle, who lived with another woman and a lot of cats on a farm near Wapsipinicon, told Clyde and Desiree and a bunch of other couples how to breathe. Clyde had had a lot of confidence in Desiree's breathing skills to begin with, as she had been doing it for more than thirty years now without any significant interruption. But even his first gently snide comment on the breathing class, a couple of months ago, had led pretty quickly to tears on her part, reminding him the hard way that as soon as he and Desiree had decided to get pregnant, they had entered into an area of incredible tenderness where he was poorly equipped to do or say anything without causing lots of emotional damage. So now he just followed the Big Boss around with his hands down at his sides, taking small steps, not saying much, and it seemed to work pretty well.

"I'll be back for it," he said.

"You gonna start today?" Desiree said.

He hesitated for a second and then said, "Yup," which, now that he had said the word to his wife, meant that he was committed for good. Clyde Banks was running for sheriff.

two

JAMES GABOR Millikan woke up every morning at six and did not move a muscle of his body thereafter for fifteen minutes. He always found the transition from the unconsciousness of sleep to the exquisitely controlled existence of his waking life to be frightening. He lay rigid, eyes open, as he ran through the checklists of his life with the same thoroughness as a pilot preparing a 747 for a transpacific flight.

And he would not think the comparison inapt. As the pilot did not want to crash and burn in midocean for lack of preparation, so too did Millikan not want to make the slightest misstatement or give the world any chance to make a misreading of him, and thereby of the United States of America. Only when he had assured himself of the status of the multiple compartments of his life did he begin to emerge from the protective cocoon of his eiderdown.

He stepped into his English slippers, which he had carefully arranged by the side of his bed the previous evening, and put on his robe over his striped pajamas. His home was on Wisconsin Avenue in Washington, D.C., right across from the National Cathedral, but this morning he happened to be in Paris, in the Hotel Inter-Continental. Nevertheless, his slippers and robe were exactly where they would have been at home. He had bathed and shaved the previous evening. He applied some Brylcreem to his thinning hair and took a swipe with his electric razor at the glittery silver stubble that had dared to emerge since midnight.

He devoted three quarters of an hour to reading several documents from his briefcase, most of them terse cables originating from major cities in the Middle East.

He went back to the suite's bedchamber and applied his cologne and deodorant, specially mixed at Whitsons on the High in Oxford. He opened the armoire. On the top shelf there were the ten folded and starched French-cuffed white shirts that were always at the ready. On the next shelf were the ten pairs of black silk stockings, the ten pairs of pressed and starched boxer shorts, the ten undershirts, and the ten starched linen handkerchiefs. On the next shelf were the three pairs of matching black wing tips that he alternated from day to day. He had five dark-charcoal pinstripe suits from Mallory's on Savile Row hanging up, which he wore in sequence, one of them always out at the dry cleaner's. He had five silk Hermès ties comfortably nesting in their rack.

He dressed in a determined and efficient manner, put on his tie, his fleur-de-lis cuff links (he was, after all, in France), his Duckers Wing tips, handmade at the shop on the Turl in Oxford, looked at himself in the full-length mirror on the inside of the door of the armoire, pulled his cashmere coat from its hanger.

Then he went down to the front desk, nodded to the doorman, and stepped out into the streets of his favorite city. He stopped on the sidewalk and breathed the cool, fragrant air of early spring—the cherry trees and early rhododendrons were peaking. He looked down the Rue Castiglione at the pink-tinted clouds over the Tuileries. He turned left and strolled to the Rue St. Honoré; the breeze shifted as he came to the corner, and he smelled roasting coffee and baking bread. He stopped at his favorite corner café, stood next to a blue-uniformed sanitation man, drank a café noir, and ate a croissant.

He walked onward, stepping carefully through the random pattern of dog shit, noting that thanks to Georges Haussmann, the gutters of Paris were always cleaner than the sidewalks. He walked with some care and looked at the windows of the boutiques that catered to capitalism's winners and their significant others: Gucci, Salavin Chocolatier, Guerlain, Bulgari, and Fayer.

He especially loved Paris early in the day, when it was still quiet, and while the city of Washington was still asleep, and (except for the nocturnal gnomes at the Agency) incapable of pestering him. That would begin around midafternoon, too late to spoil his luncheon meeting. For the next few hours Millikan was more or less a free agent, and he was at the peak of his game: articulating the gross and crude impulses of the United States of America into a foreign policy toward the rest of the world. He, not Baker over at State, understood the United States of America and the world. He, James Gabor Millikan, was the one who was here, out in the field, preparing for a luncheon meeting with his old friend, Tariq Aziz, the foreign minister of Iraq. It had been scheduled as a dinner meeting, but Aziz had been mysteriously summoned back to Baghdad and had requested a lunch instead.

He looked in briefly at the Eglise Polonaise, crossing himself as he stepped inside, admiring the ecstatic baroque saints and wannabe saints on the walls. He moved on to the Rue Royale, paused for a moment to admire the neoclassical elegance of the Madeleine on the right, then took a left toward the Place de la Concorde. The hieroglyphs on the obelisk were uncommonly clear and crisp in the light of the rising sun, as if they had just been carved last night.

To the right was the American Embassy, housed in an eighteenth-century prerevolutionary building of magnificently useless elegance. He ignored the main entrance and proceeded to the back, where the Marine guards waved him through, past parked cars to an unmarked but well-guarded entrance that led to a small elevator. He rode it up to the fourth of five floors, where he was greeted by another Marine guard and the CIA duty officer, who were expecting him.

He was where the action was: the secure rooms. Nothing important happened elsewhere. All of the other folderol in the embassy was useless pretension. The duty officer punched him through a vault entrance set incongruously in an elaborate door frame. Through the heavy door he could hear a loud whooshing noise. When the duty officer opened it, the noise drowned out all other sound, like giant garage fans: not so much loud as it was full and all-encompassing.

They were looking at a room within a room: a glass box built on four bimetallic springs that isolated it from the rest of the building.

Millikan walked quickly across the few feet of empty space surrounding the glass room; supposedly it was jammed with electromagnetic radiation that would fry your kidneys, or something, if you lingered there. Then he was inside the glass box. His assistant, Richard Dellinger, was waiting for him as well as a file marked "Eyes Only." It contained the latest reports from Langley to prepare him for whatever Aziz might be up to. As usual there was nothing there that he didn't know. They weren't exactly sure why Aziz had been called back on such short notice, but it could very well be some internal nonsense that had nothing to do with the substance of the actual meeting, and so Millikan decided not to waste effort speculating.

At half-past noon he and Dellinger went downstairs and proceeded to the Hotel Crillon, next door to the embassy. Huge flowing taffeta curtains complemented the dark-red carpets and framed the high windows that afforded a view over the Place de la Concorde and across the Seine to the Assemblée Nationale. The dining room was full of rich Japanese tourists and Arabs. The maître d' rushed up, in a dignified way, to inform Millikan that Aziz had preceded him.

Millikan made a bemused face at Dellinger. "He *must* be in a hurry."

They followed the maître d' to a small private dining room off the corner of the restaurant, containing a single table set with crisp white linen tablecloths, silver settings, and a charming little bouquet of spring flowers in the center. An Arab man with a shock of graying hair, a little mustache, and heavy eyeglasses was rising to his feet to greet them.

Millikan had known Aziz since they had both been students in England, and he counted the man to be his intellectual and diplomatic equal. Even though he represented a single-resource, underdeveloped country led by a madman, Aziz matched Millikan in his ability to articulate the gross and crude impulses of Iraq into a foreign policy toward the rest of the world.

Millikan and Aziz belonged to that most elite club in the world, even more elite than the great intelligence establishments, the financial operations, and the political systems. There were a few, an extremely few, people in the world who by sheer dint of their intelligence and their sensitivities could overcome the limitations of national identity, the normal rewards system of politics, and, most of all, the stupidities of their own bureaucracies to navigate the path to world survival. Politicians, of necessity, were the great captains of the national vessels plying the difficult and anarchic seas of international relations. But they were blind without pilots like Millikan and Aziz, men who could see both the obvious reefs and rocks of disaster and who knew the treacherous sandbars and hidden structures of icebergs. They served their states, because only states had the resources to make use of their intelligence. But for these people of all-penetrating insight, there were no masters. They were a self-proclaimed, self-regulating corps of professionals, the last of the true diplomats, the last generation of a craft that had begun in Italy after the Peace of Lodi in 1454.

Millikan understood that now, in 1990, with the Soviet Union collapsing into itself, the Chinese Communist party making the improbable transition into the Chinese Chamber of Commerce, and even South Africa backing away from chaos, the United States had one enemy: Iran, and Iran's worldwide terrorist network. Aziz knew the same thing, for his country had spent most of the previous decade in a gargantuan struggle with the vastly stronger—in virtually all respects—Iranians. He knew that only a deftly manipulated program of assistance, led both openly and covertly by the Americans, had allowed Iraq to survive. And so the two men, great respecters of each other's skills, had the added advantage of being allies in all but name.

A slight young Iraqi man sat next to Aziz—his assistant, and Dellinger's counterpart. Another Iraqi, a dead ringer for the young Saddam Hussein, stood by the door, his jacket bulging conspicuously. Standing near the table was a middle-aged Frenchman, Gérard Touvain, the French Foreign Ministry liaison.

Aziz bounded out from behind the table and headed straight for Millikan. It was a deliberate breach of protocol, no doubt carefully planned by Aziz to look like a spontaneous gesture. Gérard Touvain tried halfheartedly to intercede and make the proper introductions. He would listen in, but for both Aziz and Millikan would be no more functional than the designs on the wallpaper, and less efficient than the listening devices both knew were implanted in the room.

Millikan shook Touvain's hand perfunctorily. "Dr. Millikan," Touvain said, "allow me to present His Excellency Tariq Aziz."

Millikan gave his best warm, two-handed grasp to his old colleague. *"Zdraustvui, tovarishch,"* Millikan said—the two had served in Moscow at the same time. *"Salut, mon vieux,"* Aziz responded, and the two sat down at the table. Touvain tried to make small talk, pointing out for whomever would listen the *"belle lumière"* of the hotel. The assistants were introduced, the Iraqi bodyguard was ignored, and Touvain, after a few minutes, was politely told to beat it.

On the small table was a tray laid to Millikan's specifications with a bottle of iced Stolichnaya, beluga caviar, and plates of black bread, butter, onions, chopped hard-boiled eggs. "I thought that you might have had too much champagne by this time, old friend," Millikan explained, knowing the contempt in which Aziz held the French for, among other things, their sheltering of the Ayatollah Khomeini in the1970s.

"You couldn't be more correct, Jim," Aziz responded.

Millikan hated to be called Jim, had got into fights as a child when somebody had called him Jim, but Aziz had called him Jim for the past twenty years, and he was not about to ask him to change.

"A toast," Millikan said when the shot glasses were filled with the vodka, syrupy in its subzero cold. "To diplomacy."

The four clinked their glasses and downed the Stoli in a single gulp. They carefully prepared, consumed, and savored their slices of black bread with butter, onions, pieces of egg, and caviar. Aziz then proposed a toast. "To us, Jim, and the continued cooperation of our countries."

A half hour later the caviar was gone, the vodka half-drained and forgotten. The assistants had gobbled some bread and butter and had taken out their notepads. Millikan and Aziz, as befit kings of diplomacy, began the third course, a refreshing light lemony soup to clear the palate of the excellent but intense steak tartare that had preceded it.

Aziz looked through the dishes and candlesticks and pointed

upward to the ceiling, noting that they would both proceed on the assumption that they were not the only people listening. "How goes your task in Washington, *mon collègue*?"

"Otlichno, moi drug." Excellently, my friend. "The President understands what has to be done. With the exception of a few of the usual firebrands in Congress there is no problem. The press still understands that Iran is our major problem, although you have to understand that your boss by his very nature appeals to the more sensational of our journalists. Private sector is on board in supporting our policy. What about in your shop?"

"We are very pleased with our cooperation with you—although you understand the need to replace both the men and matériel that we lost during the last war. We have had to make some creative use of some of your assistance. I'm sure you understand."

The two liked playing this game, knowing that as they spoke, their words were being reprocessed and sent to a dozen capitals. And they had said nothing that had not appeared in last week's *New York Times*. "Is there anything more to talk about before the next course?" Millikan asked.

"No," Aziz responded. "Let's let our friends enjoy some of this good food." The stewards reentered, brought in new plates, and began the next course, a simple, hearty *saumon grillée.*

They ate well and drank better, the two old friends who knew that their performance was being observed by a surveillance camera peering out between the louvers of the ventilation grille in the wall. No papers would be slipped across the table, nothing untoward would happen, except to live well, eat well, and have a good time—a diplomatic good time.

"I have to take a piss," Aziz suddenly announced in a loud voice.

"Moi aussi," Millikan responded. "I'll go with you." The steward led them across the main dining room, down a corridor, and around a few corners to the WC, accompanied the whole way by the bodyguard, who went in first and spent a couple of minutes checking under the fixtures for bombs.

They went in, Aziz to a urinal, and Millikan to a stall—Millikan apologizing for his shy kidneys—and they loudly peed.

Millikan began to chuckle naughtily, as though the vodka had made him regress back to a rowdy college boy.

"What is it?" Aziz said loudly.

"You must come and see what is written on the wall here, it's quite amusing," Millikan said.

Aziz zipped up and went into the stall, squeezing in next to Millikan, who was standing there holding up a piece of crinkly French toilet paper on which he had written something with a water-soluble felt-tip pen. Aziz took it and read it.

It said: *Are you going to fuck me over Kuwait?*

Aziz shook his head emphatically *no*. Millikan exhaled and seemed to relax. He took the paper back, tore it up, and flushed it. Aziz said, "I want to write down that telephone number, it might be useful sometime for some of my Iranian colleagues."

They went back to the table where their assistants were becoming quite relaxed—the vodka had given way to wine. A dessert tray came and went, accompanied by coffee and tea and then cigars. By this point it was three-thirty in the Hotel Crillon.

"You'd best make sure our car is here," Aziz said to his assistant, and then, turning to Millikan, "Please send my most sincere regards and admiration to your President."

"And the same to your leader, my friend." The two shook hands heartily and emerged to be greeted by Touvain, who had been lingering at a nearby table with cigarettes, coffee, and an existential novel. The Iraqi assistant could scarcely walk. Dellinger threw himself down onto a sofa in the hotel lobby and closed his eyes. Millikan walked Aziz outside, where he was picked up in an Iraqi stretch Mercedes, the heaviest passenger vehicle Millikan had ever seen on the streets of Paris.

The limousine door had scarcely been shut behind Aziz before he was on the cell phone to someone. Millikan, meanwhile, was already composing the cable to the President in his head. He wasn't sure what it would say in every detail but, based on what

Aziz had told him in the stall, knew it would include his favorite phrase: *All is in order.*

It was fifty-eight degrees in Paris, and the spring flowers were in bloom. Dellinger was there suddenly, showing no signs of intoxication. "A walk would be nice," Millikan said.

Dellinger nodded significantly in the direction of the embassy.

Millikan raised his eyebrows. "No walk?"

Dellinger shrugged.

Five minutes later they were back in the secure room.

"What is it?" Millikan began.

"It's probably nothing, sir."

"Now, there is very little you can tell me that is going to disturb me. Aziz has confirmed that we have nothing to fear in Kuwait. He has confirmed that they are rearming to attack Iran again. My God, what would they have to gain in going into Kuwait? More oil? So what is it?"

"Well, sir, the Agency was giving a briefing on Iraq to our agriculture attaché to Baghdad, who was back in Washington for a couple of days. Nothing out of the ordinary—just a few analysts sitting around with the attaché sharing some of their recent findings with him."

"So?"

"Well, sir, it seems that one of the analysts at the Agency told the attaché that the Iraqis are misusing the three-hundred-million-dollar Food for Peace funds to—in her opinion—buy or develop weapons."

"What!" Millikan could hardly believe his ears; it had to be a mistake. "What was a military analyst doing in a briefing with an ag attaché?"

Dellinger looked stricken. "It wasn't a military analyst," he said. "It was an ag analyst."

Millikan was still too thunderstruck to become enraged. "You're telling me that some aggie took it upon himself, *first* of all, to stray into military affairs, and *then* to offer his own personal opinions about Saddam's military policies to one of our diplomats?"

"Her opinions. The analyst in question is female."

Millikan took a few deep breaths. "Pray continue," he said.

"Well, when this attaché got back to Baghdad, he told the deputy chief of mission, who told the ambassador, who told Baker, who told the President."

"Oh, Jesus Christ!" Millikan said, and slapped the table so hard it sounded like a gunshot.

"While you were in the bathroom with Aziz, I was called to the phone and given a heads up. I don't think it's important. But I thought I would pass it on to you."

That this had happened at the end of a nearly perfect day made Millikan want to scream. But he didn't scream. In his dreams, before six o'clock in the morning, he was allowed to scream. After six o'clock in the morning, he didn't scream.

But he was allowed to get pissed off. "You don't think it's important. The President has heard about it, Aziz probably rushed back to Baghdad because of it, but you don't think it's important. Goddamn it! Don't those assholes know that we're making foreign policy here? Can't I have a single meeting with my colleague without having it ruined by the inexcusable behavior of some silly bitch of an analyst?"

Richard Dellinger was not about to point out how the U.S. government worked at a time like this. He merely said, "I don't know, sir."

"We are not going to lose our Middle-Eastern policy because some bottom-fish bean counter can't keep her mouth shut. Tell the pilot to get the plane ready. We're going back ahead of schedule."

three

A STRIP mall south of Wapsipinicon was home to the real-estate offices of Buck and Grace Chandler, who had acted as Clyde's brokers on his recent purchase of an apartment building in Nishnabotna. On his visits to that office he had frequently passed the door of an even smaller and less expensive office that had been leased by Dr. Jerry Tompkins, late of the Eastern Iowa University Political Science Department (he had been denied tenure), and currently the principal of Tompkins and Associates Pollsters and Consultants.

The "Associates" were his wife and his mother. The latter, a plump woman in a Sunday dress, perched like a flagpole sitter on a small armless swivel chair in the front room, gazing fixedly at the silent telephone with its intimidating row of buttons. The former, an angular creature in a lavender jogging suit, was folded into a corner of the room with her sharp nose bent so close to the screen of a Macintosh that her waxy flesh was suffused with its cadaverous glow. The screen was covered with a grid of boxes with numbers in them. Mrs. Tompkins was pawing fretfully at the tabletop with her right hand, which, as Clyde realized, concealed one of those computer mouses. She was talking to herself quietly.

Dr. Tompkins came out from the back as if he had been quite busy and had forgotten all about Clyde's free appointment. He was a rangy fellow with a sparse beard, dressed in a limp three-piece suit and rimless glasses with large, panoramic lenses. The one free no-strings-attached consultation lasted fifteen minutes and mostly consisted of Dr. Tompkins telling Clyde that he didn't have a persona, and that, if he was going to be a public figure, he needed to get started on building one as soon as possible—a daunting task that would be infinitely easier if Dr. Jerry Tompkins was on hand to manage it. There was no small talk, fetching of coffee, or other preparatory formalities. It struck Clyde as a chilly way of doing business, at least by Nishnabotna standards; but perhaps here in Wapsipinicon people did not have so much time to burn on such unproductive activities as shooting the breeze—especially people with Ph.D.'s and computers. Clyde came away from his free consultation with nothing but a feeling of personal inadequacy and a perverse desire to return to Tompkins and Associates as a paying customer.

He had gone in there only because Terry Stonefield, chairman of the Forks County Republican party, had intimated to him that there would be a campaign budget. But a few days later Terry

Stonefield convened, on short notice, the County GOP Strategy Session '90, wherein Clyde, the other Republican candidates, Terry Stonefield, and a few other important Forks Republicans sat around a conference table at one of Terry's offices for a few hours drinking coffee and mostly agreeing with whatever Terry said. Clyde, who was not accustomed to meetings, was slow to get the gist of the proceedings, but eventually he divined that, in the view of Terry and the other Republicans, the County Commissioner's race was where the smart money was. They built the roads and bridges, assessed tax rates, and were, in general, where the governmental rubber hit the road.

Once this decision was made, an awkward silence ensued in which Clyde Banks and Barnabas Klopf, M.D., the incumbent candidate for county coroner, were the focus of much awkward, furtive scrutiny.

"You see, Clyde and Barney," Terry finally said, "politics looks different when you're on the inside. Politics is like a car. When you're on the outside, all you see is this big metal boxy thing with windows and tires and lights, windshield wipers and door handles and such—anyway, the point is that it goes and you don't understand why. But if you're a mechanic, if you're on the inside, you see the little . . . thingies and crank rods . . ."

"Lifters," Clyde mumbled.

Terry lunged at the offering like a drowning man going after a rope. "Yes. The lifters. You see my point, Clyde. When you see it on the inside, you know how to soup it up. How to hot-rod the car. And let me tell you that the way to make the car that is the Forks County GOP really get out there and lay a patch is to concentrate on that County Commissioner's race. Because I think we'd all agree"—Terry paused and looked meaningfully around the table, gathering consensus before he had even made his point—"that those darn Commissioners have coattails a hundred miles long."

"So it's coattails, then," Clyde said after a long silence.

"Clyde, you're going to make a fine mechanic," Terry said.

The upshot was that Clyde's budget was mostly transferred to the County Commissioner's race, leaving Clyde without the wisdom of Dr. Jerry Tompkins except for the vaguely remembered, complimentary admonition that he must develop a persona and become a public figure. As a sort of consolation prize, Terry Stonefield gave Clyde the phone number of a company down in Arkansas called Razorback Media, which gave Clyde an astonishingly low price on bumper stickers, as long as he had them printed in white on University of Arkansas red.

Beyond the bumper stickers, all his politicking and persona building were going to have to be done on his own time. Which was how he hit upon his campaign strategy, which brought him to the office of the county surveyor.

"Very large."

Clyde could never remember the difference between large-scale maps and small-scale maps until he read *The Hound of the Baskervilles*. There is a scene early in *Hound* where Sherlock bursts in carrying a bunch of maps of Baskerville-land and Watson asks whether they are large-scale maps. Sherlock's mnemonic reply was tattooed on Clyde's brain like a subdural hematoma.

The sheriff's department had many maps of its assigned bailiwick tacked to the walls. When Clyde had asked his boss, County Sheriff Kevin Mullowney, where those maps had come from, Mullowney had tilted his head back to look at Clyde under the lenses of his tinted bifocals. This small adjustment enabled Mullowney to make believe that he was looking downward at Clyde from a greater altitude. In fact Clyde was taller than Mullowney; Clyde had wrestled at 192, and Mullowney was always around 167 or thereabouts. Among his many other personality disorders, Mullowney had the chip-on-his-shoulder attitude typical of a wrestler who believed that he could have attained greater glory if he had weighed a little more than he really did. Since graduating from high school three years ahead of Clyde, Mullowney had compensated for this by ballooning well past the 192 mark.

"Why would anyone want a map like that?" Mullowney had said. As far as Mullowney was concerned, these very large-scale maps were secret cop intelligence that should not be allowed to fall into the hands of ordinary citizens, or even mere deputies such as Clyde.

"Looking at some real estate," Clyde had said immediately and, he thought, convincingly.

So far his decision was a private thing, a thing that Clyde had done inside his own head, and he didn't want to reveal it to anyone just yet, least of all his opponent, who was also his boss. So he said he was looking at some real estate.

"How many of them things you own now?" Mullowney said, tilting his head down to a more normal position, relieving Clyde of his intense sheriff scrutiny.

"The house we live in. A lot down the street. And then two buildings with three units each." Clyde went out of his way to use the jargon adopted by Buck Chandler, his realtor, and refer to them as units rather than apartments. It would be certain to cow Mullowney.

"They making money for you?" Mullowney asked a little less loudly. He had decided that his deputy might just be a sophisticated investment savant. Everyone knew that Clyde had been pretty good in school and had been a little surprised when he had refrained from going to college; maybe, Mullowney was seeming to think, maybe Clyde was even smarter than people had thought.

"They ain't generating any cash flow, if that's what you mean," Clyde said. Use of the money term "cash flow" in these circumstances was guaranteed to keep Mullowney's brain reeling.

"Then what's the point of owning them?" Mullowney said.

"I'm buying them on fifteen-year mortgages," Clyde said, "so the payments are pretty high."

"Jeez. We got a thirty on our house."

"Anything more than fifteen, you end up spending too much on interest," Clyde said.

Mullowney was flummoxed. This was the first time it had ever occurred to him, or for that matter anyone in his vast extended family and circle of social contacts, that if you stuck with it long enough, it was actually possible to pay off a mortgage. For Mullowney making mortgage payments was kind of like putting money in the collection plate at church every Sunday: throwing money away for a payoff that would not materialize during your actual life span.

"That's real smart," Mullowney said. "Then what? You gonna retire?"

"Well," Clyde said, "I was talking to Desiree about it and decided that I didn't want to be still breaking up fights at the Barge On Inn when I was forty-five years old."

"Oh," Mullowney said. He sounded just a little bit surprised and almost hurt to think that a person might not be happy doing exactly that.

"Do you want large-scale maps or small-scale maps?" the secretary at the county surveyor's said. Her name was on a plaque: Marie O'Connor. Marie O'Connor was apparently secure in the belief that she was the only person in Nishnabotna County who knew which was which. But when Marie O'Connor asked him that question, Clyde just quoted his Sherlock.

"Very large," he said.

"Very large," she murmured, crestfallen.

Clyde was a very large fellow. Every two weeks he stood naked in the garage, bent over the unfolded want-ads section of the newspaper, and ran a Sears electric hair clipper with a quarter-inch comb over his head, then ran the howling orifice of his shop vac over his scalp and pranced into the bathroom for a shower. His astigmatism forced him to wear glasses with very thick lenses that made his eyes look very large. Right now he was off duty, and so he was wearing jeans and very large work boots and a flannel shirt with holes burned through it from a battery-acid mishap some years back; through the holes flashes of a T-shirt could be seen on which the logo of the Texas Longhorns had been printed upside down on top of the logo of a cheerleading camp in South Carolina—Clyde bought all of his T-shirts at the monthly seconds sale down at the T-shirt plant. Clyde was also wearing an old Gooch's Best seed-corn hat, which was on his head backward because the driver's-side window of his pickup had been punched out by a drunken nephew of Sheriff Mullowney, whom Clyde had then arrested; the resulting air blast coming into the cab when he drove fast would catch the bill of his cap and whip it off his head unless Clyde turned it around backward.

"I need something where I can see individual houses and lots," Clyde said.

"I'll need the section numbers," Marie O'Connor said.

"All of them," Clyde said. "I need the whole county."

Marie O'Connor was taken aback.

Clyde had not been planning to explain his plan, but as he now realized, this was counterproductive.

"See, I'm running for county sheriff," he said. "Between now and Election Day, I intend to knock on every door in Forks County."

"I thought Kevin Mullowney was running unopposed again," Marie O'Connor said.

"Well, I just announced it," Clyde said.

Actually he had just announced it that instant. This made him feel conspicuous and awkward—nothing new in and of itself. But he had just now recognized that if he could find out Marie O'Connor's address, he could go ahead and check her house off the map. One less door to knock on.

"What are your qualifications?" Marie O'Connor asked.

"First in my class at the Iowa Law Enforcement Academy. Graduate of Wapsipinicon High School, former wrestler and football player."

"What weight class?" Marie O'Connor said, ignoring all of the other qualifications.

"One ninety-two."

"Didn't you go to State?" she asked, squinting and cocking her head at him.

"Yes, ma'am. Three years in a row."

"How'd you do?"

"Sophomore year I took third in my weight class, junior and senior year I took second."

"That's right. You're the one who kept losing to Dick Dhont."

"Yes, ma'am," Clyde said, trying to gloss this over as fast

as possible. "I'm a graduate of Iowa State Law Enforcement Academy in Des Moines, and I have five years' experience as a deputy county sheriff."

"Well," Marie O'Connor said, "you're talking to the wrong person. Kevin Mullowney's second cousin is married to my daughter."

"Oh."

"Don't you have any campaign literature?"

"Not on my person."

"Any bumper stickers or shirts or hats or something?"

"Not yet. Actually, my campaign hasn't been officially launched yet."

"Well, you got your work cut out for you."

"Yes, ma'am."

"Let's see if we can't get you all set up with some maps," Marie O'Connor said in singsong tones. Clyde wondered, hardly for the last time, whether the strategy of knocking on doors was going to be a mistake.

four

A YOUNG woman was walking by herself along Clarendon Boulevard in Rosslyn, Virginia. She was about as tall as the average adult male, and, seen from a distance, might have been mistaken for one if she hadn't been wearing a skirt—her mother had always described her as "big-boned" or "sturdy" or some other euphemism, even during her teen years when her summer labors on the family potato farm had brought her body-fat percentage down to a level she'd never see again.

For five years she had been doing a job here that involved no physical exertion whatsoever and left no time for extracurricular workouts. So now an extra layer of chunkiness had been laid over that solid frame. She moved down the sidewalk in a peculiar wide-based, stomping gait, tottering from side to side with each stride, head high, back straight. Her chin-length hair swung back and forth, and her eyes, which had not taken well to contacts, met the world from behind thick lenses.

A cold and a warm front were fighting like Democrats and Republicans for control of the Potomac Valley, and the conflict generated enormous billowing clouds, electric royal-blue skies, thundershowers, and alternating gusts of warm spring and chill winter winds that came in off the river. But the winds flowed around Betsy as if she were cast in solid bronze, peeling the vent of her Wal-Mart trench coat open to expose the not very distinctive plaid of its lining, but not diverting Betsy by even one arc second from her straight course down the sidewalk.

As always, however, the higher centers of Betsy's brain were concentrated on her job. The only thing about the weather that Betsy bothered to take note of was the pollen. They hadn't had much pollen in Nampa. Being a farm girl, she knew what it was. But when she'd first come to D.C. and seen the yellow film covering everything in the month of April, she'd mistaken it for dust—until her immune system had reacted to it, in much the same way that a city girl would react to a live rat on her bathroom floor.

It was April now, and the motley collection of professionals' gleaming Acuras and illegal immigrants' shambling Gremlins parked along Clarendon Boulevard were covered with that yellow film again. It was stuck down with static electricity or something, and no wind could take it off. A few minutes ago a spattering of rain had swept in off the river, swirling the film into abstract patterns.

Suddenly Betsy's stomping gait faltered and slowed, and she came to a gradual stop, like a ship easing into a berth. She spread her broad shoulders and hunched over. She heaved two or three times, as if sobbing, and suddenly sneezed—not a polite "atchoo" but a thermonuclear explosion so powerful that she staggered in place, nearly losing her balance, and some loitering Hispanic men on the other side of the boulevard looked up alertly, ready for action. She reached into the pocket of her trench coat and found a Kleenex, which she used to clean up the aftermath. She stomped several paces down the street to an overflowing public wastebasket. She pushed its spring-loaded door open with the back of her hand, but as she was dropping in the soaked and ruined Kleenex, a McDonald's extra-large french-fries container tumbled out, pocked against the pavement, and began to roll along the sidewalk, driven by the wind like a tumbleweed.

"Sorry," Betsy said, and began to stomp after it, like a defensive lineman pursuing a puppy. She aimed several tremendous stomps at it as she made her way down the sidewalk, drawing amused and admiring stares from the young men across the street. Finally she flattened it, bent down, yanked it out from under her shoe, and carried it half a block to the next waste container.

A few miles down the road from there was the Pentagon, and among those military people you could find quite a few who were principled enough to chase other people's litter down the street during a windstorm. But this kind of thinking was not common in other parts of the capital, and certainly not where Betsy worked. Betsy hewed to it anyway, because she had the feeling that it was the only anchor she had, and that if she gave it up, she would be torn loose like a used Kleenex in a howling tunnel of wind and end up God only knew where.

She worked in the Rutherford T. Castleman Building, near the Courthouse Metro Station in downtown Rosslyn, and lived at the Bellevue Apartments a few blocks down the hill. It took her ten minutes to walk up in the morning and eight to walk down in the evening, though she did it in seven today, because from her office window she had noticed that the citybound vehicles on I-66 had their headlights on, implying rain to the west. As she approached the front door of the Bellevue, she looked back over her shoulder and did one careful scan of the area, looking for predators. Finding none, she swept her key card out with one deft move and pressed it against the electronic pad, then shouldered the door open the moment the lock clicked. As badly as she wanted to get home, she stood there patiently watching the door until its hydraulic closer drew it shut and the lock snapped to.

She walked through the lobby that looked impossibly luxurious to her eyes, took the elevator to ten, walked down the hall, and entered her apartment. She heaved a big sigh of relief as she snapped the last lock home—she was exhausted, and it was good to be home.

Strange noises were coming from the living room: feet thumping and sliding against the floor, and fast, rhythmic, deep breathing. Betsy sidled down the short hall toward the apartment's one common room, which served as living, dining, and kitchen.

Her roommate of one week, Cassie, was dressed in tights and some kind of athlete's brassiere. Her painstakingly cornrowed hair was pulled back into a tight bun, Walkman headphones clamped over the top, and she was sweating hard as she worked her way through an aerobics routine. Betsy had been taught not to stare, but she forgot herself for a few moments. She had heard of low-impact aerobics and high-impact aerobics, and she was pretty sure that she was watching the latter, and that Cassie wasn't doing it for the first time. Her jog bra left her midriff bare, so if she had had an ounce of fat on her body, it would have shown.

Betsy was partly fascinated and partly intimidated to be sharing an apartment with this exotic person. Young, single government employees in Washington had to get used to playing the roommate game; this was Betsy's third apartment, and Cassie was her seventh roommate, in five years. The previous one had been TDY'd to Munich on short notice, so Betsy had placed an ad on a computer bulletin board, and they had sent her Cassie. Betsy's employer was picky about whom she lived with. It was best to live alone, and if that didn't work, they didn't want her trolling for roommates in public venues.

What it came down to was that Betsy had to live with people who, like her, had been pretty carefully checked out by Uncle Sam. The wallet sitting on Cassie's bedside table, containing an FBI badge and ID card, proved she was clean enough to share an apartment with Betsy.

She backed stealthily out of the living room, as if she'd intruded on some private act, and retreated to the bathroom. She took off her clothes, hanging them on the back of the door, and turned on the shower. Then she faced the mirror, raised her left elbow over her head, and gently hefted her left breast in her right hand. She leaned toward the mirror.

The door flew open; Betsy's clothes fell off the hook into a heap on the floor. Cassie was a long stride into the room before she stopped herself. "Oh! Pardon *me,*" she said. She said it sincerely. But she wasn't really embarrassed, which fascinated and somewhat irritated Betsy—who, if she had made the same mistake, would have spent the rest of the month apologizing for it.

Cassie had planted herself on the bathroom floor now and was staring fixedly at Betsy's breast, her brow furrowed, her big brown eyes burning like coals. She reached up and stripped the headphones off, then took another step toward Betsy. "What the hell is *that*?" she said, as if she were busting some criminal who'd been caught flat-footed with a bale of sinsemilla in his arms.

Betsy was so stunned by this frank intrusion that she didn't have a chance to get embarrassed. She stared at her breast in the mirror as if it were a piece of frozen evidence in a crime lab. She wasn't sure how to answer Cassie's question: she knew the answer perfectly well, but she was afraid that if she told the story, she might start blubbering. She pointed to a long, narrow bruise on the side of her breast. "Thumb," she said. Then she pointed to another one, at an angle to the first. "Index finger." A third, parallel to the second. "Third finger. Ring finger, just a shadow—no trace of the pinkie."

"Well!" Cassie said. "I could run and get a fingerprint kit. But I suppose you already know who did it."

Howard King. But Betsy didn't say anything, just heaved a big sigh, trying to head off the crying urge.

"How about the one on your back? It's straight and angular."

"Filing cabinet," Betsy said.

"Those bruises are a few hours old," Cassie said with professional certainty, "so it happened at work, not on the way home. Musta been your su-per-vi-sor." She was watching Betsy's face in the mirror as she said this, and Betsy's face answered the question for her.

"I bruise easy." Betsy dropped her elbow to her side, the examination complete.

Suddenly Cassie was excited again. "And what the fuck is *this*? What are these people doing to you, anyway?"

Cassie was pointing to a wide bruise that encircled Betsy's upper arm. Then she recognized it and calmed down. "Oh. Polygraph." Unself-consciously, she pulled her tights down and sat on the toilet. Betsy marveled at this woman, who could do things like peeing in front of a near stranger while seeming as poised as if she were sitting at a sidewalk café sipping cappuccino.

Cassie's brow wrinkled up again. "The polygraph guy didn't grope you, did he?"

"Nah." Betsy said. She could have said a lot more, but she was pretty sure her voice would quaver. Cassie, having finished with a clinical examination of Betsy's breast and arm, now zeroed in on her face. "I'm getting you a beer, Idaho," she said. "Gotta get you to open up a little."

"No, thanks," Betsy said. "I don't care for beer, thank you."

"Then you take your shower and I'll fix you something and you'll never know it has booze in it. That's what you need." Cassie finished, pulled her tights back up, and paused in the doorway. "You a *Mormon,* ain't you? I just figured that out. I always heard that the Agency was full of Mormons."

"Yep," Betsy said. "Born and raised."

"Then let's just say I'm going to fix you a drink, Ida, and it'll be your job to drink it and my job to know what it's made of. Fair?"

Betsy was not very good at turning people down, especially articulate people with strong personalities. "Yes," she said.

Cassie smiled, pivoted on the ball of one foot, reached out with a pointed toe, and triggered the flush lever. "One more immortal soul," she said, "down the toilet. See you in a few, Ida."

five

IT ALL looked real easy once Clyde got all the maps spread out on the basement floor.

The floor of his actual house would not have been a good

place for them because the Big Boss had gone into a kind of nesting overdrive where even leaving a little piece of food on the floor set her off. Spreading out a couple hundred square feet of maps would have been spouse abuse—always the furthest thing from Clyde's mind.

So instead he went to the apartment building that Buck Chandler had just sold him. It was located on North Seventh Street in Nishnabotna, several blocks west of Central Avenue, not far from the freight yard and about half an inch above the mean water table. He had thrown his big push broom into the back of his truck on the way down there, and so he started by pushing all the old dust, bent nails, and hunks of shattered drywall back into the corners of the basement. There were also a lot of cigarette ash and broken beer bottles left over from teenagers breaking in and partying in the basement.

Clyde took his very large-scale maps of Forks County and placed them edge to edge on the basement floor until the entire county was laid out in front of him, minus two square places where Marie O'Connor had been temporarily out of maps. The scale of the maps was so large that a mile on the ground worked out to almost a foot on paper. Consequently, Clyde's new strategic map of Forks County, fully assembled, was about twenty feet square.

He untied the thick braided laces of his high-top steel-toed boots, unhooked the laces from the many brass hooks that marched up his ankles and shins, wrestled the boots off his feet, and left them sitting on the floor. Then he stepped onto the map of Forks County. His socks had got damp from perspiration, and wherever he went, he left moist, wrinkled, footprint-sized patches on the map. All the tiny little black squares that represented houses were spread out around him like pepper spilled across a table.

In order to see much, Clyde had to get down on his hands and knees. The lightbulb sockets screwed onto the joists above his head were all empty. The basement had half a dozen small windows near the ceiling, which were barely above ground level.

The job that was ahead of Clyde did not look like such a big deal from there. Most of Forks County was empty, save for farm buildings spread miles apart. He could see now that he would have to resist the tendency to fritter away all his time out in the middle of nowhere, covering lots of territory but not drumming up that many actual votes. All the population, hence all the votes, were centered in the twin cities of Wapsipinicon and Nishnabotna.

Which was kind of ironic, because the cities had their own police forces. They didn't pay much attention to sheriff-related matters. It was the farmers out around the edges of the county who really needed to get rid of Kevin Mullowney and replace him with a person like Clyde.

But that was neither here nor there. For Clyde, here was Nishnabotna (population thirty-two thousand) and there was Wapsipinicon (population twenty-one thousand, plus about twenty-five thousand students at Eastern Iowa University).

The two cities each straddled a river of the same name. The Wapsipinicon came in from the northwest, flowed through the sandstone bluffs of Palisades State Park, then passed into the town of Wapsipinicon, through the verdant campus of EIU, and into Riverside Park.

The Nishnabotna came in from the north. Just north of town it was dammed up to make Lake Pla-mor. Then it ran along the railyards and industrial flatlands of Nishnabotna and joined up with the Wapsipinicon to form the Iowa River, which then flowed thirty or so miles down to the southeast and joined up with the Father of Waters, which, technically speaking, ran all the way to New Orleans, Louisiana.

"I'll just—I'll just be going," a voice said.

The voice was deep and rough and sounded like truck tires driving on a gravel road. It was coming from a dark corner of the basement, a nook that had been set into the wall as a kind of root cellar/tornado shelter. Clyde heard something moving back there.

A large, hunched, dark form emerged from the little three-sided room. Poised on his hands and knees in the middle of Forks County and looking up squinty-eyed into the dim light,

Clyde could see only his silhouette. It was hard to tell whether he was looking at a water heater, an abandoned refrigerator, or a human being. When it moved a little, he decided the latter, but in terms of size and shape it was about halfway between a water heater and a refrigerator.

The shape moved fast considering it was clearly drunk and had just got up. Clyde tried to stand, but he was still on one knee when the man dived into him, wrapping his arms around Clyde's waist, and slammed him backward into the concrete. There were ways to foil this type of takedown, but Clyde could not really use them because he had to concentrate all his efforts on not getting the back of his head smashed on the floor.

He did a half twist as he was falling backward and flung one arm above his head, so that his armpit, instead of the back of his skull, absorbed the successive impacts of his own weight and Tab Templeton's 450-some pounds.

Clyde Banks and Tab Templeton had been separated by two years of age and several weight classes when they'd been in school, and consequently had never gone *mano a mano* until both had graduated to the less scrupulously fair adult world. Since then they had gone at it a total of nine times—mostly in the back room of the Barge On Inn, but most memorably during the climactic third year of the Nishnabotna Meat strike when the strikers had got Tab liquored up, placed an ax handle in his mitts, and sent him forth to wreak some mayhem. The Heavyweight had been too disoriented to know which were scabs and which were strikers, but when Clyde had shown up to arrest him, acting on the orders of Sheriff Mullowney, Tab had suddenly realized who his opponent was and had begun to swing the ax handle terrifyingly. Clyde, for his part, was armed with his nightstick, Excalibur, which had very recently been turned from a block of yellow Osage-orange wood, dense as uranium, by his grandfather Ebenezer. The two had done battle in the center of a vast ring of cheering strikers and scabs. Clyde had—at some length, and after suffering many injuries—brought his man in.

Clyde kept shaking his head back and forth, trying to dislodge Tab's hand from his jaw and Tab kept putting it back there.

Clyde did not recognize this move at all until he finally figured out that it was not really a wrestling move per se; it was an attempt to snap Clyde's neck.

Some dim light was coming in through a window above them and glancing off the multiple layers of clothing that The Heavyweight was wearing; around his vast conical neck Clyde counted four separate collars nested inside one another and a T-shirt underneath that.

Underneath the T-shirt was something else, some kind of shiny, colorful fabric that had got dull and dirty with the years. Realizing what it was, Clyde worked his one free hand down the back of The Heavyweight's neck, grabbed it, and yanked it off.

It was a loop of ribbon with something thick and heavy dangling off it. Clyde held it up so that it rotated and glowed in the light—a yellow metal disk with a design stamped into one side and some words. Clyde didn't have the leisure to read it, but he already knew what it said:

GAMES OF THE XIX OLYMPIAD
MONTREAL 1976
WRESTLING

The Heavyweight took his hand off Clyde's chin and grabbed for his gold medal, but Clyde was ready for that; he tossed it away and heard it go *plink* in the corner of the room.

Just like that, he was gone. The terrible pressure was gone from Clyde's ribs and legs. He scrambled to his feet, snatched up his boots, and made for the stairway, keeping one eye on Tab Templeton, who was on his hands and knees in the corner of the basement, pawing through debris looking for his medal.

He found it a lot faster than Clyde was really expecting him to and followed Clyde up the steps; Clyde could feel the structure of the stairway and of the building to which it was attached sagging downward, as if The Heavyweight could pull Clyde down toward him simply by walking up the steps and tearing the house and all its contents into the central pit.

But Clyde made it out the front door and got to his truck,

which was parked sideways in the front yard. He vaulted over the edge into the truck's box, picked up the spare tire, stepped onto the truck's roof to give himself more altitude, and heaved it at The Heavyweight as he was emerging from the front door with a section map of Nishnabotna County wrapped around one of his lower legs.

It looked as if the spare tire bounced right off Tab Templeton's thick, bearded, mashed-in face, but in fact it probably just bounced off his chest. Normal body-part terminology did not always apply in the clearest sense to The Heavyweight, with his spherical physiognomy and short, fat, stunted extremities.

He brushed the spare tire off as if it were an acorn falling out of a tree, but he stopped on the edge of the front porch to take his gold medal and put it carefully around his neck. Then he dropped the medal down inside his shirt.

This gave Clyde the time he needed to sort through all the stuff in the back of his truck and find a tire chain, roughly twenty or thirty pounds of rusty iron. He held it in the middle so that about three feet of it dangled down on either side of his hand, and he stood in the middle of the truck's box so that The Heavyweight would not be able to get him by the legs.

"You scratched my medal," The Heavyweight said. He sounded amazed that anyone could do such a thing.

"I'll scratch a lot more than that if you don't lay off," Clyde said, brandishing the chain. "I don't want to use this, because it's a very bad, dangerous kind of weapon. But I'm off duty and I don't have my baton, so I got to improvise."

Clyde whirled the chain around a couple of times, just as a visual aid. It was so heavy that it almost pulled his arm out of the socket and caused nauseating pains in his sternum. He had to plant his feet wide apart to prevent it from pulling him over.

The Heavyweight observed this demonstration calmly and then shrugged. He was giving up. "You gonna arrest me?"

"Nope. Like I said, I'm off duty."

"Got any jobs you need done?"

Clyde thought this one over. "Keep people from breaking

into this place and partying, and I'll give you some more of those McDonald's gift certificates." They didn't serve booze at McDonald's.

"Okay," The Heavyweight said.

"And haul all of this debris and stuff out of the yard and stack it up in back by the alley, and I'll give you a bonus."

"Okay."

six

APRIL

KEVIN VANDEVENTER parked his rusty Corolla in the faculty lot just after five-thirty P.M., when the campus cops gave up on doing parking checks. As he walked toward the grand entrance of the Scheidelmann AgriScience Research Center—a brand-new I. M. Pei knockoff planted on the former site of the vet-med barns—he smelled the aroma every farm boy knows. After they had torn down the barns to make room for this new structure, they had hauled in new topsoil and capped it with fresh sod. But when the spring thaws came, you could still smell the underlying stratum of old, fermented manure, down deep in the soil. The smell of planting season.

As he approached the building and stepped through the enormous plate-glass doors, another set of odors took over. He paused in the main entrance hall to take in the splendor of the permanent multimedia display that had been set up there to wow visiting congressmen and agriculture ministers. He inhaled a deep draft of the building's filtered and purified air, ripe with laboratory solvents and chemical fertilizer. It smelled like Science. Totally unlike the gymnasiums, which smelled like the fierce balm that wrestlers slathered on their torn muscles, or the Fine Arts Pavilion, which smelled like the microwave-popcorn fumes that constantly escaped the maintenance engineer's room in the basement.

The Scheidelmann was named after a late and beloved dean of

the EIU College of Agriculture, who rated a small plaque by the door. In the center of the entrance hall was a rotating ten-foot globe, studded with tiny, electrified EIU pennants marking the locations of the myriad research and extension projects that were being run out of this complex. The walls were lined with floor-to-ceiling photographs depicting Twisters in action, planting rice seedlings in the paddies of Burma and giving gaunt, buck-toothed Africans practical tips on soil erosion. More than a few of these photos featured Dr. Arthur Larsen, the Rainmaker.

Five years ago *National Geographic* had published an article about Larsen in which they had estimated that his discoveries and his outreach programs had saved upward of a hundred million people from starvation, all around the globe. The regents had paid for this page of the magazine to be blown up to the size of a sheet of plywood and then engraved on a slab of solid bronze, which was now embedded in the wall of the entrance hall.

Kevin Vandeventer was entering the Rainmaker's kingdom at five-forty on a Friday night, a TV dinner from the local Quik Trip in hand, because he had experiments that needed tending every few hours, around the clock, for months at a time. Whenever he came in to tend them, he found that there was a great deal of other work that needed doing—writing and editing reports, coding computer programs, and simply straightening up around the lab.

He had to smile when he thought that he was basically there because he hated physical labor. Dad had given up on him at the age of twelve and accepted that he just wasn't cut out for the farming business. Big sister Betsy was clearly destined for higher things, and so the title of heir apparent to the Vandeventer family potato empire had fallen onto the shoulders of Bob, the youngest, who was perfectly happy with it.

Kevin did have one feature useful on a farm: he liked animals. He was always tending to them, even learning how to shoe their three horses. So when Kevin began pulling down straight A's in science courses, his dad was pretty proud. Perhaps he'd amount to something, after all. Kevin had 4.0'd himself through Boise State University, and then, after maxing the GREs, had received a full-ride research fellowship to work with Dr. Larsen—which, as he soon learned, meant working several layers beneath Larsen in the research hierarchy. But he didn't really care; he had continued to shine in the laboratory as he had in the classroom and was now rounding the turn for the home stretch on his dissertation.

He followed a maze of ground-level corridors into the Sinzheimer Biochemistry Wing and then took the elevator up to the third floor. He went to his lab in 302, put his supper in the fridge, and sat down on a high stool for a minute, collecting his thoughts, getting organized. Kevin had the gift of concentration, but it took a conscious effort to turn it on sometimes. He ate a candy bar, knowing that if he didn't, his stomach would soon begin to distract him from his work.

Then, suddenly, it was nine-thirty. Four hours had gone by as he had concentrated on pipettes and the digital readouts of his machines. His stomach had digested the candy bar and was requesting further input. He got his El Toro Beef and Beans Tostada Supper out of the fridge and headed for the microwave, four doors down the hall.

This place had been his home for four years—he kept a sleeping bag and foam pad rolled up in a cabinet and frequently slept on the floor. As one of the oldest veterans of the Sinzheimer Wing, and the only resident American citizen on the floor, he had become its unofficial mayor.

He liked the wing and its inhabitants. There were no undergrads—no female bow-heads, no young men who believed that Bud Light advertisements were cinema verité. There were none of the social-sciences professors whose development had been arrested around the time of Woodstock. This place worked twenty-four hours a day. The professors looked rumpled and tired, as if they really labored and were thinking about things. Mostly, Kevin knew, they were thinking about how to replace all of the DARPA soft money now that the Cold War was over. They drove themselves and their graduate students hard, because eighty percent of their salaries came from grants. The grad students came from other countries where leisure time was scarce and not yet considered an inalienable right. They rarely complained.

Even now, late on a Friday night, the place was alive. Most of the professors were gone, and the boom boxes in various labs were cranked up, filling the corridor with a cacophony of sound—mostly American pop music, but also multiethnic stuff in a variety of languages.

The door to 304 was wide-open, which was unusual; the grad students there were Arabs who usually kept to themselves. Even more unusual, an *oom thumpy oom thumpy* bass beat was blaring out of the open door. Kevin looked into the lab as he passed by. The windows were open to let in the fresh spring air, and at least half a dozen people were in there, all men, all Arabs, all holding paper cups filled with something bright purple. Kevin recognized it instantly: grape Kool-Aid, almost certainly mixed with pure-grain alcohol from the laboratory stocks.

The men noticed him peering in and smiled sheepishly. Kevin smiled back. One of them was sprawled out on a ratty old Goodwill sofa under the window, sound asleep. It was Marwan Habibi. He frequently slept in his lab, just as Kevin frequently slept in his. But this evening he appeared to be passed out rather than merely asleep.

It was easy enough to figure this out: the end of the academic year was not far away, some of these guys were hoping to get their hoods and tassels come May, they had been working themselves like slaves in Lab 304 for years, and they must have just passed some milestone in their research. Kevin threw them a thumbs-up and kept on going without breaking stride; he had miles to go before he slept and didn't want to be invited in for Kool-Aid. He proceeded to the little kitchen in the center of the wing and threw his dinner into the microwave.

The only one of those guys he really knew was Marwan Habibi, and Marwan was already unconscious, so there didn't seem much point in trying to join the party. The Arabs here tended to be pretty secular. Many of them enjoyed the occasional shot of whiskey. But even a heavy drinker—which Marwan certainly was not—couldn't stand up to pure-grain alcohol for very long. Kevin was impressed with how smart and how professional Marwan was. He was working on a project to control the gas-producing tendencies of the bacteria that lived in the guts of cows, which caused them to fart a lot, which in turn exacerbated the greenhouse effect. Arthur Larsen, the Rainmaker, was hardly known as an environmentalist, but he had squeezed a cool half million out of the EPA for this and packed Marwan's lab with the latest and best equipment for culturing and studying the habits of bacteria. Marwan kept door 304 closed, but from time to time Kevin invited him into 302 as he walked past, and chatted with him for a while. It was all part of his self-imposed responsibilities as mayor of the third floor.

He attacked his dinner with the flimsy plastic fork provided, finding the utensil highly unsatisfying. But the beans were great. He scraped every gram of sauce from the plastic tray and then threw the remains into the garbage can. He bought a Coke from the vending machine and headed back toward his lab. The door to 304 was closed now, but the party was still going on.

It was about half an hour later when he heard the honking of a car horn below in the parking lot. The music from 304 abruptly stopped. This was typical; the Arabs had a heavy hand on the horn button, which locals found startling and even frightening.

Kevin had his door open, so he could hear the voices of the Arabs as they departed 304. They were rowdy and happy. "Take care you don't bang Marwan's head on the door frame!" one of them said in perfect British-accented English. Kevin looked up to see them moving down the hall, carrying the dozing Marwan Habibi on their shoulders. One of them smiled sheepishly at Kevin as he went by. "A little too much!" he said, sticking out his thumb and pinkie and wiggling them.

"Tell him congratulations from Kevin when he wakes up," Kevin said.

"Oh, yes," the Arab said, "we will certainly tell him."

seven

AS BETSY Vandeventer came stomping and sneezing up Clarendon early in the morning, she could see parallel strata of light shining from the windows of the several newish office buildings that surrounded the Courthouse metro in downtown Arlington. One of them was the Castleman Suites, which she supposed had been chosen by the CIA as overflow space precisely because it looked so utterly normal. An observer familiar with the Agency might have noticed a few clues: the odd construction of the windows, which were supposedly proof against microwave and laser surveillance; the Blue Bird bus that pulled through its horseshoe drive several times a day, ferrying employees out to the main campus at Langley; the fact that the second floor, above the First American Bank branch on the ground floor, was an empty buffer zone. In most ways, Betsy reflected, it really was just another normal office building; people sat in cubicles in front of computer screens, wrote memos, jockeyed for promotions, and played politics.

The main entrance of the Castleman would get you only to the bank. Betsy entered via the parking ramp instead, walked through an unmarked, windowless steel door, and showed her credentials to a guard, who allowed her into the elevator lobby. She got off at the seventh floor, displayed her ID to another guard, and walked halfway down a corridor punctuated at wide intervals by heavy doors with electronic locks. Each door gave access to a vault of offices, each vault hermetically sealed from the next. Betsy punched the *code de semaine* into one such lock and pushed the door open. A few greeting cards, and notes of congratulations, had been slipped under her door by colleagues who worked in other vaults and who hadn't been able to make it to yesterday's celebratory lunch at the Pawnbroker.

Betsy had passed her five-year polygraph test brilliantly. Perhaps, she mused, the same low basal metabolism that made her prone to gaining weight also produced the steady traces on the polygraph that were so reassuring to her employers. The examiner had been so impressed—her responses so perfectly matched the baseline established five years earlier on her entry poly—that he had set Betsy's test aside as an example for others to aspire to.

The vault consisted mostly of open cubicles—eight in all, each equipped with a Sun workstation. These were mostly in the back, near windows. In the front were two desks for the secretarial staff. In the back corner was an office enclosed by glass walls, the domain of the branch chief, Howard King. Betsy's cubicle was gaudy with Mylar balloons and congratulatory bouquets. From her armless swivel chair she had a view over I-66, and if she put her face close to the mysterious surveillance-proof window, she could make out one tower of the National Cathedral. She took a moment to enjoy this panorama before sitting down to work.

All the way to work Betsy had been rehearsing in her head the agenda for today's Interagency Study Group over at Ag.

Betsy's mental prep for the meeting at Ag was important—she never did anything until she had run through it in her head several hundred times. Frequently she would get so muddled that, in an effort to clarify things in her own mind, she would resort to having imaginary conversations with her mother, pretending that she was at home having a cup of coffee on the breakfast table in the kitchen. "The government has been sending a lot of money to Iraq—mostly, but not exclusively, from the Agriculture Department. We do this with the understanding that the Iraqis will use the money to buy agricultural products from the U.S. So it's actually a subsidy for American farmers as much as it is a foreign-aid program. Four times a year all of the departments that are sending money to Iraq, as well as some other agencies, have a meeting to evaluate this program and to set policy objectives for the next quarter."

Simple and logical it was—a model of rational government procedure. But there was always more to it than that. If it had really been possible for her to talk about such things to her mother, and if she'd wanted to level with her, she would have had to do a lot more talking. The talk would have sounded less like a civics textbook and more like vicious gossip. Betsy had learned that these meetings usually turned out to be a chance for the various division chiefs to strut their stuff, score cheap points on crosstown competitors, and defend, or enlarge, their turf.

And when Betsy logged onto her workstation and began scanning through her waiting mail, she realized that today there was even more to it than *that.* One piece of mail was a list of participants in today's meeting. It had been suddenly and drastically revised. Today it wouldn't be just the usual division chiefs and their analyst minions. Today it went much higher. It was going to be controlled straight from the White House, and it wasn't going to be a meeting so much as a damage-control session.

The *New York Times* bureau chief in Cairo, acting on a leak by the Egyptians, had blown the whistle on the Iraqis. Saddam Hussein was being a very bad boy. He was using U.S. dollars not to buy food from American farmers but for other things. It did not take a huge exercise in forward-leaning analysis to know that he was stocking up on weapons again.

What to do about that was a policy question, and it was not for people at her level to discuss policy. It was for her and her colleagues at similar-level desks around town only to monitor cash and weapons flows, and she expected that those would be the marching orders today.

Her workstation gave her the ability to pull up vast amounts of information, so long as she had the appropriate clearances. For example, she knew that yesterday a congressional delegation, or codel, headed by Bob Dole, had met with Saddam Hussein in Baghdad. Whenever such a meeting took place, someone at the local embassy—usually a State Department employee—would write up a codel memo and cable it to D.C., where it would become available to anyone in government who had a need to know about it. Betsy typed in a short command telling the system to bring up all recent items, including the keywords "Dole" and "Iraq" and "codel," and within a few moments the document was there on her screen.

Senator Dole was quoted as having said, "I kept thinking that I was watching Peter Sellers imitating a dictator." Saddam had denied any knowledge of the Supergun project, recently very much in the news, and had said that his recent statement about binary nerve weapons had been meant merely to intimidate the Israelis. Dole was quoted again: "To see that guy talk about being a humanitarian is about as convincing as hearing Mother Teresa claiming to be a hit man." Dole had been shown official Iraqi documents "proving" that the Ag subsidies had been spent only on food supplies from the U.S. or U.S. subsidiaries.

From there Betsy could have typed in more commands and brought up more documents, following one reference to the next, tracking down leads to her heart's content.

But her heart's content wasn't part of her job description. She was only supposed to access information on a "need to know" basis.

She had learned this the hard way a month ago, when she had let her curiosity get the better of her and gone snooping in places where she didn't have any real need to know. The CIA kept careful track of who had accessed which documents. It didn't take long for word to reach her boss. His reaction had been vicious: he had waited until they were alone together in the vault, then hauled her up out of her chair and slammed her against a filing cabinet.

Someone else entered the vault. She saw him reflected in the curved screen of her workstation: a compact, trim man with a short and simple military-style haircut that looked out of place above the starched white collar of his tailored shirt. It was Richard Spector, the division chief, her boss's boss. He ran half a dozen or more vaults there at the Castleman.

He didn't bother with greetings or small talk. "Today be a good listener," he said. Even when he was saying momentous things, he always spoke in a quiet voice, as if he were only musing to himself. But it made him seem formidable, rather than mousy. "Answer direct questions directly, but try to figure out who's got what agenda vis-à-vis Iraq."

"Can you give me any more background? What should I look for?"

"This is strictly my read, not official at all. Commerce wants back into Iraq to sell some technology and to influence oil distribution. Agriculture wants to sell. That's what Agriculture does." He said this dryly, barely masking his contempt for those amoral hucksters over at Ag. He began twiddling the Annapolis ring on his left hand; its pale-colored stone caught the light from Betsy's monitor. "Defense knows something they're not sharing with us. Based on circumstantial evidence, I'm guessing it has to do with nonconventional weapons."

Spector was ex-military intelligence and was probably as qualified as anyone to read Pentagon tea leaves. "Arms Control and Disarmament Agency is, as usual, running behind the parade, convinced that they ought to be running things." Spector nodded at the window still open on Betsy's screen. "As you've already noticed, Millikan's going to be there from the National Security Council." One of Spector's tics was a refusal to use acronyms; he always spelled out the full names of agencies and departments, seeming to take great pleasure in the ones with the longest and most unwieldy titles. It enhanced his air of preternatural calmness and enabled him to put an ironic spin on everything, which made him much hated around town.

"This is big-time, isn't it?" Betsy said.

"Yeah, and I'm sorry to say that King is going to represent your branch."

Betsy was thrown off stride by Spector's frankness. "I noticed that his name had been added to the list," she said carefully. "You want me to go anyway?"

Spector nodded. "It's Howard's job to do the talking. It's your job to keep an eye on things. I want your own report—'Eyes Only'—to me by this afternoon." He checked his watch and took a couple of steps toward the door, then thought better of it and turned back to her. "You will obviously not follow the usual distribution on this."

In other words, Spector wanted Betsy's report on, among other things, her own boss's performance. Spector moved away at a racewalker's clip; seconds later Howard King showed up. Betsy had been around just long enough to suspect that this was not a coincidence. Spector had known when King was going to arrive.

"Good morning, Betsy," King smarmed as he brushed by her back on his way to the office. "Ready for the meeting? You can ride with me."

Betsy had anticipated this and said, "I left my briefcase at home, so I'll take the metro. See you there."

King muttered something indistinguishable and went into his office.

Betsy had not left her briefcase in her apartment, she had actually strategically covered it with her raincoat.

On the streets of D.C. various functionaries walked with their raincoats on and heads down, chains bearing their badges giving them identity and value in the city. The Agency people looked with some disdain on these hoi polloi civil servants. They had been told that the Agency was the crème de la crème of Washington, a veritable elite knighthood, and they didn't wear their IDs in the outside world. When Betsy presented her credentials at the Ag security desk, she was waved through with some deference.

On the third floor of the south building another security checkpoint loomed. Beyond it was the specially recrafted "secure conference room." She was still ten minutes early, but all the chairs at the large oval table were filled, except for the one reserved for the Agency.

She reached into her purse and found an asthma inhaler. Feeling conspicuous in the hallway, she ducked into a side corridor.

As the burst of expensive pharmaceuticals expanded into her lungs, she was startled by a dry, smoky-sounding voice from nearby. "You should get yourself a carburetor for that thing."

She coughed uncontrollably, forgetting to cover her mouth. "Excuse me. I'm sorry, what did you say?"

He was a worn-looking gentleman in a nice enough suit, the skin of his hands and face mottled, blotched, and lumped with age, cigarette smoke, alcohol, stress, and other malign influences. "Hi, I'm Betsy Vandeventer," she said, stepping forward and extending her hand.

"From the Agency," he said, shaking it. Betsy was startled to smell a strong odor of booze on his breath.

"Is it that obvious?"

By way of an answer he said, "I'm Hennessey."

"Oh."

"Yeah," he said. "Oh." Hennessey was infamous in the Agency.

"Pleased to meet you."

"You don't have to say that. Anyway, about that carburetor." He reached into the hip pocket of his jacket and drew out a white plastic cylinder about the dimensions of a beer can. From the opposite pocket he took out an inhaler, loaded up with the same brand of asthma medication that Betsy used. He fitted the outlet of the inhaler into one end of the "carburetor" and put the other end to his lips. "See, you spray the stuff into the carb. Then you inhale. Gives you better aerosolization. Or some shit like that. Jesus, isn't the Agency providing you guys with decent health care anymore?"

Hennessey was a spy gone bad. Turning his back on a distinguished career, he had left the gentlemen's club of the CIA and gone to work for the FBI, in the counterintelligence division. His job, in effect, was to investigate CIA employees and ruin their careers or throw them in prison on whatever pretext he could dig up. He had become a bogeyman of sorts in Agency folklore; Betsy was a little scared just to be talking to him.

"Well, excuse me, Mr. Hennessey, but I don't want to be late for my meeting."

"Hell, me neither," Hennessey said, and fell into step with her. They presented their credentials at the security checkpoint and were waved through into the room. Betsy had been relegated to the status of wall-creeper as the result of King's last-minute inclusion, so she chose a chair against the wall near King's place at the table—which was still conspicuously vacant. Hennessey, unnervingly, sat next to her.

She wasn't the only wall-creeper. Word had rapidly spread

that Millikan himself was going to show up from the White House, and several division chiefs had been aced out of their chance for glory by their superiors.

She should have been thinking about her twin assignments—officially, supporting King with facts and figures, and unofficially, making observations that she'd later relay to Spector. In the latter category Hennessey's presence there was certainly interesting. What on earth did he have to do with Ag Department credits to Iraq?

It was well-known that Hennessey and Millikan despised each other. Millikan was a noted Harvard professor who periodically came down to Washington, first to serve in the Kennedy administration and later—after becoming a leading light of the neoconservative movement—for Ford, Reagan, and Bush.

Undersecretary of Agriculture Larry McDaniel's executive secretary scurried into the room and announced, "Dr. Millikan is meeting with Dr. McDaniel, so the session will not start for fifteen minutes. I know you are all extremely busy today, and Dr. McDaniel extends his apologies. He hopes that in light of the renewed importance of this meeting, you will understand. I've taken the liberty of ordering in some coffee and muffins, so please take what you want."

For most of the apparatchiki at the meeting her announcement was a very good thing indeed. Not only would they finally be in on Something Big before it was reported in the *Post,* they would have the chance to munch on the High Fiber Department's muffins, widely known as the best in the District.

Hennessey leaned toward Betsy, venting his booze breath into her face. "Want some coffee?"

"Sure. That's okay, I'll get it—"

"Siddown!" he grunted. "Muffin?"

"Yes, sir."

Hennessey lurched from his chair, squeezing among the Schedule-C appointees who were adjusting their sleeves so that Millikan, when he graced the room with his presence, would see the proper amount of cuff showing, held together with presidential-seal cuff links. He filled Betsy's Styrofoam cup, too full. He poured his coffee about halfway and filled the rest with cream and with spoonfuls of sugar. Then he remembered that he had to get a muffin for Betsy. "Goddamn it," he said to no one in particular. "I never eat before noon." He turned to the nearest cuff-link person, a Wharton School type from Treasury. "Bud, would you stick one of those things in my jacket pocket?"

"What?" spat the Ivy Leaguer, too stunned to be offended. His gaze traveled down to Hennessey's name tag. Then, suddenly, he was delighted to be the recipient of this folksy treatment. "Be glad to give you a hand, Mr. Hennessey."

"Very kind of you," said Hennessey with no apparent irony. He walked back to Betsy, the corners of his jacket swinging with their loads of pastry and asthma medication.

Washington was the best place in the country to watch bureaucratic strangers trying to scope each other out without seeming to. But as Hennessey approached Betsy, everyone in the room stared at him openly, and when he reached her, everyone seemed to look at her. She felt her face get hot. Hennessey handed her her coffee, and she spilled some on her hand.

"What the hell," he said. "We've got fifteen minutes, might as well be comfortable." He grabbed another vacant chair and slapped it down in front of her like a coffee table. He arranged the coffee and muffin on it, then pulled his own chair away from the wall and turned it ninety degrees so that he and Betsy were half facing each other, their heads close together like a couple of lovers having a tête-à-tête at a sidewalk café. "So," Hennessey said in a quiet, conversational voice, "King has nabbed your place at the High Table so that he can be nearer to greatness. You're here anyway, probably at Spector's insistence. Spector probably figures that King's going to be so conspicuous, because of his incompetence and his sartorial deficiencies, that he'll grab all the attention. Meanwhile, you can be his fly on the wall—the cool, detached observer who reports to him later. Does that sound about right? That's okay, toots, you don't have to answer—I know you're scared shitless." He slurped his cool, pale, syrupy java. "So now's your chance to observe. What are they doing?"

"Staring at us."

Hennessey began to whisper, "M-i-c, k-e-y, M-o-u-s-e..."

Betsy felt the corners of her mouth twitching back and pursed her lips to counteract it. Hennessey hissed, "Look serious! You're on the inside of the inside of the inside, and there is nothing here."

McDaniel and Millikan entered the room.

"Case in point," Hennessey said, and scooted his chair back to its original position.

Undersecretary McDaniel sat down at the head of the table, opened his leather folder, and said, "Is everybody here?" The eyes of everybody in the room swung to the empty seat reserved for the Agency. "Is there anybody here from our brethren up the Potomac?"

"Up shit creek, is more like it," Hennessey whispered. "What you waiting for? Go sit in the chair, sister."

Betsy's heart flopped wildly a couple of beats before she realized that this was an example of Hennessey's cadaverous sense of humor. He had spent more years in the Agency than Betsy had been alive, and he knew perfectly well that if she usurped King's spot at the big table, he'd rip her head off.

The silence became unbearable when the door blew open and in walked King. He had always prided himself on being able to find a parking place anywhere in town. This time he'd clearly had trouble. He was sweating, muttering to himself, and staggered to his seat. "Sorry to be late, had some late cable traffic," he said.

Hennessey made a noise deep down in his throat. Betsy couldn't keep herself from glancing over at him. He was regarding King with a look of undisguised loathing and condescension, like a veteran theater critic watching a hack understudy blow his big entrance. King looked around the room as he pulled his chair back, trying to get a fix on Betsy's location. A moment after he picked out her face, he recognized Hennessey. His jaw literally fell open, and he sank into his chair with an afflicted look on his face.

"Let's begin," McDaniel said. "You all know the issue at hand: that our friend Mr. Hussein has been alleged to be misusing funds from the taxpayers of the United States. Dr. Millikan, would you like to give us the perspective from the White House?"

"Thank you, Larry," Millikan said. "Good morning, everyone. Glad our representative from the illustrious Department of Transportation could make it today: Mr.—" Millikan stopped, knitted his brow, and turned his head toward Howard King, squinting at his name tag, unable to quite make it out.

A look of flabbergasted horror spread slowly across King's face. "King," he rasped. "Howard King. Uh, pardon me, Dr. Millikan, but I'm from the Agency."

Millikan had seemed brusque and hurried when he had started, but now he leaned back in his chair and slowly poured himself a tumbler of water, seeming to derive some enjoyment from letting Howard King twist. "Arms Control and Disarmament?"

"No, Doctor—"

"United States Information?"

"No, Doctor, Central Intelligence."

"Oh, that Agency. I knew something was missing. Yes, of course. Forgive me, Mr. Howard King," Millikan said. Having finished keelhauling Betsy's boss, he sat up straight and turned away to address the center of the table. "I will get straight to the point. There is a lot of nonsense being reported in the press about Saddam Hussein and his ambitions. Some of it is being presented by our Israeli friends, who are understandably concerned by Saddam's regrettable, though culturally typical, rhetoric. Some of it is being spread by the administration's political enemies, who are talking their customary nonsense about the President's lack of vision. I am here to tell you that Saddam Hussein is still a keystone in our Middle-Eastern foreign policy. Two administrations supported him in his struggle against the Iranians, who have nothing but ill will toward us. Senator Dole took a personal letter from President Bush to Saddam Hussein expressing our concerns about perceptions of his actions and statements that may or may not be accurate. Mr. Hussein has promised to get back to us on our concerns.

"Now, the reason I am here today is to try to get all of us reading from the same page. You are tasked," he said, patting a stack of envelopes, "to provide, in three days, input to anticipate criticism of USG export-import credits to Iraq; to provide plans expanding and diversifying the agricultural and commercial credits presently extended to Baghdad; and to establish your implementation plans."

Millikan's assistant, White House Staff badge dangling like a gaudy fishing lure as he walked around the table, picked up the stack of envelopes and passed them around. Each was marked "Secret" and contained a freshly minted NSC Decision Directive. "Now," Millikan said, "I have a meeting with the President in thirty minutes. Are there any questions or comments?"

The knowledgeable players of the game knew that Millikan wanted questions and comments as much as he wanted to get dog shit on his Duckers Wingtips, but custom dictated that he make the request. McDaniels began to close the meeting when King, who had been stunned into a coma, said, "You can be sure that we'll be team players on this." At which point he turned and glared meaningfully at Betsy.

Millikan mumbled, "I'm sure we can count on you," sounding almost as if he were clearing his throat. His assistant sprang to the door and hauled it open for him, and then Millikan was gone, headed for the President's office, leaving behind nothing but an indefinable aura of Greatness that was like pure oxygen to most of the people in the room.

McDaniel looked around the room and said, "Thank you for coming. We look forward to your contributions."

"I'd give anything to read your report on this," Hennessey said to Betsy as the meeting broke up. "Tell old Spector I give him my best."

eight

DESIREE WAS fixing a bit of breakfast. Clyde was perusing the sports section of the *Des Moines Register*. Maggie sucked on a pacifier and dozed in her baby chair.

Clyde was still wearing his deputy sheriff's uniform. He had just come off the night shift. Ever since he had announced his candidacy for sheriff, his boss and opponent, Kevin Mullowney, had assigned him to the night shift, or to jail duty, every day. These were considered the least desirable duties a deputy sheriff could perform. Clyde agreed that guarding the county jail was an ordeal, but he didn't mind the night shift so much. He wasn't getting any sleep anyway.

Last night he'd been given responsibility for the region lying to the north of the city of Nishnabotna, which basically amounted to lazily circumnavigating Lake Pla-Mor looking for interesting people and situations, and then shining the cop light on them. The vacation cabins along the lake's shore were an inviting target for burglars, the parks and boat ramps a favorite haunt of teenaged lovers, fighters, drinkers, and drug abusers. All of these people were happy to make themselves scarce as soon as Clyde rolled up and pinioned them in the blue halogen beam of his cop spotlight. Sometimes he had to garble something harsh and unintelligible into his PA before they would get lost—the young women covering their faces and giggling uncontrollably, the young men valorously flipping him the bird.

It had been rainy last night, and so things had been slower than usual along Lake Pla-Mor. If an irate taxpayer were to corner Clyde Banks today and demand that he justify the amount that had been spent, during the last eight hours, on his salary, overhead, and benefits, Clyde would be able to offer only that he had recovered one of the university's rowboats.

He had noticed it while proceeding along Dike Street, which ran along the top of the dam on the Nishnabotna River that had brought Lake Pla-Mor into existence. The boat, a big old dinged-up aluminum beast, had apparently drifted down the lake and got hung up in a mess of reeds and cattails not far from the spillway. Clyde knew that the water was only knee-deep there, and so he had parked his unit nearby, pulled on some waders from the trunk, sloshed out, and grabbed it. He payed out its bow rope, clambered back up on the shore, and then towed the boat away from the dam until he reached a swimming beach a few hundred yards farther north.

The boat had been stolen from the university boathouse on the other side of the lake, which had to be one of the most popular burglary sites in the entire county. It was almost a mandatory rite of passage for young men from either the high school or the university to break into it at some point during their lives, steal a rowboat or canoe, and go out on the lake for some aimless, drunken fun. From the beach where Clyde brought this particular boat to shore, he could look directly across the lake and see the streetlights that had been put up in the boathouse parking lot as a pathetic self-defense measure. He considered simply rowing this boat across and putting it back where it belonged, which would have taken a while but would have been more useful and productive than his usual night-shift activities. But one of the boat's oars was missing. So he dragged it up on the beach as far as he could. This was not very far, because the boat had a couple inches of rainwater in the bottom, and a bit of gravel, so it was heavy. He tied the painter to the leg of a picnic table and made a mental note to call the boathouse in the morning and let them know about it.

Desiree mumbled something that was lost in the self-righteous harrumphing of the Mr. Coffee.

"Come again?" Clyde said.

"Get rid of that car," Desiree said. "It's not a good kid car."

Clyde dropped the paper and stared at his wife's back, which now, only three weeks postpartum, was just as skinny as it always had been before. "You mean the pickup truck?"

"We need the pickup truck to haul things," Desiree said. "Baby furniture. Stuff for fixing up your buildings."

"So you're saying—"

"We have to get rid of the Celica," Desiree said. She said it as if it were a new idea, and hers. In fact, Desiree had bought the Celica to begin with. Clyde had been trying to get rid of it ever since. But he knew that it would be unwise to agree right away, because this might be construed as gloating.

"Are you sure?" he said craftily.

"We can't deal with a two-door. It just doesn't work with a baby seat. Ask Marie. Marie and Jeff had two two-doors, and they had to get rid of both of them."

"If you say so," Clyde said, and when Desiree did not change her mind and protest right away, he felt quietly satisfied. An issue of long standing had now been settled, and Clyde had been given carte blanche to settle it his way.

While standing in various roadside ditches of Forks County, holding a flashlight as the medics wielded the Jaws of Life, he had got a pretty clear idea of which cars were well built and which weren't. If getting T-boned by a one-ton pickup at a rural crossroads didn't reveal all of a vehicle's structural deficiencies, then the Jaws of Life sure did.

Forks County was an especially good place to learn these lessons. County Sheriff Kevin Mullowney was not the kind of politician who spent a lot of time worrying about policies, but he did have one hard and fast rule: never arrest drunk drivers. Follow them home if you like, but don't arrest them. Methodical application of this rule over a twelve-year reign had led to a situation in which Forks County had the lowest drunk-driver arrest rate, and the highest traffic fatality rate, in the state of Iowa.

So for quite some time, especially since the pregnancy, Clyde had been itching to swap the Celica for something with a little more stopping power. He had tried many arguments out on Desiree, told her many gory car-crash anecdotes. Desiree always had a devastating rebuttal handy: the Celica was "cute" and "a neat little car."

Now, this very morning, with her mind occupied with long-range strategization, she had made the crucial error of telling him to ditch the Celica without saying anything about whether the replacement needed to be cute. Clyde changed the subject to something very different, ate hastily, excused himself, stripped all known copies of Celica keys from all known key chains, snatched the title out of the bill-paying desk, hopped into the cute little thing itself, and careened down the street. Just in case the Big Boss had second thoughts and tried to run him down, he did not look into the rearview mirror until he was out of shouting and waving range. Another torrential rainstorm had just commenced, which helped.

Fortunately, Desiree always kept the Celica pretty clean on the inside, so that it would stay cute. Clyde threw the few remaining personal items into a garbage bag, ran the vehicle through a car wash so that the rain would bead up attractively on its hood, and then drove straight over to the First National Bank of NishWap, a structure that had been gleamingly modern twenty years ago and now looked older than its nineteenth-century neighbors. It had a gravel parking lot in back, and before going inside, Clyde swung through that lot one time, looking for a particular vehicle.

It was still there. Clyde grinned and whacked the Celica's steering wheel with the palm of his hand, feeling that everything was going his way for once. He parked right next to it; it was so heavy that he almost felt the Celica rocking toward it on its flimsy suspension, drawn in by its gravity.

The vehicle in question was a 1988 Buick Roadmaster station wagon. It was red inside and out. It possessed many luxury features, none of which Clyde cared about. He had done much theoretical car-shopping during the last nine months. At first he had paid careful attention to the various features and options. But as time went on, his mind became more focused, and he became fixated on one single number: namely, throw weight. And this vehicle right here weighed more than anything else you could buy. To exceed it, you had to go all the way back to the Lincoln Continentals of the mid-1960s. This beast had enough mass to drive all the way through a car like the Celica with only minor turbulence; but just in case—on the off chance you might hit two or three Celicas at the same time—it had an airbag, too.

"I'll trade you my Celica for the Roadmaster, straight up," Clyde said.

That Jack Harbison, branch manager, did not immediately chortle and scoff at this suggestion told Clyde that he almost certainly had himself a deal. For the first time in more than half a year, Harbison saw a way to get rid of the Murder Car.

The late owner of the Murder Car, a longtime EIU football booster and season-ticket holder, had come home unexpectedly early from a Twisters game and surprised his wife and her lover in bed. A fight had ensued. His head had got bashed in. Wife and lover had lined the inside of the Roadmaster with lawn and garden bags, laid the husband out in the middle, put more bags on top of him and an old rug on top of that. By the time they had got him out to Palisades State Park, he had died of asphyxiation or brain swelling—Barnabas Klopf, the coroner, flipped a coin and put down brain swelling. They had dragged him out over the tailgate and put him in a shallow grave at the edge of the woods. But the edge of the woods was just where hunters and their dogs were likely to be during the months that coincided with the football season, and so not more than a week later the body was found by someone's golden retriever. Clyde himself had helped haul the body bag out to the main road.

Now both of the killers were down in Fort Madison for a long, long time. The First National Bank of NishWap had foreclosed on the auto loan and repossessed the station wagon, and it had sat in their lot ever since, an object of morbid fascination to schoolboys who made lengthy detours to ride past it every day on the way home from school, but not very inviting to anyone else.

Except Clyde. Jack Harbison came out and gave the Celica a wary test drive, consulted his blue book, put his glasses up on his forehead, and rubbed his eyes. "Done," he said resignedly, and within minutes Clyde was headed for home behind the wheel of the Murder Car.

nine

AFTER THE meeting at the Agriculture Department, Howard King followed Betsy Vandeventer all the way out of the building, insisting that she ride back to the Castleman Building in his car. She tried to avoid him by taking the stairs, but he plunged in after her, shouting at her like a furious schoolmaster. "Betsy! Stop where you are *immediately* and listen to me!"

She surprised herself by overriding her instincts and continuing down the stairs. King stood his ground until she was almost down to the ground floor, then pounded down after her, his comb-over and his necktie flapping. It wasn't that Betsy had somehow broken free of the need to be a good girl. It was that something had changed since this morning. Howard King no longer had any authority. Spector's orders had hinted at it, Millikan's keelhauling had made it obvious, and now King's own desperation served as proof.

He followed her halfway to the metro stop, hot in the spring sunshine, failed hair transplants dotting his sweat-beaded scalp. Once, twice, he almost reached out to grab her. Both times he controlled the urge, inhibited by the strolling office workers all around them, the tour groups piling out of the buses. She turned her back on him one last time and headed down into the metro.

When she arrived on the seventh floor of the Castleman, she stopped to chat with the security person on duty by the elevators, an ex-cop. "Morning, Miss Vandeventer," he said.

"Morning, Martin," she said. "Too nice a day to be locked up in a vault."

"That's true," he chuckled.

"Has Mr. King come in yet?"

The look that came over Martin's face when she mentioned Mr. King was the final and conclusive proof, if she wanted any, that something bad was about to happen to her boss. "Oh, yes, ma'am," he said. "Mr. King came in early this morning."

"I mean recently—within the last half hour."

"No, ma'am."

"Well, he'll be coming in soon," Betsy said, "and I think he may be very . . . emotional."

Martin nodded reassuringly. "I understand."

She went into the vault, said hello to a few colleagues in other cubicles, accepted congratulations from a couple of them who hadn't been around yesterday for her five-year polygraph celebration. She settled into her own cubicle and signed on to her workstation to find an urgent memo waiting for her: it came from DCI, the Director of Central Intelligence, and it was an invitation for her to attend a Deputies Committee meeting several days hence, to discuss the intelligence community's views on Iraq. There was a number she was to call on secure line number two.

The DCI's executive assistant took the call and confirmed the invitation. "Let me know if you have any questions."

Through the vault door Betsy could hear a commotion coming down the hall. "I have one question already."

King punched a wrong code into the lock, cursed, did it again, and shoved the door open.

"Shoot," said the DCI's assistant.

"Have you cleared this with my branch chief?"

"Cleared what?" King demanded. Behind him Martin prevented the door from closing and stepped quietly into the vault, his gaze fixed on the back of King's head.

"There's no need," said the assistant. "But to cover you, there is an advisory to him on his computer mail. Tell him to read that."

"Cleared what?" King demanded, stepping threateningly close to Betsy.

"The DCI's executive assistant said you should check your computer mail," Betsy said.

The mention of the DCI forced him to moderate his tone. He spun on his heel and went into his office, cursing under his breath. He logged on, pulled up his mail, and exploded. He stormed out and said, "You big cunt!" then stopped in his tracks as Martin interposed himself between him and Betsy.

"Mr. King, I sure was hoping to make it through the day without having to file any incident reports with my superiors," Martin said.

King did something unexpected: closed his eyes and breathed deeply several times. When he spoke again, his voice was quiet and defeated. "Nothing," he said, and went back to his office. Betsy did not dare to sneak a glance at him until several minutes later. He had opened the tasking envelope from Millikan and was poring over it, apparently intending to handle the job himself rather than passing it on to one of his subordinates.

Betsy informed her officemates that she would be in the library and retreated to the third floor. It was a pathetic excuse for a library, but it worked nicely as a place where analysts could get away from their bosses. She had brought some blank paper along, which she used to write out an account of the day's occurrences, using the Cross ballpoint pen her parents had given her as a high-school graduation present. When she thought it seemed good enough, she went up to the fourth floor and handed it to Spector's secretary, saying, "He wanted this."

The secretary—an old Agency hand—said, "I know, dear." She handed Betsy an interoffice envelope. "The courier just brought this to you from the DCI's office."

Betsy accepted it, her gaze going immediately to the "Eyes Only" stamp. "Thanks."

She went back to the library. The seventh floor was still a little too emotionally charged. She opened the envelope to find a set of marching orders with her name on them. "The White House wants your views on Iraqi misuse of USG funds. Be prepared to make an oral report on the sixteenth. In order to be prepared for this assignment, you are now seconded to the DCI's personal staff 04/13/90 to 04/20/90. You will do no further work in the Castleman Building until your return on 04/21/90."

By now it was half-past noon. She ventured back to the seventh floor, knowing that King would be gone to lunch. A few minutes after she arrived, Spector cruised in. "Why don't you take the rest of the day off? The next week is going to be pretty intense. King knows about your new orders." He looked about the vault. The other analysts shoved their faces into the screens of their workstations as if they hadn't been listening. Spector took one hand out of his pocket and beckoned to her. "Come this way."

Betsy stood up and followed him into King's office. He shut the door and walked slowly around the office, looking at King's stuff appraisingly. "None of what you do is to come back to this building," he said. "When you return, you'll go back to monitoring Southwest Asian Commodities. King won't be here."

"Pardon me?"

"We've floated him an administrative editorial excellence award. He'll be promoted to a fifteen and assigned to run the Collections Office in Mobile, Alabama."

Collections officers were the CIA's ears to the ground. Their basic function was to pay uninvited visits on people who had recently been abroad and ask them if they'd seen anything interesting.

Betsy could not hide her amazement. Spector said, "You've

been here long enough. We can fire analysts. We can't fire managers. And you know why. So don't ask."

"See you in a week, then," Betsy said. She was already trying to think of what she'd do with a free spring afternoon.

"Be careful. You'll be swimming with the sharks now."

The notion that she would never see Howard King again, never have to worry about him again, had left her so elated that she hardly heard Spector's words. But she noticed Spector looking at her intently. "Thanks for the warning," she said. "Can I call you for help?"

Spector, unexpectedly, reddened. "You can call me for advice."

The next morning she took the Blue Bird bus from its stop outside the Rosslyn Metro out to Langley. The orders had said she was on the DCI's personal staff for the week, but that was a sort of marriage of convenience, existing only on paper. They assigned her a windowless nook, far away from the office of the DCI or of anyone else important, and they left her completely alone. No one ever came by. That didn't mean that someone wasn't checking up on her; every time she logged on to her workstation, every time she punched a key on the keyboard, a record went into a file somewhere, and the DCI, or Spector, or whatever important person was responsible for putting her into this nook for the week, could get a very clear picture of how and what she was doing simply by pulling up that file.

The same Somebody had also temporarily upgraded her access privileges, and so, with the exception of nuclear-related and undersea-warfare compartments, she had virtually free run of all the information she could ever want.

She did not waste any time taking advantage of it. Spector had told her that she was asking the right questions, so she followed her nose, sure that there would be no Howard King to get in her way, confident that no hovering snoops would notice an anomalous pattern of requests and blow the whistle on her.

What was Saddam doing with all the money that Ag had sent him for food? The weapons guys had chased down most of that information, tracing the dollars to banks in Cyprus, Austria, Jordan, and, unbelievably, Nepal. The Agency knew where the Chinese-missile money was going, where the German-chemicals dollars were going—including one really clever diversion through Libya. They knew where the North Korean nuclear-research cash was flowing, where the French-computer checks were going, where the American-food bucks flowed. The Iraqis did have the good taste to buy some food from big American suppliers: Soo Empire Grain, Louisiana Rice, and Great Lakes Co-op. But there were still three hundred or so million dollars unaccounted for. That kind of money wouldn't get Saddam very far in the nuclear department, but chemical and biological weapons were much simpler and cheaper—much more his style. Three hundred million could buy a lot of nerve gas, a lot of anthrax.

She pulled up the tracking documents of the various departments involved: Agriculture, which maintained that all the money not spent on American food products was still in the Baghdad treasury; Commerce, which maintained that Ag was hiding something—that there were funds that should have gone to buy American technology; ACDA, which noted the Chinese weapons flowing in, but said that there was still a lot in the treasury; the Pentagon, which had tracers on all its surplus weapons sprinkled around the world and was watching them converge on Baghdad. She sent a request to a local Collections person and had him ask the Mossad liaison in D.C. if they would care to share their read on the dollars flow; within forty-eight hours the answer came back that four times the amount of money allocated the Iraqis out of the most recent batch had been spent. She called up HUMINT sources in what was left of the contacts the Agency had in the Middle East and got nothing, except one tantalizing hint that a number of Iraq's best microbiologists were gone, that an entire chunk of the curriculum at Baghdad University was being taught by Pakistani and Palestinian adjunct professors.

At midnight on the fifteenth, the night before she was supposed to appear before the Deputies Committee meeting, she was still thrashing around. She'd accumulated a huge dossier of hints and dead-end leads, but nothing that led to any firm conclusions. Any idiot could plainly see that the Iraqis were up to something. If she'd been an elected official, that would have been enough to go on. But she was just a lowly analyst, she had to be objective and scientific, and she couldn't get by with hints and suppositions.

She logged off her computer, dragged her weary body over to the elevator just in time to see the next shift come on board at the situation room down the hall. Langley never slept, reflecting Dean Rusk's observation that when we were asleep, two thirds of the globe was awake and raising hell.

A Red Top cab swung by to pick her up at the front entrance. She stood there by the statue of Nathan Hale, smelling the forsythia and honeysuckle in bloom, trying to figure out what she'd say tomorrow. Figuring out Saddam's game was the easy part; making the big shots believe her was a different matter.

The cab took her home down the G.W. Parkway. She was so tired that she closed her eyes and fell asleep. In what seemed like hours she was awakened by the Bangladeshi cabbie.

"Madam, pardon me, please wake up. Madam, please wake up. Oh, good, that will be seven-fifty."

Betsy was embarrassed and gave the cabbie a ten, partially because she felt stupid for having fallen asleep and partially out of gratitude for the driver's gentlemanly behavior.

As usual Betsy woke up at six the next morning. She felt splendidly rested. As she was climbing out of the shower, she heard a dim mechanical purring noise through the wall. It took her several moments to realize what it was: a phone ringing. Not a modern digital chirp but a throaty "drring, drring, drring," loud enough to shake plaster off the walls.

But they didn't have any old-fashioned telephones in the apartment, just cheap boxy Radio Shack models.

Then she remembered. When she'd moved into this place, she'd been poking around in the broom closet, looking for a place to cram her winter clothes, when she'd stumbled across an old black telephone. It sat on top of a flat black box, which was hooked up to a narrow orange cable, which ran out of a hole in the wall.

Her former roommate—also CIA—had been living in the place for a year and was holding the lease. "That was here when I moved in," she said. "I guess it must have been installed for the previous tenants and the Agency never got around to removing it. There are probably phones like that stashed away in apartments all over northern Virginia."

When Betsy had taken over the lease, she had mentioned the phone to Security, and they'd said they would send someone out to pick it up, but they never had. Every new roommate who passed through the place discovered the phone, picked it up, found that the line was dead, and never touched it again. She and Cassie stacked their hats on it.

Betsy tripped over some towels, stumbled into the closet, swept the hats off the receiver, and picked up the black phone. "Hullo?"

Spector's strangely distorted voice came over the earpiece. "I'll meet you down at level three of your parking garage at six forty-five. I'll be driving a tan Ford Fairlane." Then he hung up.

Betsy had been maintaining a fragile calm in the face of her upcoming deputies meeting; now even this facade was completely shattered. Something must really be up. Her whole day was off balance. Her twenty-minute routine took thirty-five. She had forgotten to get her clothes ready the night before. The iron was broken, so she couldn't press her blouse. She broke into her summer clothes to get a lightweight number to wear under her no-nonsense blazer. She finally got herself put together and went to the elevator with her *Post* in hand.

Parking-level three was the last stop on the elevator ride, and when she arrived, exactly at six forty-five, Spector wasn't there. The exhaust fans throbbed and hummed, drowning out even her own thoughts, and she waited for five minutes, getting more and more nervous. Finally the government-issue Ford rounded the curve and pulled up beside her.

Spector leaned across, opened the passenger's-side door, and said casually, "Get in. Have you had any breakfast?"

They drove down to Nineteenth Street and over to McDonald's. The drive-through was choked with cars, so Spector handed Betsy a ten-dollar bill and said, "Egg McMuffin, orange juice, cinnamon roll, and large black coffee." The only people she saw at McDonald's were some cops, and two street people sharing a meal, drinking dozens of artificial creamers, and eating the contents of what appeared to be twenty packets of sugar. Soon she was back in the car.

They drove up the parkway to the first pull-off overlooking the Potomac. They got out, looked down at the rowers in their shells below and the golden sun, already high in the sky, casting a haze over the District.

"Enjoy," Spector said. "You're going to have an interesting day."

"Interesting in the Chinese-curse sense?"

"Absolutely. You are now a target—from at least three places. One, the career bureaucracy. King has spread the word about what a disloyal, insubordinate bitch you are. Two, Department of Agriculture. Glaspie took your words to heart and told the President. He is pissed off—not at you, but at Saddam. The Vice President has been all over the Foreign Assistance Office and Aid for International Development. They have contacted their buddies in Policies and Programs, who are pissed off—not at Saddam, but at you. Three, senior analysts. They were so busy trying to intuit the White House line—Millikan's line—and fit their analysis to that procrustean bed, that they totally missed all that you noticed. The question is not whether you are or are not right. The problem is that you scooped them. And they are pissed."

"But what about Millikan—why does he hate me so much?"

"Because Ronald Reagan was a big supporter of Saddam Hussein."

"I don't follow."

"Someone had to get the goods—the weapons, the money, the matériel, the intelligence—into Saddam's hands. Not as a one-off, you understand—the Iran-Iraq war dragged on forever, and the sheer quantity of stuff we handed over to the Iraqis during those years beggars the imagination. Handing it over was the job given to our friend James Gabor Millikan. Not that he didn't want the job, of course. He was glad to do it. But it's safe to say that it turned into a much bigger deal than he was anticipating when it all started—and then he had no choice but to see it through to the bloody end. It's in the nature of Washington, Betsy, that these things get structured in such a way that there is one, and only one, designated fall guy. One sacrificial lamb who will take full blame if the policy ever goes sour. In the case of our policy of shipping guns and money and highly classified intelligence to Iraq, the fall guy was Millikan. And ever since he's been waiting for the other shoe to drop."

"And he's afraid that I'm going to drop it."

"Bingo."

"Okay," Betsy said, "that explains Millikan. In a weird way it almost makes me feel sorry for him. But what about the DCI—where does he stand in all this?"

"He's a weenie. He cut his teeth under Casey. His understanding of the role of the Agency is to prove whatever it is that downtown wants proved. Anything that does not fit is either 'forward-leaning analysis' or else wrong. But since CIA doesn't do wrong things, it will probably be forward-leaning analysis."

"So what's going to happen to me?"

"You'll be sacrificed. For the good of the Agency, don't you know. But each of them will want their piece of you."

Betsy felt light-headed and tried to swallow a big lump in her throat, the same lump she used to get when Mom took her to the dentist to get her cavities drilled out.

"Look, I've been watching your work, and I know where you're going with it," Spector said. "And you're right. But that's not germane. Tell me if I'm wrong, but aren't you going to come up with the notion that there is a massive Iraqi research effort in nonconventional warfare under way? And that not only is it funded with our agricultural credits, but it's being carried out largely on our soil, in our academic institutions?"

"God, you're good."

"No, you're good. But in the immortal words of the new chief of collections in Mobile, Alabama, 'You've exceeded your task.' So say nothing. When they ask you for your report, say that you have not got all the results you need. They will proceed to stomp all over you. The Director of Central Intelligence will be pissed off because you did not fall for the trap of being brought out to headquarters to release your findings prematurely. The Office of Science and Technologies head will be pissed off at you because you have found something that his shop should have found, but because you'll say nothing, he won't even have the pleasure of venting his wrath. The Policy staff will be pissed off at you because you have scooped them. And on and on. You will take some shit for not exposing your body to their poisoned arrows, but if you say nothing, you will be alive to fight again another day."

Betsy had not touched her McMuffin. She was sick. For the moment Nampa, Idaho, seemed like an awfully nice place to her. Spector finished his meal and was sipping at his coffee. "I've saved the worst for last. Our friend Ed Hennessey has come up with the same conclusions you have. He needs our foreign information, and you need his help on the domestic front. Hennessey may be the Agency's most hated man in Washington—he's let it be known that he's found a lot of bad actors among our ranks, but he's playing his cards close, so everyone's afraid of him. Millikan hates him, too, for reasons that would take all morning to enumerate. You were seen talking to him the other day. My dear, you are in deep shit. You've got only one friend in town, and it's not me."

"Then why are you telling me this?"

"Because I ultimately work not for the Director of Central Intelligence or for Millikan, but for the President, and the President knows how these things work. He knows how totally irrational this system is and how much there is a need to change things. But this is the only system there is. He wants you to hang in there. I'm instructed to cover for you insofar as possible."

Betsy began to shiver; chills ran up and down her body, and she didn't know if it was from the damp April morning or sheer terror. She had never been this afraid before.

"I'm not real good at pep talks. I got out of Operations because I wasn't comfortable with sending people to virtually certain deaths. You are not going to be physically murdered—if you were, you'd get a star on the wall. You are going to be career-murdered. You will probably not get another promotion, and you will spend the rest of your life doing soybean studies. But you are in a situation that comes to few of us. You can, honest to God, make a difference."

"Why..."

"Yeah, I know, why if it is so dangerous doesn't the system take care of the problem? Don't forget, during the Cuban missile crisis John Scali of the American Broadcasting Company, meeting a Soviet diplomat at a restaurant, probably saved the world from nuclear destruction. This is not quite so dramatic. But it is important. And the system simply can't handle it. We have to do everything back-channel, both because of the peculiar chain of command and because we think there's a mole somewhere in the system. Eat your breakfast."

They sat there for fifteen minutes, watching the sun coming up over the city, listening to the increasing rumble of the incoming traffic. Finally Spector went to his car phone. Moments later a Red Top cab pulled up.

Betsy was shaking. Nothing in her life had prepared her for what was to come. Spector squeezed her elbow, gave her the most earnest, serious, eye-to-eye-contact look she had ever received from a Washington person. "Do good, kid. My ass is on the line, too. Unlike you, who stumbled into this, I'm a volunteer. See you next week."

Betsy walked over to the cab. It was the same cabbie from last night. "Good morning, madam," he said brightly. "Did you get a good night's sleep?"

"Not good enough. And you?"

"Oh, yes." Giggling. "Oh, yes, a very nice night's sleep."

ten

AFTER HIS big encounter with The Heavyweight, which put kind of an ominous spin on the overall decision to launch his campaign, Clyde decided he had had a little bit too much of the

Big City for the time being and that he would begin out in the hinterlands of Forks County. Somehow he reasoned that it would be easier there. He could go way out past Palisades State Park to the northwest corner of the county and start visiting farmhouses one at a time, out there in that flat territory on the west side of the Wapsipinicon, where two thousand acres was considered to be a small farm.

Another advantage: this would put him as far as possible from Lake Pla-Mor. Recent events there had given Clyde's opponent, Kevin Mullowney, some ammunition. Mullowney had been bruiting it about Forks County that Clyde's recent three A.M. rowboat recovery had been botched so miserably as to suggest that Clyde might be UNFIT TO BE SHERIFF.

The rowboat had been collected from the beach where Clyde had left it by the manager of the university boathouse, who towed it back, hauled it up on the ramp, and, with the help of a couple of strong rowers, turned it over to dump out all the rainwater that had collected in the bottom. Other debris had tumbled out, too: a few handfuls of gravel and some shards of a broken bottle. Fearing that barefoot boaters might cut their feet, the manager had swept all of it up and dumped it into the garbage can.

Two days later the missing oar had been noticed floating along with the great spinning whorl of flotsam and jetsam that always formed at the spillway. From time to time the Corps of Engineers would come along and rake all this unsightly debris away and haul it to the dump. The oar, clearly stenciled as EIU property, was plucked out by a diligent employee and eventually found its way back to the boathouse. It was an old splintered wooden oar, rough and creviced at the tip. Someone at the boathouse noticed that clumps of black hair were wedged into the cracks. Upon further analysis some shreds of human scalp were found in there, too.

Everyone knew instinctively where the body was. It was in the Rotary—the horizontal vortex that formed where the Nishnabotna River struck the face of the dam and curled under. The Rotary was marked with red buoys and lurid danger signs for half a mile upstream, but every year it seemed to claim another clueless high-school student or drunken frat boy. Once a body got into the Rotary, it could spin round and round for weeks before it was spat out, all decomposed and bloated and chewed up by the gar and carp and pike that lived in the lake.

The garbage can at the boathouse was emptied out and its contents personally inspected by Sheriff Mullowney himself, who worked best under the clinical illumination of television lights. The gravel from the bottom of the rowboat looked as if it had come from a public boat ramp way up at the northern end of the lake. The shards of glass did not come from a liquor bottle; they were quartz laboratory glassware. And there was a key chain in there, too, consisting of a car key, a house key, and an office-door key from the university, on a simple split ring. The office key was found to fit a laboratory door in the Sinzheimer Biochemistry Wing of the Scheidelmann AgriScience Research Center. The office was that of one Marwan Habibi, who had not been seen for two weeks.

Clyde Banks knew perfectly well that he hadn't done anything wrong—even if he had noticed the key chain in the boat, it wouldn't have given him reason to suspect a murder had happened. But Sheriff Mullowney seemed to have convinced every working journalist in eastern Iowa that Deputy Clyde Banks had blown an opportunity to break a probable murder case.

This, more than anything, had given Clyde the impetus to get started on his campaign. And for some reason it felt less embarrassing to do it out here, in the rural northwest corner of the county. If he started in some built-up area where the houses were close together, he would be seen making his way down the block. People sitting out on their front porches enjoying the spring breezes, people out mowing their lawns or playing basketball in the driveways, would watch him coming their way, hitting one house after another, and wonder what on earth he was doing. Word would get around.

Of course he had to remind himself that this was the whole idea of a political campaign. Word was supposed to get around. But Clyde had never been the type to draw attention to himself.

In high school he had hung around a little bit with attention-getting people who acted in plays and played musical instruments, almost all of whom had now moved to distant places where that kind of thing was not considered outlandish. The only people left behind at home were the ones who did not act that way. So for a man to go around knocking on every door in the county and putting his name and even his face up on signs in people's yards seemed very peculiar—not a good way to earn the respect of the citizenry.

The northwesternmost house in Forks County was pretty easy to find. He just drove west on 30, the Lincoln Highway, until he reached the border between Forks and Oakes counties, which was marked out by a straight gravel road running north-south, then took a right on that road and drove north until he saw a sign saying Maquoketa County. Then he shifted the wagon into reverse and backed up about a hundred feet. A farmhouse was on the right side of the road. Clyde backed directly into its driveway, leaving the Murder Car pointed outward so that he could escape rapidly if the place turned out to be occupied by one of the roughly eight thousand Mullowneys who lived in Forks County. But when he climbed out, he could see that the name Frost was on the mailbox. He went up and knocked on the door.

Only one person was in the place, a man in his fifties or sixties who looked vaguely familiar to Clyde. When he pulled the front door open and looked at Clyde through the screen door, his mouth was open and turned down at the corners like one of those thespian masks. He was lacking teeth, and this made his mouth seem especially large, further emphasizing the mask analogy. Also, his eyes were wide-open and greatly magnified by a pair of exceptionally thick eyeglasses, and he seemed to be staring at Clyde with kind of a haggard, amazed, slack-jawed look.

"Deputy Banks," the man said. "Why are you here?"

"Hello, Mr. Frost," Clyde said. "Sorry to bother you."

What should he say now? It seemed kind of rude for Clyde to ask if he could come in. He should leave that up to the individual voter. Besides, he had said only that he'd knock on every door in Forks County, not go into every living room. He was going to have to learn how to do this stuff quickly if he was going to hit every door between now and November.

"I just wanted to talk to you for a second," Clyde said.

Mr. Frost opened the storm door wordlessly and backed out of the way, holding it open with one arm, apparently indicating that Clyde could come into his house. So he walked into Mr. Frost's house. It was dark and fairly empty, and it smelled of mildew and old cigarette smoke not well vented to the outside.

He turned around in the middle of the living room and saw that Mr. Frost was still standing there by the front door, staring at him with that expression of tragic astonishment. By now Clyde was beginning to convince himself that this all had to do with the shape of Mr. Frost's mouth without dentures. If Mr. Frost had his choppers in place, it would change the shape of his whole face, and he would be beaming confidently at Clyde.

"How are you today, Mr. Frost?" Clyde said.

"Don't feel so good," Mr. Frost said.

"Oh, well, I'm sorry to hear that." Now Clyde felt like a heel. "I'll just do what I came to do very quickly, then."

"Go ahead and get it over with," Mr. Frost said.

"As you know, Mr. Frost, I'm a deputy county sheriff and have been for the last five years."

Mr. Frost let out a soft, aching moan as the word "sheriff" was making its way across the living room. He walked over to a footstool and sat down on it and grabbed his left forearm with his right hand and began to squeeze and rub it.

"You ain't gonna handcuff me, are you?" Mr. Frost said. "Please, I won't make no trouble."

"Oh, Jesus, Mr. Frost, that's not why I'm here!" Clyde said.

"God, my arm hurts like hell," Mr. Frost said.

"Oh, man," Clyde said, and put one hand up to his face and began to rub his eyebrows, staring at the old cigarette-burned carpet. "I'm really sorry, Mr. Frost. I'm new at this, and I should have just told you right up front that I didn't come here on official business."

All of a sudden he remembered where he had seen Mr. Frost before. Mr. Frost had beaten up his wife a couple of years ago on their farm south of town and broken one of her cheekbones so that her eye got out of place. Clyde had arrested him and taken him down to the station, and later Mr. Frost had pleaded to a lesser charge and got off with six months. Now it kind of looked as if Mr. Frost was living alone.

Mr. Frost was just gaping at Clyde with his mouth still turned down. He had stopped rubbing his forearm and put one hand on his chest. As Clyde watched, he made that hand into a fist and pressed it against his breastbone.

"Did you punch me in the chest?" Mr. Frost said.

"No, sir, I did not touch you. I'm sorry if—"

"I feel like barbecued shit," Mr. Frost said, and slumped back so he was leaning against the wall. Clyde noticed that he had got all sweaty. Once again Mr. Frost made the chest-punching motion.

Clyde remembered a piece of nurse lore that Desiree had told him, which was that when heart-attack patients came in, they almost invariably made chest-punching motions.

"I'm calling an ambulance," Clyde said. He went over and picked up the phone. It was dead.

"Didn't pay my bill," Mr. Frost said. "Paid all my money to the alimony."

"Then we have to get you to a hospital," Clyde said. "Come on."

He went over and picked up Mr. Frost in a fireman's carry, slinging the old man over his shoulders like a bag of charcoal briquettes, and carried him out to the station wagon. Mr. Frost had gone limp, so Clyde buckled him in to keep him upright. Then he started the engine and punched the gas and sent the Murder Car chortling through deep gravel onto the road, southbound.

The next farmhouse was just half a mile down the road, but Clyde figured that he could get to the hospital faster than he could call up an ambulance and have them come out there, so he just drove into Wapsipinicon at about a hundred miles per hour, noting with professional embarrassment that no sheriff cars even noticed this breach of posted speed limits.

He came into town on U.S. 30, which was known as Lincoln Way in populated areas, passed the main campus on the left, then the mile-wide parking lot of the Events Center, with the auditorium and then Twister Stadium and then the coliseum rising out of the asphalt, past the Twister's outdoor and indoor practice fields, then hung a screaming left onto Knapp Avenue and went up about half a dozen blocks and pulled into the medical center, following the red signs to the emergency room at Methodist Hospital, which was so brand-new and so good that it was not called an emergency room but a trauma center. Clyde could find the trauma center with his eyes closed; he went there all the time, on business.

He did not feel it would be decent to leave the grounds until he knew how things turned out with Mr. Frost. But he also knew from experience that drinking foul, watery coffee in the hospital cafeteria was not a good way to kill time, and so, after a decent interval had passed, he parked the wagon in the visitor lot and went for a stroll.

A few moments' walk took him down into the greenbelt along the Wapsipinicon. A bike path ran along the bank, with occasional bizarre-looking suspension bridges (engineering-student projects) over to the EIU campus on the opposite side. Clyde strolled across one of these and soon found himself on the sculptured quadrangle of the two-year-old marble-sheathed Henry Scheidelmann AgriScience Research Center, the House That Larsen Built. It was a campus within a campus, free from the unwashed mobs of undergraduates who thronged the rest of the university's twenty-five hundred acres, populated mostly by foreigners with stratospheric IQs. Clyde sat down on a bench that said it had been donated by the government of Nigeria and watched them coming and going in their dashikis and saris and turbans and white lab coats, and wondered whether Frank Frost was still alive, and if he was, whether he had any idea that a place like this existed just a few minutes' drive away from the run-down farm where he had chosen to seclude himself from the world.

Clyde sat on that bench for fifteen minutes, watching the foreign students come and go, and thinking not about Frank Frost but about the missing Marwan Habibi.

He stood up, stretched, then ambled into the main entrance of the Scheidelmann. He dawdled around the giant electric globe for a few minutes, looking at the electric pins thrust into so many exotic parts of it, every one of them a place where Eastern Iowa University had somehow got itself tangled up with some other nation's government and laws. He consulted a map on the wall and made his way into the Sinzheimer Wing, then up to the third floor, to door 304, which had been sealed off with yellow crime-scene tape.

"Can I help you?" said a voice. An American voice. Clyde looked up, startled, to see a young man standing there, holding an unopened can of Coke and a small bag of chips. He was about Clyde's height but probably forty or fifty pounds lighter. He had large pale-blue eyes and strawberry-blond hair and a history of acne that was not entirely history. He had an alert, birdlike look about him.

"Pardon?" Clyde said.

"You've been standing here for ten minutes," the man said. "I'm Kevin Vandeventer. That's my lab right there." He nodded at the adjoining room.

"Clyde Banks," Clyde said, and shook Kevin Vandeventer's hand. Then, as an afterthought, he added, "Deputy county sheriff and candidate for sheriff."

"Oh. So you're here on the investigation."

Clyde remembered something. "You talked to the Wapsipinicon detectives already, didn't you?" Clyde had read the report of Vandeventer's interview during his recent efforts to play catch-up and not look like a complete idiot.

"Yeah." Vendeventer shook his head. "Boy, it's a real shame about Marwan. I'm hoping they find him alive and well—but that seems less and less likely."

Several dozen questions had already come to Clyde's mind. But almost all of them had been asked by the Wapsipinicon detectives. Vandeventer's answers had been detailed and grammatically perfect—interviewing scientists was a piece of cake. Besides, it wasn't Clyde's job to be grilling witnesses—he had to go out and win an election first. And he wasn't winning any elections here in this corridor inhabited by foreign students who couldn't vote.

"Gotta run," Clyde said. "Vote Banks."

eleven

THE CABBIE drove the five miles up to the CIA entrance off the parkway and stopped a bit past the curve that concealed the guardhouse from the highway. Betsy, deep in thought, had not got her badge out, but she didn't need to. The cabbie and the gate guard knew each other. He drove past the Bucky Fuller Auditorium, into the U drive, and dropped her off at the Nathan Hale statue. Betsy reached into her purse for the fare, but the cabbie waved his hand—"No need, madam, the gentleman took care of it. Have a good day." Then, motioning toward Nathan Hale, he said, "Remember, be glad that you have only one life to give for your country."

She was early and the day was beautiful, so she found a nearby bench to collect her thoughts. How curious, she mused, to have uttered one sentence and caused all this. How curious, too, was Spector, and what he had said about the President. Could that be for real?

How should I play this? she asked herself. She remembered her first graduate seminar at the University of Idaho. She was the only woman in an econometrics seminar. She knew very little at that time about economic modeling and number crunching, but she knew that the men in the class had real contempt for her. She was new, she was not pretty, and she was there for the thrashing. She had remained quiet, had given her paper, and had been hammered without mercy. The professor who ran the seminar, and who hated her mentor, Larkin Schoendienst, urged his men on much like Caligula urging on the gladiators at the colosseum. She had survived. But she had felt raped.

She was a good girl, but she wasn't stupid enough to repeat that experience. Betsy would follow Spector's advice. She would say, "Gee whiz, sir, I just don't know." Or, "Gee whiz, sir. I haven't got the whole story." She was as much at risk here as she had been out in the irrigated potato fields of the Snake River basin. There were rattlesnakes all over here, too, except that she didn't have her pellet gun and dog, Katie, with her. But she had her survival skills. Her spirits began to rise. She fished in her purse and pulled out her billfold. Cassie had wanted to see what pictures Betsy carried and had let out a whoop when the only one she saw was of Katie, a Labrador mix, sitting in the back of the pickup with her doggie grin on and red tongue hanging out. Betsy looked at that picture and a broad smile spread across her face. It felt strange. She hadn't smiled in days.

Spector was right. She would not make the mistake she'd made with the attaché back in March. She would not exceed her task. She would not fall into the bureaucratic trap. She would complete her task to the letter and walk out bloodied but unbowed.

As she walked in, the limousine carrying the DCI—her boss for the last week—pulled up. She had seen him once before, when he had come to the Castleman Building to eat pizza with the staff, something his personnel people had encouraged after Casey had stroked out. She smiled at him, he opened the door for her. As she walked in, she heard him ask an assistant, "Who's that?"

"That's her."

"Vandeventer?"

She stepped aside and let him and his people go through security together while she dug her badge out of her purse. When she went through, the DCI was waiting for her. He introduced himself and said, "We look forward to hearing your report today."

"Oh, thank you, sir. I feel so honored to be able to share my findings at that level."

"By the way, you should know that Dr. Millikan will be coming out to join us."

"Oh! So much the better!"

"See you on seven," he said, exchanged a *What a ditz* look with his aide, and headed for the executive elevator.

Betsy crowded onto the staff elevator, which stopped at all the intervening floors. She finally got to seven and went straight to her nook. She logged on and paged through her bioweapons report, the best she'd been able to come up with over the last week. No doubt the DCI's minions had already copied it and pored over it, highlighting all the soft spots—of which there were many.

She closed that document, pulled up her soybean report, and printed all forty pages of it on the laser printer. She carried it to the other end of the hall and had fifteen copies printed up. While the machine was running, she went to the rest room to straighten herself up. Through the frosted-glass window she heard a helicopter descending on the nearby helipad. Millikan had arrived.

She went to the supplies closet and got twelve binders for her report, then back to the photocopy room to collate them, humming to herself as she stacked the pages and snapped them into the binders. Then she sensed a hostile presence, smelled the same kind of perfume that her least-favorite third-grade teacher had always worn. It was the DCI's executive secretary, Margaret Hume. Betsy turned and said, "Hi!" as chirpily as she could.

Hume merely glowered and blocked the door. Behind her she could see Millikan walk by with his entourage, followed shortly by the director of the Iraqi task force out of Operations—she didn't know his name. The director of the Office of Program Analysis and Coordination. The director of Economic Analysis. The director of Science and Technology. The deputy DCI, liaisons from DIA and NSC, the deputy director of Operations. All of them men in dark suits, moving quietly and purposefully, all waiting for her performance. She should have been too intimidated to stand up.

"Time for me to go," Betsy cooed sweetly.

"When it's time," the steely Mrs. Hume replied.

"Maggie," Betsy asked, taking great pleasure in watching the anger flare in the thirty-year veteran's face, "do you think the Agency is guilty of treating its female employees unfairly?"

"Absolutely not. The Agency loves its people."

"Yes, I've noticed," said Betsy, getting up. "I've got to go."

"Not till it's time."

"Maggie," Betsy said, "I grew up moving irrigation pipe and digging potatoes. I weigh two hundred pounds. It's time for my meeting. In about five seconds all two hundred pounds of me is going to come through that doorway as fast as I can walk, which is pretty fast. Now, please don't tell me that I have to resort to physical intimidation to get out of this room."

Betsy turned her back on Margaret Hume, gathered up her binders into a stack, and cradled them in her arms. She turned to the door to find the executive secretary still doggedly planted there in her path. Betsy fixed her gaze on a point somewhere behind Margaret Hume's head and strode forward, building quickly up to the full head of steam that she used when stomping down the hill from work. At the last minute Mrs. Hume lost the game of chicken; realizing that Betsy wasn't kidding, she backed awkwardly out of the way. Betsy heard the satisfying snap of a heel coming loose from Mrs. Hume's shoe. She slumped against the corridor wall and Betsy pushed by. "Have a lovely day, Maggie."

She arrived at the door of the conference room just as a lackey came out for her. "You're here?" he said with some surprise.

"It's time for the meeting, isn't it?"

She walked into the room with its splendid kidney-shaped Florentine-marble table. Every chair was taken. She turned to the lackey and said, "Where am I to go?"

"Over there," he whispered, gesturing to the spotlighted podium.

"Gentlemen," the DCI began, for there were surely no women there except for Betsy and, bringing up the rear, the limping Margaret Hume, "our stated agenda today is what to do with Iraq's export-import credits. As you know, there is severe pressure from certain circles on the Hill to cut these sources of support for Mr. Hussein. The President has already received our reports on Mr. Hussein's use of funds both foreign and domestic, both internally generated and externally donated." He paused, as if to consider the rhetorical elegance of what he had just said. "As most of you know, we reached no stated consensus on what to do and recommended further study on the Hill of this issue."

Polite, barely perceptible smiles spread around the room. The DCI had just stated that the intelligence community had cobwebbed the anti-Iraqi forces. There were enough pro-Iraqi factions on the Hill to schedule hearings that would last until Saddam died of old age.

"Consequently, the actual agenda for today is to consider Ms. Vandeventer's reports on possible misuse of agricultural funds by Iraq. If you'll open the envelope in front of you, you will see the history of this particular question. In February, Ms. Vandeventer was on a briefing team for our agricultural attaché to Baghdad. After finishing her report she added her concerns about the distribution and application of the Food for Peace grants. Word made its way up the chain to the ambassador, who communicated her concern to the secretary of state." He looked around and saw that there was nobody there yet from State. "Mr. Baker considered it important that that concern in turn be communicated to the President. Dr. Millikan, will you continue the story?"

Millikan cleared his throat. "I hate this time of year in Washington. The allergies set off a river in my head." The assembled directors indicated their sympathy. Betsy, the only one standing, began to notice that her nose was running, too. She felt a sneeze building.

"As you know," Millikan continued, "the making of middle-eastern policy is a difficult task. We count heavily on you to help us. We know of your difficulty because of the devastation of our HUMINT resources after the Iranian Embassy takeover and the death of Colonel Buckley.

"The goal of our policy is simple. It is to keep Iran in check. Their brand of Islamic fundamentalism, their population and resource base, and their terrorist network around the world constitute a clear and continuous threat to us and to our new Soviet colleagues in Central Asia. As unpleasant as it may be, we have only one counterweight to Iran, and that is Iraq and the theatrical Saddam Hussein."

His face began to redden. "It's tough enough to handle the Israeli lobby and their pressures, and the liberals and their bitching about George's lack of vision, and the press with their sniping attacks. But when we get sandbagged by bottom-fish analysts, this is too much. We have to be on the same page! Is that clear?"

The exalted directors around the table were taking a tongue-lashing from the White House. Betsy watched this passively, much as she might be watching C-Span at home. She knew that she was the object of this attack, but she didn't feel as if she were in the same room. Millikan talked more and more and began to turn red and pound the table as he lashed out at incompetent underlings, disloyal subordinates, and the helplessness of government to clean out bad employees. He then stood up and pointed directly at Betsy, who imagined herself as Joan of Arc, tied to the stake, smoke curling up into her inflamed nasal passages—

She sneezed. It was a good one. It came out when Millikan, like Pavarotti going for a high C, was ready to drive his point home. A long thread of mucus flew out over her upper and lower lip, and everyone in the room looked away from her. She fumbled for a Kleenex.

The room was paralyzed. The deputy director of Operations blurted, "Gesundheit."

Betsy said, "Sorry."

Millikan had lost his train of thought. He could not sustain his anger at anyone this pathetic. He could only shake his head in disbelief and look helplessly at the DCI.

"I'd like to thank Dr. Millikan for his insights and for his typically acute analysis of a serious problem in policy formation. Ms. Vandeventer. You have been our guest here for the past week. I'm sorry you're feeling poorly—as soon as you've got yourself together, could we see your report?"

"Of course. Maggie, would you pass these out?" Betsy said, dumping the heap of binders in front of the crippled dragon lady. Hume had fully recovered her composure, and she hobbled around the table cheerfully dispensing the copies.

Betsy began. "The level of classification for this briefing is FOUO—for official use only."

"What? Nothing important is FOUO," said one of the suits.

"If I may continue," Betsy appealed to the DCI.

"Go ahead."

"I will welcome questions or requests for elucidation at the end of my presentation."

She then read her paper on soybean markets, present and future, in Southwest Asia. As she patiently explained that there was a healthy market for American soybeans, if the U.S. could keep the Indians from entering the market, the men around the table began to mutter and look across at each other. Their staffers in chairs around the edge of the room began to growl in sympathetic response.

Millikan finally broke in. "You know goddamned well that this is not what you're here for. You're here to expand on the line you gave the attaché about Saddam using our Ag funds for improper purposes."

"Oh, sir, that's not what I was tasked for. I was dealt with harshly by my branch chief, Mr. Howard King, who has since received a promotion for his good work. He told me forcefully never to exceed my task again, never again to mention anything outside my job of tracing commodities flow. I'm doing some interesting work on the lentil market now. Would you like to hear something about lentils?"

"You mean that you won't discuss your notions of improper Iraqi use of USG funds?"

"With all due respect, sir, I cannot exceed my task. Now, if you gentlemen would like to contact my branch and task me to pursue Iraqi use of USG funds, I would be glad to. But I'm sure that you all are considering that."

Millikan interrupted, softly and slowly. "Then why did you tell the attaché that Mr. Hussein was misusing USG funds? Don't play stupid with me."

"I told him that he had misused funds because part of the allocation was to be a direct cash transfer, after Baghdad initialed the agreement, to Soo Empire Grain in exchange for eight hundred thousand tons of soybeans. Mr. Hussein bought coffee from Brazil instead. At that point it ceased to be part of my task."

Millikan sensed there was no reason to continue the discussion, turned to Gates, and said, "I'm pleased that the branch chief instructed Ms. Vandeventer on proper procedure. Please send my commendation to his file." He sent one long, chilly glare in Betsy's direction until she broke eye contact in favor of staring down at the podium.

The DCI looked around the room and asked, "Are there any other questions to be asked of Ms. Vandeventer before she goes back to the Castleman Building?"

There were none. The NSC had been bought off. They put their knives away. There would be no ritualistic blood sacrifices. The DCI motioned Margaret Hume over and asked, "Would you show Ms. Vandeventer to my office? I'd like to talk with her after this is over."

"Thank you for your report," said the Operations head with barely concealed amusement. He knew a fog job when he saw one.

"You're dead in this business," Mrs. Hume said, leading her down the corridor. "You might as well outprocess right now while you've still got a breath in your body. You also owe me a pair of shoes."

Betsy took a seat in the DCI's office, looking out over the trees of McLean down toward the Potomac. Off to the south she thought she could see the top of the Washington Monument.

"Did you hear me?" asked Mrs. Hume.

"Sorry about the shoe," Betsy said absentmindedly, "but I am a clumsy person. Could you get me a cup of coffee? Black, please."

Hume hissed in a deep breath, as if preparing to shoot flames from her mouth, and then almost whiplashed when she heard her boss's voice right behind her: "That sounds good. Get one for me, too, Maggie. Thanks so much."

The DCI came over and sat behind his desk. He did not seem angry, just professionally neutral. "Quite a performance. You had at least six long knives coming after you, and if Millikan had drawn blood, you would have been slaughtered."

"Why didn't you do something? Why put me through this?"

"There is an inherent and unstoppable bureaucratic dynamic. It's almost visceral. Your one simple comment to the attaché had an impact like a hand grenade. If one GS-eleven can figure things out, then how do you explain the need for all this?" With his left hand he indicated the central compound. "I know that I can count on your discretion, but we're going to take a pounding on our misread of the Sovs over the past ten years. I came on the watch fairly late in the game, and there are bureaucratic and political momenta that I can't even begin to touch."

"I don't mean to be naive, but isn't this a stupid way to get things done?"

"Yes, but it's all we've got."

His secretary came in with the coffee, and he launched into a totally disconnected discussion of the need to maintain order among the ranks, the importance of the hierarchy, and so on. She left, and he busied himself for a moment with the cream pitcher.

"So everyone says I'm finished. Am I finished?"

"In the long run, yes," he said. "In the short run you still have an assigned role. It's all part of that momentum thing. Go back to the Castleman after lunch—you're acting branch chief now."

They exchanged some completely inconsequential small talk about Idaho geography. Before she had lingered long enough to become unwelcome, Betsy excused herself, shook the DCI's hand, walked out past Hume, past the offices on the seventh floor, wondering if she'd ever be there again. She took the lift down to the first floor, walked out past security, and went to the waiting area to wait for the Blue Bird.

A familiar voice came from a bench near Nathan Hale. "Good morning, madam. How is your day? Do you need a ride?"

twelve

MAY

HAVING GROWN up in the explosively fecund Dhont household, Desiree already knew more about parenting than Clyde ever would. Intimidatingly enough, she had launched into a concerted research program, buying or borrowing dozens of advanced baby-management books, surging out way beyond her former level until she vanished over Clyde's horizon.

Some of the baby books were well-worn standards from the Nishnabotna Public Library, and some were slick new handouts obtained from the Child Development Department. Clyde had once, furtively, picked up a document while sitting on the pot and begun to peruse it. The language was clear enough (especially to one accustomed to the Victorian complexities of Sherlock), and you didn't have to be a rocket scientist to get the basic ideas. He scanned through to the end of the book with renewed confidence. By spending a little bit more time than usual sitting on the pot and reading these books, he might, in the fullness of time, surprise and delight his spouse by suddenly displaying a hitherto unsuspected grasp of parentology.

Then he picked up another one and discovered that it contradicted the first one directly. He understood why Desiree spent so much time on this: you had to get a few hundred of these things under your belt so that you could sort out the nonsense from the wisdom.

When the little one took to waking up in the middle of the night and crying, he found that many wee hours that normally would have been lost to wasteful sleep could now be spent improving his mind, reading the works of several august Ph.D.'s in Baby Science. All of them held diametrically opposed opinions about how to get your baby to sleep at night, and all of them had blindingly impressive academic credentials, so sorting out truth from fiction was not a simple task.

He had one small advantage: namely, that in the course of his work he routinely came into contact with Ph.D.'s from the university. Ph.D.'s, he had found, did not seem so intimidating after you had jump-started their cars, got their cats out of trees, and arrested a few of them for beating up their Ph.D. wives. So he went directly to the content.

It seemed like a good bet that if the writer of such a book was a fool, this fact would be bound to come out somewhere in its several hundred pages. Like a feckless student shoplifting his way through an academic year at EIU, a fool writing a book would be bound to screw up somewhere along the line. Clyde read the books with the relentless penetrating scrutiny of a detective, not looking for information so much as evidence. The presence of a screaming baby in his near vicinity concentrated his mind and gave him a kind of judicial clarity of thought; finding an internal contradiction or even a badly written sentence, he would snap it shut, with a popping noise like the bang of a gavel, and Frisbee it across the carpet into the reject pile. Finally he was beginning to find his niche in this parenting thing. Desiree was too soft and accepting; she read all of this contradicting stuff and tried to give all of it a fair hearing. But he had more of an unyielding Old Testament approach and did not hesitate to cast suspect materials into the Lake of Fire.

Over the course of many such nocturnal research sessions he was able to narrow the field of baby-sleep experts down to one guy, a Ph.D. from back East. Clyde liked this guy because he seemed clearheaded and was not overly sentimental. He got the sense that this guy was giving it to him straight. What the guy said was that babies had to learn how to go to sleep on their own, and that if you rocked them or bottled them to sleep, they'd never learn how. In other words: let the baby cry. Sooner or later it'll figure out how to go to sleep on its own.

This was a good theory. There was only one problem: the guy said you weren't supposed to let them cry until they were four months old. Maggie had been born in March.

That was why Clyde spent a lot of April and May driving around with Maggie in the Murder Car at three and four o'clock in the morning. Driving in the car was the only way he had yet found to calm the kid down; and if it didn't work, at least his neighbors wouldn't know about it.

It was useful in another way, too: it gave him plenty of time to think about the last hours of Marwan Habibi's life.

The Rotary had finally spat Habibi's body out last week, badly decomposed and half-eaten by fish. He was still wearing a leather jacket, whose pockets had been filled with gravel from the boat ramp, but his body had bloated to the point where it floated in spite of this improvised attempt to weigh it down. Clyde had, naturally, been given the job of hauling the remains out of the spillway box while Kevin Mullowney stood on top of the dam in a nimbus of TV light, looking tough but concerned. Clyde had accompanied the body bag down to the office of the Forks County coroner, Barnabas Klopf, M.D., who had stirred through the remains while Clyde loitered in the background, trying to find something else to look at. Clyde had seen a few bodies but never anything like what was left of Marwan Habibi.

"Aw, damn," Clyde said, reading a label on a drawer. "What's Kathy Jacobson doing here?"

"She's dead," Barney Klopf said.

"I'm sorry to hear that." Mrs. Jacobson had been a fixture at the Lutheran church that Clyde had attended until his marriage to Desiree had forced him to become a papist. "When did she pass away?"

"Just yesterday. Had a heart attack in the kitchen while she was making lutefisk."

Clyde didn't say anything, but he felt some satisfaction at this; if Kathy Jacobson could have picked a time and a place to die, it would certainly be in her kitchen making lutefisk.

"Mallory Brown," Clyde said, continuing to browse the drawers. Mallory was a black Korean War vet who always carried the flag in the Veteran's Day parade.

"Two days ago. Stasis Asthmaticus."

"Who's Rod Weller?" Clyde asked, coming to another drawer.

"Lawyer from Davenport. Yesterday. Heart attack while bowhunting for carp."

Barney was running for reelection, also on the GOP slate, and so when he finished the autopsy, for the first time in his career Clyde actually gained some benefit from being affiliated with the Republican party: he was the first person to know about the coroner's report, which stated that Marwan Habibi had probably died as the result of having his head staved in by several blows from a heavy bladelike implement, not unlike an oar. Clyde announced this fact to a waiting camera crew when he exited the building. But it probably did him as much harm as good; it just reminded everyone about the rowboat.

Clyde drove to Lincoln Way, headed east through the industrial flatlands of east Nishnabotna and through the strip malls on the periphery of town. The colored lights seemed to hold Maggie's attention and stun her into momentary silence, or maybe she was simply looking straight out the windshield at the galactic magnificence of the Star-Spangled Truck Stop, whose giant electronic signboards could be seen for miles away; they had been specifically engineered to wake up even deeply slumbering truckers on I-45 and give them ample time to decelerate and take the Nishnabotna exit.

Once past the Star-Spangled Truck Stop, they were plunged instantly into total darkness. The boundary between city and farm was abrupt in this part of the world, and strip-mall parking lots typically ended in cornfields.

Heading south on I-45, they clipped through the southern extremity of Nishnabotna before crossing the Iowa River. Almost immediately, Clyde took the exit for New 30, which took off west-northwest across empty cornfields and the occasional tiny cluster of houses until it joined up again with Old 30, aka Lincoln Way. At this point Clyde would veer off onto a ramp, slow the Murder Car way down, and hang a hard right, bringing it all the way around to an easterly heading on Lincoln Way. This intersection was shared by a used-car dealership, a Casey's minimart, and a down-at-the-heels roadhouse that seemed to change ownership every few months. Or at least that had been the pattern until last year, when a couple of women had bought it and turned it into a cowgirl bar—the sort of cowgirl bar where cowboys were about as welcome as diamondback rattlesnakes. The place was popular among women affiliated with the university. But Nishnabotnans had heard about it and liked to titillate themselves by gossiping about who had been sighted there.

One night, finding that the gas needle was on empty and that Maggie was not sleeping anyway, Clyde stopped at the Casey's for a fill-up and a cup of coffee. As he topped off the tank, squeezing the trigger to fire additional quart or half-gallon bursts of gasohol down the pipe, he heard loud Patsy Cline music spilling out of an open door on the side of the cowgirl bar. Looking up at the sound, he saw a couple of cowgirls sharing an amorous moment against the side wall of the building. One of them had her back to Clyde; she had long blond hair and looked like a college student. Her friend was leaning back against the wall of the bar and had grown-up hair, frosted and set. It was Grace Chandler, who, along with her husband—local sports legend and defrocked broadcaster Buck Chandler—had sold Clyde his apartment building. She was a vivacious and pleasant woman, smarter than her husband. She had always seemed sad to Clyde, until now.

From the Casey's, Clyde could drive all the way through the middle of Wapsipinicon and Nishnabotna on Lincoln Way, a stretch of road lousy with stoplights. At this time of night no cars were active to trip the sensors buried in the road, and so the lights were running on automatic program. As long as he hewed to the speed limit, Clyde could drive all the way through those thirty-two stoplights without stopping or even slowing down. When he sensed that he was riding a wave, he would simply set the vehicle's cruise control at thirty-five and keep the station wagon aimed straight down the center of the road.

But occasionally some nocturnal driver would pull up on a cross street and trip the sensor, throwing the entire chain of traffic lights into a state of chaos. Since the land was flat and Lincoln Way was straight, all of the lights, for miles into the distance, were visible at once. The results were almost palpable. Clyde could see the headlights of the interloper, lurking in the side street, and he could watch the lights turning red in chain reaction up and down the length of the street.

Attached to each light was an apparatus that consisted of a little electronic box with a long, narrow tube sticking out of it in each direction, pointing down the street. Recessed way back in each tube was a photocell. The photocell stared up the tube, looking at the street with tunnel vision.

Emergency vehicles all had strobe lights tuned to flash at a particular frequency. When the photocell noticed such a light, it would trip the stoplight and make it turn green. This was how emergency vehicles were able to scream up and down the length of Lincoln Way even at rush hour without ever encountering a red light.

Whenever Clyde saw lights beginning to turn red on Lincoln Way in the middle of the night, he would reach down and wrap his fingers around the knob that controlled the station wagon's headlights. He would jerk the knob back and forth several times, rapidly flashing the headlights, and as if by magic, lights would turn green, in chain reaction, all the way down the length of Lincoln Way, all the way (he imagined) to the East Coast, and he would glide by in the big station wagon, glancing at the interlopers stopped at the cross streets, glaring at him suspiciously.

Once he found himself stopped at a red light anyway, because he was thinking so hard about Marwan Habibi that he had forgotten to flash the lights. He glanced at the cross street to see who the hell was out at three o'clock in the morning, screwing up the preordained behavior of the traffic lights. It was a powerful, jacked-up Trans Am belonging to one Mark McCarthy, a misdemeanor specialist whom Clyde had arrested on several occasions. The Trans Am was departing an especially inexpensive neighborhood of Nishnabotna, where he was known to live, from time to time, with his common-law wife and occasional children.

Someone—or something—was definitely in the passenger seat next to Mark McCarthy. But Clyde was unable to tell who, or what, it was until McCarthy pulled forward and made a left turn directly in front of him. Looking in through the windows of McCarthy's Trans Am at close range, Clyde was clearly able to make out a pale-pink baby seat with an infant strapped in it, wrapped in its fuzzy blanket sleeper, sucking on a fresh bottle.

The key witness was Vandeventer, who had seen Marwan Habibi carried out of the lab early on the same night he had been murdered (the same night that the rowboat had been stolen). Vandeventer had got a good look at Marwan and was sure that his skull had been intact at that point—and, indeed, there could be little doubt of this, because the damage observed by Barney Klopf during the autopsy had been severe, and obvious even to Barney, a notorious abuser of pharmaceutical substances.

Vandeventer had ID'd the other Arab students who had been present at the party in Lab 304, and all of them had been interviewed—but their words were taken with a grain of salt, because all of them were suspects. The students agreed that after leaving Lab 304 they had proceeded to a house, where Habibi had woken up and continued with the celebration.

Fingerprints were lifted from the rowboat and the fatal oar and matched with those of one Sayed Ashrawi, who was one of the students ID'd by Vandeventer. Further interviews with the other students established that, at about one o'clock in the morning, Ashrawi had volunteered to take Marwan Habibi home—he was relatively sober, the designated driver of the bunch, and Habibi had once again lapsed into incoherence. After that neither Ashrawi nor Habibi had been seen until eight o'clock the next morning, when Ashrawi had shown up for a meeting of a local Islamic students' group. But a look at Ashrawi's credit-card statement showed that he had purchased gasoline at an Exxon near Lake Pla-Mor at five in the morning.

All of the other students had alibis. Ashrawi was arrested and even now languished in the Forks County Jail, refusing to eat the unclean jailhouse food and praying to Mecca five times a day as the other inmates flung curses at him.

Clyde didn't dare say so in public, but he was pretty sure that Ashrawi was an innocent man.

thirteen

SAVING A hundred million lives, or at least believing that he had done so, was not half-bad for a man who had begun life in a bootlegger's hut in the hills of McCurtain County, Oklahoma. Arthur Larsen's father had taught him one lesson and one lesson only: how to dodge. How to circumvent the bizarre and meaningless hurdles that were constantly thrown in one's path by Authority. And, where dodging wasn't possible, how to jump through the unavoidable hoops with the absolute minimum of effort.

It was an ideal philosophy of life for a bootlegger, but Arthur Larsen found that it worked even better in the academic world—even as early as grade school. He was valedictorian of his high-school class, not because he was the smartest but because he had sussed out the system and had no qualms about manipulating it. He found his way to Oklahoma State University, where he worked a full-time job and still managed to complete the B.S. and vet-med requirements in six years. His record was so outstanding that Cornell gave him a full E-ticket ride for his Ph.D. studies in veterinary pathology.

By this point he was doing serious science. You couldn't fake that. But as long as that one rule was followed, you could dodge within that system as well as any other. Larsen developed a shrewd sense of just how little substance you could put into a research paper and still get it published. His first efforts were not well received, but he kept cranking them out anyway, and after a few years the minuscule flakes of data began to pile into drifts. By the time he got his Ph.D., the snow job was complete. He moved to Eastern Iowa University and, having conquered the research racket, turned his attention full-time to what would become his crowning achievement: supreme mastery of the black art of grantsmanship.

And where grants weren't enough, he found other ways of making money. Larsen and the Iowa State treasurer ran a four-hundred-head herd of Black Angus as an experiment, sold the proceeds—sans taxation—and cleared a small fortune. By the time 1990 had rolled around, Arthur Larsen had raised two monuments to his achievements: one, the Scheidelmann AgriScience Research Center, and two, a research park south of town that served as home for two dozen small high-tech start-ups. At least half were spin-offs of Larsen-sponsored research and had Larsen on their board of directors. The research park was a small masterpiece in and of itself; it was built with state money on university land and lavished with tax breaks and sweetheart loans by the state legislators, whom Larsen herded through the place like so many Black Angus, dazzling them with visions of a Silicon Barnyard.

What he could do within the framework at EIU he did at Scheidelmann, and what he couldn't he did in his spin-offs. These were the two pillars of the Larsen colossus, a fabulously complex web that occupied a six-person law firm full-time just to keep all the taxes paid and all the important laws more or less unbroken.

Kevin Vandeventer had plenty of time to review these facts and statistics in his mind as he sat in the waiting room of Professor Larsen's office suite one morning in early May, waiting for a ten A.M. appointment that kept getting pushed back, five and ten and fifteen minutes at a time. He was slowly working his way up a queue consisting of some half a dozen other graduate students—all South Asians and Africans. Each of them, including Kevin, was responsible for some of Larsen's grant money—half a million here, three million there. Each was responsible for making sure that those dollars were reprocessed and converted into a certain number of published research papers, and, wherever possible, press releases extolling the lifesaving benefits of modern agricultural technology. Each had to check in with Larsen every few weeks and brief him on recent progress. Larsen tended to schedule all such appointments in a block so that he could sacrifice a whole day to it and keep other days free for golfing with the board of regents, piloting his Beechcraft to Taos, hornswoggling venture capitalists, taping interviews with national news programs, or jetting off to China or India to be feted by the highest echelons of those governments. Those things were the fun part of being the Rainmaker. Managing these grants, and grinding out Ph.D.'s, were like the compulsory figures in an ice-skating competition.

There was not much friendly small talk in the waiting room. These people had been sent there because they were smart, not because of their social skills. Many of them were probably competing against each other for the pool of grant money hauled down by the Rainmaker, and those who weren't might be from nations that were mutually hostile, or even at war.

The receptionist's intercom chirped. Kevin blinked and tried to shake off the midafternoon lethargy; he was at the top of the queue. The receptionist spoke on the phone for a few moments, looking straight through Kevin, and then hung up. "He apologizes again—a call just came in from New Delhi that he absolutely has to take—just a few more minutes."

Kevin made himself comfortable and did not fret about it. His role in life was to get shunted from one grant to the next, a pawn on Larsen's giant board, filling whatever roles Larsen needed filled at the moment. Now it was his role to wait.

As a case in point, he had, sometime in the early part of 1989, been written in as a research assistant on a three-hundred-thousand-dollar NSF grant. He didn't know this during the life of the grant. He had first become aware of it a couple of months ago, when he had received a W-2 form claiming he had been paid twenty-five thousand dollars that he had, in fact, never received.

He had gone to Larsen's comptroller, who worked in downtown Wapsipinicon, at the law firm that handled his affairs. He had pointed out, with all due respect, that he shouldn't have to pay taxes on money he had not received. He had done this, he'd thought, with great good humor, thinking that the whole absurd situation might be good for a chuckle. But the bookkeeper wasn't amused—he wasn't even surprised.

"Do you have a tax man?" the bookkeeper said.

Kevin laughed. "Heck, no. My taxes are so simple, I—"

"You do now," the bookkeeper said. "Bring me all your other W-twos, ten ninety-nines, business expenses, and so forth, and I'll take care of it."

"Take care of it?"

"I'll make sure that your tax return is filed properly, and on time," the bookkeeper said, slowly and clearly. "And the taxes on this"—he wiggled the mysterious W-2—"will not trouble you."

"Dr. Larsen will see you now," the receptionist said.

Kevin scrambled to his feet, snatched up his laptop, and strode down the marble-lined corridor to Larsen's office, a basketball-court-sized room in the corner of the building with a 180-degree view over the Wapsipinicon Valley and the EIU campus. The walls that were not made of windows were lined with honorary plaques, and with autographed photos of Larsen hobnobbing with secretaries of agriculture, Nobel prizewinners, and foreign heads of state.

He had done these meetings before—he knew the drill. First of all, thirty seconds of chummy small talk with the Rainmaker. After that some kind of internal alarm went off in Larsen's head, his eyes glazed over, and he became clipped and distracted. If you saw it coming, and got down to brass tacks before Larsen had time to become irritated, you were golden.

Today, though, was a little different: there was an unusual item on the agenda.

"This Habibi thing," Larsen said. "You've handled that well so far. Nice work."

Kevin shrugged. "Cops asked me questions, I told them the truth."

Larsen gave him a wink and a knowing chuckle, which Kevin found disturbing. "You've handled it well," he repeated. "DA wants to throw the book at Ashrawi and keep him down at Fort Madison until he dies of old age. Looks like he'll probably just be deported instead—then he's the Iraqis' problem."

"Uh, I think that Ashrawi is Jordanian."

Larsen stared fixedly at Kevin for a few moments. "All those borders are bullshit—drawn by imperialists in the recent past. So don't waste my time quibbling about whether he's Iraqi or Jordanian or Kuwaiti or what have you. All I want is for him to go back over there and not trouble me and my operations again. And if you hear any hints or rumors about further developments in this case, you come to me first—you understand? We've dodged a bullet here, but we can't afford to let down our guard just yet."

It hadn't occurred to Kevin that they had dodged any bullets. A murder had happened, the bad guy was in jail. But he could see Larsen's point. This kind of thing could have serious repercussions for Larsen's finely tuned PR operations.

"Out with it!" Larsen snapped.

"I've had a couple of visits from Clyde Banks—one just yesterday," Kevin said.

"Clyde Banks? What the hell is he doing coming here?" As a pillar of the local GOP, Larsen knew very well who Clyde Banks was.

"He was asking me about some of the details in my statement to the detectives."

"Which details?"

"Well, for example, when the others were carrying Marwan out of the lab, one of them said, in English, 'Don't bang Marwan's head.' Clyde was asking me about that."

"What kind of questions was he asking?"

"He wanted to know whether the Arab students normally talked to each other in English, or if they normally spoke Arabic."

"And you told him?"

Kevin shrugged. "I said normally they spoke Arabic."

Larsen's face began to turn red.

"But," Kevin hastened to add, "I mentioned that there were many dialects of Arabic, and so if Arab students from different countries were trying to communicate, they might occasionally lapse into English."

Larsen took a deep breath. "You did good. You did good." Larsen swung his chair around ninety degrees and looked out the window. "Clyde ask any other goddamn questions?"

"He was curious about the habits of the Arab students. Such as, Was it normal for them to drink alcohol? And I said that they drank on occasion. Um, he asked whether they normally left door 304 open. I said no, but they were having a party that night, so maybe they left it open to get some fresh air. And he sort of poked around my lab for a little."

"What do you mean, 'poked around'?"

Kevin shrugged. "He's just curious. Most people have never been inside a working laboratory. I remember he noticed that I had a box of latex surgical gloves in my drawer, and he asked me whether that was a common thing."

"Shit," Larsen said, and spent a full minute staring out the window in silence.

"Well," Larsen finally said, "your research."

Kevin stepped forward to place two documents on Larsen's desk: a thin one and a thick one.

"The thin one is mostly graphics," Kevin said. "If you flip through it, it'll give you a general sense of the key milestones we've passed and the key challenges we face." "Milestones" and "challenges" were two of the primary Larsen buzzwords. "The thick one is a complete report on the progress of the research to date, for your files."

Larsen picked up the thin one and opened it. A loose sheet of paper slid out into his lap. "That's kind of like the executive summary of the executive summary," Kevin explained. "A bullet chart of milestones and challenges, and some back-of-the-envelope calculations on the body uncount."

"Body uncount" was the ultimate Larsen buzzword. He had become obsessed with it during the run-up to the *National Geographic* article, when he had spent many a long night and weekend cracking the whip over his graduate students, getting them to work up an estimate of how many lives he had saved, which they could feed to the university public-relations department, which could feed it in turn to the reporter who was writing the article. So the body uncount had officially started five years ago at a round hundred million and had been climbing steadily since then. It was now a part of standard operating procedure with all of the Rainmaker's projects that his lieutenants had to keep a running tab on the body uncount as they went along—how many lives they could save by developing and implementing whatever new idea they were working on. Anything less than ten million was considered not worth the overhead.

The number on the summary sheet was twenty-five million. Larsen pulled a face and nodded appreciatively, then flipped through the thin document. "Holy cow," he blurted, and flipped through it again. The graphics were computer generated, three-dimensional, in vivid color.

Kevin shrugged. "I was playing with some new graphics packages on my Mac. Hooked it up to a color printer down at Kinko's. Hope you don't think it's too, uh—"

"Too what?" Larsen said.

Kevin had gone and got himself into a tight spot. He squirmed and said nothing.

"It looks fine to me. Hell, it looks better than fine," Larsen said. "This is exactly why I like you, Kevin, is that in addition to being a fine scientist you have a creative flair—you can actually communicate your results. Believe you me, that is an unusual trait."

"Thank you, Dr. Larsen."

A phone call came through. Larsen picked up the handset and said, "Yep," six times in a row, then hung up. "By the way," he said, leaning forward and lowering his voice, "thanks for being understanding on the tax thing and for not making waves. It was a bookkeeping screwup."

One of Larsen's flock of secretaries scurried in and gave him a letter, which he signed. Then Larsen gave his full attention to Kevin. "When you were waiting to come in here, what kind of folks did you see in the waiting room?"

"My fellow graduate students."

"Notice anything about them?"

"They're all really smart."

"C'mon, man, what color were they?"

Kevin shrugged uneasily. "A variety of browns."

"Do you realize that you're the only American doing work for me?"

"Well, no, but now that you mention it..."

"The shithead high-school system in this country produces such wretched products that the universities have to spend all their time bringing them up to what used to be a senior in high school in Little Dixie." After this burst of eloquence Larsen shut down for a minute or so, took another cryptic phone call, stood up, and looked out the window. "Kevin," he said, "I want you to be my special assistant."

Kevin had no idea what that meant; he imagined fetching coffee, or running a copy machine. "What do you want me to do?"

"Run the shop for me here when I'm in Washington, or go to Washington in my place when I'm running the shop."

Kevin laughed nervously. "Dr. Larsen. What do you mean, 'run the shop'?"

"Oh, come on, now. You sit here and you look at three things: milestones, challenges, and body uncount. You've got that down pat, it's all right there!" He flicked his fingers at Kevin's summary sheet. Then he took a step closer to Kevin and lowered his voice. "Look, let's not bullshit around. My Asian kids are first-rate. They're great scientists. But I can't send them back to work the Hill, the NSF, Ag. But you—you're young, personable, you know your science, you can make pretty graphs, and, not to put too fine a point on it, you're a white man who speaks English. Will you do it?"

"But I haven't finished my dissertation."

Larsen blinked in surprise. He'd forgotten about this. Then he heaved a big sigh and rolled his eyes. He had deep-set farmer's eyes surrounded by creases—such a pale shade of blue they were almost gray. Those eyes glanced up and to one side as he called upon his obstacle-dodging skills, which had never yet failed him.

An inspiration struck. He walked back to his desk and picked up the thick document: *Bovine Transmission of Heavy-Metals Pollution Through the Food Chain: Recent Progress.* He flipped through it, pausing to look over some of the graphs and charts, and spent a minute or so scanning the bibliography.

"This will do. It's a contribution. Give it to Janie to put in dissertation form. We've got a software package to do that somewhere."

"Excuse me, Dr. Larsen?"

"Submit it. I need you to be a Ph.D. We can have the grad school waive the deadline requirements. I need you now."

Three weeks later Dr. Kevin Vandeventer, Ph.D., stepped out of the Courthouse Metro Station in Arlington, Virginia, a garment bag slung over his back and a plastic Hy-Vee grocery sack dangling from one hand. He walked down Clarendon and arrived at the Bellevue Apartments a few minutes later. He dialed his sister's apartment and got lucky: Cassie answered the phone; the surprise was preserved. She buzzed him in.

In the elevator he pulled his Ph.D. robes, mortarboard, and hood from the grocery bag and put them on over his traveling clothes. Thus attired, he marched majestically down the hallway. Cassie was waiting for him by the door; when she got a load of his outfit, she let out a hoot and began giggling.

"What's going on?" Betsy asked.

"Betsy, come here! You've got a *distinguished* visitor."

Betsy came out of the bedroom and flinched involuntarily when she saw the imposing creature in the robe. When she recognized her little brother's face, she was delighted, and when she saw the cardinal, green, and harvest-gold Ph.D. hood, she was floored. She almost knocked him over with a hug. "Why didn't you tell me?"

He looked away awkwardly. "It happened pretty fast. How you doing, Bets?"

Tears sprang out and trailed down her face, making him feel even more awkward. "When did this happen?" She let go of him, stepped away, and caught a deep breath. "I'm so proud. Have you told the folks?"

"Thought we would call from here. They can come out for the formal hooding next month. Larsen takes about a half hour to process his people through."

Cassie stood back wide-eyed, like a kid at Halloween who had just seen a goblin costume for the first time. "Dr. Idaho," she said, then dropped suddenly to the floor and crawled up under his robes.

"Let me unzip this thing so you don't suffocate," Kevin said, awkward and unnerved. Cassie's head popped out of the neck opening, next to Kevin's, and the picture that Betsy saw was one that she'd remember for life.

"Stay right there," she shouted as she ran for her little camera.

"My pleasure," Kevin said, hugging Cassie.

Betsy came back and snapped shots from various angles. "I'm gonna make sure Dad gets an eleven-by-sixteen of this."

Cassie began to note that Kevin was not letting go. "Well! Give a man a Ph.D. and suddenly he takes prerogatives!" she said. "Excuse me, Doc, but my people have got something about getting caught by people in robes." Kevin let her go and she slipped out. Kevin was in a state of bliss.

"Let's pop that bottle of champagne we bought for Betsy's promotion," Cassie said.

"Sounds good," Kevin said.

"I said, *for Betsy's promotion,*" Cassie said, getting a little provoked.

"Oh. You mean the fifth-year poly thing?"

"My boss got transferred out," Betsy said, "and Cassie's making a big deal out of the fact that I've been made acting branch chief."

"Branch chief in the Company! Pretty good for a potato picker," Kevin said tepidly. Betsy could tell her brother was a trifle deflated at losing the spotlight.

Cassie aimed the bottle through the open balcony doors and launched the cork toward the Pentagon with a satisfying explosion. She poured the Sovetskoe Champanskoe Vino into the jelly glasses—everything else was still drying in the dishwasher. "A toast to Dr. Kevin and Officer Betsy." They drank the sweet champagne down, agreed that it was just fine, and had another round instantly.

"Take it easy, Doctor boy," Cassie said in mock alarm, watching Kevin suck it down. "My dad told me there's nothing so quick and fun as a champagne high or as quick and nasty as a champagne low."

The champagne high lasted for several hours, or maybe they had other reasons to be in a good mood. Cassie called Domino's and ordered a pizza. Twenty-five minutes later the doorbell rang, and Cassie returned from the front door with two fresh, hot pizzas and a young woman—their neighbor from down the hallway. Betsy had made small talk with her in the elevator several times but never invited her in. "Look who's hanging around in our hallway," she said. "This is Margaret—sorry, I don't even know your last name."

"Park-O'Neil," she said. "Sorry to intrude," she said to the others, "but this woman dragged me in here."

"You look lonely," Cassie said, "and we got too much pizza and too much champagne."

Betsy couldn't help noticing that Kevin was very quick to his feet to shake Margaret Park-O'Neil's hand. She had to admit that her brother cut quite a figure in his Ph.D. robes, which, besides giving him great authority, seemed to put meat on his lanky bones.

"Sorry, I didn't know it was a formal," Margaret said. "Should I go back and dig up mine?"

"Ooh, excuse me! *Dr.* Park-O'Neil," Cassie said. She looked at Betsy. "You and me, we just got to go out and get ourselves some damn education."

During the next couple of hours the neighbor came in for a lot of attention from Betsy's brother. From spectating on their conversation Betsy learned that Margaret was half-Korean and half-American, an Army brat with a doctorate in East Asian history, working, naturally, for the CIA. She was a funny, down-to-earth, and likable woman who knew how to wear clothes.

She reminded Betsy strongly of an Asian-American woman Kevin had been deeply in love with for two years during his college days, whom he'd brought back to Nampa several times to meet the family, and who had eventually broken up with him, throwing him into a year-long funk. She had no doubt that, whether or not Kevin was conscious of it, he had noticed the resemblance, too.

Margaret stayed for a decent amount of time and then excused herself on the grounds that this was a school night. "Yeah. Time for all good little federal employees to go to bed," Cassie said, carrying the pizza boxes into the kitchen and ramming them into the trash. Kevin went to the broom closet and got out the sleeping bag he always used when he was there; Betsy rolled it out on the couch and donated her spare pillow.

She noticed him standing there looking at her with his eyes glistening. She stepped closer and gravely and formally shook his hand. "I'm proud of you, Kevin. Congratulations."

"Let's go out on the balcony," Kevin said.

"I'll need a wrap," she said. "I don't have a robe and hood." She plucked Mom's afghan off the back of the couch and threw it around herself, then followed her brother out. He was leaning against the railing looking out over the lights of D.C.

"This still blows me away," he said.

"What's that?"

"D.C. We landed coming down the Potomac tonight. And like you told me, I sat on the left side of the plane, window seat. I can spot the beltway, and when the moon is out like tonight, I can even see the cathedral. But the view of the Mall toward the Capitol is so beautiful, I wanted to cry, and tonight I could see Lincoln's head through the skylight and Jefferson's hand. And then a cab ride and here I am with my sister, who I used to sit with on top of the house looking at the mountains through Dad's old binoculars."

Betsy felt herself beginning to sober up. A lot of questions were swimming to the top of her mind. "Kevin. How did this happen so fast?" she asked gently.

"You and me, winding up here?"

"You getting your Ph.D."

Kevin was full of himself and champagne and the still palpable memory of Margaret Park-O'Neil. He told Betsy a remarkable story. He told her about Professor Arthur Larsen and his empire, how Kevin had, over the last year, been elevated to the point where he reported directly to the Rainmaker over the heads of tenured professors. He told a very odd story about a rogue W-2 form and how Larsen's hotshot bookkeepers were now looking after his tax work. This was the point when Betsy's alarm bells went off.

Kevin was still close enough to his sister to sense her unease. "Don't worry, Bets," he said in a tone that was supposed to be reassuring but came off as condescending. "It all passes audit."

The champagne crash hit Betsy at that moment. That was one of Howard King's lines. How many sleazebag feds had she heard say that after they bent rules? In how many budget meetings had she heard the phrase "pushing the envelope, but not so far that we do hard time"? She still remembered one contractor who had written himself in for forty percent more than had been allowed and said, "In private sector I wouldn't do this, but here they'll never catch it. Never forget, dearie, that the margin for profit is found in that zone beyond the written law and before the point where the enforcement system kicks in."

Betsy felt sick. Her brother was now one of them.

"Don't worry, there's a good reason to do this. We are feeding the world."

And yourselves, too, Betsy almost said. But she did not. She did not want to spoil her brother's triumph.

"Oh, there's a lot of hype with Dr. Larsen's body uncount. No one really believes he's saved that many lives—least of all Dr. Larsen. You have to understand that stunts like that are necessary—part of how you do business. But there's some truth there underneath the hype, Bets. This research does a lot of good."

She was tired. She'd have to sleep on his news. She merely reached out, hugged her brother, and held him as she used to do when Dad would lose his temper and shout that he'd never amount to anything. "Watch your step, Kevin," she whispered.

"I will, sis. We're a long way from Nampa, and sometimes it gets a little complicated."

They stayed for another few minutes, watching the MD-80's and 757's land at National, seeing the lights reflect on the blossoms that were still left on the trees, smelling the sweet air of D.C. Then Betsy suddenly sneezed so loud that an echo came off the apartment building across the way. "Time for bed, bro. Whatever you're doing here for the Rainmaker, I'm sure you've got to be bright and sparky. You can use the bathroom after Cassie gets done. Don't forget to hang up your suit."

They went in. Betsy kissed her brother on the cheek again, told him how proud of him she was, and then went to bed. But she did not fall asleep until long after the eastern sky had begun to brighten.

fourteen

ONE MORNING at 3:52, according to the station wagon's dashboard clock, Clyde was cruising southward along the Interstate 45 portion of his circuit when he witnessed a one-car accident. A four-door was coming toward him in the northbound lanes, drawing attention to itself in more than one way. To begin with, it had its parking lights on, but not its headlights. Second, it was going so fast that Clyde could tell it was speeding from a mile away. It looked as if it must be doing about 120. Third, it was weaving lazily from lane to lane, straying well into the left and right shoulders when the driver felt like claiming a little extra elbow room.

Finally it weaved just a bit too far to the left, all the way across the paved shoulder. The driver sensed something was wrong; even from the front Clyde could see its brake lights flare. Its tires bit dirt, yawing the car violently into the shoulder. The driver fought with the wheel for a few moments as the car plowed through the ditch, kicking up dirt and rocks, but finally it struck a boulder or something and veered sharply away from the road, erupted over the lip of the ditch, smashed through a wire fence and into a field of tall corn, which swallowed it up as if it were an actor vanishing through a curtain.

Clyde slowed, pulled over into the right lane, eased the wagon into the median, and executed a perfect cop turn, rumbling up into the northbound lanes with enough turbulence to bounce Maggie around in her seat but not enough to wake her. He followed the skid marks on the pavement to the gouges in the ditch, and the gouges to the gap in the fence, parked the wagon on the shoulder, and set the emergency flashers. He took a flashlight and some flares out of the glove compartment, fired up the flares, and tossed them onto the road. He took Maggie, still in her child seat, out of the car, and set her up on a fence post well away from the highway, in case the Murder Car got rear-ended by a semi while he was investigating.

The occupants of the car had been lucky that it had not flipped over and suffered much worse damage. Instead it had remained on its wheels and burned off kinetic energy by boring a surprisingly long tunnel through the corn. Along the way it deposited a trail of Marlboro cartons, like Hansel and Gretel dropping bread crumbs. Apparently the trunk had been full of them and had popped open as the car had been wrenched this way and that in the ditch. As Clyde followed the trail of white-and-red cartons glowing brilliantly in the beam of his flashlight, he could hear low voices conversing. The car's wild trajectory had scared him half out of his wits, and he was irked to find that the actual occupants of the car were now laughing. He could not make out what they were saying, and as he drew closer, he realized that they were speaking in an unfamiliar language.

"Hello!" he called.

The voices became quiet for a moment. "Hyello?" someone answered carefully.

Finally he could see the car. They had turned the headlights on, illuminating a solid wall of corn plants, shoved all four doors open, knocking down more corn in the process, and had gathered in the car's wake, which was the only clear place they could stand. There were several of them. Clyde twisted the bezel of his flashlight to get a wide-angle beam and gave the scene a careful look before coming any closer. It was a big, new Buick LeSabre with a Hertz sticker.

He counted five men. All of them were smoking, which struck him as poor judgment in the present circumstances.

They all held their cigarettes between thumb and index finger, like darts. They stood there smoking and bleeding and looking ridiculously nonchalant. One of them stepped forward. He was tall and blond and had a very thin, hatchetlike face and gray-green eyes. At first glance he looked like a teenager, but as time went on, Clyde's estimate of his age steadily climbed all the way up to about forty.

"Sheriff," Clyde said.

"Zdraustvui," the man answered. "This means 'Greetings, friend!' in Russian. I am Vitaly. God bless you for coming to save

us, Mr. Sheriff." He stepped forward and shook Clyde's hand limply.

"Clyde Banks," Clyde said. He realized that the odor he'd been smelling wasn't gasohol from their fuel tank. It was booze on their breaths.

Another man came forward with a fresh Marlboro carton in each hand, holding them out as gifts. Clyde politely turned him down.

"How 'bout if we get you guys to the hospital?" Clyde said.

"Not important, my friend. We go to the airport." Vitaly tapped his watch.

"There's plenty of time. The flight to Chicago leaves at eight A.M."

Vitaly seemed to find this funny and spoke to his cohorts in Russian. Clyde heard the word "Chicago" in there and realized that Vitaly was translating. The men all laughed.

"My friend, the flight to Kazakhstan leaves as soon as we get to the airport," Vitaly said.

Clyde finally figured it out at that moment and felt stupid for not having figured it out before.

The Forks County Airport served as home base for an Iowa Air National Guard unit that specialized in heavy transport. Its twelve-thousand-foot runway happened to be perfect for the unbelievably large Soviet-built transport planes known as Antonovs, and there were a couple of companies in Nishnabotna that occasionally used them. One was Nishnabotna Forge, ninety percent of which had gone out of business in the seventies, but which still operated a small production line in one corner of their empty, echoing plant. They made a type of steel tubing much prized by oil drillers in distant, godforsaken parts of the globe, who sporadically felt a frantic demand for the product. So the Forge would occasionally call in the Antonov, load it with steel tube, and send it off to the Brooks Range or to Central Asia. The Antonov would come larruping across the skies of eastern Iowa, triggering tornado sirens and spraying the corn with a fine mist of oily soot, kick out its giant landing gear—multiple long rows of fat black tires—and slam down on that big runway to pick up its load.

Clyde had never met or even seen the crew before. It was rumored that they slept on the plane.

"Maybe someone ought to have a look at that before you take off," Clyde said, nodding at the one with the crooked arm.

"We must get back to *Perestroika*," Vitaly said. "You see, that is the name of our airplane, in honor of Gorbachev. *Myi biznesmeny*—we are businessmen. We are afraid—your hospital—too expensive."

Vitaly was not the only person who was worried about hassles and red tape as the result of this accident. A bunch of Russians—who crashed a rental car and damaged a farmer's property while driving drunk, in the process of smuggling some cigarettes—the thought of all the reports he would have to fill out made Clyde want to swoon.

So he led them out of the cornfield, retrieved his daughter from the fence post, flipped down the backseat of the station wagon, and packed the Russians into its spacious cargo hold. He could hear them making humorous comparisons between the Murder Car and *Perestroika*. They carried as many cigarette cartons as they could and packed them in among their bodies. Vitaly leaned over the seat and made faces at Maggie and marveled at her perfection while his crew ran back into the cornfield and scavenged more cigarettes. Clyde took out the first-aid kit Desiree had packed, which was the size of a suitcase, and found an inflatable arm splint, which he applied to the one crewman's damaged limb, to the fascination and astonishment of the fliers.

Finally they were ready. He drove them the last two miles to the airport, pulled onto the runway, and drove up alongside the flank of *Perestroika*, which loomed as high as the bluffs of Wapsipinicon. Vitaly insisted that he and Maggie come inside for a tour. Clyde went in with some trepidation, worrying that this gang of pirates would close the hatches, take them off to Arabia, and sell them into slavery, perhaps throwing in some Marlboros and steel tubing as freebies. But although Vitaly was manipulative and blatantly untrustworthy, he was not evil, at least in that kind of spectacular way, and the moment Vitaly had seen Maggie, he had obviously decided that he and Clyde were friends for life.

The interior of the plane was the most sloppy and ramshackle thing Clyde had ever seen; it was a flying fraternity house, with cases of Soviet brandy and various other forms of contraband stashed everywhere. The wiring had been patched with lamp cord and duct tape, and everything was greasy with hydraulic fluid, which had dripped or sprayed from faulty connections and frayed hoses.

On the other hand, it could carry a locomotive thirty-five hundred miles at almost the speed of sound, so who was he to knock it?

Just the same, he got well away from the airport before the Antonov took off.

fifteen

LARKIN SCHOENDIENST, professor of Ag Econ at the University of Idaho, and Betsy's mentor, had, in an earlier life, worked abroad for many years as an agricultural attaché in various embassies throughout the Third World.

Actually, he had been working for the CIA in the Operations Division, and after many adventures, which he frequently alluded to but always declined to talk about, he had suffered a breakdown. The Agency had provided him with a greased path to a nice office in Moscow, Idaho, with a view over the otherworldly landscape of the Palouse Hills, and set him up with 125 percent disability, plus his professor's salary, plus whatever he could pull down selling information and analysis back to the Agency. He divided his time between a furnished room above someone else's garage in Moscow, and a condo in Ketchum a stone's throw from the ski lift.

Betsy had arrived in Moscow, Idaho, at the age of twenty-one, fresh from Brigham Young, where she'd earned a B.A. in Russian. Larkin Schoendienst had been named as her adviser. He was, by a very wide margin, the most morally ambiguous person Betsy had ever met. Now that she had her M.A. and was in Washington working for the Agency, she understood that nothing was an accident; Schoendienst was a procurer for the CIA, and he had taken Betsy under his wing because she was a Russian-speaking Mormon from a sheltered home, the ideal candidate for Agency grooming.

So Betsy had a lot of qualms about Larkin Schoendienst and was pretty certain that, when he finished drinking himself to death, he was going straight to hell. But she loved him anyway. He had encouraged her, protected her, and, in one long, boozy session at a campus bar the day after she'd been awarded her degree, he had given her what he called the keys for survival in D.C.

"If you want to survive there," he had said, "never suggest solutions, never take credit, and be a bit to the right of the President—whatever President—because they leave and you stay."

She had shrugged off his cynical statements at the time. She thought that the CIA, with its unparalleled access to everything, would be a neat place to work. And so it was. For a while. But the more years she spent there, the more of Schoendienst's little bits of advice came unexpectedly to mind. And after she was named acting branch chief and moved into Howard King's office, where the telephone still reeked of his aftershave, the relevance of her adviser's words became clearer every day.

In her first orientation meetings down at the Farm, she had had the notion beat into her that it was not her job to offer ideas. It was her function to be tasked by "downtown." It was there in the Constitution: the elected people, not the civil servants, make policy. "It is not ours to ask, it is ours to answer."

That was the CIA line, and Betsy came out of the Farm believing it. But as time went on, she remembered Larkin Schoendienst's take on it: "The people who know the most are not allowed to ask questions—or even to make suggestions. The least common denominator sets the standards. Just wait until you see Washington, Betsy—these goddamn car salesmen and small-town lawyers come into town every two years not knowing their ass from a hole in the ground, and this enormously sophisticated and powerful and dangerous system is at their mercy. The Agency distorts information to fit the half-assed policies they scheme up."

She called up all the visa records from Immigration, combed through them, picking out the student visas, identified all visas granted to South and Southwest Asian students, and then fed the results into a cartographic system, making a 3-D plot of the information. The result was a picture of the continental United States with the topography exactly reversed: the coasts were low plains, and the Great Plains states were studded with precipitous crags, centered on places like Elton, New Mexico; East Lansing, Michigan; Stillwater, Oklahoma; Wapsipinicon, Iowa.

She knew most of those universities well; they were the kinds of places where she and her fellow agro-Americans tended to apply for grad school. Narrowing the search to cover Iraqi students only, and running the cartographic program again, she got a similar result, with fewer and starker peaks: Auburn, Colorado State, Texas A&M, Eastern Iowa.

During numerous blowing-off-steam sessions over cases of bad zinfandel on the balcony of their apartment, Cassie and Betsy had arrived at conclusions similar to Larkin Schoendienst's. Cassie, from her job at the Hoover Building, and Betsy, at the Agency, each had access to certain information that convinced her that she actually knew what was going on, at least within the confines of her designated compartment. They were sworn not to divulge specifics to each other. But they agreed that at any one time there were in town at least five people, desk officers six levels down from the President, who actually knew what was going on.

There was no lack of information. The combined forces of the intelligence community—with all its spectacular satellites, sneaky HUMINT heads, NSA intercepts, independent contractors such as Dr. Schoendienst, the never-flagging torrent of governmental studies and statistics from national and international bodies, privileged information from multinational firms, and the best mainframes and libraries in the world—provided all the information that anybody needed.

There was no lack of smarts among the analysts, either. But the six-level editorial process so distorted what they wrote that several times Betsy could not recognize items that were attributed to her in the President's Daily Briefing.

The problem was the managers. Not for them the open struggle of ideas in the marketplace of policy. It was turf politics, building alliances not to further the general good of the body politic, but to cement advantage to gain entrance to the exalted level of the Senior Executive Service Corps, to use whatever administration that was there to feather their own nests—not to solve problems, but to use problems to strengthen their position.

"Watch out for the iguanas," Larkin Schoendienst had told her. Betsy hadn't understood the reference until recently. But now she saw iguanas all over Washington, people who sat sunning on their rocks, destroying anything or anybody who came within tongue's reach, but doing nothing.

So now she was a branch chief (interim), working directly beneath Spector. But her higher status wasn't helping her catch any bad guys, especially since Millikan had convinced the President that by all means we had to prop up Saddam. To the contrary, she'd spent much of the last month out of town, down at the Farm or out at Airlie House, attending courses on how to be a branch chief.

Once back in the office, she found that at least half her days were taken up by meetings of one kind or another and the other half by paperwork and editing the work of her subordinates. The message was not lost on her: someone had decided that she couldn't get into any more trouble as long as she was buried in administrative tedium.

She got the worst of both worlds—because she was only interim, she received no pay increase. Her only break was that King would not do her yearly evaluation. She encountered unspoken hostility from all of King's old friends who had learned of her perfidy. Still, she enjoyed the change from soybeans, and a casual observer would conclude that she had adjusted well to the shift from worker bee to manager.

But casual observers weren't there at four A.M. when she checked in. She had a standing order with her Bangladeshi cabbie now, who was faithfully at the entrance to the Bellevue Apartments every morning at three fifty-five. He was always cheerful and had taken to bringing her a fresh pastry every day.

On this, her private graveyard shift, she continued asking the "right question"—trying to find where those millions of dollars of unaccounted-for taxpayers' money had gone, searching through the noise for patterns. She continued to access the mainframes of the other agencies involved with Iraq and to make as much use of the HUMINT folks in the Middle East as she could get away with. She was especially interested in who was being proposed to come to the United States for study.

She had clearly established one trend that no one else had noticed: faculty and staff from other Muslim countries were being brought into Iraq on adjunct status to teach courses in biological sciences. The names on the visa applications usually did not match those of the absent academicians, but the physical descriptions did.

She also gained access to the names of prominent Iraqis in the arms business. These were compiled by making a run of all registrants at arms fairs worldwide for the past ten years and then doing a match on brochures advertising their products. By pulling up IATA passenger lists she could see who was going where.

She tried to task other directorates and branches within the Agency, but she made the mistake of putting her name on the requests. She was turned down forthwith.

Despite these and other frustrations, she became increasingly certain that her hypothesis was right. The Iraqis were putting a lot of money—and, perhaps more important, a lot of brainpower—into biological warfare. She asked Spector to get infrared satellite imagery inside Iraq. He was turned down because he didn't have a sufficient need to know. She went to the Defense intelligence liaison at Langley and asked for clearance to contact people at DIA and was turned down. She asked for clearance to contact people at the National Science Foundation. She was turned down. She back-channeled to the DCI. He did not respond.

She had one of her subordinates apply for clearance to contact the USIA, without using the poisonous name of Betsy Vandeventer. Clearance was granted.

Over the weeks she had compiled a Dirty Dozen list—the twelve Iraqis who, based on her intuition, looked most suspicious. She used her USIA access to pull up their J-9 forms, which they had had to fill out in order to apply for their student visas. These had been scanned, digitized, and filed away in the USIA's archives.

Each J-9 contained a description of the applicant's plan of study, including the names of the institution where he would be working and of his faculty adviser.

Of the Dirty Dozen three were in Elton State University in New Mexico. Two were at Oklahoma State in Stillwater. Three were at Auburn.

The remaining four were at Eastern Iowa University. All four were studying under Dr. Arthur Larsen. Two were microbiologists. One was in veterinary medicine. One was a chemist. Pulling up one form after another, Betsy saw, on each, the signature of Ken Knightly, EIU's dean of international programs, and beneath that the distinctive scrawl of Dr. Arthur Larsen, which also graced her brother's newly minted Ph.D. diploma.

And that was where she had to stop, because the CIA's activities were restricted to outside the borders of the United States. It was a rule that was bent from time to time; but given the number of mortal enemies Betsy had in the Agency, some of whom had the power to monitor her activities at the workstation, she knew she couldn't go any further without ending up in prison. Her research had brought her to the edge of FBI turf, and all she could do now was stand at the border and peer in through the fence.

She got home late after an obligatory dinner with some Agency people, reached for her FacsCard, and then remembered that she'd given it and her key to Kevin. She went to the phone and dialed. Kevin answered the phone. His voice was slurred but happy. In the background she could hear the theme music of *Late Show with David Letterman*. "Hi, sis. Which number do I push?"

Kevin, still in his suit, welcomed her in with great dignity. "How was your day? Besides a very long one, right?"

"Ah, you know, Kevin, same old same old."

"Nah, I know that you spent the day destroying what was left of the USSR's economic and moral infrastructure."

"Guilty as charged. How was your day?"

"Neat. Scored pretty well over at NSF, lunched and schmoozed"—a word he'd picked up recently—"with some of Larsen's buddies over at Ag. And then, for something completely different, cocktails over at the Jordanian Embassy."

"Really," Betsy gushed, "you had a wonderful day. What was the most fun?"

"It was all fun, to be part of this place. I know that I got a good reception only because I represent Larsen in this process. But the embassy reception was special. They really know how to make a person feel important."

Betsy began to interrupt him, but Kevin continued.

"Now, I know that you're part of this—"

"Not on your life. I never mix with foreigners of any type, friend or foe," she said. "But I just wanted to remind you that a diplomat's job is to be charming."

"Well, he was. I met with the embassy's cultural attaché. Let me get his card." He fumbled through the handful of cards that marked his progress through town. "Ah, yes, here it is, Hassan Farudi. Nice guy."

"What were you talking about? If I may ask."

"Sure, I'm not sworn to secrecy like you. Lots of people want to come and study with the Rainmaker. I'm trying to process a new batch. Most of them did their earlier work in European or English—I guess England is part of Europe—universities. I have to check them out with the Jordanians—they act as kind of a clearinghouse for the Arabic countries in international exchanges."

"What'd the Jordanians have to say about these guys?"

"Oh, hell, they're all fine. Just farmers like you and me, Bets, who want to learn how to build a better cow. That's all routine stuff. We had a nice dinner together, had a few drinks, bullshitted about politics."

"Really?"

"Yeah." Kevin laughed. "The Jordanians definitely have a different take on things. They were talking about how they and all the responsible countries are working against the Iranians, who they say are working with the Israelis." He gave her a conspiratorial look. "Does that sound right to you?"

"It could be. But I don't know much about that stuff."

Kevin gave his sister a wink as if to say, *I know that you know, and I know that you can't say what you know.* "Anyway, I'll go over to USIA tomorrow to the office where all the student visas are handled and give them the relevant paperwork. You'd be amazed how much you can speed up the wheels of government just by hand-carrying forms across town. That's why Larsen's so good—he understands these things." Kevin yawned and stretched lazily. "You getting up at four again tomorrow? I heard you go out today."

"I'll try to," Betsy said. "I have a lot on my mind."

sixteen

JUNE

THE CALL came in at four-thirty A.M. Clyde had backed his unit into a narrow dirt road between fields, facing east, and so when he opened his eyes and grabbed the microphone, he could look straight down a tunnel of corn into a translucent pink sky. As he was depressing the thumb switch on the microphone, it came into his head, for some reason, that the sky looked the way it must have looked to little Maggie when she had been in the womb and Clyde had taken out his big battered black cop flashlight and played its light against the flawless porcelain dome of Desiree's belly.

The call had come in from a farmhouse about five miles away. A motorist had struck a deer and gone into the ditch. Clyde arrived in a few minutes and saw the business laid out very clearly: short skid marks veering right onto the soft shoulder, trenches cut into the deep grass by the tires, the car stopped in the bottom of the ditch, crumpled at the right front corner where it had tried to climb out and instead had dug into the trench's steep bank. The deer was lying dead across the yellow line. It was huge, probably an eight-point buck, though this detail would have to remain hazy in Clyde's report, because extensive antler damage made it hard to get a meaningful count. If Clyde were still a bachelor, he would give some thought to having the buck's mangled head mounted in its current condition as a nice bit of cop humor.

After Clyde had set out a few road flares, he went and found the driver, who was holed up at a farmhouse half a mile away on the far side of the bridge over the creek. She was a nurse at the hospital, a colleague of Desiree's, on her way into town to do some night work, and the buck had simply come out too fast for her to avoid it. She had a stiff neck, which the farmer's wife was treating with ice.

Towing the car out of the ditch would be the responsibility of the owners, which they would see to in a few hours when the garages opened up. Getting the debris off the road was Clyde's problem.

Clyde grabbed the animal's legs and rolled its body this way and that, verifying his impression that there had been almost no bleeding. Most of the points had been sheared off the buck's antlers, but the armatures still remained more or less intact.

Clyde backed his unit up to the animal. There was some cop baggage in the trunk, which he moved to the backseat. He hoisted the buck's head so that it rested on the rear bumper, one antler now scraping on the pavement while the other stuck out into space. He raised one foot and stomped hard on the antler. It snapped off near the base and clattered into the trunk. Clyde flung it into the ditch. Then he repeated the process with the other antler.

Clyde was able to heave the buck's center of mass over the lip of the trunk with a couple of great leg thrusts. After that it was just a question of arranging its extremities in such a way that he could get the lid closed.

The sun was just coming up when he backed into the driveway. He sneaked into the garage through the side door and hit the button for the opener, praying it wouldn't wake up Desiree and the baby. He backed the unit into the garage and closed the door, then turned on all the lights.

He had a dirty old nylon rope among his tools, which he threw over one of the bare joists of the garage. He popped the trunk of the unit and tied a noose around the neck of the dead buck. He put on some leatherwork gloves to protect his hands, then took up the loose end of the rope and put a couple of turns around the trailer hitch on his pickup truck, which was parked parallel with the unit. With the nylon rope wrapped around his leather gloves he pulled and pulled until the entire body of the buck lifted free of the unit's trunk and swung out across the garage like a venison pendulum, knocking over several bicycles like dominoes. The joists creaked. The buck swung back and thudded into the back of the unit.

He went out into the backyard and got Maggie's wading pool, which was made of stiff pink plastic decorated with off-brand cartoon characters. He rolled the pool in through the side door and centered it beneath the dangling hooves of the buck. Then he stole into the kitchen, selected the longest knife in Desiree's set, and ran it through the electric sharpener on the back of the can opener once or twice.

Clyde gutted the buck as Ebenezer had taught him, letting the blood gush into the wading pool and the guts tumble in after it. Some blood splashed onto his uniform, but this was hardly out of the ordinary; truly violent crime was rare hereabouts, but large dead animals on the highways were ubiquitous.

He placed a phone call to Ebenezer, who was already up preparing for his daily auroral golfing trip with John Stonefield. Clyde knew that his grandfather would not be happy to have his golf trip preempted by this job; but he knew just as well that Ebenezer would not utter a word of complaint nor hold it against him. Within fifteen minutes Ebenezer pulled into Clyde's driveway and entered the garage carrying an old toolbox where he stored all of his butchering knives, and under the other arm a long white roll of butcher paper. He set about dismembering the buck and cutting the flesh from its bones while Clyde began to clean the hair, and traces of blood, from the trunk of the unit. The two men worked for an hour and a half on their respective jobs, standing some eight feet apart in the quiet of the garage, and exchanged very few words during that time. Ebenezer was occupied with whatever dark thoughts occupied Ebenezer. Clyde was thinking about Marwan Habibi and his apparent murderer, Sayed Ashrawi.

The business in Lab 304 stank to high heaven. Clyde simply could not bring himself to believe that Marwan Habibi had really passed out from alcohol and been carried out of that laboratory alive, come awake at someone else's house for some more partying, and then been murdered in the boat by an oar-wielding Sayed Ashrawi.

Vandeventer insisted that Marwan's skull had been intact when he had been carried out of the lab. And Vandeventer was a scientist who had seen Marwan from a few feet away, in good light. There could be no doubt of this.

There were no gaping holes in the story as Mullowney and the Wapsipinicon detectives had pieced it together. But there were oddities. Why had the students left door 304 open that night? If you're drinking grape-flavored grain alcohol in the lab and one of your buddies has passed out from it, don't you want to hide that?

Why had one of them spoken in English as they'd carried Marwan out of the lab?

But the big question, which came close to being a smoking gun as far as Clyde was concerned, was, Why had Sayed Ashrawi, after committing the murder, gone to an Exxon station at five in the morning and used his credit card to buy $6.20 worth of gas?

If you've just committed a murder and the tank of your getaway car is empty, then you have no choice but to buy gasoline—but you pay for it with cash so it can't be traced.

Ashrawi had bought only 5.2 gallons—not enough to fill the tank of his car. Why had he bothered to get gas if his tank wasn't empty? Pretty stupid behavior for a graduate student.

Maybe he couldn't afford to fill it up. But if he was using a credit card, did it really matter? The next day he had gone out and charged a new VCR at Wal-Mart, so it wasn't as if he were bumping up against his credit limit. This was another noteworthy detail—usually foreign students began buying VCRs and other major appliances just before they graduated and headed for home.

Clyde had another theory: Marwan had died right there in his own laboratory. The other students wanted to conceal that fact, for some motive that Clyde hadn't worked out yet. They needed to carry Marwan's body out of the place somehow, which was impossible without attracting suspicion—the place had security guards and cameras by all the doors. So they had convened at the lab and thrown a fake party, leaving the door open so that their neighbor, Kevin Vandeventer, would know about it. They had carried out the corpse, throwing in some patter in English, again for Vandeventer's consumption. They had brought a supply of latex surgical gloves with them. They had gone to the lake and stolen the boat, making sure that only Ashrawi's fingerprints showed up on it. They had crushed the dead man's skull with the oar, put the rocks in his pockets, thrown him out of the boat, and then bought gasoline with Ashrawi's credit card just to leave a neon-lit trail straight to him and him alone.

In other words, they were sacrificing Ashrawi to keep the rest of the group out of trouble, so that they could stay in Forks County and keep doing whatever the hell they were doing.

The big hole in Clyde's theory, which Mullowney would not hesitate to point out should Clyde be rash enough to speak it aloud, was that it was impossible unless Sayed Ashrawi had agreed to the whole plan and served as an accomplice in his own framing. And what kind of a person would do that?

Desiree came down, her white flannel nightie looking out of place in the garage and even more so in the presence of the butchering operation. She noticed, but did not bat an eye at, the wading pool. Clyde was watching her face at this moment because he feared that by using the pool he might have crossed one of the mysterious boundaries separating proper from improper behavior, so invisible to him and so obvious to her. But she wandered up, sweetly unsteady from just having awakened, leaned against him and gave him a kiss, came away with buck hair on her nightie and a glow in her eyes, and Clyde's heart swelled and ached with maniac love. She brought them coffee and promised them breakfast. Ebenezer, weighing the cut and wrapped cuts of venison in heaps on their bathroom scale, announced that he had removed 180 pounds of meat from the animal and selected perhaps a quarter of it for his own Deepfreeze. He declined breakfast, perhaps having absorbed enough of the buck's substance through his own pores to give him a morning's nourishment, then took off for the golf course in hopes of catching up with John Stonefield on the back nine.

Clyde got the unit back to the sheriff's department in time for the end of his shift, filed his report on the accident, then drove home and began to work on the problem of the wading pool. Maggie was awake now, and he was very glad to see her.

seventeen

"WE'RE GOING to the Jersey shore!" Cassie said one Wednesday in mid-June. "Clear your calendar for the weekend, lady."

Betsy had to admit that, even with her constitution, the fourteen-hour days were catching up with her. "Why not the Eastern Shore? Why go all the way to Jersey?" she said.

"Because one of the people we're going with has a family place there—in Wildwood. And I've got four other people coming. Nobody with less than Top Secret Code Word clearance, all of them able to have a good time without talking about their work—or our work. You've got no option. We're getting up at six Saturday morning and heading up to Jersey."

Betsy was impressed—her roommate was going to get up at six in the morning. She had a very good rest of the week—not only did she have the beach weekend to look forward to, but things were actually beginning to change at work, too. The oil tanker of policy had begun a slow change of course, and Betsy, keeping watch on its decks, could sense it from subtle shifts in the wind. On Thursday morning word spread through the intel community that next week State would block five hundred million dollars in loan guarantees because Ag had been forced to admit that irregularities—including kickbacks to USG personnel—had occurred, and that previous grants had not gone to sugar, rice, and corn. Betsy got to savor that for a few minutes, imagining what kind of a mood Millikan must be in this morning. But the rest of Thursday was consumed by meetings, and one sensitizing session on understanding women employees.

On Friday, Spector stuck his head in her office door—she hadn't seen him in a month—gave her a wink and a thumbs-up, and disappeared. Toward the end of the day a courier arrived with an "Eyes Only" envelope from headquarters. *One of these "burn before reading" jobs,* Betsy thought. She opened it—it was a handwritten note from the DCI. Stamped above the message was the warning, SHRED AFTER READING. NOT FOR CIRCULATION. NOT FOR DUPLICATION.

This is a heads up. Lie low. Somebody has been monitoring your activities and knows every request you've made. Break contact with your project for at least a month.

Very interesting, she thought, as she headed to Thelma the secretary's desk to make use of the shredder. "Love letters?" Thelma teased.

"Kind of. I'm outta here. Have a good weekend."

She walked out of the Castleman Building. It was the first hot day of the season, and the sky had that yellowish haze it had when the ozone soup cooked up. She took the long way home, detouring past the Iwo Jima memorial, putting things together in her head.

The White House still wasn't acting on her findings. Anything she had put through the system had been beaten back. She had to figure out some way to go outside the system, because if she did not, a lot of people might die.

At one meeting she had been talking with a branch chief from Science and Technology who had been paying her more attention than was strictly professional. The conversation had got around to bacteriological warfare. She played dumb and talked about how one of their cows had been killed by anthrax back on the ranch. The S-and-T guy had snorted. Anthrax was not what they were worrying about; it was genetic markers—germs or toxins that could kill members of one ethnic group, but not another. "That's what Saddam's after."

"Then why is the Army developing all of that anthrax vaccine?"

"Those people, they're still fighting the last war. The future is genetics. Why don't we go out to dinner tonight and talk some more about this?"

"Sorry, I've got Bible study tonight. Want to come?"

She had looked into the genetic-markers thing and found that it was a real threat, but at least ten years in the future even for the Americans. The S-and-T guy was just trying to impress her. But one of his comments stuck with her: "They're still fighting the last war." The Soviets had done a lot of anthrax work, NATO had stockpiled a lot of vaccine—were Saddam's people smart enough and good enough to see that some alternative bug might be more effective? Saddam's nuclear people had been remarkably creative in coming up with unexpected ways of enriching uranium.

She was close. But there were just no connects.

Cassie was definitely in a party mood when Betsy got home, dancing around the room to a Janet Jackson CD turned up loud. When Betsy came in, she turned the volume down a couple of notches and set them up with a couple of Stoli straight shots.

"We're gettin' outta this bureaucratic ghetto! We're gonna see salt water."

Betsy turned on the Weather Channel, changed into shorts and a T-shirt, and sipped her vodka.

The phone rang. Cassie hit the mute button on the stereo and picked it up. She listened for a moment, then covered the mouthpiece and looked quizzically at Betsy. "Did you call Acme Wildlife Management?"

"Wildlife Management?"

"Yeah. It's a pest-control company."

"No. Are they here?"

"Yeah. Downstairs. I didn't call them." Into the phone Cassie said, "There's gotta be a mistake." Cassie paused, then turned to Betsy and said, "He wants to talk to you."

"Ms. Vandeventer? Jack Jenkins of Acme Wildlife Management Services, Inc. Your parents read in the paper about the forecasted infestation of roaches this year in the District and they gave you a free treatment."

Betsy blushed. Mom's ability to embarrass her was undiminished by time and distance. "Okay, come on up."

"What's that all about?" Cassie asked.

The vodka and the long week and the fatigue all came on Betsy at once, and she broke out in giggles. She couldn't stop once she got started. She blurted out, "My folks read that there's an infestation of bugs in—"

Then it hit her, and she wasn't laughing anymore.

"Come on, love, what's this all about?"

"It's very simple, they're coming up to remove bugs. But I don't think my parents called them."

Jack Jenkins the Acme man showed up, complete with two assistants, all of them dressed in Acme Wildlife Management coveralls and caps. But they didn't bring the usual array of chemicals and sprayers. All of their equipment was electronic.

"Nasty spring for roaches, Ms. Vandeventer. Your parents were right to be concerned about you. You know, if you find one, there are fifty thousand of them behind it. Would you mind if we close the shades?" He went ahead and closed them without waiting for an answer, and closed the balcony doors and windows, too. "Some of our sprayers will interfere with your television set," he said, scooping the remote control off the coffee table and terminating the Weather Channel. In the meantime his assistants were moving furniture away from the walls.

They began to walk around the apartment carrying wands with small LED screens built into the handles. They found a lot of "roaches." Betsy and Cassie just sat close to each other on the living-room sofa and watched.

Jack Jenkins gave them a sheet of paper with the usual "burn and flush the ashes down the toilet" warning.

We think that you have listening devices from at least four different sources here. We know that all of your balcony conversations are monitored from the eighth floor of the Belvedere, and we're reasonably sure that you're being targeted by mobile microwave surveillance systems.

Betsy showed Cassie the note and then wrote, "Who's doing it?" Jack Jenkins shrugged and threw up his hands, a predictable response even if he knew the answer. Betsy went into the kitchen and burned the note under the vent fan of the range hood, then washed the ashes down the garbage disposal. She returned to the sofa, sat with Cassie, and watched the men at work.

All outlet covers and switch plates were taken off, with interesting results. One device was found in the base of a lamp, another on the TV cable connection. All of this seemed utterly routine and everyday to the Acme men.

Then one of the guys hissed, "Shit. . . ." He grabbed a chair, pulled down a smoke detector from the wall above the front door, and pried it open. "Video," he said. He mouthed to his chief, "This ain't ours."

Jack Jenkins prepared another note.

We hadn't expected this. Some Bureau stuff here, and some foreign goods of unknown provenance.

Betsy looked up at him sharply. "Good stuff," Jenkins mouthed, and gave her a sardonic thumbs-up.

One of the men was unscrewing the mouthpiece of the phone Cassie had brought up from Atlanta. He took from it a ceramic pyramid about a centimeter on a side and showed it to the chief. Jenkins wrote another note.

Israeli. Makes your phone a continual transmitter—there's probably a master unit a hundred feet away.

A half hour later and they were done. "You shouldn't have any more bug problems, ladies. Glad to have helped."

Betsy saw them out and turned around to find Cassie weeping silently on the couch. Betsy sat down next to her and started crying, too. She had never been so humiliated. Three months of private life had been entertainment for a bunch of shitheads. All of their private conversations were on tape. This just wasn't worth it.

"You know what, though?" Betsy said. "We were good girls the whole time, Cassie. We were perfect. We never talked about anything we weren't supposed to. They've got nothing on us—whoever they are."

"Fuck 'em! Fuck being a good girl!" Cassie shouted.

"Watch it. Acme probably put as many bugs in as they took out."

"I don't give a shit," Cassie said. "Let's get out of here. Let's go down to the car and just go."

"No way. Our car's bugged, too. I'm going to take the metro down to National and rent a car. You pack for both of us and we'll get out of here."

Betsy grabbed her purse and a windbreaker and stomped down to the Rosslyn Metro Station. Fifteen minutes later she was walking into the Avis office. "I want to rent the best car you've got. I don't have a reservation."

Cape May was a priceless little Victorian resort town. Wildwood, just a few miles to the north, was its antithesis, its streets lined with motels done in spectacularly garish Jetsons-style architecture and crammed with rowdy, drunken, gold-chain–wearing, backward-baseball-cap–sporting, cologne-reeking, loud-car-stereo–playing, chest-hair–showing teenagers from South Philly. During their progress through the city Betsy and Cassie were followed by carloads of such persons on several occasions, who shouted lewd propositions at them and held up signs saying Show Us Your Tits. At any other time in her life Betsy would have been scared. But she was with Cassie, and Cassie had a gun. So they laughed it off.

"What kind of a place did you bring me to?"

"Isn't it great?" Cassie said.

Cassie's friends' house was a flat-topped cinder-block structure with circular windows that were probably meant to look like portholes. Cassie had a key to the place. They dragged their stuff in, made a run to the local convenience store for high-priced, high-calorie, low-nutrition, low-fiber foodstuffs, and then to a liquor store for more Stolichnaya. They watched a Rambo movie on HBO, then picked out beds and fell asleep.

At six o'clock Betsy's internal alarm clock went off, and she went outside to see a wonderful dawn over the ocean. The house was about two blocks from the beach. All of the loud people from South Philly seemed to have gone inside for the time being.

She left a note to Cassie and walked past restaurants and knickknack shops to the beach. She walked along the tide line, interrupted only by the cries of the seagulls and one lone jogger who was too fixated on the tunes coming out of his Walkman to notice her. Betsy was comforted by the shore, and she had a moment of peace. She breathed deeply out of the very bottom of her lungs. She thought of nothing at all. Cassie had been right. She needed this.

She wanted to swim, but the air was still a bit chilly. She walked back to the house. Wildwood was slowly coming to life. Cassie was still zonked, curled up on her left side, her hair becoming entwined with her eyelashes. She, too, was breathing deeply and peacefully. She, too, was healing.

They made a morning beach visit, Betsy in her big straw cowboy hat and Cassie in her Atlanta Falcons cap. They went back to the house to fix some lunch, and Cassie's friends finally drove up in a BMW, beeping its horn excitedly.

Cassie leaned out the kitchen window and heckled them for being late. "You people don't know how to have fun. Betsy and me, we can have fun. We've been here a whole damn day!"

Betsy felt shyness coming over her—a familiar feeling. She had felt completely content with just Cassie there and wouldn't have minded if these people had canceled.

There were four of them. As Cassie had promised, they were all in the national-security game, too. Cassie had already provided Betsy with capsule descriptions, so she knew who was who: Jeff Lippincott, an Agency man detailed to the USIA Visas Division, whose uncle owned the house. His girlfriend, Christine O'Connell, an Annapolis graduate who worked as an analyst at DIA. And two guys: Marcus Berry from the Bureau, and Paul Moses—an NSA cryptography specialist.

"How did you get to know these people?" Betsy had asked last night.

"They all go to my church," Cassie shot back. "Marcus is mine, by the way. Paul's for you—he's a hunk."

Betsy had been so embarrassed by this that she had practically melted into a puddle. Now, as the four came into the house, full of energy and good cheer, she blushed just to remember it.

Just the same, she had to admit that Paul Moses was a hunk—though not in a conventional movie-star way. He was a huge guy, with hands that showed he had worked. Round-shouldered, shy, good-natured. Straw-blond hair and blue eyes.

Cassie had already supplied her with an opening line and forced her to rehearse it.

"You're a farm boy, aren't you?"

"How'd you know?"

"I'm an old potato farmer from Idaho."

"And I'm a wheat farmer from the Palouse country."

"Probably a Cougar, too."

"Guilty. I went to WSU because it was twenty miles away from home. Did you ever see Kamiaken Butte?"

Indeed Betsy had. She'd gone to a model UN in Pullman and had admired the views of the Moscow Mountains and Kamiaken and Steptoe Buttes from the windows of the student union building.

"My folks farm right up the north slope of Kamiaken. Gotta tell you I miss the Inland Empire."

"So you're at No Such Agency."

"Yeah, they keep me in a cage and hook my umbilicus up to a Cray and we crunch numbers all day."

"I have about as interesting a life."

"Not true. You're kind of infamous. I got warned about you." And then in a taunting, teasing voice, "You go outside your compartment, you go outside your compartment."

Betsy blushed rarely, but when she did, it was a beaut. Her pale skin turned the intensity of her hair. Nobody had teased her in years.

"Better be careful. I'm a career killer."

"Oh, yeah," Moses said, "I can see you're bad to the bone." Both of them laughed. "Seriously, I don't give a shit. I've had my go at D.C. I've been on the inside of the inside long enough. It's time to go back to Whitman County and grow that hard red wheat."

"You're really leaving?"

"After another year. I promised my dad I'd stick with it for four years. He wanted to make sure that when I came home, I'd come home because I wanted to. And I want to. This life is absolute bullshit. Want a beer?"

Betsy wanted a beer. She could feel herself tumbling for this guy.

"I brought some Grant's Ale—from Yakima. If I have to hear about the superiority of Sam Adams one more time, I'm going to puke. You're the first northwesterner I've met out here, so I'm going to monopolize you. Hey, guys," he shouted to the other four, "leave us alone."

For the rest of the day they talked about Palouse-country sunsets, black Labradors, Chinook winds, honest people, their hatred of bureaucracy, and fishing for steelheads along the Snake River. They did a comparative study of their high-school classes, laughed at yuppies, exchanged horror stories, and not once did they spoil it by mentioning anything even slightly classified.

They walked along the beach halfway to Cape May and back, smiling at three-year-olds playing in the surf, savoring the old, old couple who hobbled barefoot along the tide line, picking up shells, getting pissed off at kids playing their boom boxes too loud, watching the seagulls wheel and dive for garbage. Late in the afternoon the sun vanished behind storm clouds, and they turned around and headed back. It was nearly dark by the time they returned to Wildwood. Some drunken yahoos passed close to them, but Paul's bulk and Betsy's lack of fear convinced them to go elsewhere. They finally encountered Cassie walking along arm in arm with Marcus Berry.

"Christine got called back to D.C., and Jeff went with her. Some kind of military-spook shit," Cassie said. "Some weekend, huh?"

It was starting to rain. They walked through the gaudy strip of businesses along the beachfront and found their way into an Italian restaurant with a decent seafood menu. Continuing their unspoken policy of not talking about work, they had a normal, healthy, totally inconsequential conversation over dinner, rambling from movies to sports to the relative merits of Macintoshes versus PCs.

Cassie insisted on picking up the tab. Fumbling in her belt pack for her wallet, she came up with a white envelope. She blinked at it in momentary surprise, then handed it to Betsy. "Oh, I forgot," she said. "Before he left, Jeff asked me to give you this." Betsy turned the envelope over in her fingers; it was blank and unmarked. She folded it in half and stuck it in one of the innumerable pockets in her hiking shorts.

"Let's get home," Marcus said. "We've got a bottle of Sovetskoe Champanskoe Vino on ice."

"I can't drink that stuff," Paul said. "The sugars fire up my asthma something terrible. But you guys go ahead, I'll drink a beer."

Paul and Betsy talked asthma all the way back to the house until Cassie threatened to draw her service weapon and silence them if they mentioned it again. The rain began to come down in earnest and the wind kicked up; their clothes were not nearly warm enough now. They gathered in the house's living room, poured three champagnes and one beer, and Marcus proposed a toast: "To being outside D.C." They touched cups and Paul added, "To better days."

More toasts followed. For a while they made a token effort to talk in a foursome, but the attraction between Cassie and Marcus was as obvious as that between Paul and Betsy. Cassie announced that she was going to the bathroom to take a shower and walked out of the room, casually flicking off the lights as she departed. A few moments later Marcus followed her, and they didn't come back. Betsy found that her head fit naturally and comfortably on Paul's shoulder, and Paul found that his long arm went nicely around her big shoulders, and as the evening went on, they found any number of other ways to get closer.

They made out on the couch for a long, long time, serenaded by an endless parade of thumping car stereos out on the streets of Wildwood, gradually making their way to first base, second, third... and finally they were naked together. Paul was not in any hurry, which was nice. Betsy let him know that she was ready. Paul excused himself sweetly, ran back into the bathroom, and fumbled through his shaving kit for some condoms. When he came back, he had lost his erection. Nothing they did would bring it back—even though he'd been stubbornly hard from the first moment Betsy had put her head on his shoulder. "Sorry," he finally said, "just one of those things."

"That's okay," she said. "I've waited thirty years, I can wait a little longer."

"Oh. Well... I'd be lying if I claimed I'd waited that long."

"That's okay. I don't insist that everyone be as pure and innocent as little old me," Betsy said.

"Well... considering the kind of people you're hanging out with now, that's probably a good policy," Paul said.

eighteen

WHAT KIND of man would act as an accomplice in a plot to frame himself for a brutal first-degree murder, in a foreign land where everything was stacked against him?

Clyde kept asking himself this question and, whenever he pulled jail duty, kept watching Sayed Ashrawi in hopes of getting an answer. Most of the inmates in the Forks County Jail were foul, violent, abusive, stupid drunks. They had to put Ashrawi in a separate cell to keep him safe from these people—the Arab was a slight man with a concave chest. Not the sort who could realistically haul the 160-pound Marwan Habibi into a rowboat, beat him to death with an oar, or accomplish any of the other prodigies of which he was now being accused.

After Ashrawi was jailed, he went for three days without eating any food, because the jail's food was not what he called *halal*. Then some of the other Arab students began to bring in some tidbits that he was willing to eat. His most frequent visitor was one Dr. Ibrahim Abboud, who already had a Ph.D. from a university in England and was working on a second. It was Abboud who had spoken in English for Kevin Vandeventer's benefit as they had carried Marwan Habibi's corpse out of Lab 304. Clyde had him pegged as the ringleader of this little conspiracy and took a particular interest in his jailhouse visits.

But this was for naught because Dr. Ibrahim Abboud had Clyde pegged, too. It appeared that Abboud was the only person on the face of the earth, with the exception of Desiree, who did not automatically underestimate Clyde's IQ by a good fifty points upon first seeing him. So Abboud was all knowing smiles and guardedness whenever Clyde was in the room. Clyde asked him once where he obtained *halal* food in a place like Forks

County, Iowa. Abboud, for once, dropped his guard. "From a Jewish rabbi," he said.

When Ebenezer had finished stripping the roadkill buck down to bones and cartilage, and selected his own thirty or forty pounds of flesh as commission, he had turned all the remaining meat over to Desiree, except for one watermelon-sized bundle, which he had dumped into Clyde's arms: "Odds and ends."

That bundle was now resting in a Styrofoam cooler in the back of Clyde's pickup truck. Though he would never mention it to Ebenezer, he had also thrown in several other cuts of meat, painstakingly salvaged by the old man, that Clyde knew from experience to be shot through with sheets and cords of deer structural material that made for difficult chewing and worse digestion. Ebenezer was the only nonaborigine who ever bothered with these parts and had invented his own terms for them: "neck nugget," "pelvic potpourri," and so on.

This was Saturday, Desiree's day to sleep in. As soon as Maggie had begun to stir that morning, Clyde had rolled out of bed, extricated her from her crib, wrapped her in a blanket, and spirited her out of the bedroom like a ticking bomb. Now, one nap-and-bottle cycle later, she was strapped in her baby carrier, a streamlined plastic module with a handle so that you could carry the child around all day and never actually have to touch her. Clyde swung it into the pickup and docked it with its mother ship, a color-coordinated pedestal already strapped in place on the passenger seat. Industrial baby-handling technology continued to march forward at a pace matched in few other fields; friends of theirs with two-year-olds had car seats and baby carriers that might as well have been lashed together from sticks and rawhide, so primitive did they seem in comparison with the wonders that had begun to appear in their home after the first of several Dhont-sponsored baby showers. Clyde had little doubt that if he and Desiree ever had another baby, they would have to take all this stuff and beg homeless people and Ethiopians to take it off their hands for free, to make room for the new generation of technology.

Clyde stirred his hand through a rusty tire chain on the bed of the pickup, found its end, and draped it carefully over the top of the Styrofoam cooler so that it would not blow away when he got the vehicle up to cruising speed. Then he opened the driver's-side door, shifted it into neutral, rested one foot lightly on the parking-brake pedal, and released it silently. He leaned one shoulder against the frame of the open door and shoved the truck forward with a long, slow thrust of both legs. It began to coast down the gentle slope of the driveway. He climbed in and allowed it to roll out into the street before slamming the door and starting the engine, two activities that, in a truck of this vintage and in this condition, would be sure to wake Desiree if performed within the garage.

Maggie began to fuss aimlessly as they passed down into the old redbrick city of Nishnabotna and the great stacks of the Matheson Works rose to port. She had done well so far, considering that Desiree was not there to subject her to the continual stream of cooing, nose kissing, toy jiggling, and peekabooing that normally filled Maggie's senses every waking moment. Clyde's demeanor was, to put it mildly, more reserved, to the point where Maggie could have been forgiven for supposing that her father had tripped and fallen in the driveway and the truck had been coasting driverless toward the river ever since.

When Clyde had first seen the way Desiree played with the baby, he had been humbled that she possessed such talents so lacking in himself. He had been even more humbled when Desiree had mentioned to him—offhandedly, and not in a way intended to inspire guilt—that all of this was not playing but "stimulation," that each silly game was not improvised but planned to foster one important part of the infant's brain or another. Desiree's playing all came with footnotes. Clyde could only suppose that if he were to raise Maggie by himself, the girl would grow up to be a lopsided mouth-breather who walked into closed doors.

"Konrad Lukas and Sons" had been painted on the brick wall of their destination sometime around the turn of the century. Below, where it had probably said "Abbatoir" or "Slaughterhouse," the words "Specialty Meats and Custom Slaughtering" had been painted in much more recently.

The cooler would require both of his hands, so he took the radical measure of unsnapping his daughter from the baby carrier/car seat module and transferring her to the reversible backpack/frontpack baby carrier module. He slung her onto his back, tossed the tire chain off the cooler, and carried that box of odds and ends around to the front of the building.

Outside the butcher's was the largest collection of university-related vehicles Clyde had ever seen in Nishnabotna. Mixed in were a few cars that clearly didn't belong: a new Cadillac and a Volvo station wagon whose license plates marked them as being from other counties in Iowa, an hour or two distant. The car closest to the entrance was a big Chevy Caprice sedan, a model typically used for cop cars; but this one was navy-blue and bore no special equipment or insignia except for a yellowed cardboard sign on the dashboard reading Clergy and bearing a Star of David. This car had Illinois plates.

He came around the corner of the building onto the brick sidewalk, separated from the brick street by a stone curb at least two feet high. A dark-suited, bearded fellow wearing a black fedora was just emerging from the front door of Lukas Meats, carrying a large leather satchel. He threw the satchel into the trunk of the Caprice, climbed in behind the wheel, and drove away.

Clyde was startled by some of the people standing in the front room of Lukas Meats on this Saturday morning. The men wore the same Kmart Blue Light Special clothing that all the other grad students wore, but the women were swaddled in yards and yards of dark fabric, some with only the ovals of their faces showing, some peering out through horizontal gun slits. For the most part families had come in their entirety, the men doing the driving, disbursement of money, and control of larger children while the women carried infants and told the butchers what they wanted. Meat was flying out of the place by the boxload. No one bought less than ten pounds, and the average order was probably more like twenty. Two butchers were at work handing over the meat, and one clerk was ringing up the sales.

One of the men would have been conspicuous even on the streets of his own home village, wherever that might have been. Something had happened to him, something hard for Clyde to put his finger on, but clearly awful. His complexion hadn't been good to begin with—lots of acne scars—but his face bore a disfiguring pattern of heavy scar tissue. His lips and nose looked okay, but the sides of his cheeks had been burned and healed haphazardly. He had a truncated ear on one side, and the hairline on that side of his head was badly deranged, his curly black hair fading in and out crazily over substrata of lumpy, marbled red skin. The damage continued beneath the collar of his shirt and at least as far as his left hand, which was missing three fingers. The index finger was still there, and the thumb was present in a stunted, mangled, and crudely patched form. The man was gaunt and surprisingly tall, probably almost as tall as Clyde, who was six feet three. He was with a considerably younger woman whose plump, attractive face was encircled by a large silk scarf that dangled down her back, covering her hair.

They were buying a huge box of meat. When it was ready, the woman turned away from the counter, and Clyde saw that she was enormously pregnant. The man grabbed one end of the box with his good hand and slid it off the counter, holding up one knee to support the end while he groped for a fingerhold with his damaged hand. When he raised his knee in this fashion, the leg of his trousers rode up on his calf and exposed a few inches of flesh-colored plastic. But it must have been a below-the-knee amputation, because once he got his finger hooked into the box, he walked over to the cashier with only a slight limp.

Maggie pawed at her pacifier, which flew out of her mouth and skidded across the floor. Clyde was chagrined that he had not made use of the baby technology available to him by the infinite bounty of the extended Dhont family; they owned many clip-on pacifier shock cords intended to prevent this sort of incident, but in his haste to get Maggie out of the house lest she detonate prematurely and wake Desiree up, he had forgotten to install one.

The pregnant woman bent over carefully and picked up the pacifier. She turned to the cashier, a blue-eyed Lukas female in her fifties. "Is there a WC?" she said.

"Pardon me, honey?" said the cashier, leaning forward and cupping one hand to her ear.

"Rest room," said the husband, more for his wife's benefit than the cashier's.

"Back there through the door," said the cashier.

The pregnant woman circumnavigated the counter, seeming to glide along on a cushion of air in her tentlike garment. A Bunn coffee machine was sitting on the counter with a stack of Styrofoam cups next to it and a bowl for contributions. One of the glass carafes was full of hot water. The woman plucked it off the machine as she went by and carried it into the bathroom with the pacifier.

Clyde heard the sound of water running. Maggie was beginning to fuss; he turned around, said something meant to be reassuring, but couldn't make eye contact without breaking his own neck. Presently the woman emerged from the bathroom and replaced the carafe. She turned toward Clyde, smiling warmly. Clyde was slightly taken aback until he realized that she was smiling not at him but at Maggie. "May I?" she said, holding up the steaming pacifier.

"Please. Thank you," Clyde said. The woman did something behind his head, and Maggie became quiet and calm as she built up to full suction. The woman remained for a few moments as her husband finished paying for the meat, making eyes at the baby and talking to her in a low voice, speaking an unfathomable language. Then her husband was by the door, holding the box, repeating a word to her a few times, patient but firm.

"Thank you, ma'am," Clyde said as she was on her way out. Her husband had shouldered the door open and was holding it there with his back while she made her way out. Clyde made eye contact with him; he was looking back at Clyde calmly, in an appraising and almost absentminded way. Clyde nodded to him. "Have a good day, sir. Vote Banks."

Maggie fell asleep. As Clyde approached the counter, he shushed Todd Gruner, the butcher, who, surprised and excited to see a fellow representative of Christendom, was about to greet him too loudly."How you doing, Todd?" he whispered.

"Nice to see you, Clyde. What's in there, a coon?"

"Bats," Clyde improvised. "Been catching them round the porchlight with a potato sack." He took the lid off.

"Huh. Neck nuggets. Looks like old Ebenezer's work," Todd said. "Need us to make you some sausage?"

"Yup."

"We got a new spice mix that's real good. It's extra spicy."

"Don't want extra spicy."

"Regular, then. Where'd you get a buck this time of year, Clyde? Poach it?"

"Had it flown in from Australia. It's deer season in the Southern Hemisphere."

"Well, I should have it ready for you, oh, Monday afternoon."

"See you then," Clyde said. "Vote Banks."

It had occurred to Clyde that he might score some additional relationship karma by driving into Wapsipinicon and going to the European bakery there on Lincoln Way and buying some cinnamon rolls. It was not out of the question that he might even get back with said booty before Desiree woke up, which would earn him a double karma bonus.

Shortly after he turned south on River Street, he noted three Nishnabotna Police Department vehicles blocking the right lane a couple of blocks ahead, and Lee Harms standing there in his cop uniform waving traffic around the obstruction.

Clyde gunned the truck forward crisply, ignoring the gesticulations of Lee Harms, who had not yet recognized him, and stopped it behind a police unit.

He saw right away that another officer, Mark Ditzel, had a

suspect facedown on the pavement and handcuffed. Ditzel had his nightstick out; it had blood on it. A bulky woman in a tent-like dress was standing with her hands on the fender of the Toyota, shouting at the police officers in a language that Clyde did not recognize. A police dog from the local K-9 unit was busying herself with something that was not in the Toyota, but on the pavement next to it, up on the curb.

Clyde got out. He set Maggie on the hood of Ditzel's unit, right in front of the driver's seat, and stepped forward into the middle of the fray. He recognized the woman now: she was the one who had cleaned off Maggie's pacifier. He had not recognized her at first because the scarf had been pulled down off her head during the action, and her face was distorted with tears of rage.

Ditzel had his knee in the middle of the husband's back and his face about two inches away from that of the prisoner. He was holding his bloody nightstick up as if about to deliver an additional blow. Ditzel's face was flushed, and speckled here and there with droplets of blood not his own. Clyde flinched as a whiff of pepper spray drifted into his nostrils.

Ditzel was fulminating into the prisoner's face, spit flying from his lips. "You do not interfere with an officer! You do not touch or strike an officer! If you do so, I am justified in taking you down hard! You understand that, or you want some more of this?" Ditzel's eyes were red, and clear fluids were streaming from his tear ducts and nostrils; some of the pepper spray had got into his face as well, and this had done nothing to brighten his mood.

The man said something Clyde could not quite make out. Ditzel's eyes got even wider, this time in astonishment. "Very well, sir, I'll just have to take some additional *measures*." He grunted the last word, tensing his diaphragm as he swung the nightstick downward in the general direction of the prisoner's kidney. But it never struck home because Clyde Banks, anticipating the move, grabbed the end of the stick before it really got going. Remembering a maneuver he had practiced during his stint at the Iowa Law Enforcement Academy, he twisted the stick round against the grain of Ditzel's fingers and pried it out of his hand. Then

Clyde flung the stick over the Toyota. It clattered on the sidewalk and slid to a halt against the boarded-up facade of Walgreen's.

Ditzel was utterly terrified just for a moment, thinking he had been disarmed by an accomplice, and then he recognized Deputy Sheriff Clyde Banks and was too startled to be angry just yet. "Clyde," he said in an amazingly calm tone of voice, "what the fuck are you doing here?" Then, beginning to get pissed off: "What the hell did you do with my stick, man?"

"Giving you a chance to cool off and think about it," Clyde said.

Just then the woman took her hands off the fender of the car. She flung herself toward the K-9 officer and his dog, who were also on that side of the car. The dog chose to interpret this as a hostile gesture and drove her back with violent barking and lunging.

Both Clyde and Ditzel went after her. Ditzel went all the way around the front of the Toyota. Clyde vaulted over the hood in such a way that he came to earth directly between Ditzel and the woman. Clyde moved quickly toward her, maintaining a moving pick between her and Ditzel, and put one hand on her shoulder. She shrugged him off and windmilled that arm, trying to push him away, then turned around and recognized him.

"Look what the dog is being allowed to do!" she cried, pointing at the ground.

The box of meat had been removed from the Toyota and set on the grass of the parking strip, which was now littered all around with sheets of bloodied butcher paper. Some of the meat still lay in the center of its wrappings, and some had been dumped out onto the ground. A few cuts still remained undisturbed in the box.

Clyde caught the woman's hand in his, tucked it under his arm, and trapped it between his arm and his body. In this fashion he led her forcibly to the flank of the Toyota. He took her hand and pressed it against the top of the car, held it there with one hand while he reached around behind her with the other, got her other hand, and put it next to the first. Now he was behind her, wrapped around her like a cape, though he was so big and she so tiny that there was an air gap of several inches between them. Into her ear he said quietly, "I can take care of this if you calm down and do not move. If you take your hands off the car again, I have no idea what is going to happen."

"Well enough," she said.

Clyde released her hands and backed off a few inches. When she did not move, he relaxed and turned his attention to the dog.

The K-9 officer pulled another cut of meat from the box, unwrapped it, and laid it out on the ground. The dog prodded it with its nose and licked it. The officer had donned clear plastic gloves, which were now smeared with blood, and as Clyde watched, he pulled at the meat, tearing it apart and letting the dog sniff at it some more. "Good girl," he said, and tossed the dog one of the torn-off pieces.

While the dog was enjoying this well-earned morsel, Clyde stepped forward, picked up the box, and set it on top of the Toyota. It still contained one enormous piece of wrapped meat about the size of a large turkey. "Hey, what's up, Clyde?" said Officer Morris, the K-9 specialist.

"Why?" Clyde asked after a long pause, turning to nod at the box of meat.

"Well, you know, Clyde," Morris said. "You know why we got Bertha."

"Drugs. But this looks like meat to me."

"Oh, no, Clyde," Morris said. He started laughing, a somewhat forced laugh, and actually slapped his knee. He straightened up from his squat and gave a command to Bertha, who sat down and stayed. "Clyde, I've known you for years and I figured you for a smarter officer than that. You know we got a lot of marijuana coming in here to Forks, and you know that's why we spent all that money on Bertha."

"I'm with you so far," Clyde said.

"Well, what you got to remember is that not all criminals are stupid. Some of 'em are pretty damn smart. They know about Bertha. So they hide the goods now, Clyde. They hide the stuff in cans of coffee or anything they think will throw off the scent. Now, if you wanted to throw a dog off the scent, what could be better than hiding a big ol' head of sinsemilla inside an even bigger hunk of raw meat? Pretty clever, huh?"

"What makes you think he's got dope to begin with?"

"It's gotta be coming in from somewhere," Morris countered.

"Hell, Jim, it's coming in from ten miles away. Most of the dope in the United States is grown in the corn belt. You know that. Now, why would anyone go to the trouble of importing the stuff all the way from—wherever the hell these people are from—when there's acres of the stuff growing right here in Forks County?"

Morris broke eye contact. Clyde could see he was defeated. But the conversation was interrupted by more commotion from the opposite side of the Toyota. Clyde ran around to find Ditzel kicking the handcuffed suspect in the ribs. "Fucking sand nigger! That's all you are! You got that? So don't be giving me any more of your lip, because we don't take lip from sand niggers in this town."

"Officer Ditzel, if you strike that man again, I'll put your ass in a sling," Clyde said.

He could not believe he'd said it. Neither could Ditzel. For Clyde to imply that he would rat on a fellow police officer was like announcing that he was going to have a sex-change operation. It left everyone within earshot stunned and forced them to reevaluate everything they had ever known about Clyde Banks.

"Ba ba ba ba ba," said Maggie from the hood of Ditzel's unit.

Ditzel looked at Maggie, his astonishment growing even deeper, and then a sneer developed on his face. "Well, what the fuck are you doing here anyway? I don't remember calling for backup from a deputy—or his partner," he said, pointing at Maggie.

"Rendering assistance," Clyde said, "and advice."

"Advice? Well, thanks very much. This was going fine before you got here."

"Doesn't look fine," Clyde said, nodding at the suspect.

"I stopped him 'cause he wasn't wearing a seat belt. Maybe they don't have a seat-belt law where he comes from, but we do here. Then he started acting suspicious. So I asked him to get out of the car, him and his woman, and called for K-9 to check out the car, and that's when he got surly. Then, when the K-9 showed up, he started actively resisting, so I took him down. So this is a clean bust all the way, and I'm not in need of your advice, Deputy."

"See this?" Clyde said. He began tapping his nail against a sticker on the Toyota's window.

Ditzel leaned out to see and opened his mouth as if this would improve the acuity of his vision. "So? Parking sticker."

"You wouldn't know this, 'cause you're Nishnabotna, but I learned how to read the codes on these things working in Wapsie sometimes," Clyde said. "This one's for the law-school parking lot."

"I'll be darn," Ditzel said.

A profound silence fell over the scene. Clyde could hear wind rustling in the leaves of the oak trees.

Eastern Iowa University did not even have a law school. The law school was in Iowa City. But Clyde Banks, who had known Ditzel since they had gone to kindergarten together, knew that Ditzel could be relied upon not to know this.

"C'mere," Clyde said, and jerked his head back toward his truck. He turned his back on Ditzel, plucked Maggie off the unit as he went by, and went around back of his truck. He set Maggie down on the bed of the truck and replaced her pacifier. Ditzel met him there a moment later.

"You know how these lawyers can make a stink," he said.

"But he's just a camel jockey," Ditzel protested, his voice now much higher.

"Even better, given the state of our judicial system. Just think of it. An oppressed minority with a pregnant wife versus a redneck cop."

Ditzel opened his mouth to protest, but Clyde stopped him with an outstretched hand. "Not my words," he said. "To me you are Officer Ditzel, an experienced and decorated law-enforcement veteran. But when they haul your ass into court, all that's going to be forgotten and you are going to be presented as a redneck cop. Believe me. I've been over there in Wapsie, and I know how these people think."

By now Morris had come round with his dog. Clyde looked over at the woman, who was eyeing the box of meat, an arm's-length away. She glanced his way. He slid his glasses down on his nose and gave her a warning look, then pushed them back up and turned his attention to the officers.

"So what are you advising?" Ditzel said.

"Well, now, think about it. He didn't buckle up. You nailed him for that. He gave you some guff and you spanked him. You've had a good day, my friend!" Clyde reached out and slapped Ditzel hard on the shoulder. "You got all the satisfaction you're ever going to get. Now, you could take it the next step and spend the rest of the day in front of a typewriter and then get hauled into court and be accused of being a redneck cop and everything else that would follow. Or you could cash in your chips right now while you're ahead. Let them go."

"It'd kill me if there was some weed in the bottom of that box," Morris said ruefully.

"Yeah!" said Ditzel, who had almost given up until Morris had mentioned the drugs. "We gotta get to the bottom of that."

"There ain't nothing but meat in there," Clyde said, and told them briefly of what he had seen at Lukas Meats.

"So that's a Jew?" Ditzel said, astonished and scandalized.

"I would guess Muslim. But I think they follow the same rules as far as meat," Clyde said, "so they all buy their meat on the same day, when the Jewish butcher comes to town. That's where all that meat came from, and if the Lukases have been hiding dope in their meat, then I reckon it's the Lukases we ought to be checking out with the K-9 unit."

Providentially, Maggie started to cry at this moment. Clyde brought her round to the front seat of the pickup and snapped her in, then climbed in and watched through the dirty windshield as Morris put the box of meat in the back of the Toyota and helped the woman into the passenger seat. Ditzel removed the man's handcuffs, hauled him to his feet, and shoved him toward the Toyota. Clyde started the truck, backed up, and swung it out into the left lane, idling forward very slowly as he drove past the scene. The man had a big laceration across his forehead, the kind of thing that always bled like crazy, but by now it had clotted up enough that he could drive the car safely. He seemed absurdly calm as he climbed back into the car, as if he had just stopped in at a rest area to take a leak.

Then Clyde's view of the scene was eclipsed by the broad body of Lee Harms, still directing traffic, who leaned down and looked into the window above Maggie's car seat as Clyde went by. "Nice going, Clyde," he said. "Looks like you got the Muslim vote all sewed up."

"Vote Banks," Clyde said weakly, and hung a big U-turn on River Street, headed home to Desiree. He did not feel like getting cinnamon rolls.

nineteen

JULY

THE CURVY drive leading up to the Wapsipinicon Golf and Country Club had been lined with small plastic American flags thrust into the ground, many of which were already listing badly before the wind that was howling across the prairie. The plastic flags made a brittle rattling sound as they were strafed by the wind. Clyde came around the last one of those curves and saw three men wearing fancy black outfits with bow ties. The sight made him falter; he lifted his foot from the gas, and the wagon's transmission made hissing and sighing noises as a few bucket-loads of hydraulic fluid looked for someplace to go.

"What's wrong, honey?" Desiree said. Her face was burnished and lovely; she'd spent the last weekend with the National Guard running around in the sun treating fake chemical-warfare casualties. Her arms, back, and the ravishing Dhont deltoids had been concealed by the Army uniform, and she had fretted about their incongruous pallor when she had put on her sundress; but Clyde thought she looked wonderful. He would never dare tell her, though, that she looked even cuter in her combat fatigues. There was something about Desiree's body rattling around in yards and yards of scrunchy camouflage fabric that sent him over the edge; the green and brown brought out the highlights in her hazel eyes.

"Let's say Maggie's sick," Clyde said, looking into the backseat hopefully. Maggie had vomited on the epaulet of Clyde's best sheriff uniform not thirty seconds before they had left the house, and even though they had wiped most of it off, the mysterious proteins had congealed to a hard shine. But Desiree had pronounced this a normal vomiting episode, a sign of robust good health; and, indeed, Maggie was, unfortunately, pink-faced and happy.

"It's just a cookout."

Clyde looked in the rearview mirror. The view in that direction was nearly filled by a navy-blue Lincoln Town Car, navigated and piloted by Bob Jenkins of Bob Jenkins Lincoln Mercury, who came to a stop behind them. He recognized the Murder Car and turned to his wife animatedly. His wife had got a new hairdo; Clyde could tell because she moved stiffly, as if a mad bomber had wired tubes of nitroglycerin into her permanent wave.

"They had these a lot in California," Desiree said. "It's valet parking. All we have to do is get out and they'll park it."

"I know what it is," Clyde said darkly.

"Then why are you holding up the Jenkinses? You don't want Rick Morgan to drive the wagon?"

"Nah."

"You forgot something at home?"

Rick Morgan, straightening his bow tie, made eye contact with him; he was trapped now.

"Howdy, Clyde. So you're the one that bought the Murder Car!"

"I guess so," Clyde said, clambering out. Desiree was already at work in the backseat, disengaging the baby pod from its docking unit.

"Well, we'll take real good care of it," Rick Morgan said, sliding into the driver's seat as if he owned the vehicle.

"It takes off pretty good in first because that big old four-sixty has good low-end torque, so it'll surge when you give it the gas," Clyde said, "then level off pretty quick."

"Okay, Clyde," Rick Morgan said. He seemed startled and dismayed.

Clyde shut the door on Rick Morgan. "You'll notice that I didn't slam the door," Clyde said. "That's for a reason. It is because the door is so heavy that it has a tremendous momentum of its own."

"I read you loud and clear, Clyde," Rick Morgan said, and gunned the engine too hard. The wagon reared up and bolted. Clyde imagined he could hear the transmission fluid flashing into live steam and bursting valves. But it was too late now. Desiree was standing there holding the baby on one hip, waiting (as Clyde eventually realized) for him to offer his arm. He did so and led Desiree up to the door.

"Vote Banks," Clyde muttered to another bow-tie wearer as he went inside, putting one hand on the door himself even though it was being held for him. The notion of able-bodied men requiring servants to open doors for them was not one that Clyde would ever come to grips with.

The country club had been built during a phase of architectural history that Clyde vaguely remembered as the Flagstone Period. As he walked across the clubhouse floor, the theme music from *The Flintstones* came into his head and he had to consciously force himself not to start humming it.

This area was all low tables and sofas. A few people were there, mostly older folks and women with conspicuous hairdos, or possibly wigs, that could not be taken into the windy conditions outside. The back wall of the room was all picture windows and led to a very large flagstone patio with a pool to one side and a view over the golf course. A cylindrical pig roaster was smoking away, tended by a youth brought in on loan from the Hickory Pit restaurant, and a few dozen Republicans were milling around drinking what Clyde assumed to be cocktails and trying to dodge the long, ropy plume of smoke that shot out of the roaster and veered this way and that as the wind shifted—like escaping prisoners trying to stay out of the beam of the prison searchlight. A wall of beautiful thunderheads rose many miles to the west, violet below, their tops incandescent peach and magenta. The sun was going to sink behind those clouds soon, bringing a premature end to the day.

Clyde saw the next hour of his life plotted out as if on the whiteboard in the roll-call room down at the sheriff's department. He would go out and mingle uncomfortably. Everyone would stare at Desiree and the baby. The baby would begin to get hungry in approximately forty-five minutes. Desiree would take her inside, plop herself down on a couch directly across from an old Republican lady in a blue wig, and, just like that, whip out a tit and start feeding the kid. The old Republican lady wouldn't say a word, but the repercussions would come anyway, and pretty soon Clyde would be called in for a friendly man-to-man with Terry Stonefield and be informed that so-and-so was waiting for an apology. Desiree would refuse to apologize, and so Clyde would do it on her behalf and then so-and-so would not be satisfied—she would still be angry, but now she would be angry at Clyde—and Desiree would be angry at him for having apologized, and Terry Stonefield would be angry with Clyde, also, for not having handled it better.

This being the case, it seemed fitting and proper for him to have a drink. So he ambled to the bar in the corner.

From that location he was able to see a nook where John Stonefield and Ebenezer were wordlessly ramming great unruly tangles of tobacco into the bowls of their pipes. Standing near them, a mixed drink in his hand, talking at some length but getting no response, was John Stonefield's son Terry, chairman of the Forks County Republican Committee, chairman of the board of several venerable Forks-area businesses, sometime state senator, gubernatorial candidate, and two-term U.S. congressman. He was dumpy yet delicate, wearing a navy blazer and khaki trousers and a striped tie with a stars-and-stripes pattern.

By the time Clyde had got his drink—a bottle of Steinhoffer Pilsner—Terry had turned around, noticed him, and beckoned him over. Hands were shaken all around. Neither John Stonefield nor Ebenezer had said anything yet, or all day, so far as Clyde could tell.

Clyde was not sure when John and Ebenezer had started golfing together, but he did not put much effort into trying to figure it out. He had noticed that old people were much more interesting and complex than he had ever suspected as a young man and that there was no telling what secret connections and machinations they might be up to. Ebenezer had lost a son-in-law (Clyde's father) and John had lost a son: his oldest, his fair-haired boy and heir apparent, had been shot down in Korea and never found. But Clyde knew, from tiny droplets of information leaked out here and there, that John had filled Ebenezer with a great deal of secret knowledge about the Stonefield family, the quirks and personal failings of its members, and the inner workings of its business empire.

None of it was likely to impress Ebenezer. Ebenezer was a plain-dealing and -speaking sort. In his mind all transactions more complex than, say, buying a plate of scrambled eggs at the Hy-Vee breakfast counter, and all relationships more complex than a lifelong, purely monogamous marriage between two virgins, belonged to a vast but vaguely defined category called "shenanigans." He had let it be known, once or twice over the years, that the Stonefield family, in the decadent years since Terry's older brother had gone down in flames, and John had turned matters over to Terry and gone into retirement and seclusion, had become tangled up in any number of different types of shenanigans. He always said this regretfully, as if he did not mean to seem judgmental. But Clyde had been judged by Ebenezer many times over the years, usually with the end result of getting walloped by a belt or stick, and so he knew that Ebenezer must have strong opinions hidden somewhere.

John Stonefield now spent most of his time in his farmhouse above the river outside of Wapsipinicon, reading outlandish newspapers mailed in from places like London and emerging only to play golf with Ebenezer. But he got together with Terry and the rest of his family from time to time and must have mentioned the Banks family during his conversations. Clyde knew as much, because one day late in 1989 Terry Stonefield, who had never known him from Adam, had suddenly invited him out to lunch and had made it clear that he knew a great deal about Clyde Banks and his domestic and career situations. The full majesty and power of the Forks County Republican party would be behind Clyde Banks should he choose to run.

So when Clyde stepped into the little nook where Ebenezer and the elder and younger Stonefields were, he felt like the last piece of a jigsaw puzzle that these men had been putting together over the last several months or even years. It didn't take a genius to figure out why; incumbent Mullowney was a bad man and a bad sheriff. On the other side of the equation, the sheriff's job was prestigious and carried with it a great deal of power, most of which was of an unofficial and unwritten nature. It would be a good thing for anyone to have a relative, or a friend of a friend, who was the sheriff of Forks County.

"Look at those anvils," Clyde said, shaking his head. All four men stared out the window, sizing up the approaching storm front.

"Must be topping fifty-five thousand feet," Ebenezer said.

"How's the campaign going, Clyde?" Terry said brightly.

Clyde said nothing for a moment, reckoning that his true answer should not be spoken in the presence of John and Ebenezer.

"Saw some of the stickers around town. Guess that means you hooked up with Razorback Media okay."

"Hooked up with 'em, all right," Clyde said.

"I keep looking out my window waiting for you to come up my road, Clyde," John Stonefield said.

"What the hell are you talking about?" Ebenezer said.

"Well, he said he'd knock on every door in Forks County. Hasn't knocked on mine yet, 'less I was out when he did."

"I figured I'd catch you on Sunday, sir," Clyde said.

"How's that?"

"Thought I'd join you and Grandpa for golf, if you wouldn't object," Clyde said.

"You got your swing straightened out?" John Stonefield said darkly.

"Haven't made it out to the course since last Father's Day. But I've been visualizing a good stroke. They say that works."

John and Ebenezer exchanged a brief poker-faced look and concentrated for a moment on their pipe-stoking and -lighting efforts. This was to say that they both understood Clyde had paid them the compliment of starting to bullshit them.

"Does it work to get you elected?" Ebenezer said.

After this John and Ebenezer became even more reticent than usual, apparently on the theory that, whatever they had to say to Clyde, they could say on Sunday when they weren't berating him over his poor golf game. Sensing the shift in mood, Terry and Clyde drew away from them, moving back toward the center of things.

Clyde sensed that there were a great many people who were eager to step forward and shake Terry's hand, but who were restraining themselves forcibly lest they interrupt some high-level impromptu strategy session involving the inner workings of the sheriff campaign. Clyde, never the sort to inconvenience any such people, decided he would get to his point as quickly as he knew how.

"I was down at the jail yesterday," Clyde said.

"The jail? What were you doing there?" Terry said sharply.

"Working," Clyde said.

Terry looked mildly irritated. "Oh, yeah. Of course."

Clyde hated working at the jail and knew that Sheriff Mullowney had been giving him lots of jail duty just to harass him, but Ebenezer had taught him not to whine. So he skipped over that part. "I was talking to Mark Becker."

"Who's Mark Becker?" Terry said, suddenly intrigued at the prospect of adding a new name to his mental Rolodex of behind-the-scenes movers and shakers.

"One of the prisoners," Clyde said.

Terry screwed up his face with disgust and looked away. When he turned back, he was wearing an expression of patient, fatherly disappointment. "Now, why are you talking to people like that?"

"When I'm on jail duty," Clyde said defensively, "I can't help but talk to 'em. Mostly they talk to me, though." Jail talk made high-school locker-room talk sound like an episode of *Firing Line*. "Anyway, Mark said he was on West Lincoln Way picking up litter as part of his community service—"

"Wait a minute, Clyde. Get the story straight. Why was he in jail if he'd already been sentenced to community service?"

"Community service was last week. For a previous infraction. Then I arrested him for disorderly a couple of nights ago. He'll probably get jail time for that."

"Oh, I see. So Mark Becker is a career criminal!" Terry said, outraged.

"That's giving him too much credit," Clyde said. "If I told Mark Becker he had a career, he'd probably stop being a criminal and do something else."

"So what did Mark Becker have to say to you, Clyde?" Terry said, looking around significantly at all the people who wanted to bust in on the conversation, somehow giving each one of them a warm smile and a bit of eye contact. This unnerved Clyde, and so he let it all out in a rush.

"He was saying that fifty percent of the litter he picked up on Lincoln Way was 'Vote Banks' bumper stickers. He said he picked up bags of 'em."

"Sounds like a box fell off a truck somewheres," Terry Stonefield said.

"No, these were used. The backing had been peeled off. These were stickers I had handed out at church, around the neighborhood and so on, and people had put them on their cars and they fell off when it rained last week."

Terry Stonefield considered this for a moment, then laughed nervously. He got an amused look on his face, and Clyde could sense that he was about to make light of the situation. Clyde realized it was time to pull out his ace in the hole, let go with his *cri de coeur*.

"Mark Becker told me," Clyde said, "that he saw a dust devil moving down the median strip of Lincoln Way made up of Clyde Banks bumper stickers."

Terry suddenly turned on his Serious Look. He stepped closer to Clyde. "Clyde, did you just try giving Razorback Media a call?"

"Their phone's disconnected," Clyde said. "Little Rock Triple-B says they skipped out on their lease."

Terry mulled this one over and pulled at his face. "How'd you pay for those darn stickers?"

"Desiree's credit card."

Terry brightened. "That a First National Bank of NishWap credit card by any chance?"

"Sure is."

"Well, there you go. They got a policy."

"Policy?"

"You buy anything with that card that's defective, stolen, dropped off a truck by the UPS man, shattered by lightning or any other act of God—they'll refund you in full. Good talking to you, Clyde," Terry Stonefield said, and shook Clyde's hand with his left while reaching out to another supporter with his right.

Clyde got back to Desiree just in time; she was reaching up under her shirt, preparing to whip out a tit in the middle of the room. Clyde plucked Maggie lightly out of her hands, rummaged in the baby bag for a bottle, and carried her up an open stairway to a mezzanine that looked out over the ground floor and the patio. He and Maggie were the only people up there, and Clyde immediately felt calmer to be looking down on the Republicans from a healthy distance.

Maggie went to sleep in his arms; time passed; Desiree came up and agreed that it would be acceptable to leave now. The immense anvil thunderheads to the west loomed high above the rolling hills covered with eight-foot corn, rolling like massive weapons of destruction spewing out lightning in all directions, bearing down relentlessly on the quarter- to half-million-dollar homes lining the golf course.

twenty

POLICY KEPT shifting against Saddam, and Betsy's position was vindicated. That made her happy even though Spector had been at pains to make it clear to her that she would never get credit. She had gone outside of her task, and in the government it was better to follow the lines of authority than to be right. She remained as much an outcast as she had been earlier. And she received no help from any of the branches that could give her the information she needed. But she kept probing, bringing up what sources she could, reading widely to find some sort of confirming link that would tie together the misspent American aid dollars, the wandering academics, the technology of nonconventional warfare, and a few Midwestern universities.

The Iraqis had many of their best people in the States, and she could not understand why. Normally they would send promising youngsters here for training and then bring them back to home soil to do their actual work. But several Iraqi scientists who should have been in the prime of their careers were stationed in the U.S. She could only suppose that here they could get access to equipment or other resources not available at home.

But the implication was that these people were actively developing weapons—or, at least, the underlying science for a weapons program—on U.S. soil.

For a while she traced down the possibilities of a new form of anthrax as a weapon. She had read studies classified as confidential describing how the Iraqis were retroengineering the process of developing weapons-strength uranium—that instead of taking the technology forward, they had actually gone back to 1946-model Oak Ridge technology. Could they be taking a similar tack with biological weapons?

She jumped into the CDC files and dug out all she could on the development of anthrax toxins. She spent three weeks on this line of inquiry but got nowhere. When she would ask Science and Technology for help, they would stonewall her. The DCI refused to disturb the bureaucratic rhythms. The Pentagon would not even consider giving her any help.

One morning at five o'clock, when she was banging on her screen with a foam-rubber sledgehammer that Kevin had given her, Spector walked in. "I was going to ask how things were going. But sometimes nonverbal communication is more effective."

She looked at him with blood in her eye, got up, walked over to the vault door, and shut it. "Why don't you people help me?"

"We can't."

"Look, I'll take no credit. I'll turn everything over to somebody in S and T."

"They don't want it. They know you've touched it."

"Can't we move on any front?"

"No. Millikan has spread the word that you're to be insulated. Isolated. Ignored."

"By name?"

"No, that would be gauche. He has done something much more effective: he's laid out the wiring diagram on investigations into this issue. You're not on it. Except insofar as it includes your section, as a footnote of sorts—but it's laid in such a way that anything coming from this vault will have to pass through three layers of review before it actually goes anywhere. You've been cobwebbed by the best."

"What about going to the President?"

Spector blinked in disbelief and did her the favor of not laughing. "Folklore has it that the President, because of his Agency experience, is relatively sympathetic to the plight of the low-level analyst. This has caused many people in your position to harbor unrealistic ideas about going straight to the top. But there are thousands of low-level analysts who dream of doing that."

"Is there anybody else working on this angle?"

"Not to my knowledge."

"What do I do?"

"Keep plugging away. And be careful. You and your roomie are real good at not talking openly about what's going on. But your tone and your nuances—especially your nuances—communicate volumes. Since your run out to Wildwood, the whole nature of your conversational tone has changed. Remind me, now that you're a branch chief, to show you the voice-wave analysis systems. They're damned good, much better than polys at reading people. Anyway, your patterns have changed."

Betsy leaned back and looked out the window at the dawn. He

was right. Paul Moses had changed things, but it had nothing to do with the search she was carrying out. There would be no point, though, in trying to convince Spector of that.

"I'm going to keep working on it," Betsy said.

"Good. Just wanted to let you know where you stand. You want to let me out of this place?"

June had gone by with her days divided among serious work (four A.M. to eight A.M.), branch affairs (eight o'clock to noon), and meetings ad nauseam (noon to four). She was slapped on the wrist by Spector because her branch's productivity had declined under her tenure. "That's because you have me doing all this nonsense," she responded.

"Doesn't matter. You've got to keep the words coming."

Weekends were spent with Paul when Paul wasn't busy with his own work. After the events in Wildwood he had drawn away from her to a safe distance and become more of a buddy than a boyfriend. They exchanged the occasional snuggle or smooch, but even that level of intimacy seemed to make him uncomfortable. At first she assumed he was still embarrassed over his episode of impotence. But as time went on, she began to worry that it went deeper than that and resolved to have a talk with him when she could find time.

Betsy and Cassie began to make plans for their annual Fourth of July bash. With a bit of effort one could see the fireworks display from their balcony, so they always had a few people in. This time they were going to have the Wildwood group plus Kevin, who would be in town for the first week of July running errands for Larsen. Needless to say, their neighbor, Margaret Park-O'Neil, would be there, too, so they could entertain themselves by watching her and Kevin make eyes at each other.

Paul came early and brought a huge bag of ice. He bantered with Cassie in the kitchen, then sneaked up behind Betsy and gave her a hug.

The door buzzer kept sounding as the rest of the crew showed up. Soon enough booze was consumed and food eaten that the conversation was going at a dull roar. Jeff Lippincott and Christine O'Connell had got married in the interim—each still keeping his/her name. Marcus Berry had come back in from the Midwest, where he seemed to spend a lot of time on assignment, to spend the holiday with Cassie. Kevin and Margaret Park-O'Neil resumed exactly where they had left off—Betsy gathered that they had been exchanging a great deal of e-mail in the last month.

They turned on Channel 26 to watch the concert from the Mall and kept on talking and drinking. Betsy watched Kevin carefully. He had never handled his booze well, and it didn't take long for him to reach the point where he was speaking very loudly and slowly, as if he had to taste each word before it got out of his mouth.

Kevin was trying very hard to impress Margaret, who at least looked impressed. He was telling her, in various ways, how important he had become. About his friends at the Jordanian Embassy. About the really important people coming in from all over the world to study or lecture or do research at American universities, and how he was bending rules and cutting deals with petty bureaucrats to help get them in, and how this was all part of Larsen's international mutual back-scratching game, which would lead, like a pyramid scheme, to even deeper connections, larger grants, and greater accomplishments. As he talked louder and slower and became less aware of his impact, the room grew quieter and quieter until, aside from Kevin, the only sound that could be heard was "the 1812 Overture" coming out of the television's two-inch cardboard speaker. "And Dr. Larsen is giving me a huge bonus. He got some new business from Jordan, and I get a five percent commission."

Two minutes earlier he had alluded to this business from Jordan and had mentioned that it was "a couple of million dollars." Everyone in the room had heard it.

Now the words "five percent commission" floated in the air for what seemed an eternity. Then a huge aerial bomb exploded above the river, so loud that Kevin startled back and sloshed his drink into his lap. "Time to go watch the fireworks," Betsy said.

"Don't lean too far over the rail, it's a hundred feet down to the concrete."

Margaret scurried into the kitchen and got some paper towels to get Kevin dry, an operation that caught Betsy's eye if only because the drink had spilled into his lap.

In a strange way Betsy was more disappointed with Margaret than she was with her brother. She knew her brother. She knew that he was young and full of himself and just going through a phase, and that eventually he would snap out of it and be embarrassed by his behavior—and rightly so. But Margaret had seemed pretty sharp. That she was fawning over Kevin called her judgment into question—her judgment, or her sincerity.

Kevin stood up abruptly and headed for the bathroom. Margaret watched him go, then turned sheepishly to Betsy, perhaps reading the look on her face.

"My dad's got a drinking problem—a typical master-sergeant thing," she said. "So I guess this is incredibly pathological of me. I apologize."

This went some way toward alleviating Betsy's suspicions. "We never had booze in the house when we were kids," she said. "Now he has to drink as part of his job. I wonder if Larsen knew what he was getting into when he hired my brother."

Margaret said, "He's really sweet. But I hope he doesn't go down the same road my father did." Then she blushed, perhaps realizing she might have gone too far. "I'd better go now."

Paul emerged from the bathroom with one arm around Kevin and half carried him to the bedroom. He came back, looked very seriously at Betsy, and said nothing. Jeff Lippincott came in from the balcony; the fireworks were over, and Betsy had missed them. Jeff hugged Betsy and whispered in her ear, "Recheck my note."

"My God," Betsy murmured. Jeff had given her an envelope during the trip to Wildwood; she had put it in her pocket and then forgotten it, preoccupied as she was with Paul. Since then she had washed the shorts.

She left Cassie in charge of the party, knowing that it was in good hands, and entered the bedroom, where Kevin was snoring loudly on the bed, smelling of vomit. She dug her shorts out from deep in the ironing basket and removed the warped and fuzzy envelope. There was a sheet of paper inside, hard copy from a laser printer, fortunately waterproof.

Jeff had given her a list of names—Arabic names. Jeff was Agency, but he worked at USIA, checking visa applications, and Betsy had come across his name more than once when investigating the flow of Iraqi scientists into American universities.

Some of the names she recognized—they were people she already knew about, people on her Dirty Dozen list. But some were new to her.

Next to the column of names was a column of dates, labeled "Date of Entry." Most of the dates were one or two years in the past. But some of them were marked July 1990. These names were the ones Betsy didn't recognize.

Kevin had just been bragging about the big shots he was going to be bringing into the country in the coming month. None of this could possibly be a coincidence.

twenty-one

FAZOUL, THE maimed foreign student, was throwing his own Fourth of July shindig down by the river at Albertson Park, so-called because it lay across from Albertson's grocery. The invitation specified Picnic Shelter Number Nine, a quarter mile in, close to the bluffs above the Nishnabotna. The small parking area there was full, and a couple of dozen cars were parked quasi-illegally along the shoulder of the road leading to it.

As Clyde, Desiree, and Maggie reached the parking lot next to the big shelter, they saw a banner printed out on long strips of computer paper, hung from the eave of the shelter, with letters—shapes, really—printed on it in green. He figured it was Arabic. Beneath it were smaller letters in some other script he'd never seen at all, lots of curlicues. He saw men who looked straight out of *Lawrence of Arabia,* dressed in white robes with towels draped over their heads; men wearing aprons and leather vests, wearing square, boxlike hats the size of McDonald's drink holders; men in shorts and Nikes wearing T-shirts with things written on them in English and other languages; men dressed in suits and ties. Some of the women were completely veiled in chadors, just columns of black with huge black eyes peering out as through gun slits—Clyde thought of the EIU Twisters mascot, a tornado on legs, with a male cheerleader concealed inside looking out through a narrow aperture. Other women were showing their faces, and there were tawny women running around barefoot in shorts and T-shirts. Kids were everywhere, all of them dressed as if they'd just gone on a shopping spree at Wal-Mart. Clyde could hardly plant one foot in front of the other for all the kids.

All these people began to applaud. Suddenly everyone was looking at him. The applause was joined by a bizarre warbling sound from the throats of the women. He slowed, then stepped back a pace.

A large, heavy man with a goatee, dressed in a white robe with a towel over his head, was standing just in front of him; he had turned around to face Clyde and was applauding lustily, the sleeves of his robe shaking. A taller, darker, and much gaunter figure dodged around this man and headed straight for Clyde; it was Fazoul, dressed in jeans and a denim jacket. He reached out and grabbed Clyde's right hand for a two-handed shake, the index finger and thumb of his truncated left hand gripping Clyde's forearm in a surprisingly strong pincer. After a long and strong handshake, he pivoted on his fake leg, threw an arm around Clyde's shoulders, and started leading him toward the shelter.

"Sorry we're late. Had to go to another thing first," Clyde said.

"Oh? I am doubly indebted if you cut short some other engagement to come here."

"I'm glad you gave me an excuse to get out of it," Clyde said. He was still reeling from the Republicans.

They'd already made a place for Desiree up at one of the picnic tables in the shelter. Clyde supposed it was a special table because they had thrown a colored rug or something over it—not a carpet remnant from Sears, but something that looked as if it had been made by hand someplace far away. Atop the table was a rustic cradle made out of strips of leather and hunks of bent wood, lined with the thickest and plushest sheepskin Clyde had ever seen. He assumed it was for Fazoul's son, but it was empty now. Half a dozen or so women, including Desiree, were gathered in the vicinity of this table, manhandling and cooing over a couple of different babies, none of whom was Maggie.

Clyde was handed an enormous tumbler full of a white fluid with translucent hunks floating in it; this turned out to be iced buttermilk with sliced cucumber, and it was astonishingly tasty.

"Where's Maggie?" he said to Desiree between gulps.

"I don't know," she said. "Isn't this nice?"

Clyde allowed that it was. In spite of himself he scanned the area for his baby and thought he glimpsed her fifty feet away, on the grass beneath an oak tree, where a dozen women had sat down in a circle, forming a sort of human playpen where five or six infants and toddlers were staggering around falling over each other. Several babes in arms were being passed back and forth, around the circle, jiggled, rocked, and cajoled. One of them looked like Maggie.

Fazoul sat down across the table from him, straddling the bench and lifting his peg leg onto it with a grimace.

"It took us longer than expected to start the fire last night, so you are just in time," Fazoul said.

"Last night?"

"You like to barbecue?"

"Sure, I guess so."

"Come with me, please." Fazoul planted his peg leg on the floor again and pushed himself up with his arms. Clyde followed him in the direction of the line of great trees that crowned the bluff. As they walked through a small crowd of women, someone came up and deposited a large bundle in Clyde's arms: someone else's baby, not more than a couple of weeks old. Fazoul seemed not to notice, so Clyde kept walking.

"You would think that a bunch of physicists and engineers and other savants would not have such trouble making fire," Fazoul said, "but how quickly we forget such things!" Fazoul laughed and shook his head in disbelief. "The number of tree roots is astonishing."

"You got a barbecue pit going back in the woods?"

"Exactly," Fazoul said.

"You know, you can rent a roaster down at Budovich Hardware. Saves all that digging."

"Unless it was a brand-new roaster, we could not be sure it had never been used to cook pork," Fazoul said. "So your gallant efforts to protect the lamb from the dog might have gone to waste."

"Oh." Clyde was starting to put it together. "I see."

"I have a son!" Fazoul exclaimed, and nodded at the bundle in Clyde's arms. "We always hold a feast to celebrate. We needed a *halal* lamb for this feast—it had to be slaughtered in just the right way. This was done for us at Lukas Meats on the morning you and I met. The police dog rendered much of our meat unusable on that day, but you prevented it from defiling the carcass of the lamb, which was the most precious to us."

"And you're roasting it in a pit."

"We have been doing so since, oh, something like one in the morning." Fazoul checked his watch, a heavy stainless-steel number, and yawned.

"Is this your first?" Clyde said.

Fazoul broke eye contact and stared off into the forest. "Fifth."

"Oh. Are the other four here today?"

"No," Fazoul said after an awkward pause, "they were not able to attend."

They arrived at a clearing near the edge of the bluff. Nishnabotna was visible across the river, through a sparse picket line of big trees. They were shielded from a direct view of the packing plant by the dense summer undergrowth that competed for the light that shone on the rim of the cliff in the morning. Four men were standing around a place where smoke and steam came out of the ground, seeping through a thick cap of leaves. All of these men were dressed in Western clothes, and one of them was actually a Westerner.

"Dr. Kenneth Knightly, dean of international programs," Fazoul said.

"Honored to meet you, Clyde," Knightly said, stepping forward to shake hands; but seeing the baby in Clyde's arms, he settled for an exchange of nods.

"Pleasure," Clyde said. Fazoul went on to give the names of the three foreigners, and Clyde forgot them immediately.

"I contacted your boss—Sheriff Mullowney—and told him about what a fine thing you did," Knightly said. "Gave him my personal thanks and that of the president of the university. He said you'd always been one of his finest deputies."

Clyde hardly knew where to begin, so he held his tongue and soon thought better of trying to unburden himself to Dr. Knightly on the subject of his job.

Fazoul picked up a rake and used it to claw the cap of leaves off the barbecue pit. A mushroom cloud of steam rose out of it, smelling wonderfully of cumin and other spices. Down in the pit was something wrapped in more leaves, surrounded on all sides by a thick jacket of black-and-white coals that glowed like neon tubes in the deepening prethunderstorm gloom. Fazoul and his three coreligionists commenced a serious but heated debate in whatever their language was.

"New High Altaic," Knightly said, reading the curiosity on Clyde's face. "New because it's a modern dialect. High because it originally came from the high mountains of Central Asia."

Knightly spoke with a Texas accent and wore actual cowboy boots—down-at-the-heel ones scraped round the edges and marked here and there with road tar. He was wearing a Gooch's Best seed-corn cap to protect the large bald area on the top of his head, and he was smoking a straight Camel with the hunched, apologetic posture of a longtime smoker who has tried and failed to quit. Clyde felt that he could ask Knightly questions without being made to feel like an unlettered townie.

"How about Altaic?" he said.

Knightly grimaced, looked at Nishnabotna, and took a long drag on his cigarette. "Well, that gets us in deeper. Fazoul and his homeboys are Turks."

"What part of Turkey they from?"

"Most Turks have never set foot inside the country called

Turkey. I s'pose I could be old-fashioned and call them Turkomans just to make that distinction a little clearer. There's a whole lot of different kind of Turkomans, Clyde. They start in Constantinople and go all the way to China. There's Turks in Siberia and Turks in India."

"Sounds like they really got around."

"They did get around. The Turks are the biggest ass-kickers in history. They kicked everyone's ass at one point or another. I mean really kicked their asses. You know who Genghis Khan was?"

"I guess."

"Well, Genghis Khan was a Mongol, and he wouldn't have been diddly except that he got the Turks on his side early. I could go on and on. Anyway, the point is that they're all over the place, there are a lot of different subgroups. Fazoul and company are from a subgroup that started out in the Altai Mountains a long time ago and made a name for themselves—literally—in the Vakhan Corridor, which is where Afghanistan and China and Russia and Pakistan all come together. They are Vakhan Turks. But they have been a lot of other places since they got that name."

"And now they're in Forks County," Clyde said.

Knightly laughed out loud and ground out his cigarette. By this point Fazoul and his friends had lifted the smoking bundle from the pit, so Knightly wielded the sharp toe of his cowboy boot to kick the butt of the Camel into the hole. He and Clyde watched as it smoked, turned brown, and suddenly burst into a little star of yellow flame.

A moment later it was snuffed out as one of Fazoul's men pitched the first shovelful of black earth into the pit. They filled it in quickly; the first fat drops of rain had begun to tumble down like water balloons from the purple-black thunderheads whose bases were now directly over their heads. Clyde pulled the corner of the baby's blanket over its face, and all of the men—the four Vakhan Turks and the two Americans—made for the shelter as quickly as they could. By the time they emerged from the trees, it was raining steadily, and when they were within a few yards of the shelter, it began to come down in a seamless mass. All of the partygoers had gathered together under the shelter's hipped roof, forming a solid rectangular bloc. Clyde had lost track of Fazoul and excused his way through the crowd for several minutes, rocking the baby in his arms, until he found Farida, Fazoul's wife, sitting next to Desiree.

After Clyde had turned the baby over, Desiree flung one arm around Farida's shoulders, leaned sideways, and put her face right up next to Farida's. "What do you think?" she said.

"Beg pardon?" he said.

Desiree refused to say, just posed there right next to Farida, the two women staring up at him with the same mischievous expression. They looked like a couple of naughty sisters. Lightning struck nearby, strobing a still image of the two women deep into Clyde's brain.

"I'll be darn," Clyde said. Then he actually felt a chill moving up his spine, and a tingling around the back of his skull where his hairs were trying to come to attention. And it wasn't because of the thunder rolling in from the nearby ground strike, or the ozone smell of the thunderstorm.

It was common knowledge that Desiree had been adopted from someplace exotic. Her dark hair, the almond shape of her hazel eyes, her ability to tan rapidly and evenly to a lovely terracotta shade, all marked her out as being not from around here, and certainly not borne of a Dhont.

Mrs. Dhont claimed not to have any idea where Desiree came from. If she knew, she wasn't telling. She believed, perhaps with good reason, that her daughter's adopted heritage made no difference at all and should not even be mentioned in conversation. If Desiree had been blond and blue-eyed, Mrs. Dhont probably never would have admitted that she was adopted at all. This was a policy arrived at internally by Mrs. Dhont, operating behind the veil that separated women from men, following the arcane rules and, perhaps, instincts that women applied to matters regarding family—rules that could not be explained or justified, leading to decisions that could not be questioned or appealed.

Sons just obeyed. But daughters turned into women and

passed through that veil, where they could enact their own decisions and carry out their own programs, sometimes regardless of what precedents Mother had laid down.

Clyde had never imagined that Desiree harbored the slightest degree of curiosity about her origins until this moment. And now he knew that she'd been fretting about it all along. He also knew, now, that he was married to some kind of Turkoman.

Clyde had a theory that women had a book, a homemade, photocopied three-ring binder called "Surprising Things to Do in a Relationship," which they passed around to one another, adding pages from time to time, hiding it under the bed. He figured that Desiree could run home tonight and add a new page.

The lamb was unwrapped from its leaves, carved, and served. The rain came down so hard that the ricochet from the deepening puddles under the eaves soaked the people sitting around the edges of the shelter. Gusts of wind came through with the momentum of freight trains on the Denver–Platte–Des Moines, inflating the raiment of certain partygoers like spinnakers and sending avalanches of plates and food down the lengths of the tables. Several of the foreign students were at work out on the grass, wearing raincoats improvised from garbage bags, struggling to erect a tent of wooden poles and skins.

He sought out Knightly, who was just winding up a conversation in Arabic, or something, with a man in a robe.

"I was just explaining to this gentleman," Knightly said, "what those poor Vakhans are doing out in the rain. I suppose you want to know the same thing?"

"I figured that gentleman would already know," Clyde said.

"That gentleman's ancestors rode camels around on the desert of Arabia. Of course, now they're oilmen. But Fazoul's ancestors rode ponies on the grasslands beneath the snow-covered peaks of the Altai Mountains in Central Asia, a few thousand miles away. Different people, different customs. Fazoul's people have been doing this for their newborn sons since, oh, a couple thousand years before Mohammed trod sand."

"They gonna do a ceremony or something?"

"Yeah. Sort of like a consecration. They dedicate the son to

God, formally declare a godfather and any other namesakes or important people in the kid's life." Knightly turned toward Clyde and squinted at him. "You're gonna be in there."

"I am?"

"Yeah. One of the baby's middle names is Khalid."

"So?"

"So that's the closest they can come, in their system of pronunciation, to Clyde."

Clyde suddenly wished that beer was available at Muslim feasts. "I'll be darn," he said.

Fazoul limped over to the shelter, picked up the baby, and carried it through the rain into the tent. Two of his cohorts ran to one of the parked cars and pulled a trunk out of the back, ran it over to the tent, and pulled the flaps shut behind them.

By the time Clyde was ushered into the tent, it had been fully furnished with a rug, cushions, lanterns, and other amenities—even a couple of framed photographs with small votive candles burning underneath them. One was a landscape shot of some mountain countryside; it had gone all blue with age. The other was a picture of a man, not a formal portrait but a candid shot snapped in the heat of action. Clyde guessed from the set of his features and his clothing that the man was a Vakhan Turk, probably a bit less than forty years old but with a bearing of great authority. He was on a road somewhere, a dirt road through a rough country of volcanic rock and scrub trees, and in the background were others on motorcycles and beat-up Jeeps.

He was the handsomest man Clyde had ever seen, even though Clyde was not in the habit of noticing or admiring this trait in other men. His cheeks and chin were covered with black stubble salted with gray,and the rest of his face was caked with dust and dried sweat. He was grinning broadly at something, as if he had just pulled something over on someone, and the way his skin wrinkled, or the way the photo was arranged, gave Clyde the impression that he didn't smile very often. The photo was cropped to show only the man's head, shoulders, and upper torso; but Clyde was startled finally to notice, in the bottom right corner, a dark, hard-edged shape: barely recognizable as the flash arrestor on the muzzle of a gun, which this man was apparently carrying under his left arm. It was evidently attached to a worn braided leather strap that ran over the man's left shoulder.

Following the others' cues, Clyde knelt on the rug. Besides Fazoul, two other Vakhan males were there. Fazoul's son was laid out on the sheepskin cradle Clyde had noticed earlier. Fazoul called the meeting to order, wailing in a surprisingly high and reedy voice. Clyde recalled seeing a movie long ago in which a man was apparently being tortured up on a high tower in the middle of a Muslim neighborhood.

It was just like the first time Desiree had dragged him to Catholic Mass, and Clyde had been completely confused the whole time, surrounded by people who knew the whole program by heart and who ran through it as easily as Clyde tied his shoes in the morning. They didn't speak Latin, but they might as well have done. Clyde had learned, on that and other forays into the papist universe, to adopt a solemn expression, sit very still, and do what other people did when called upon; and he found that it got him through this Vakhan ceremony, whatever it was, just as well as it got him through Mass. He heard the name of Khalid pronounced, and they looked in his direction, and he heard another name pronounced, something like Banov, and they looked at the photograph of the left-handed gunman. The rain battered the tent, making a roar like a hundred drums rolling at once during an especially grand halftime show; lightning flashed through the seams, ozone-scented air leaked in under the edge and made the lanterns flicker.

He was just settling in for a good hour of additional folderol when Fazoul suddenly relaxed and broke into English. "That's it, then," he said. He scooped up his son from the cradle and walked on his knees through the flaps. He clambered to his feet and held his son above his head, and Clyde winced, thinking of the danger posed by lightning. He could dimly hear a roar of approval from the crowd under the shelter.

By the time Clyde got out of the tent, almost all the people had fled to their cars. He helped Desiree carry Maggie and all the baby support systems to the station wagon, then walked back to the parking lot near the shelter and, stepping into his role as lawman, began directing traffic. The partygoers, so cheery and gentle on foot, had all gone crazy as soon as they had got behind the wheels of their cars, honking wildly at each other as they fought to escape the lot. Clyde took to whistling through his fingers and waving his arms dramatically, and when they recognized him, they stopped honking and accepted his authority.

After a few minutes Dr. Knightly strolled up, dressed in a slicker, which apparently concealed a generous store of Camels in some dry place. He hunched over and got one lit, then thoughtfully arranged himself downwind of Clyde. "I came early, so I'll be the last one to get out," he said. "I'd rather drive backward on a freeway at midnight with no lights than go bumper-to-bumper with these people."

"You ever live in one of their countries?"

"Aw, shit, Clyde," Knightly said, and shrugged. "Yeah, Turkey for a while. Did some time in China, too. Green Revolution stuff. Travel gets real old after a while." He sucked deeply on his cigarette, as if the mere memory of these travels made him eager to hasten his own death from cancer. Or, Clyde thought, perhaps the memory of driving in those countries had made him fatalistic. Knightly took to worrying the toe of his boot into the ground. "I'm not much good at this," he said by way of warning, "but I do want to thank you sincerely for what you did for Fazoul. It is not out of the question that you might have saved his life."

Clyde chuckled. "Nishnabotna cops ain't that bad."

"I don't mean to say they would have killed him, Clyde. I mean to say that if Fazoul had been provoked any more, he might have become irrational and done something that would have landed him in jail—then got him deported."

"How's that come to saving his life?"

Knightly was taken aback by this question and stared down at the coal of his cigarette for several moments. "It's a tangled thing, Clyde," he finally said. "I sometimes forget how tangled it must seem to someone like you, a lifelong Forks County boy. Let's just say that the Vakhan Turks are one of those ethnic groups that don't have a homeland of their own, so in order to come here and study, they have to carry passports from other countries in that area. If they get into a mess here and get themselves deported, they will be forcibly taken back to a country that may not want them. Which might have them on a list of people who, if they ever show up at a border, are to be taken straight to a windowless cell somewhere and never let out alive."

Clyde had only a small number of oaths in his arsenal, of which "I'll be darn" was about the strongest; and as it did not seem adequate here, he said nothing at all.

"That's why these people have done you the very exceptional honor they did today," Knightly said. "By the way, Khalid was perhaps the greatest warrior in the early history of the Muslim world—right up there with Saladin. They called him the Sword of the Faith. So there's also a play on words at work here. Just thought you ought to understand that."

By the time the traffic jam had cleared out and Knightly had given Clyde a lift back to the station wagon, Maggie had crashed in her car seat, and Desiree was looking a bit drowsy herself—she was engaged in the practice of "resting her eyes," which Clyde had never been able to distinguish from sleep. Clyde drove them home. Desiree was awakened by the sound of the garage door rumbling open and got Maggie tucked into the crib while Clyde changed out of his full-dress uniform and into a plain old deputy's uniform.

"What happened in that tent?" she said, gliding into the dark bedroom smelling like milk.

"Ceremony. Like church, I guess," Clyde said.

"So what did you think of the two picnics?" she said in a clearer voice, cocking her head in a mischievous way to let him know that this was very much a leading question.

"If I tell you all of what I think about the difference between Republicans and Muslims," he said, "we'll never get to sleep. Let's talk about it tomorrow."

twenty-two

KEVIN VANDEVENTER drove his new Camry from O'Hare back to EIU, a trip of two and a half hours, and spent most of the time talking to himself. Here he was, a newly minted Ph.D. who would never have to teach a gut biology course, wearing a new suit, driving a decent enough car back from a trip to D.C., where he had entrée to a number of embassies and was on a first-name basis with fairly significant personages at State, USIA, and Ag. But as the Vivaldi pounded away at him from the Camry's fine stereo, he wondered why he felt that strange discomfort—something eating at him, as if he had done something really bad but couldn't quite make out what it was.

Maybe it was becoming throwing-up drunk at his sister's apartment, just when things were getting good with Margaret. He made a mental note to dry out. He was acquiring too much responsibility to risk doing something like that at a business lunch. Mother had always said that Dad's side of the family was full of alcoholics. "One drink, one drunk. But you know, they were always sweet," she would say, looking at Dad. But when Dad drank—generally after a late frost destroyed the emerging potato plants—everybody avoided him.

Kevin was a sweet drunk—during college he had frequently awakened next to girls he didn't know, who had always assured him of this. As he drove over the Mississippi, looking at the barge trains headed downstream, he resolved that he would have to get a grip on himself—learn what to drink, and how much of it.

The Chicago stations were dying out, and all he could pick up was country and western, which he didn't like. He turned off the stereo, fished a pocket tape recorder out of his briefcase, and began to dictate his trip report for Professor Larsen. One of the secretaries in Larsen's pool would type it and expertly clean up the phrases that weren't very coherent. "Arrived D.C. 3 July for appointments at USDA's Foreign Ag desk. Checked out the rumors that there might be some recision on our subcontinent wheat-rust grant. Your golfing buddy Congressman Fowler has great staff. They homed in on that sucker just as it was coming into committee and covered our butts. The *National Geographic* piece still works wonders, though it has precious little to do with science."

Whoops, better erase that. He backed the tape up while passing a couple of semis at eighty-five miles an hour, fishtailed a bit, and got back into the right lane just in time for a red Corvette to whoosh by him doing at least one hundred. "Reggie Marsh, desk officer for Brazil, sends his regards. Then across the Mall and down a ways to State and a chat with our friends at USAID. They wanted us to make sure to keep in contact with your Iraqi students so that in case of more hostilities between them and Iran, they could serve as channels for technology and funding and (reading between the lines a little bit) intelligence. Hugh Reinckens, one of your former students, sent his regards. FYI, he isn't doing so well careerwise."

He pulled over at a rest stop, emptied his bladder, bought a Coke, and climbed back in for the final half hour of the drive. "University liaison at USIA bitched at us—they are getting picky about some of the documentation on our current stable of Jordanian grad students. Someone in town is pressuring them to the effect that some of those students should have their papers rechecked or else lose their student visas. Probably fallout from the Habibi murder. Anyway, I asked for a half year, because most of the Jordanians will be gone by Christmas anyway. In a classic example of right hand not knowing what left hand is doing, the folks at the student visa office checked our three brand-new Jordanians right through.

"Went to the Jordanian Embassy to talk to the cultural attaché. He was very pleased to hear about the three new students. Didn't want to talk much after that.

"The next day I celebrated our nation's independence.

"On the fifth I made the rounds of National Academy of Sciences, Ag, AID offices in Rosslyn, NSF, and Food for the Future. Good reports across the board—everyone is pleased with the work we're doing for them, eager to continue supporting that work. NSF wants to funnel some cross-discipline work your way—I'll pass the papers along."

After that Kevin had spent three days making the rounds of the embassies of countries in Africa, South America, and Asia where EIU had set up research stations. He glossed over these meetings in his report. There wasn't much to say about them. Everyone was happy. They had no reason not to be—much of the money channeled through Larsen's operation ended up in the private Swiss bank accounts of the officials concerned. Kevin barely remembered these meetings anyway, since many of these people had served him drinks. The mere memory of this made him powerfully thirsty—the dry, cold air blasting from the Camry's air conditioner, combined with the hot sun coming in through the left-side window, had left him dehydrated. A big glass of iced tea, perhaps with a shot of whiskey in it, would go down well. He could think of little else as he blasted across the town line into Wapsipinicon and headed for his duplex north of the university. He punched the button on his garage-door opener, pulled inside, and entered the place through his kitchen door. The blast of the air conditioner almost knocked him down—he had forgotten to turn it off before he'd left. The electric bill would be a thing of excess. Dad would never have left any room or building without first turning off everything that was there to be turned off.

There were fifteen calls on the answering machine, most of them telephone sales—lots of no-load mutual funds. Apparently he had found his way onto some list of newly affluent suckers that was circulated among marketing companies.

Larsen had called to tell him to check in as soon as he got back. He left a message on Larsen's answering machine. "Everything went great, I'll have the report on your desk by noon tomorrow."

Mom called to say that she wanted a full report on Betsy in D.C. He called and assured her that Betsy was okay, that he was okay, that D.C.was beautiful with all of the fireworks (none of which he had seen).

And then a vaguely familiar voice, clearly Midwest born and

bred. "Howdy, Dr. Vandeventer, sorry to bother you again—this is Deputy Sheriff Clyde Banks. Came in to the jail this morning and found out that Sayed Ashrawi had been deported in the middle of the night. He's back in Jordan now, I guess. Just wondered if you had any comments. Good-bye."

There was something deeply troubling to Kevin about the whole Habibi murder, and especially about the doggedness of Clyde Banks in pursuing the issue. Hearing Banks's voice coming out of his answering machine, he felt the pit of his stomach tighten up right away. He should have stayed in D.C., where all he had to do was ride around in taxis and have foreigners buy him drinks. He felt suddenly sweaty. He went to the fridge, pulled out a container of iced tea that had been sitting there for a week and a half, and poured some into a Flintstones jelly glass. Then he opened the high cabinet above the fridge, took out a bottle of Jim Beam, and dumped some in—he thought it looked like about one jigger, maybe a shade more. In his haste to get home he had forgotten to buy groceries or even to stop at a drive-through, so he grabbed a handful of saltines from a cupboard. His bowels went into action at the mere sight of food, so he strode to the bathroom, set the jelly jar and the crackers down on the counter, dropped his pants, and took a seat.

Banks had not divulged his theory of the Habibi case to Kevin, but Kevin could read between the lines easily enough: Banks believed that Marwan Habibi had been dead that night in Lab 304—that Kevin had seen not a drunk and unconscious colleague, but a warm corpse. It followed that all of the other men in Lab 304 that night had been not jovial party animals but cold-blooded plotters hatching a scheme to dump Habibi's corpse in the way least damaging to them, their activities, and—by extension—Larsen's rainmaking operation.

It was a preposterous theory. But the mere idea that Kevin might have been that close to a bunch of foreign agents coldly manhandling a dead man around the Sinzheimer gave him chills.

His cordless phone was sitting there on the counter in front of him. Kevin picked it up and dialed the direct-line number of one of his buddies in the Jordanian Embassy in Washington. There must be some simple explanation of the sudden deportation of Sayed Ashrawi. But the voice at the other end was that of a secretary. She politely but firmly rebuffed him. She must have been a new hire, because this was the first time Kevin had been treated so rudely.

The doorbell rang. Kevin didn't move, hoping that whoever it was would go away. But he had left his garage door open, so everyone who came by knew perfectly well that he was at home.

He pulled his pants up and went to the door. The image in the peephole was that of the paperboy.

"Hello, Scott," Kevin said, hauling the door open.

"It's Craig," the paperboy said. "Uh, you owe me for two months—fourteen fifty."

Kevin had taken his wallet out of his pocket when he'd come in, so he went back into the kitchen to get it. It was still full of crisp twenties from a D.C. cash machine, so new, they stuck together treacherously. He walked back to the front door, trying to pick them apart, and when he looked up, he was startled to see that Craig had been joined by a large and sturdy man with a stubbly haircut, looking sweaty and awkward in neatly pressed jeans and a striped dress shirt.

"Deputy Banks!" Kevin said weakly. "Just got your message—I just got back a few minutes ago." He thrust a twenty at the paperboy and hardly noticed when the change and receipt were handed back to him. "The business with Ashrawi—I don't know what to tell you. I tried making a phone call—"

"This isn't about that," Banks said, blinking in surprise through his thick glasses. "As you may've heard, I'm running for sheriff, and I'm trying to knock on every door in Forks County. And now it's your turn."

The paperboy had moved on to the next duplex. Banks looked at Kevin appraisingly. "You okay?"

"Just got back from D.C. Bad airline food," Kevin essayed.

"They tell me it's pretty bad," Banks said. "Speaking of which, mind if I use your bathroom? Too much iced tea."

"Sure," Kevin said.

"I already know the way. All these duplexes are the same," Banks said. He entered the duplex, seeming to nearly fill the doorway, and found his way back. Kevin heard a clattering sound and a muffled curse. When the deputy came out a minute later, he looked sheepish. "Knocked your glass and your crackers into the sink," he said. "I owe you."

"Don't worry about it."

"Can I at least mix you another drink or something?"

"Please don't give it another thought," Kevin said, appalled that Banks had smelled the whiskey.

"Say, as long as I'm here, I was wondering if you could tell me again what old Marwan Habibi was working on in that lab."

"A kind of bacterium that lives in the bovine digestive tract," Kevin said automatically. He had dropped into Interrogation Mode without even thinking about it.

Banks blinked in surprise again. Kevin reminded himself that, as of four hours ago, he was back in the Midwest, where he was actually allowed to take his time in conversation, where hasty responses might strike some people as suspicious. He wished Banks hadn't spilled his drink.

"Could they live in a human?" Banks asked.

"I don't know the specifics. But I'd be surprised if they couldn't," Kevin said.

"Could he have died from those bacteria, then?"

"Not unless he died from farting too much, Deputy."

Banks didn't seem to find that very funny. But he did change the subject. "Seems that Ashrawi was suspected of having killed someone in Jordan—some kind of family-feud type of deal. Supposedly, while he was sitting in our jail in Nishnabotna, some new evidence happened to turn up over there, and they just had to bring him back so that their courts could have first crack at him. Then we can have him back. What do you think they'll do to him—cut his head off?"

"I believe you're thinking of Saudi Arabia," Kevin said.

"I'm not sure we could have convicted him anyway," Banks offered.

"Really? I thought you had great evidence."

"Well, I did, too, until the quarterly death statistics came out at the beginning of July."

"Quarterly death statistics?"

"For the whole state of Iowa. Health department plots all the deaths on a little map. Color coded. Most of the dots are on nursing homes and they're green, which means, more or less, that the person died of old age. A few red dots in Des Moines and the university towns—those are AIDS deaths. Yellow dots for traffic accidents."

Kevin wanted Banks to go home. Banks was supposed to be here on a brief campaign stop, a charade that had now vanished. This mercilessly detailed explanation of the death map had to have a point. Kevin kept waiting for the nightstick to come out and crack him over the head.

"Could I please have a glass of that iced tea?" Banks said.

"Sure," Kevin said, and got up.

"No whiskey in mine, thanks," Banks said as Kevin left the room.

There were no clean glasses, only a thermal coffee cup from APCO to which he'd lost the lid. Kevin filled it with the tea, threw a couple of cubes into it, and came back to find Banks leafing through some scientific papers he'd left on the coffee table.

"So you were saying?" Kevin finally said.

"Well, usually each quarterly map looks the same as the last. But during the second quarter of this year, it was different."

"Different how?"

"Along the Iowa River, between Nishnabotna and where it joins the Mississippi, there were a whole lot of deaths from lung and heart ailments. Way more than usual. Now, the state health department came and checked it out, but you know bureaucrats—their dream is to have a quiet day. So they said that the lung deaths were a consequence of the flu epidemic, and the heart deaths were a statistical anomaly."

Kevin couldn't help noticing that Banks pronounced the words "statistical anomaly" easily and perfectly, as if the sheriff's department forced every deputy to pass a monthly diction test.

What do you think they'll do to him—cut his head off? Banks was good at playing stupid.

"You have a different theory?" Kevin asked.

"Funny thing is, none of the deaths occurred upstream of Lake Pla-Mor," Banks said. "And none occurred prior to the night you saw Marwan Habibi carried out of Lab Three-oh-four."

"Ah," Kevin said.

"Half of these cases were in Forks County, so our county coroner, Barney Klopf, signed the death certificates. And I know old Barney, so he let me have a peek at the records. And you know what? The lung deaths looked just the same as the heart deaths. There was no difference between 'em."

"Is that your opinion, or—"

"And you know another thing? All of those people had had contact with fish from the river before they died. Lutefisk makers, fishermen, fellows out shooting carp with bow and arrow."

"Oh."

"Well, I got lots of doors to knock on," Banks said, "so I think I better see myself out. Thanks for the tea. And don't go eating any fresh carp, all right, Kevin?"

Kevin retrieved his glass from the sink, went to the kitchen, and made himself another drink. As he was doing so, it occurred to him for the first time to wonder whether Banks had just made up that whole story about the death map. It didn't make much sense, when he thought about it. Kevin couldn't believe he'd fallen for the ruse.

twenty-three

JUST AT the moment Clyde was halfway between his unit and Thomas Charles "Tick" Henry's screened-in porch, Henry's dog made its presence known by coming round the corner of the garage, raising its hackles, crouching, and beginning to emit a low growl almost like the purr of an idling diesel. The dog had not revealed itself until Clyde was halfway between the unit and the front door, exposed on a barren glacis of creeping Charlie, crabgrass, and faded aluminum beer cans. Clyde unsnapped his holster.

The important thing was not to show fear.

Clyde changed direction and lunged straight toward the onrushing dog, which, like all other bad dogs he had ever seen, was some kind of offshoot of the race of German shepherds (or, as people around there called them, perhaps ironically, police dogs). Tick Henry's dog was so startled that it actually faltered; and when Clyde shouted, "Get the hell out of here!" into its face, it planted its feet and came to a complete stop, its scraggly dewclaws snagging long skeins of creeping Charlie so that the whole surface of the lawn moved around him.

There was a moment of silence, and Clyde heard a low hissing noise from the screened-in porch. The sound of someone drawing on a cigarette. Clyde looked that way, but the only illumination now came from the big hissing farm light on the garage, which was enshrouded by a more or less infinite number of small insects. Larger black shapes briefly eclipsed it from time to time: bats going after the bugs.

Finally the dog's ears rotated to the side a few degrees, flattened just a bit. Instantly Clyde stomped forward two more strides and shouted, "Get the hell out of here!" The dog turned, ran away, and looked back at Clyde, beginning to wag its tail.

"You maced my dog!" shouted Tick Henry, kicking the screen door open. "You maced my dog!" He stepped out into the yard, moving stiffly on the front steps, hindered by his football-ravaged knees. He must be pushing fifty, Clyde realized.

"You maced my dog," Tick Henry said. It was clear from the conviction on his face that he was one of that breed of mankind, frequently encountered in Clyde's line of work, who could make themselves believe anything simply by uttering it three times.

"I don't carry Mace," Clyde said, "because I got a gun. And if your dog had taken one more step toward me, I would have shot it."

"That's police brutality!"

"If you could read, Tick Henry, you would know that I ain't police but sheriff's department. You know the difference?"

"Huh?"

"The sheriff's department's main job seems to be serving papers on the likes of you—and your houseguest," said Clyde, stepping forward and waving a court summons in the air.

Tick Henry said nothing at all, just drew on his cigarette and squinted at Clyde. The farm light went out for a moment as an especially large bat, or perhaps even an owl, eclipsed it.

"I know he's in there," Clyde said. "Everybody knows you've been sheltering him."

"So Grace went out and got herself a goddamn lawyer," Tick said, and shook his head in disbelief.

"Everyone's entitled to a lawyer," Clyde said. "Buck could have got one if he'd been on his toes. Then the divorce could have happened right here. As it is, it's going to happen in Seattle—more hassle for Buck."

"Seattle? Grace took off to Seattle?" Tick Henry shook his head again. "I suppose Seattle's dyke paradise or something."

"Let's get this over with," Clyde said. "Where is he?"

Tick jerked his head back toward the house. Clyde gave the dog one last warning glare and then climbed up onto the screened-in porch.

Buck Chandler was fast asleep on the living-room recliner, illuminated by the light from the tube, which was showing a baseball game on the West Coast.

Buck had been an intermittently brilliant quarterback in high school and had been demoted to tight end when he'd matriculated at EIU and joined the Twisters, which was a much easier team to join back in his era. He and Tick Henry had scored quite a few touchdowns between them; in 1961 the Twisters had actually beaten both Iowa and Iowa State in the same year, which had not happened since and would probably never happen again.

After graduation he had done a stint in the military, then came home and knocked around town for a while, selling cars and insurance, and eventually became the Voice of the Twisters, announcing all the football and basketball games on the local 250-watt AM station. As a youth Clyde had listened to these broadcasts every Saturday afternoon while raking leaves or shoveling snow. But a few years ago the rights to broadcast the Twisters games had been bought up by a big media company out of Aurora, Illinois, and Buck Chandler had lost his job and his identity. He and Grace had eventually got into the real-estate thing. Grace had passed the realtor's exam immediately. Buck had taken six runs at it. When Clyde had gotten around to buying some real estate, he had sought out the Chandlers to act as brokers, not because they were the best company but because he felt sorry for Buck.

And now Grace was off in Seattle making a new life, and Buck was passed out in a recliner in Tick Henry's living room, reeking of whiskey.

Clyde unfolded the divorce papers and put them on Buck's chest.

"Hope you're proud of yourself," Tick Henry said.

Clyde walked back to his unit, backed out into the highway, and departed. He had not even made it to the next section-line road before the dispatcher had called him up to inform him that Tick Henry had called the sheriff's department to complain that a deputy had threatened to shoot his dog.

"Threatened nothing. I promised to," Clyde said.

"Did you serve the papers?" the dispatcher said. She was a shirttail relative of Mullowney's, implacably hostile.

"I did," Clyde said. The dispatcher did not respond. Various deputies had been trying to serve those papers on Buck Chandler for six weeks. Clyde Banks, the Summonater, had, for the umpteenth time, come through where others had failed.

twenty-four

AUGUST

AUGUST 1 was not a good day for James Gabor Millikan. Saddam Hussein was marching into Kuwait. Millikan was being clobbered. All of the geopolitical brilliance he had expended in the service of his country was for naught. First he had been tripped up internally by a GS-11 who should have been shot for disrupting the elegance of his carefully laid out policy scenario, and then externally by the imbecilic actions of Saddam Hussein, who had not played the role he should have played.

Millikan carried a heavy burden, that of omniscience—and he carried it gracefully, most of the time. He always had known what was best. He always had known that God had intended for him to be the mind behind the throne, the man who would actually have the ideas, who would save the country but who would selflessly not claim credit. It was a tough role, but one he savored. Now his classic geopolitical formula to bring peace to the Middle East, to block the Iranians, to foil what was left of the Soviets—all of this was unraveling. And worst of all, as he set up the President's schedule for his vacation in Kennebunkport, he had to include the bottom-fish analyst who had done so much to upset his plans and his timing. As he sat at his keyboard looking out of his office in the Old Executive Office Building toward the White House, he was bitter.

Millikan was not a Saddam Hussein enthusiast. It could be truly said that except for some colleagues at St. Antony's and Harvard, he was an enthusiast for no human being except himself. Millikan wanted to achieve in foreign relations the elegant perfection that mathematicians achieved in calculating the digits of pi. He did not deal in terms of individual human beings; he did not, in the long term, believe that human beings, or what they thought, had anything more to do with the carrying out of state policy than had the ants and their little universes in affecting individual human life. He saw a large and imposing calculus dominating the affairs of state, and he saw himself as the Newton to apply that calculus to manipulate international affairs.

As he laid out the national-security arrangements for the President's vacation, he knew that his Middle-Eastern scenario had failed. The question now was how to change policies in midstream without getting wet, how to find someone to blame for the debacle. But he had to remind himself that it was not his debacle: it was the failure of a man for whom he had contempt, George Herbert Walker Bush, and his total inability to move. Bush had scuttled the chance to take advantage of the Gorbachev opening, and Millikan felt deeply each and every one of the knives deftly shoved into his back by George Shultz's people.

While he was staging the normal-seeming vacation of the President at the Maine compound, he had tasked his assistant, Richard Dellinger, to go back through his collected, classified memos to remove any record of his appearing to be too pro-Iraq, a difficult task, given the fact that he had been one of the foremost proponents of Baghdad. But Millikan knew his Orwell.

In the face of the fact that Saddam had invaded Kuwait, that the administration had already cut both open- and back-channel communications with the PLO, that he had already lost whatever leverage he had on the Hill, it was apparent that he had to do something to maintain his high ground. Gnawing at the back of his mind was the knowledge that Hennessey had a dossier on him a foot thick, that Hennessey could nail him anytime he wanted by throwing him to the wolves of the Democratically-controlled congressional committees, that he could spread rumors that would make him out to be the long-sought Big Mole in the national-security network, that Hennessey had, as the result of his shocking, unprecedented, and possibly illegal lateral jump to the FBI, become the heir of all the secret photos that J. Edgar Hoover had assembled on the Harvard boys and all the Oxford types. He had to find some way to short-circuit Hennessey, get back on top of the curve on Iraq, convince the President that he was really serving well. He needed a hook.

As he gazed over the top of his workstation out the window at the White House, it suddenly struck him what his salvation would be. How he could simultaneously outflank Hennessey, impress the President, and grab the next-best issue of the war—the public fear of the Iraqis' poison gas and bacteriological-warfare capabilities, soon to be widely publicized by the scare-mongering press.

It was at moments like this that Millikan always felt a certain sense of satisfaction and renewed self-esteem. He drafted a National Security Council Decision Directive setting up an interagency task force to include Hennessey from the FBI, Spector and Vandeventer from the Agency, some of the folks from the chemicals branch at NSA and the Pentagon, and some of the germ people from the NSF. They would start work immediately, in Kennebunkport. He typed it up for that morning's meeting. He knew that it would be approved without question. If American boys were going to die, the administration had better look as if it at least knew there was a danger. If they died, Millikan looked good, because he'd been on top of it from the beginning. If they didn't die, Millikan looked good, because his task force could claim the credit.

twenty-five

"WE HAVE a report of a bloody horse on the south Boundary Avenue extension," said the dispatcher's voice. Clyde was slumbering so deeply that, when he woke up, he was not sure whether he had heard it correctly. Surely she had said "runaway" and not "bloody."

He had stayed up late listening to the dumbfounding news of the Iraqi invasion of Kuwait on his transistor radio, which was still squawking away on the dashboard. The news reports, his own dreams, and the words of the dispatcher must have got all mixed up in his sleepy head.

"It's in the vicinity of the vet lab," she continued. "Sounds like it might be another case of you-know-what. All units respond."

"All units?" Clyde said aloud, staring at the ceiling of his unit. He was only talking to himself. At the moment "all units" amounted to three Forks County sheriff's deputies.

When Tab Templeton had materialized before the gates of Nishnabotna Meat like a biblical apparition, liquored up and swinging an ax handle, a single deputy—Clyde—had been dispatched to deal with the problem. If Charles Manson, Abu Nidal, and a pack of rabid wolves had been sighted on Lincoln Way, the

Forks County sheriff might have found the situation sufficiently grave to merit the dispatch of two deputies. And now they were sending three after a horse.

Deputy Hal Karst came on the radio, not bothering to disguise the fact that he'd been laughing. "We gonna just grab that horse by the reins, or actually rassle it to the ground?"

No answer. The dispatcher was flummoxed.

Hal Karst continued. He was in his late forties, the oldest deputy on the force, and he didn't care what the dispatcher or Mullowney or anyone else thought of him. "You want us to rassle it, Clyde can take point, and me and Jim'll help. But if you just want us to grab the reins, I can handle that all by my lonesome, and Clyde and Jim can go back to sleep." Hal was an old farm boy and still kept horses of his own.

"Hal, go after the horse," the dispatcher said, sounding more than a bit frosted. "Clyde and Jim, you are to throw a dragnet over the area."

Clyde jackknifed to a sitting position and hollered, "A *dragnet*?" He snatched the microphone with one hand, killing the little transistor radio with the other. "Did you say *dragnet*, Theresa?" He did a poor job of concealing the grin in his voice. He had never heard this word actually used in an official context. Then he got himself under control and didn't say anything more. They were recording his transmissions, and if he got overly lippy, they could play it on the radio and TV and make him look like a bad deputy.

"Sheriff's standing orders," Theresa shot back, "in the event of another mutilation case."

"Oh, shit," Clyde said to himself. So it really was a bloody horse.

Deputy Jim Green came on the horn for the first time. "Which one of us gets to be Joe Friday?"

"That's enough horsing around!" Theresa said. "Clyde, you handle the northern end. Jim, you come in from the south. Converge on the vet lab. Report anything unusual."

Clyde was several miles north of town, in the hilly, sparsely wooded country between Palisades State Park and Lake Pla-Mor.

He pulled out onto the road and accelerated south, wiping fog from the inside of the windshield with one hand, then groping for the switches that turned the lights. He would have been justified in using the siren, but the farmers didn't like being woken up in the middle of the night and always complained.

On second thought he went ahead and turned the siren on. When they complained, they'd blame it on Mullowney.

And Mullowney would call them back very respectfully, or (since this was an election year) perhaps even stop by their house personally in his unit, pausing in their driveway to pop a mint into his mouth so that they would not smell the alcohol on his breath. He would enter their house, taking his Smokey Bear hat off respectfully, and accept the proffered coffee and pie only with the greatest reluctance, and would apologize to them deeply for the disturbance caused by the nocturnal sirens; but, he would say, a bit of noise in the night was a small price to pay, and all the citizens of Forks County must be ready to make small sacrifices, playing their own little parts in the War on Satan.

Kevin Mullowney had declared War on Satan only yesterday. The *Times-Dispatch* had carried his news release on the front page, unedited except that they had corrected all the spelling and grammatical errors that had slipped past Mullowney's typist (his third cousin once removed). When the sheriff became aware of the invasion of Kuwait, he would be chagrined, for it would surely drive the War on Satan back to the second page for the next week at least.

The news release had been accompanied by a large photograph of Kevin Mullowney paying a surprise visit to a head shop in campustown, where he inspected a rock-band poster emblazoned with a pentagram. One of Mullowney's flunkies held the poster up between the sheriff and the owner of the store—a sallow, bearded fellow with an earring. Mullowney had both index fingers in action, a sure sign that he had roused himself to action; with one he was tracing the pentagram on the poster, and with the other he was pointing at the chest of the owner, nearly prodding him in the sternum. The owner was blinking when the flash went off, and his eyes were neither open nor closed but somewhere in between, giving him an alarmingly moronic, possibly drug-addled appearance.

The War on Satan was, of course, actually a counterattack—a purely defensive measure. Forks County had (Mullowney explained) been infiltrated silently over a period of years, and only recently had the local satanist contingent felt confident enough to come into the open. They had announced their presence by initiating a campaign of cattle mutilation.

The first attack had been a couple of weeks earlier. A heifer had been found missing by its owner, who had discovered a hole cut in his fence and followed a trail of blood down into a creek bottom where the victim had concealed herself. Some mysterious runes had been carved into her flanks.

The second incident had been about a week later. A horse had been led from a stable at a local riding school, through a gate that had been cut open, down to the woods along the riverbank, and had had an upside-down, five-pointed star carved into its shoulder. This second incident demonstrated a pattern even Kevin Mullowney could not fail to notice, and the War on Satan had been launched as soon as he had sobered himself up enough to dictate the manifesto to his typist.

Now perhaps the mutilators had struck again, probably at the vet lab—a federal installation, tied to EIU's Vet Med College. This made sense; the vet lab had lots of livestock and, being a government operation, tended not to supervise them as carefully as farmers would. It was exactly where Clyde would go if he wanted to mutilate some animals without being caught.

Deputy Karst came on the horn. "I'm in the area and I see tracks," he said. "I'm along the eastern edge of the Dhont farm. I'll tie it up to a fence or something, then return to my unit and notify you so's you can send out a veterinarian."

Clyde went straight down Boundary Avenue, along the western edge of Wapsipinicon. The northern stretch passed along nice neighborhoods, where, he hoped, many influential constituents were erupting from their beds as his unit screamed past, and concluding that Sheriff Mullowney's War on Satan was sheer madness.

A mile south of Lincoln Way was Garrison Road, which formed the southern border of the city; everything south was farmland. But instead of the wall of corn that usually marked such boundaries around here, the south side of Garrison Road was a motley spectacle of peculiar and outlandish crops planted in small patches and individual rows, and greenhouses of various types: some traditional ones built of glass, others just poly film stretched over improvised frameworks. These were the EIU College of Agriculture experimental farms, and they stretched for another mile south to the next section-line road. Beyond that was the National Veterinary Pathology Laboratory and Quarantine Center, in the vicinity of which the bloody horse had been sighted. Hal Karst was probably traipsing around that area right now, proffering odds and ends of his sack breakfast to the terrified critter.

If Clyde were a satanist, and had just finished mutilating a horse at the vet lab, he would make his escape northward across the experimental farms, which were unpopulated, poorly fenced, and never patrolled. Clyde checked around the area for the injured horse but, finding nothing, returned to the vet lab.

The gates there were well secured—there was a guardhouse, manned only during the daytime, and to get in at night, you had to shove a magnetic card into a little box that would raise the gate for you. A closed-circuit TV camera recorded all comings and goings. This was of little interest to Clyde. But the perimeter of the vet lab was almost two miles in length. It was surrounded by a chain-link fence topped with barbed wire, but much of it was so dark and so remote that anyone with a pair of bolt cutters could get through it at will.

Three sides of the vet lab were bounded by highways of greater or lesser importance, but the southern border was formed by the main line of the Denver–Platte–Des Moines Railroad. If Clyde were a satanist, he would turn off Boundary Avenue onto the dirt track that ran along the railway siding, drive down that track until he was well away from the road, and cut the fence there. It was where all the teenaged boys went to drink beer and smoke marijuana.

As soon as he pulled off Boundary onto the track, he saw

recent-looking tire marks in the dirt and stopped the unit where it was so that he would not destroy the evidence. He plucked his nightstick, Excalibur, from its mount on the dashboard and, after some dithering, decided to leave the shotgun where it was. He turned on the spotlight and shone it down the track, then proceeded on foot.

Sure enough, there was a fresh cut in the fence about a hundred yards in from the road. It was high and wide enough for a horse. The mutilators had apparently gone into the vet lab, selected their victim, led it out through this opening, and cut it up there; the ground in front of the fence cut was all churned up with horse and human footprints, and sprinkled with blood. Tomorrow around ten o'clock, when Sheriff Mullowney had recovered from the night's drinking sufficiently to stand erect, this was where he would come to be photographed by the *Times-Dispatch* and videotaped by the TV crews from Cedar Rapids and Des Moines. He would squat to examine the footprints, point significantly at patches of blood, and finger the cut ends of the fence wires attentively.

Clearly, the perpetrators had come in a vehicle; clearly, they were long gone. Clyde trudged back to the unit and got on the horn. "Got a pretty good crime scene along the railway cut, just off Boundary," he announced. Then he got a roll of yellow crime-scene tape out of the bumper and strung it around the area.

As he returned to the unit, he could hear radio traffic on the PA speaker. Deputy Jim Green and the dispatcher were discussing the whereabouts of Deputy Karst. He had left his unit by the Dhont farm a good half hour ago and not reported in yet.

A bad road accident in the southern part of the county demanded Jim Green's attention. Clyde backed his unit out onto Boundary and headed south across the tracks toward Dhont territory. Less than half a mile south he came across Hal Karst's unit pulled onto a little farm road that separated one Dhont field from another. Hal had left his spotlight shining at an angle across the soybean field to the right of the dirt road. Beans were a low-to-the-ground crop, and a runaway horse would be more likely to go into a bean field than a cornfield, where the ripening tassels would be above its head.

Clyde parked his unit on the turnout of the dirt road, behind Hal Karst's, then reached in the open window of Hal's car, grabbed the handle on the spotlight, and swung the light slowly back and forth across the bean field. As the beam came round nearly parallel to the dirt road, two closely spaced red sparks suddenly jumped out of the darkness, so far off in the distance that he could barely resolve them. They blinked out, then on again. Either the Dhonts' bean field had been invaded by a large and exceptionally calm buck, or else this was the horse. It was near the fence, and it didn't seem to be going anywhere. Maybe Hal had succeeded in tying it to a fence post. Clyde aimed the spotlight directly down the center of the road, expecting to pick out the burly form of Hal walking back toward his unit, sweaty and out of breath from chasing the horse around the field. But that was not exactly what he saw. He did see Hal Karst, only a stone's throw away—clearly recognizable by the light-tan color of his sheriff's uniform. But Hal was not walking up the road. He was lying down in the dirt and he was not moving.

The nature of police work in Forks County was such that when a deputy saw a colleague down on the ground and not moving, he did not immediately think about death and violence, as a big-city policeman would. It seemed much more likely that Deputy Karst might have tripped and fallen on his face. But though he was moving around weakly, he made no real effort to get up.

Clyde lunged in through the window of Hal Karst's unit, grabbed the mike from his dashboard radio, and said in a tight voice, "Hal is down. Hal is down. Send an ambulance." Then he dropped the mike onto the seat and took off running.

Hal Karst was thrashing weakly from side to side. He had fallen first on his face but had rolled over several times since then and was now coated with dust from the road. He had crossed his arms over his body and was clutching his ribs and gasping for air. "What's wrong, Hal?" Clyde said, but whatever was wrong with

Hal seemed to concern his heart and lungs and rendered him incapable of speech.

Clyde yanked the big black cop flashlight from his belt and shone it over Hal's face and body, looking for a clue. He was startled to see blood smeared on the hands and uniform shirt, and for a moment his heart jumped as he thought that perhaps the bad guys were still out there and had done something to Hal. Controlling the panicky urge to shine the light around him in a search for perpetrators, Clyde took stock of Hal's situation as calmly as he could. He did not see any wounds, and the blood was thinly smeared around, not coursing out the way it would if Hal had been knifed or shot.

Hal's motions were getting steadily weaker. Clyde shone the light on his face, which had gone all pale. Hal's lips were violet. His eyelids were drooping. Clyde dropped the flashlight, put one hand under Hal's neck and lifted it up so that his chin tilted back. He reached a couple of fingers down into Hal's mouth and made sure he hadn't swallowed his tongue. Then he clamped Hal's nose shut, bent down, pressed his lips over Hal's, and forced air into his lungs.

Clyde spent a long time there giving Hal Karst mouth-to-mouth resuscitation. After a minute or two he reached down with his free hand and groped his way around Hal's chest until he could find a pulse. It felt weak and fluttery, as though the heart of a hummingbird were beating in there, and so Clyde started alternating CPR with the mouth-to-mouth, ramming the heel of his hand into Hal's sternum very hard so that the rib cage bulged with each thrust.

The amount of blood did not increase, and Clyde finally figured out that it was just a red herring. This wasn't Hal's blood, it was the horse's. Hal had got it smeared on him when he had been getting the horse calmed down.

Then he had started walking back down the road to his unit, still breathing hard, his heart pounding away violently, and finally the old ticker had given out on him. Hal was not just the oldest deputy on the force but also the heaviest, forever coming in last on the physical-fitness tests. He had been eating the farm diet ever since he was born: real cream in his coffee, straight from the cow, and planks of home-cured bacon for breakfast, tenderloin sandwiches for lunch, doughnuts for snacks, steak for dinner. Everyone had been waiting for this.

Finally the ambulance came; it parked out on Boundary, and the crew came sprinting up the road carrying their big fiberglass gear boxes. They hooked him up to a number of tubes and machines right on the spot, getting a read on his vital signs and radioing the information back to the trauma center at Methodist Hospital. Clyde listened to this traffic and knew that the news was bad. They tore the uniform shirt off Hal's body right there in the dirt, a gesture that somehow offended Clyde even though he understood it. They took out the paddles and they shocked him once, twice, three times, each time shooting a different combination of substances into his heart with a giant horse needle. After the third time Clyde suddenly felt an overwhelming urge to start crying. He turned his back on the scene and walked up the road until he reached the horse, whose eyes were still glowing in the beam from Hal Karst's spotlight. Great patches of coagulated blood had thickened on its flanks and on the side of its neck, obscuring whatever marks had been carved into it by the mutilators. But whatever Hal had done and said to it seemed to have calmed it down, and it was patiently snuffling through the line of grass and weeds along the fence wire, looking for something worth eating. Clyde stood there and talked to it for a while about nothing in particular, until the tears had drained away from his eyes and he no longer had the tightness in his chest. He unwrapped the reins from the fence post where Hal had placed them and led the horse up along the fencerow toward Boundary. By this time they had taken Hal away, and nothing was left at the place where he had died except for a great deal of colorful litter: the torn-open wrappings of various medical supplies scattered all over the road like a bouquet that had been dropped from a procession. The wind was picking up as dawn approached, and the litter was already starting to stir and to tumble back up the road.

Clyde picked up his flashlight and a few other items he had

dropped, then continued leading the horse up the road. Just as he was reaching Boundary, a pickup truck happened along, a white one with black letters on the door identifying it as a U.S.-government vehicle. It was towing an empty horse trailer, which almost jackknifed around into the ditch as the truck stopped abruptly, right in the middle of the lane. Two men jumped out, not bothering to close the doors: a white man and a black man, young and trim, with neat, short haircuts and in good shape, to judge from the way they sprinted toward him. "Thank you, Deputy," one of them said as he was still several paces away; then he reached out with one gloved hand and took the reins from Clyde's hand. "Come on, Sweet Corn," he said to the horse, leading it forward with a firm tug. Sweet Corn roused itself to a faster gait, and the man jogged alongside it back toward the trailer.

The other man from the truck stayed where he was, looking at Clyde. But he wasn't looking at Clyde's face as if he were interested in conversation. His eyes were traveling up and down Clyde's body, inspecting him. Finally he focused on Clyde's name tag.

"Deputy Banks," he said distinctly, as though committing it to memory, "thank you for your assistance."

"Hope Sweet Corn's okay," Clyde said.

"She's a lot tougher than you'd imagine," the man said.

Clyde stopped, faced the man, straightened to attention, and snapped out a salute. Uncertainly, the man returned it. As he did, Clyde could not help noticing that he was wearing latex surgical gloves.

"Thanks again," he said weakly, turned away, and jogged toward Boundary. The other military man—for they were definitely military—had already got Sweet Corn loaded into the trailer. They took off as quickly as they had arrived, leaving Clyde alone with two units to look after. The sight of Hal Karst's abandoned vehicle made him depressed, so he busied himself stringing crime-scene tape around the place until reinforcements began to show.

twenty-six

BETSY HAD worked with Spector enough to know when things were really bizarre. Usually Spector had the taciturn, understated approach to life, death, joy, and tragedy that American men had all picked up watching TV and movies during the *Peter Gunn* and *Dragnet* era. He could even handle the possibility of his ship going down if Betsy screwed up in a big way. But today, as he walked into her office, he was visibly shook up.

He shut the door, sat down, ran his hands over his translucent buzz cut, and silently passed a sheet of paper across the desk to Betsy. It was an "Eyes Only" memo. Betsy focused in on the letterhead: the National Security Council. The memo didn't take long to read.

"Goodness!" she exclaimed.

Spector was staring at her in astonishment. "Goodness?"

Betsy started sorting through the documents on her workstation, trying to figure out what tasks she could delegate to her staff to keep them out of trouble, and to keep the flow of words up during the next three days. "See you at National, then?" she asked.

Spector said nothing, just stared at her coolly.

"Or should we drive down together?" Betsy continued.

"You've got a real talent for denial, or something," Spector finally said. "This hasn't sunk in yet at all, has it?"

"I don't think I'm in denial," she said. "I'm just trying to concentrate on the here and now."

Spector grinned. "That," he said, "is definitely a form of denial. See you there." He stood up, took a couple of deep breaths, grabbed his military-issue aluminum briefcase, and departed.

She spent another hour delegating three days' worth of tasks and planting emergency contact numbers. She said good-bye to Thelma the secretary, walked down to the apartment, left a note for Cassie, packed, and lugged her briefcase and garment bag down to the Rosslyn Metro Station.

Ten minutes later she was at National, wishing she hadn't packed so much.

If she'd been hopping a Delta or USAir flight, she'd have known exactly where to go. As it was, she blundered around the place for a while. They had signs up for people who wanted to find a rest room or a baggage claim. They didn't have any signs for people like her. It was fortunate that her good-girl instincts had prompted her to arrive almost an hour early.

Eventually, by process of elimination, she found herself at the civil-aviation wing. She trudged through a couple of commercial maintenance operations, now cursing herself for every extra blouse and pair of shoes she had stuffed into her bag. Some kind soul directed her through a door marked Staff Only, and she found herself in a waiting room manned by the same kind of Agency security personnel who sat by the elevators at the Castleman Building. Betsy was the only person there. A couple of dark-tinted windows looked out toward the apron, where a government Gulfstream jet was being worked over by its crew. Betsy recognized the construction of these windows: the same beefed-up, surveillance-proof numbers that always implied the presence of Agency people.

Half an hour later Spector came. He was followed by some hassled types from the NSA who had been helicoptered down from Fort Meade; an Army and a Marine colonel who had taken the metro down from the Pentagon, and—at the last possible minute, bringing up the rear, wiping sweat from his balding head with a dirty handkerchief and puffing on his asthma inhalers—Ed Hennessey.

A woman in a blue uniform entered through a different door, bringing an exhalation of muggy, diesel-scented air with her. Her uniform was almost calculated to be nondescript and bore no discernible insignia or name tag. "Welcome to the Kennebunkport Express. I'm your pilot. My name is Commander Robin Hughes. Please follow me to the plane. Please stay as far away as possible from the open hangar doors." Robin Hughes had the enviable poise and self-possession that Betsy had learned to associate with women who had graduated from one of the three service academies.

They had all been chatting and even joking until this moment; suddenly, now, they became hushed and reverent. Robin Hughes turned and led them out the door and into the hangar where the Gulfstream was sitting, ready to go. The hangar's doors were wide-open, and Betsy understood why they had been told to stay back from them; if they got any closer, a tourist or reporter standing in one of the concourses would be able to pick their faces out with a telephoto lens.

The little jet had two rows of seats. They had barely settled into them when Commander Robin Hughes began to taxi out onto the apron. This was air travel with an unfamiliar twist: no waiting. No one came back to demonstrate how to fasten their seat belts, no one hassled them about their seat backs or tray tables. Robin Hughes blithely cut in front of an outraged Trump shuttle and a slightly mystified American Airlines 757, swung the plane around to its takeoff vector, and pinned the throttles. The plane ripped down the runway and jumped into the air like a bat out of hell, and they were a thousand feet above the Potomac no more than sixty seconds after they'd chosen their seats. It was, in other words, not like flying commercial.

It was not a talkative bunch. Everyone had a window seat. Some took advantage of it, gazing and pondering, others snapped open briefcases as soon as the plane was airborne and hunched over documents and laptop computers. Betsy saw the wide mouth of the Delaware below and even caught sight of the vee-shaped wake of the Lewes–Cape May ferry, giving her fond memories of the weekend when she had met Paul Moses.

Ed Hennessey was sitting across the aisle from her; he jammed his seat back into the face of one of the NSA people and fell asleep, wheezing and snoring loudly enough to be heard over the engine noise. By sitting up straight and craning her neck, Betsy was able to see a glimpse of Manhattan through his window.

She sensed someone was looking at her. It was Spector. He

was sweating and chewing gum obsessively. He shook his head in amazement. He was permanently dumbfounded by his Idaho girl. Looking out the window at the pretty view!

They were already descending toward Kennebunkport. Cape Cod was on the right, the sandbars around Provincetown perfectly resolved. Hughes came on the intercom, telling them they were about to land, and jokingly apologizing for the quality of the cabin service. "I request that nobody leave until the buses have pulled into position and we've been given the go-ahead. It's important, for national-security reasons, that you not be seen together."

Something about this statement tore a large rent in the curtain of denial that had been hanging before Betsy's eyes.

National-security reasons.

Saddam was in Kuwait. The United States was, for all practical purposes, in a state of war.

For the people in this airplane to be spotted in this place, in this combination, could, in some as-yet-unimagined way, cause people to die.

She turned back and looked at Spector. He was eyeing her now with a hint of a grin. The growing shock must have been obvious on Betsy's face.

The plane taxied way, way back to the far end of a runway. Betsy didn't even know what airport they had landed at; somewhere with lots of trees. Robin Hughes swung it around so that the door faced toward the trees, away from any buildings. Very shortly a couple of school buses and a blue government van arrived—ten times the seating capacity they needed. The buses, empty except for their drivers, maneuvered back and forth on the apron, forming an L-shaped barrier that would block the view of anyone spying on them back in the trees. The van pulled up very close to the Gulfstream. Doors were flung open, a signal was given, and everyone hustled up the aisle, down the steps, and into the van.

Except for Hennessey, who was still sound asleep, and Betsy, who stayed behind trying to wake him up. No one else on this plane, with the possible exception of Robin Hughes, had any stomach for the job of trying to wake up this leprous pariah. Devil take the person who was seen being nice to him; God help the person who incurred his resentment. The combined efforts of Betsy Vandeventer and Robin Hughes were needed to get him on his feet and down the steps without breaking his neck.

The buses peeled away and parked themselves somewhere. The van was a tinted-window special with two security men on board, not making any effort to hide their Heckler & Koch submachine guns. As they pulled out of the airport, another vehicle fell in behind them—a massive Suburban with government plates.

The sight of the weapons, and of what was obviously a government war wagon behind them, tore down most of what remained of Betsy's curtain of denial. She began rubbing her palms against her skirt; they were sweating even though the air-conditioning in the van was turned up high. Her heart was pounding and she had a lump of apprehension in her throat.

The van took them several miles through rocky country with occasional, surprising views of the ocean. They turned into progressively narrower and windier roads, edging closer and closer to the sea, glimpsing large waterfront homes from time to time. They turned onto a drive and passed through a security checkpoint. A few hundred yards later they pulled up before a barnlike structure, a sort of utility and machine shed, surrounded on all sides by trees. It looked simple and bucolic except for the forest of antennae sprouting from its roof.

A large roll-up door opened. Standing in the center of the dark aperture was a man in an impeccable dark-charcoal pinstripe suit: James Gabor Millikan.

Spector leaned over to Betsy and whispered, "Watch this."

Hennessey had boarded the van last and had the front passenger seat. He shoved his door open and climbed stiffly out of the vehicle, ignoring a Marine who held out one hand to help him down. He walked toward Millikan, and Millikan walked toward him. Everyone on the van had his face pressed to a window; those who were unfortunate enough to be on the wrong side stood up to peer over the others' shoulders.

Millikan extended his hand to Hennessey, grinning broadly.

Hennessey looked taut and grim and tired, like a man walking into a hospital for prostate surgery. But he shook Millikan's hand firmly and, as an afterthought, patted Millikan on the back, as if to say, "You got me this time." Inside the van everyone exhaled.

They climbed out of the van one by one. Millikan was still making small talk with Hennessey; he had positioned himself so that he could look over Hennessey's shoulder and watch them emerge. He ignored all of them except for Betsy. When he zeroed in on Betsy's face, he nodded to himself, as if mentally checking an item off a checklist. "Welcome to Kennebunkport, Ms. Vandeventer," he said. Betsy did not think that he sounded terribly sincere.

A White House aide, a perky young woman who seemed out of place around all of these saturnine spooks and burly machine-gun-toting guards, stepped toward Betsy holding a White House blazer, extra large. She introduced herself—Betsy forgot her name instantly—and explained, "You're coming to dinner tonight, and you have to look like a staffer. Care to try this on for size?"

Betsy tried it on. It fit perfectly. She was glad to have it; late afternoon above the ocean in Maine was much cooler than running toward National Airport at midday carrying heavy bags.

A government sedan awaited. Millikan stepped toward Betsy. She almost flinched, half expecting him to sock her in the jaw, but instead he offered her his arm and nodded significantly toward the car.

She took Millikan's arm and looked back at Spector, who saluted her and said, "*Bon appétit.*" It was clear that the rest of the new arrivals were going to be dining on the Colonel's Best Extra Crispy Chicken, with gravy and biscuits.

Millikan continued to be the very picture of refined manners during the brief drive to the house. He was in an expansive and jovial mood. "The President, as you well know, likes raw intelligence. He has great respect for the analytical branch of the business and wants to meet you. But you should not misinterpret this." Millikan held up one finger and shook it in a gentle and self-mocking way. "This is a social event—not an opportunity for you to circumvent the system. You are to keep substantive conversation to a minimum. You've been named part of the working group on nonconventional warfare—a signal honor. That group is a team, and I am the leader of that team—everything important goes through me. Do you understand?"

Betsy, still remembering the abuse that Millikan had showered on her, nodded her head and said nothing.

"You bypassed me once, but you'll never do that again. Do you understand?"

Betsy said nothing. The car pulled up to the residential compound; Marines opened the doors.

"Remember," Millikan said, "as long as we are out-of-doors, you are a White House staffer."

Marlin Fitzwater was giving a briefing to the press. Off to the side the first lady was entertaining some kids with Millie tricks. A tall man with a high forehead was poking around in a large net bag of life preservers and other boat stuff. He straightened up, mumbling, "Well, I thought I'd put the darn things in here, but I'll be goddamned if I know where they went." He focused on Millikan. "Oh, howdy, Jim. And good evening, Betsy. What say we go for a run in the boat?"

Betsy could sense Millikan tensing up.

"Ha, ha!" the tall man said. "I forgot Jim hates the water. He won't admit it, but he does. You can stay home, Jim. Bar'll fix you a drink."

"It's quite all right," Millikan said. "I'll come with you and Ms. Vandeventer, Mr. President. I would just ask that you not try to make the boat flip over this time."

On cue a White House staffer, a young man in a blue blazer, stepped out of the house and approached them. "Dr. Millikan? Telephone call for you, sir."

Millikan glowered. It was clear, even to someone as new to Washington as Betsy, that all of this had been staged. "Unfortunately, I won't be able to take you up on your invitation, Mr. President. Enjoy the ride, Ms. Vandeventer."

"You look like a large to me. Er, maybe a medium," said George Herbert Walker Bush. He rummaged in his net bag and pulled out a couple of life jackets. "Try these on for size. We probably won't need them, but"—anticipating the joke—"must be prudent."

Bush and Betsy went down to the dock, where a small contingent of Coast Guard and Secret Service waited next to the President's Cigarette boat. "Bet you didn't have anything like this in Iowa," Bush said.

"Idaho," Betsy blurted before she realized what she was doing. But Bush seemed easygoing, not the type who would mind being corrected. She was so embarrassed that the next sentence came out in a tumble. "Hell's Canyon—jet boats. They have them there. Big jet boats in the canyon."

"Oh, yeah. I know 'bout that. Big controversy down there with those jet boats," Bush said.

The motors were already idling, getting warmed up. Bush made sure that Betsy was properly squared away with her life jacket, then eased the boat away from the pier and ran the throttle up. The boat shot out and started pounding through a light chop. The water was rougher than Hell's Canyon, the ride much wilder. Betsy shrieked as the spray slapped her in the face, and found it difficult to get her breath back, such was the speed of the boat. The President spent a few minutes trying to hit every large wave that came within range, trying to get the nose of the boat pointed as close to vertical as he could make it. Betsy spent half the time genuinely terrified and cried out more than once.

Then he cut the throttle and let them drift.

"Good work, Betsy. I know about all the nonsense you've been going through. Keep plugging away."

Betsy was still catching her breath. She felt relaxed and energized now and suddenly understood that the boat ride wasn't just a boat ride. It was a tool Bush used to shake visitors out of the daze that came with being in the presence of the most powerful man in the world.

"Thank you," she said.

"What's the story on this Iraq bioweapons thing? Been on my mind recently."

"Dr. Millikan said I should keep it general."

"I'm the President, not Millikan, and you tell me what you want to." The President throttled the boat back up, not nearly as fast, and began to run it in long, lazy figure eights.

Betsy laid out the whole thing from her first discoveries in 1989, trying to concentrate on the facts and not stray into whining about how the system had failed, how Millikan had treated her. The President said nothing, merely frowned. Finally he said, "Don't you just wish that we could simply go after the bad guys? But all of this stuff is like a bad tumor, with millions of tentacles. We cut out the main tumor, the rest grows back."

"Well. That's as may be, Mr. President. But—" She stopped, unable to bring herself to disagree with him.

"Spit it out, Betsy."

"Well. I'm not supposed to do domestic. You know that."

"That's a very important rule, Betsy. Got to take that rule very seriously."

"But there are some things I've become aware of accidentally."

Bush snickered. "Accidental intelligence is my favorite kind, Betsy. Good stuff."

"That is, I wasn't doing domestic intelligence gathering or exceeding my task. I learned of this because of a family member who stumbled across it—or maybe I should say, stumbled into it."

"Gimme the upshot."

"Something's going on at Eastern Iowa University in Wapsipinicon. There are some people there who should be watched."

Bush nodded. "Got the Wapsipinicon thing covered."

Betsy was stunned, delighted. "You do?"

"Yep."

"Who's covering it, if I may ask?"

"Bureau. Hennessey."

"Hennessey?"

"Got a man on the ground there." Bush nodded toward the house. "Bar's waving at me like mad. Better get back." He ran up the throttle so fast that Betsy screamed again. "Gonna have a nice dinner," he shouted. "A nice social thing."

twenty-seven

DEPUTY CLYDE Banks stood stolidly in a column of steam that writhed and swirled all about him, wielding a spatula in each hand, stirring through a heap of shredded potatoes as if trying to find a pearl of great price that had somehow fallen into the frying pan. It was a great big industrial frying pan about the size of a satellite dish, and the flame ring underneath it was consuming so much gas that the buckle of Clyde's belt was beaded with condensed water vapor. The giant industrial-range hood above his head howled like a tornado siren, drowning out the ceaseless catcalls of the prisoners.

Mrs. Krumm, the official cook of the Forks County Jail, sat in the corner, another cigarette in her mouth and a disposable lighter in one of her hands, trying to bring those two things together despite the constant shivering to which her advanced age, nervous disposition, and incredible nicotine consumption made her liable. Mrs. Krumm wanted to retire from this job and probably should have a long time ago, but she needed the money, and so she clung to the work as if it were the last carton of Virginia Slims on the face of the earth. Whenever Clyde was assigned to jail duty—increasingly often, since it was considered the worst of all duties—it was evident to him that Mrs. Krumm was just not physically capable of doing the work.

Clyde should have been thinking about the sheriff campaign, but there was not much to think about there. His bumper stickers had all long since fallen off and blown away to Illinois, or else washed down into storm drains and formed a new variegated red-and-white lining for the regional sewer system. He had it on good authority that raccoons and other midsize animals were lining their nests with "Vote Banks" bumper stickers. The only thing left was the doorbell-ringing campaign. Whether or not this was useless, Clyde was determined to see it through to the bitter end.

So the campaign did not occupy his mind anymore, except

that he would visualize the next block of houses or row of apartments in Wapsipinicon that he would visit when his shift was over. He was much more inclined to ponder the recent events in Kuwait.

For about a week the whole invasion business had been just another conversation starter for use in coffee shops and convenience stores, a welcome respite from many years of talking about the weather or the condition of the old one-lane bridges on County Road E505.

For Clyde, however, the war had suddenly come much closer to home this morning, over breakfast, when Desiree had made some passing mention of calling up the reserves.

Desiree had been in the Army Reserve for several years. She gave them a weekend a month and an annual two-week stint; they sent along a check; and that was that.

But now it sounded as if it might be a hell of a lot more than that.

It was inconceivable that they would need to call up the reserves to deal with a piddly-shit country like Iraq. But they said on the news that Iraq had the fourth-largest military in the world. The U.S. Army, accustomed to facing down the Soviets in Europe, could surely handle even the fourth-largest military with one hand tied behind its back. But they said on the news that the military was short in several key areas—such as medical personnel. Clyde's mind had been seesawing crazily back and forth like this all day long.

They couldn't possibly call up the mother of a little baby.

Why not? They called up fathers of little babies all the time.

The potatoes were burning; the prisoners had smelled their lunch going up the chimney and set up enough pandemonium to be heard even under the range hood. Clyde grasped the handle of the frying pan with both hands, swung it around, and dumped the potatoes into a huge stainless-steel serving bowl.

When Clyde turned around, he was startled to see another person in the room—a tall black man, stoutly constructed but not overweight, wearing a suit with a very clean, heavily starched white shirt.

"Deputy Banks? Marcus Berry, special agent, Federal Bureau of Investigation," the visitor said, holding out a business card. Clyde accepted it and shook Berry's hand. For a moment he was confused; he irrationally thought that this had something to do with Desiree, that the government had sent this man out to take her away. That made no sense at all, but the notion of it shook him up anyway.

"Wanted to talk to you about the horse mutilation," Berry said, "if you have a minute."

"Mrs. Krumm, would you mind serving the prisoners lunch?" Clyde said.

Mrs. Krumm gathered up her lighter and cigarettes, pulled herself to her feet with a deep sigh, and got to work.

"I've been over your report," Berry said. He was all business, which impressed Clyde favorably. It would have been common for a black man in Berry's position to spend a while shooting the breeze, talking about the prospects for the Twisters' football season and so forth, on the assumption that the brain of a Nishnabotnan would still be reeling from the shock of actually having seen a black person and would need several minutes to get back into some kind of decent working order. But Berry gave Clyde a bit more credit than that. "I hope you don't mind my saying this," he continued, "but usually I hate reading reports by local deputies and small-town cops."

Clyde nodded, having read a few himself. Many fine human beings worked in local law enforcement, but Sir Arthur Conan Doyle they were not.

"Your report on the Sweet Corn incident was impeccable," Berry said. "You've got my vote come November."

"Thanks," Clyde said. "Don't recall knocking on your door yet, but I guess I'll cross your name off the list."

"Too late," Berry said. "You knocked on it while I was out. Left me a brochure. Anyway, as I said, your report was an exceptionally thorough account of some exceptionally conscientious police work. So I don't have as many loose ends to tie up as I normally would. But there's always something." He reached into his briefcase and pulled out a copy of Clyde's report.

There was something that startled Clyde about seeing a copy of his work coming out of the briefcase of a federal agent. His shock was redoubled when Berry began to page through it, and Clyde saw that it had been marked up and highlighted. Questions had been scrawled in the margins, and though Clyde could not read them, he could distinguish two or three different hands. Yet there was only one person in the local FBI office, and Clyde was talking to him.

"First of all, let me express my condolences about your friend and colleague Hal Karst."

"I appreciate that."

"He sounds like a fine fellow. Wish I'd had the opportunity to know him."

"Hal was a good one," Clyde said.

"I don't really imagine you want to talk about it with me," Berry said, "and I apologize for raising a difficult subject, but I thought I ought to say something."

"No offense taken," Clyde said.

"This fucking shit sucks shit!" shouted one of the prisoners from the cellblock.

"Okay, down to business," Berry said without batting an eye. "There are a few big institutions down in that part of the county—the high-tech park, the Vet Med College, and the Federal Veterinary Pathology Labs. Before you went to the scene of the incident, you visited all three of those places. Why did you do that?"

"I'd read the reports on the first two mutilation incidents," Clyde said. "They were well organized, so I thought I'd swing through the logical escape routes and look for any unusual vehicles."

"But you didn't see any."

"None that I knew to be unusual."

"What were you looking for?"

"Oh, if I'd seen a van or something stopped in one of those lots with its engine running, pointed at the exit, and the windows steamed up, that would have caught my attention."

"But instead all you saw were the kinds of cars you'd expect to see in such places."

"I hit each one with my spotlight. Didn't see anyone sitting in any of those cars. No steamed-up windows. Nothing that stuck out."

"No black van?"

"Nope," Clyde said.

A cow had been mutilated two nights ago in Cedar County, half an hour's drive away, and a black or navy-blue van had been sighted in the vicinity. Sheriff Mullowney had wasted no time in proclaiming that the War on Satan had already forced the evildoers to take their business out of Mullowney's jurisdiction.

The van had left no tire tracks in Cedar County. But the tracks left along the railway siding on the night of Sweet Corn's mutilation had been identified, and it was a type of tire that might commonly be found on a van.

Those tracks suggested that the van, or whatever it was, had turned south on Boundary after leaving the scene of the incident; in other words, it had headed away from Wapsipinicon, probably to limit the chances of being noticed by someone like Clyde. Deputy Jim Green, heading north on Boundary, hadn't passed any vehicles at all coming his way; but he had seen one turning off Boundary onto a section-line road ahead of him and heading off to the east. That road led to a junction with New 30 and Interstate 45 some four and a half miles distant. Once reaching the interstate, the vehicle could easily have fled north toward Rochester or south toward St. Louis, or just turned back into Nishnabotna a few miles to the north and made its way back to wherever the satanists lived.

So it seemed quite clear that there had been one vehicle, a dark van; that it had been right there along the railway siding; and that Clyde's probe of the nearby parking lots, while not a wholly bad idea, had been a waste of time. It was funny, then, that Berry kept asking about it. "What would you consider to be an unusual vehicle in those locations—setting aside the obvious things?"

"There's janitors who work those buildings at night. I sort of recognize their cars. Other than that the only thing you'd see would be the grad students' cars. Sometimes high-school kids will go there to make out or smoke dope—you can tell them right away because they park in the far corner of the lot and the cars are different."

"Different how?"

"Either it'll be a hot rod, or else a nice car someone borrowed from Dad. Whereas the classic grad-student car is a ten-year-old import station wagon."

"Why?"

"Because most of the grad students are foreign, and most of them have families."

"And you commonly see such cars there at night."

"All the time. They work on these research projects in the labs and have to be there at odd hours."

"Okay," Berry said, seemingly satisfied. He flipped forward a couple of pages in the report. "Let's turn to the actual scene of the mutilation, along the railroad tracks. I know you've already covered this in your report. But I'd like you to go back and search your memory one more time, trying to recall if you saw any sort of debris or litter or any other man-made junk lying around on the ground there."

"Well, as I said in the report, that area is used by a lot of kids who go there to drink beer and smoke pot," Clyde said. "So there's always a lot of litter strewn around the area. It's very difficult sometimes to tell ten-minute-old litter apart from the litter that's been there a few days."

"You know that the horse was hobbled?"

"Hobbled?"

"Yes. The veterinarians found marks around its legs."

"I didn't examine the horse that carefully. But now that you mention it, it stands to reason."

"Did you see any straps on the ground?" Berry said. Then he added, "Or anything else that might have been used to hobble a horse?"

"Well," Clyde said, "which is it?"

"Say again?"

"Was it straps, or something else?"

"I'm asking you," Berry said.

"You said that there were marks on the legs of the horse. Were they strap marks, or some other kinds of marks?"

Berry shifted uncomfortably. Clyde had trapped him without really meaning to. Berry had given away information that was supposed to remain secret.

"I didn't see any straps on the ground," Clyde finally said, "or anything else that might have been used to hobble a horse."

twenty-eight

FAMILIES LIKE the Bankses passed objects like ropes and tarps down through the generations the way other families did houses or silver. Clyde knew that the Big Black Tarp had been acquired by Ebenezer around the time of the War and that it had originally been used to cover Manhattan Project machinery that had rolled into town on a flatbed truck in the middle of the night in 1944. He knew that the Little Brown Tarp had been purchased by his father from a surplus store around the time of the Korean War and used to cover the family's possessions when they'd moved to Illinois and back. In the oral tradition of male Bankses, each of the tarps was as storied as a tapestry or handmade quilt, and when Clyde noticed a bent grommet or a patched tear or an oil stain, he needed only think about it for a few moments to remember which camping trip, move, natural disaster, or construction project had occasioned it.

To Desiree they were just dark, dirty things that lurked in the garage reeking with an ominous, gunlike odor, and so as Clyde used the Big Black Tarp to cover up Desiree's possessions in the back of the pickup truck, he found himself worrying about what would become of the tarp when she reached her new home in Fort Riley, Kansas. It would be like her to drag the tarp over to a Dumpster and leave it there as if it were nothing more than a sheet of plastic from the hardware store. Fort Riley must be crawling with new arrivals now, most of whom had a more practical bent than Desiree, and some sharp-eyed master sergeant would surely snap it up within minutes, dry it out in his driveway, and store it lovingly in his garage.

Clyde worked late into the night, worrying about his tarp. Desiree kept bringing more things out; she brought out her sewing machine so that she could sew things for Maggie. She had insisted, quite rightly, that she drive the truck and not the station wagon; the wagon was the family car, a much safer and cleaner vehicle for Maggie to be squired around in, and the truck was the right vehicle to take to war.

Clyde was worried about the truck, so he changed the oil and checked all the other fluids and rehearsed Desiree on how to change a flat tire. He was worried that rain would get in and destroy her things, so he laid the Big Black Tarp out on the empty bed of the truck, loaded her things on top of it, then folded the tarp over the top when she had promised–insisted–that she had brought out the last of her things. Shiny luggage, clothes in white garbage bags, shoe boxes filled with family photographs, framed photographs stashed in glossy department-store bags, the sewing machine, a couple of spare pillows in bright flowered pillowcases, a disconnected telephone with its cord wound around it, the garment bag containing Desiree's full-dress uniform, a stack of novels and magazines, all vanished beneath the oily shroud of the Big Black Tarp.

It started to move, seemingly of its own accord. Clyde looked up, startled, and saw Dick Dhont. Dick had pulled up and parked on the street, come up the driveway without saying a word, and grabbed an errant corner of the tarp. It was about a quarter to one in the morning.

The tarp was more than large enough to cover Desiree's things and to wrap generously around the sides, but both men knew that Desiree liked to limit her speed to between eighty-five and ninety miles per hour, unless she was in the city, where she would hold it to under thirty. Without having to discuss it, they set to work tying down the tarp so that it wouldn't flap loose as Desiree barreled down the interstate.

They walked several more times around the truck and each

man concluded with some reluctance that the job was finished, Desiree's things were immobilized as securely as a freshly pinned Dhont wrestling opponent, and there was nothing more to worry about. Dick Dhont rummaged under the seat of the truck, found Clyde's five-year-old Rand McNally Road Atlas, opened it up to the map of Kansas, and carefully arranged it there on the seat next to where Desiree would sit tomorrow. Clyde was ashamed that he had not thought of this.

Dick went inside to check on Desiree; he had to work in the morning and would not be able to see her off. Clyde sat down in the grass in the front yard and waited. A batch of plastic went bad out at Nishnabotna Plastics and erupted from the tower like a detonating oil well, filling the neighborhood with faint, ghostly light. Dick came out of the front door after a few minutes, closed it gently, then turned and ran to his car. He sat behind the wheel for a few minutes, his shoulders hunched and heaving, then started the engine and drove away, forgetting to turn on his headlights.

Clyde turned off the garage light and went inside. He found Desiree lying on the couch in the living room with Maggie nestled up against her. Her nightgown was unbuttoned and one breast was peeking out. The sleeping Maggie nuzzled at it. Her lips began to suck on air, and a little smile came onto her face.

Clyde had been working the night shift so frequently of late that he did not imagine he would have much luck getting to sleep; the adjustment was just too difficult to make. So he made himself comfortable in the living room, turned the TV around toward his chair so that its flickering light would not disturb the girls, and watched TV for a while, mostly CNN. It all had to do with Desert Shield. President Bush was buzzing around Maine in his boat, and convoys of heavy military vehicles were converging on air bases around the country, mostly in the Southeast. There was a little feature story about a schoolteacher in Ohio who had been called up, and who had appeared before his class in his Army uniform to give a last lecture, explaining to the kids where he was going and why. The kids looked stunned, much the way Dick Dhont had.

Then the doorbell had rung and its sound was dying away and the front door had been flung open. It was Mrs. Dhont and two of the Dhont wives. It was morning. Clyde tried to sit up in the La-Z-Boy but found Maggie had been deposited on his chest all wrapped in pink blankets. Desiree was not in the room anymore. She was taking a shower. He heard the whine of the house's plumbing and could smell her shampoo.

Becky, the eldest Dhont wife, came and plucked Maggie off Clyde's chest and cuddled her, leaving Clyde there alone, as if he had some preordained role in the upcoming ceremony that had nothing to do with looking after Maggie. Mrs. Dhont and the other Dhont wife busied themselves in the kitchen making a hearty Dhont breakfast. Knowing that Desiree had strayed from the family dietary traditions, they had brought the necessary staples with them: two-inch-thick patties of homemade pork sausage, eggs still warm from the chickens, bottles of raw milk with cream still making its way to the top.

Clyde found himself with nothing to do. He went out and walked around the truck a couple of more times.

When he came back inside, Desiree was out of the shower, her hair wet and smelling of peaches. She had changed into jeans and a T-shirt for the drive. They spent a few minutes smooching and flirting in the bedroom as if this were any other day, then went down, hand in hand, to breakfast. The Dhont females had prepared a meal adequate to feed the entire Seventh Army Corps. Clyde expressed rote amazement but was hurt on the inside; it reminded him too much of what was to come.

Still, he thought as he chewed his sausage, it wouldn't have been any better if Desiree had pulled into the drive-up window on the way out of town for an Egg McMuffin. There was nothing wrong with marking the occasion, with bringing all of the heavy emotions straight to the forefront, as women in general and the Dhont women in particular tended to. It just wasn't a Banks way of doing things, and he would never adjust to it.

After breakfast Desiree drank a whole big tumbler of water, the way she always did when she was about to breast-feed, and took Maggie into the den for a quarter of an hour. When the two emerged, Maggie was gurgling and happy, and Desiree had tears running down her face, knowing that she would never breast-feed her daughter again—now that she was going away, her milk supply would soon dry up. She hugged and kissed her mother and sisters-in-law very hard, then handed the baby over to Clyde, who handed her over to Becky. Clyde followed Desiree out to the garage, feeling light-headed.

" 'Bye," she said. "I'll call you from the road somewhere." She hit the starter and the engine whined for a long time and Clyde's heart jumped as he hoped it might not start; then the engine caught, and he felt himself go limp and helpless. Desiree gunned it a few times, the way Clyde had always told her not to, then backed it slowly out of the garage.

All of the neighbors had come out onto their front porches and were waving American flags and handkerchiefs and yellow ribbons at her. She honked the horn, shifted it into first gear, and drove away, holding down the horn button intermittently as she moved down the block, occasionally turning around to wave at Clyde, her little fingers fluttering in the truck's rear window above the shadow of the Big Black Tarp all crisscrossed with ropes.

Then she was gone. Gone to war. Everyone in the neighborhood looked at Clyde, standing there in the middle of the garage door. He turned his back on them and, finding himself trapped with nowhere to go, climbed into the station wagon and punched the opener. The garage door closed behind him. He closed the station wagon's door and found himself alone in a dark, quiet place. He leaned forward until his brow was resting on the wagon's maroon dashboard. Finally his body began to heave and shudder, and he cried for the first time since he was fourteen years old.

twenty-nine

SEPTEMBER

"THIS YOUR first one of these?"

Dean Kenneth Knightly, piloting his rust-ravaged ZX across the Mississippi River bridge on I-80, glanced over at Kevin Vandeventer, who was sitting in the passenger's seat with the window rolled halfway down, trying to fight back Knightly's cigarette smoke. Though the wind blowing in through the rust holes in the floor did that better than any window.

"These what?" Kevin responded with a bit of an offended edge in his voice. He didn't like the dean, his scuffed cowboy boots, his unfiltered Camels, his Texas accent, his blue blazer from Kmart. In short, he did not like the fact that the dean, despite his high position, made no effort to disguise his agro-American roots. "I've gone back to the beltway a number of times for Dr. Larsen, but I believe this is the first time I've had the opportunity to attend this particular meeting."

Knightly was tickled. He didn't like this mousse-haired tadpole anymore than Kevin liked him. Partly, he didn't like him for the simple and obvious reason that he was an arrogant little shit with a freshly minted Ph.D. and a closet full of suits with the outlet-mall price tags still on them. But that all came with the territory. He really didn't like him because he worked for Larsen, and Larsen was crooked.

"Well, then, let me tell you a bit about where we're going today, representing *the* Eastern Iowa University. We'll be attending the thirty-eighth—I believe the program has it in Roman numerals, I believe that is ea-ecks, ea-ecks, ea-ecks, *vee*, eye, eye, eye. It is among the oldest postwar white-slave exchanges in the world, although most of the people we move now are brown, black, and yellow."

He was just trying to provoke Kevin, and Kevin was too provoked to figure it out. "It's fine for you to be cynical, but our job, in our shop, is saving lives and making the world a better place."

The dean began to laugh. "What's the Rainmaker up to now? A quarter of a billion lives?" He finished a cigarette and poked the butt through a rust hole in the floor of the car. "Look. Don't get me wrong. There are some good things that come out of your shop, as you call it—people get fed, students get trained. But there are some wonderful babies born out of whorehouses, too. And you, Dr. Vandeventer, are working in the intellectual, multinational equivalent of a whorehouse in which, in the pursuit of legitimate goals, your pimpo magnifico, the fucking son of a bootlegger, provides services for a massive profit, breaking laws, treaties, moral and ethical guidelines—and working against his own country's national interest."

"Jesus!" Kevin exclaimed. He'd always been trained to be nice, polite, and not bring disagreements out into the open—especially with someone he was about to spend the whole day with, cooped up in cars and airplanes. He was knocked off balance by Knightly's sudden double-barreled attack.

"Oh, he does have the best accountants between Chicago and Denver working for him. Just don't give me that 'making the world a better place' jive. What about all those fake Jordanians you've brought in?"

"What are you implying?"

"Hell, Dr. Vandeventer, I know the region. I've fucking *been* there. I know the accents. I know the way those people talk, walk, dress, and think. And if those people are Jordanians, then you're Kim Basinger."

"They are all legally cleared international students, certified by the Jordanian government and confirmed by our embassy in Amman. They are legally in this country and have the proper visas."

"Yeah. Sure. Well, I've got my own network and my own experience, and I can tell you that most of those people are Iraqis. And you know what? I suspect that deep down under all of this making-the-world-a-better-place crap, you know that they're Iraqis."

Kevin's face reddened, and he clenched his teeth and was shocked to realize that tears had begun to form. This was a little too much like the old days on the potato farm, being tongue-lashed by his father.

Knightly was right. Kevin didn't know it totally—it wasn't a conscious realization yet—but he had begun to piece things together in the back of his mind.

Along with the incipient tears his nose had begun to run. He cried too easily, goddamn it. He pulled a handkerchief from his pocket, blew his nose, and blinked back the tears. He thought he'd done a good job of controlling himself without Knightly noticing. But when Knightly resumed his rant, his voice was much gentler, as if he'd noticed it and felt bad. Kevin was indescribably humiliated by this.

"Look, Kevin. Maybe I'm just jealous. I'm in the same game—though at a different level, and I'm legal. But it's the same game. That's what this meeting is about."

Oddly, Kevin felt himself starting to relax. Ever since the magic with his W-2 forms, he'd had questions, but he'd never let himself ask.

Knightly continued. "Let me tell you about the National Association of International Science Students, NAISS—we pronounce it 'nice.' Larsen's PR department must have thought that one up. You'll see people from virtually every school in the United States and officials from virtually every country in the world. It's a market. The foreigners—especially the really poor countries—will let us take their smartest people for a few years and use them—kind of like an indenture—but we make money out of it. Then we send them back with some initials after their names, and funny hats that they can't wear, eternally alienated from their cultures and their identities. We take these talented people and the money they bring with them, we use them to run our labs and teach our classes and do our research for four or five years, and then we send them back to become our satellites. Sort of like the athletic department and their wonderful student-athletes off whom they make millions of dollars, wrecking their bodies in the process, and then ejecting them into the world.

Anyway, NAISS is the market in which the bureaucrats and the universities piece together agreements that guarantee the supply of gray matter from Timbuktu." Knightly shook his head wryly. "And *we* say we're doing *them* a favor. You have any idea what would happen to our system if the flow of these foreign kids stopped?"

They didn't talk much more as Knightly slammed his ZX across the rolling territory of northern Illinois, through the outskirts of Chicago, and into Midway Airport. Kevin tried to put all this out of his mind by running through his mental checklist for the dozenth time. He'd turned off the air conditioner in his apartment, the oven and burners were off, the iron unplugged. He'd left forwarding addresses and numbers. Larsen's full-time, in-house travel specialist had reserved him a room at the Rosslyn Holiday Inn, right across the Key Bridge from Georgetown where the meeting would take place, and only four blocks from Betsy's apartment building—and Margaret's.

Once he had cleared his mental desk of all the reassuring normality, reality came back, and the fear and anxiety with it. For the last several months he had been constantly worrying that the IRS would audit him. The Habibi case, and Clyde Banks's ongoing interest in the subject, also bothered him. Now to these nagging low-level anxieties was added a much more profound fear of this business with the new Jordanian students. Prior to the arrival of these new people in Wapsipinicon in mid-July, he had been on the phone with his friends at the Jordanian Embassy every day—sometimes several times a day. Since then they hadn't called him once, and when he called them, they were always in meetings, or out of town.

It had occurred to him that if he ever did find himself in trouble, he could expect very little help from the Rainmaker. Larsen treated Kevin with the same respect as he treated the keyboard of his laptop—something useful, functional, and eminently replaceable. The more authority Larsen gave him—the deeper into this business Kevin got—the more Larsen withdrew from him personally. Kevin's bowels spasmed and he felt short of breath.

He went through his mantra. *I'm really okay. Nothing has changed. I just have to watch my drinking and stay calm. I've done nothing wrong.*

They went on board with their garment bags and found places to stuff them. Their seats were together. Dean Knightly took the window seat and seemed to enjoy the view of the Chicago skyline contrasted against the deep-blue waters of Lake Michigan. He could peer almost directly down into his beloved Wrigley Field, where the Cubs were being slaughtered by the Pirates.

After the flight attendants had come through with sandwiches, Knightly picked up where he'd left off. "Look, NAISS has all of these panels, luncheons, banquet speakers, and the like. You can go if you want to. You'll either run into people like yourself, many of whom are just looking for a way to drink on someone else's tab and get laid in someone else's bed, or the NAISS gerontocracy, who want to have their hands shaken and get awards for their distinguished service. The real business will take place in the bars and hotel rooms. I like to watch the people work each other and to see my old friends—all two of them. So you won't see anything more of me after we hit National."

That was fine with Kevin, who wanted to see only one person in Washington. To his great delight Margaret had left a message at his hotel, saying that she would swing by after work so they could have a drink together. Kevin had every reason to think he could stretch the drink into dinner—and if he could, what was to prevent him from stretching dinner into something more intimate?

He took a shower and shaved for the second time that day, leaving his face hot and razor burned, then made dinner reservations in a funky Caribbean restaurant in Adams-Morgan.

He met Margaret in the lobby, and they took the elevator to the top floor of the hotel. She looked too good to be true—he couldn't believe she'd just come off a long day at work. Betsy always looked blown and frazzled when she came back from work—maybe it was because she insisted on walking everywhere.

Margaret blew past the "Please Wait to Be Seated" sign and grabbed the choicest table in the bar, by a window looking down toward Roosevelt Island. Margaret ordered club soda; Kevin ordered Stoli straight up and hold the water. "And we need some finger food."

"Finger food," the waiter echoed, coolly mimicking Kevin's country vowels. "Thumbs or pinkies?"

"Pretzels and nuts, asshole," Kevin said. The waiter raised his eyebrows, turned, and walked away, punching keys on his electronic order pad.

"Not a good evening, huh?" Margaret said, resting her hand on his for a moment. The sensation ran up his arm and exploded in his brain. "What's bothering you?"

Kevin sat back. He wanted to stare at Margaret's face all night long, but she was looking back at him with a penetrating gaze that forced him to look away. Instead he looked out the window at the traffic jam on the parkway and the Roosevelt Bridge, the planes landing at National. "It's a long way from Forks County, Iowa," he said. "And Forks is a long way from the potato farm. A lot of people come here to D.C. like it's nothing—they use the city like a public phone booth. To me this is a big deal." He shook his head. "Shit. I'm so jealous of Betsy. The work she does. The access she has. She talked to the President!"

"Kevin, if you only knew..."

"Yeah, yeah, I know her job has a big downside, too. But so does mine. If *you* only knew about *my* downside!" He laughed. "I put up with it because it gets me here. To D.C. Where I can look down the river every night to the Jefferson. And go out with incredibly beautiful women like you."

"*Women?* You've got more than one?"

Kevin blushed, horrified to have made such a gaffe. But Margaret laughed—just teasing.

He'd never opened up to her this way before. Until tonight he'd been all pretense. He had done his best to make her think that he really was one of those beltway insiders. It felt wonderful to unburden himself. Margaret didn't seem to mind—she hadn't jumped up and stormed out of the place yet. In fact she was smiling at him warmly, eager to hear more. "Tell me about the downside," she said. "What's troubling you?"

"I've probably made some bad choices, Margaret. If I get out now, I can get a job as an untenured teacher at some dipshit four-year school in central Mississippi. If I ride this wave I'm on, I might get out okay."

"Depends on where the wave is going," she said.

"Okay," Kevin said, and drained his glass. "I'll tell you about it. Hell, you're CIA, you're fire-walled from all domestic affairs, and this is domestic, so this shouldn't interfere with your work—right?"

Margaret shrugged. "Can't talk about my work," she said.

"I know about your work," Kevin said. "You sit in front of a workstation and write reports, like my sister." But Kevin didn't really care. It all had to come out now. So he started telling her about everything—how he'd found his way into the Rainmaker's empire years ago and worked his way to the top, and how an odd bit of work had come across his desk in May, involving some new Jordanian grad students who absolutely had to get into the country no later than mid-July, and who seemed to have an infinite amount of money and influence behind them. About all of the strings he'd pulled, bureaucracies he'd manipulated, little white lies he'd told, laws and regulations he had bent to make it happen. How, having used him for this one purpose, his Jordanian friends had cast him aside like a used condom, and how Larsen himself was becoming ever more distant in recent weeks.

At some point he realized he'd been talking for a solid hour and had made his way through three or four Stolis. He paid the bill and led Margaret down to the garage where he had parked his rental car.

"Now that I've shucked my pretense of being the ultimate Washington insider," he said, "do you think you could give me directions to Adams-Morgan?"

"Easy," she said. "Give me the keys and I'll drive."

"It's a rental—you're not an authorized driver," he said.

"Neither are you, when you've had five shots in an hour and a half," she said. "Shall we take a cab?"

"Okay, okay," he said, and handed her the keys.

She drove them across the Key Bridge, through the strange mixture of posh and tawdry that was Georgetown, and got them onto the Rock Creek Parkway. "Secret shortcut to points north," she said, accelerating around a curve into the darkly forested vale. A few minutes later they shot up a steep exit ramp and resurfaced in a different part of the city. Margaret took them eastward, into the border zone between the affluent west side of the District and the war-torn east side, and onto a crowded and neon-lit street of ethnic restaurants, fast-food outlets, newsstands, and bodegas. It was the antithesis of Wapsipinicon, and it was pretty exotic even by the standards of D.C. Margaret braked to a stop in front of the restaurant. "Hop out," she said, "and grab our table. I'll park."

"Are you kidding?" he said. "I'm just enough of an old-fashioned macho shithead that I'm not going to let you walk around here alone."

"Have it your way," she said, and then spent fifteen minutes circling for a parking space. The widening gyre of their search took them into darker and less pleasant parts of the neighborhood; finally they found a space on the street, underneath a streetlamp, a block away from the main drag. It looked dark and hazardous from inside the car, but when they got out and began walking down the sidewalk, it didn't seem so bad. There were a lot of pedestrians about, Hispanics of all ages and both sexes.

The restaurant was great—Kevin had called it right. Dynamite Caribbean beer, ice cold. Chicken, black beans, rice, curried meat wrapped in flat bread, grilled marlin. They did not talk anymore about Kevin's troubles—instead they talked about his research, and his dreams.

In the back of his mind Kevin was dimly aware that they had spent all their time together talking about him and that he barely knew anything about Margaret. But it wasn't his fault. It was hard to get the woman to open up when her work was classified, and her family background was apparently a tender subject to be carefully avoided. He made a mental note to redress this imbalance one of these times.

But not right now. Everything was going too well.

Kevin racked up the meal and the drinks on his Gold Card, and they stepped out into the night. The crowd on the streets was different now, mostly young people, not the cross section of ages they'd seen earlier in the evening. And when they turned off the main street and headed into the desolate neighborhood where they'd parked, they found the sidewalk deserted—except for a couple of young Hispanic males carrying a car battery they'd just stripped from a vehicle.

"Hope it wasn't ours," Kevin said, and couldn't help laughing.

Margaret let go of his arm and unzipped her purse.

"What are you doing?" he said.

"Getting the car keys," she said.

They walked another few yards.

"So where are they?" he asked.

"What?"

"The car keys. You said you were getting them."

She said nothing. Then Kevin took the car keys out of his pocket and jangled them. "You gave them to me, remember?" He laughed delightedly, but she didn't seem amused. In fact she didn't seem to be paying attention to him at all.

"Where's that damn streetlight we parked under?" he said, looking up the street.

"Three cars ahead of us," she said. "It's gone out for some reason." She stopped in her tracks. "Kevin, I don't like this. Let's get out."

"Get out? What do you mean?"

"I mean, back to the main street."

"Margaret, the car's right there. If you want to get out, we should get in the car and go."

This seemed obvious enough to Kevin. For some reason Margaret wasn't buying it. She stood there indecisively for a few moments, then strode forward and snatched the keys from Kevin's hand. "Let's do it," she said.

She was in her seat and shoving the keys into the ignition before he'd even got his door open. By the time he'd sat down and closed the door, she was furious about something. "Goddamn it!"

"What's up?"

"Car won't start."

"Want me to give it a try?"

"Sit back and don't move!" she said in a strong voice, a voice of someone who was used to giving commands. Kevin looked over at her, astonished, and saw that she was gazing out the windshield.

Kevin looked up and saw a man on the sidewalk right outside the car, a bulky man wearing a hooded sweatshirt with the hood pulled up around his head. He had brown skin and a thick mustache and dark glasses. He was pulling something out of his waistband.

There was a crisp metallic sound in his left ear. He looked over to see that Margaret had reached down between her legs into her purse and pulled out something big and heavy.

It was a gun. A semiautomatic. Right in front of Kevin's face. He could see the maker's mark and serial number stamped on the barrel. She had just chambered a round. The hammer was cocked. She shouted something, not at Kevin but at the person outside. Two different male voices began shouting in an unfamiliar language outside the car. They seemed startled and upset. But Kevin's eyes were fixed on the gun in front of his face. He actually saw the hammer spring forward.

For a long time, then, he didn't hear anything except explosions.

The windshield shattered immediately. It held its shape but turned into a web of finely spaced hairline cracks, so that it was nearly opaque. The figures outside were vague shadows, desperately out of focus. Kevin had noticed another one in the street, on Margaret's side of the car.

The cracks in the glass all flashed brightly when flames erupted from the barrel of Margaret's gun or the guns outside the car, and at these times the entire windshield seemed to become a sheet of fire. From place to place the glass had a large circular hole in it. The number of holes increased as the explosions continued.

After a while he realized that he hadn't heard any explosions in a long time. They were still sitting there, he and Margaret, just as they had been a few moments ago, when she'd been about to start the car, about to drive back to Kevin's hotel room for some to-be-specified additional socializing. Except that now most of the windshield was gone and the car was full of smoke. The key chain still dangled from the ignition, swinging back and forth like a pendulum.

He remembered, then, the thing Margaret had shouted after she had pulled out her gun, and just before the explosions had started. She had been shouting, "FBI! FBI!"

"What was all that about?" he said.

Margaret didn't answer.

thirty

OTHER THAN the sporadic visitations of the mighty Antonov transport ship, the twelve-thousand-foot runway at the Forks County Regional Airport was used only for a couple of weeks each year, when the Guard unit would perform its annual maneuvers. Boys would converge on the airport, leaning their bicycles against the fence, watching the C-141's and occasional C-5A's stain the runway with long streaks of molten rubber.

The Guard unit had been mobilized immediately after the invasion, and the runway had begun to see more use. Doug Parsons, the shop teacher at Nishnabotna High School, was pulled away from his classes and put back in uniform and back in the cockpit, flying C-141's hither and thither, first on short hauls within the continental United States and then on epic journeys to Saudi Arabia.

A good deal of traffic was going to and from Fort Riley, where Desiree had been stationed, and so she was able to make it back to Forks County three different times during the month of September—easing her concern that her fast-growing baby daughter might forget her face and voice. When a week and a half went by, and Desiree was unable to find a flight back, Clyde bought a plane ticket and took Maggie on a stress-ridden three-leg flight down to Fort Riley. They stayed illegally in the officers' quarters for a couple of nights and then flew home.

Each individual moment of September seemed to last forever. When Clyde was at work, he worried about Maggie, who was usually in the care of one of the Dhont wives. There was nothing really to worry about, but he worried anyway and could not wait for his shift to be over. When he was out campaigning, going door-to-door with Maggie strapped to his back, he checked his wristwatch between houses and was always crestfallen to see how little time had gone by. And the time spent taking care of Maggie was worst of all. He loved the little critter, but he just couldn't concentrate on her the way Desiree could. The baby was the center of Desiree's attention; she could concentrate on Maggie and Maggie alone for hours at a time; the baby chased all other thoughts from her mind.

It wasn't like that for Clyde. He and his wife had worked out an arrangement whereby she handled the tactics of child rearing and he handled the strategy, always walking a couple of paces ahead of them, club in hand, looking out for tar pits and saber-toothed tigers. He was always thinking about how to rewire the ceiling fixtures in the apartment building so that he could get some tenants in there next month and get some cash flow to divert into Maggie's college account, keeping track of the oil-change schedule for the station wagon. He tried to retool his brain for Desiree's role and just couldn't do it. He'd sit there spooning mush into the child's mouth, and instead of making each spoonful into a little event unto itself, and lavishing praise on Maggie for her advanced mush-slurping capabilities, he would just move that little spoon back and forth like an industrial robot, staring at a squirrel out in the yard or some other irrelevant focus point, saying nothing whatsoever.

Desiree wrote letters, even though they talked on the phone every night and saw each other almost every week, so that Clyde ended up getting each individual piece of news three times. Even though the Army appeared to be gearing up for war, the nurses were not unusually busy. She had been posted not at the main base hospital, but at an outlying clinic, filling in for other nurses who had been sent off to California for desert exercises. She was much more apt to see the spouses and children of soldiers, and retirees, than soldiers themselves. After a couple of weeks, though, her role changed.

> First big batch of reservists hits town next week. We are gearing up to in-process them. Translation: your wife will spend the next couple weeks sticking needles into butts. So I'll pack up my stuff again and move to new quarters nearer the main hospital. No more private rooms, I'm afraid. Army called up a batch of cardiovascular surgeons and put them in barracks with no blankets. They flew off the handle, but Army doesn't care because Army has them and there's nothing they can do about it. Making some friends with the other nurses now. Found out I was wearing my rank in the wrong place. But everyone's a little rusty, and things are always looser in the Medical Corps, so they didn't make me peel potatoes or anything. But I was warned that things will get stricter if/when I get closer to the action.

Despite the fact that each individual moment of September seemed to last forever, the month as a whole flew by. Starting on Labor Day, Dr. Jerry Tompkins, as a way of garnering some free publicity, had begun to release weekly polling results to the newspaper, and they showed that Clyde's popularity had surged to within a few points of Sheriff Mullowney's in the weeks following Desiree's move to Fort Riley. This was small comfort to Clyde, who no longer cared about the election. It did help give him the energy to keep campaigning for another week or two, until more poll results came out showing that his standings had dropped to a bit short of where they had been to begin with. Man-in-the-street interviews on the front page of the *Times-Dispatch* suggested that, in the view of the electorate, Clyde ought to be concentrating on taking care of his baby and not out campaigning, or for that matter trying to run the sheriff's department.

> I see butts in my sleep: white butts, black butts, hairy butts, smooth butts, pimply butts. Some of the owners of these butts squawk and fuss, but generally they take it pretty well.

> Some of these people were even more surprised than I was when they were called up. They believed (like me) that the call-up would never happen. Some of them are claiming hardship, which makes me PO'd because some have fewer hardships than we do. All the motels and campgrounds are full of wives and kids. If you bring Punkin down again, we will have a harder time sneaking you into the BOQ. Maybe we could rendezvous in Kansas City.
>
> Do you remember the Post Gas Chamber?

Clyde remembered it. It was a low concrete-block structure standing off to itself near the entrance to the post, identified as such by a stark general-issue Army sign. When Desiree had picked him and Maggie up at the airport, she had slowed down and pointed it out to him, and they'd laughed at the very Army-ness of it.

> Well, it's been busy, if you can believe it. They march the men in there, give them gas masks, expose them to tear gas, and then make them practice getting the masks on under "combat" conditions. Hopefully they won't make us medical weenies do it. But they say Saddam has a lot of NBC capabilities, and so we are going to get a lot of training in MOPP gear and chemical mass casualties and all the rest. Talked to a doc who says they are hitting the books and learning all about good old anthrax. I wonder why. Anyway, I told him I grew up on a farm and am immune to it.

That was just like Desiree: turning it into a joke. Clyde put his hands over his face when he read that and wondered whether anyone else in the Medical Corps was laughing.

The doorbell rang just then, and Clyde got up and ran to answer it, fearing that a second ring might wake Maggie from her nap.

"How do people die in Forks County?"

Dr. Kevin Vandeventer was asking the question. He had shown

up unexpected, much as Clyde had materialized on Kevin's doorstep a few weeks earlier. But Vandeventer wasn't running for anything and so had no clear excuse. He looked about ten years older than he had during their last conversation.

"Beg pardon?" Clyde said through his screen door. Vandeventer hadn't got around to saying hello-how-are-you yet. Clyde could see that Vandeventer was all worked up and did not really want this man bringing his troubles into the Banks home, which was troubled enough. Maggie was inside napping, so Clyde stepped outside and joined Vandeventer on the front porch. It was about ninety-five degrees out there. Clyde immediately began to sweat freely—something that Vandeventer had evidently been doing for hours.

"How do people die around here?"

"What are you getting at? Would you like some iced tea?"

Vandeventer didn't seem to hear the offer. "In D.C. it happens several times a year that some black kids will come over to the west side of town, mug a white guy in a suit, and end up shooting him to death in the bargain."

"Dang," Clyde said.

"So when that happens, of course everyone's shocked and outraged and all that—but the important thing, Clyde, is that *no one is surprised.* That kind of thing doesn't make anyone *suspicious.*" He leaned forward into Clyde's face as he delivered this punch line, then bounced back away from him with a triumphant look on his face.

"Sounds pretty suspicious to me."

"But what I'm saying is, if you wanted to assassinate someone, and you set it up to look like just another one of those crimes, no one—not even the D.C. police—would have any reason to suspect it was anything different."

"Okay," Clyde said, after cogitating for a while. "So the reason you came round this afternoon is to ask me if you wanted to assassinate someone in Forks County without making the cops suspicious, what kind of crime would you set it up as?"

"Precisely."

Clyde sucked his teeth and squinted off into the distance,

getting his brain in gear. But Vandeventer interrupted him. "Just let me say that if anything of the kind happens to me, Clyde, look a little deeper. I know that when Marwan Habibi died, you were the only cop in Forks County who bothered to look a little deeper. And I have confidence in you."

"Are you saying someone's trying to assassinate you?"

"That's exactly what I'm saying."

Clyde looked searchingly at Vandeventer, then decided to let this pass for the time being. "Well," he finally said, "usually when I see a stiff in my line of work, it's a stiff in a smashed-up car." He was about to launch into a canned peroration about Sheriff Mullowney's abysmal record when it came to catching drunk drivers, but Vandeventer didn't seem to be in the mood for it, and, besides, it appeared that Clyde had already earned his vote. "Also," he offered, "a lot of people get drowned in the rivers, especially in that Rotary at the dam where Habibi spent a couple of weeks caught in the spin cycle. Then there's hunting accidents, but this isn't the time of year for that."

"Well, Clyde, just for the record, I don't plan to go swimming or hunting."

Clyde's cop instincts were finally coming into play. "Who do you think is going to assassinate you?"

"The Iraqis," Kevin said.

From time to time Clyde got the job of driving a prisoner down to the state mental-health facility in Iowa City for testing, observation, treatment, and, sometimes, an open-ended stay. Consequently, Dr. Kevin Vandeventer was not the first Forks County resident—not even the first Ph.D.—who had insisted to Clyde that he was the target of secret, carefully disguised assassination attempts by foreign governments.

He had learned a few rules of thumb for identifying certain broad categories of mental illness and now began to apply his rudimentary knowledge to Kevin Vandeventer. He seemed sincere, rational, and convincing. But these guys always did—especially the ones with Ph.D.'s.

"I hadn't known until now," Clyde said carefully, "that Baghdad was running those kinds of operations inside our borders."

Vandeventer laughed, much too loudly. "You and me both, Clyde, we're both babes in the woods. Shit. The university is one big nest of foreign spooks."

"I know it is," Clyde said. In part he was just trying to placate Vandeventer so that he would go away and leave the Bankses alone. The absence of Desiree was a howling void in their household and their lives—a sucking chest wound. Clyde felt like a soldier on a battlefield who has been shot in the abdomen and is using both hands just to keep his insides from falling out on the ground. All he wanted was for Desiree to be back in this house. And so when people came to the house who were not Desiree, it just emphasized her absence and aggravated the pain. He frankly could not care less about Kevin Vandeventer and his impending assassination.

But Clyde wasn't precisely lying. In the months since he had recovered the fatal rowboat from the rushes of Lake Pla-Mor, in the course of following the Marwan Habibi murder case, and of getting to know Fazoul and his family, he had come to realize that Eastern Iowa University was, as Kevin averred, a snake pit of foreign intrigue.

And he could hardly care less. He had overwhelming problems of his own.

"If you see anything goofy, call the cops," Clyde said. "If you have evidence that foreigners are involved, call Marcus Berry down at the FBI."

Kevin nodded eagerly, as if this were all incredibly new advice to him. He kept staring expectantly at Clyde, his eyes glittering.

Clyde heaved a big sigh. Through the screen door he could hear Maggie shifting around in her crib, beginning to fuss. "If that doesn't work, give ol' Clyde a call," he said, wishing that he could kick himself in the ass even as he was saying it.

Kevin nodded and took half a step back. But he was still waiting for something.

Clyde said, "If you turn up dead or mangled, I will attempt to look beyond the obvious."

"Thank you, Clyde," Kevin Vandeventer said. Like every other paranoid schizophrenic Clyde had ever humored in this fashion, he then said, "Watch your back!" And he turned his back on Clyde and walked down the front steps of the Banks home in the cautious, measured gait of a man who was convinced he had a bull's-eye painted between his shoulder blades. Or maybe he just didn't want to work up a sweat.

thirty-one

LARKIN SCHOENDIENST had told Betsy that in D.C. there were two ways to murder policy without appearing to have committed a crime. One was cobwebbing, in which a person with an idea—usually a young and bright person with a good, new idea—would fall victim to the surrounding bureaucrats, who would exclaim, "Why, that's a good idea!" and throw out a web of reporting requirements, consulting requirements, or new budgeting procedures. Soon the person and his idea would be totally immobilized by a shimmering silken cocoon, to be put away and devoured another day.

The second method was the interagency task force.

"You have to remember, Betsy," Schoendienst would say, "that D.C. is not about solving problems. If we solved problems, there would be nothing else left to do and we would all have to go out and do something honest—like fry hamburgers. No, D.C. is about keeping jobs, which we do by *managing* problems. There is no higher achievement than making a problem your own, managing that problem, nurturing that problem along until you've made it to retirement and hopefully mentored a whole new generation of young bureaucrats to whom you can bequeath the problem. The purpose of the interagency task force is to bring the resources of several agencies and many bureaucrats to bear on a promising new problem that needs special care and nurturing."

By that time Betsy had grown used to the cynicism of this alcoholic old man, but his words came back to her forcefully during the first meeting of the group in the big antenna-covered barn at Kennebunkport. It soon became evident that this was a dog and pony show for Millikan—a chance for him to demonstrate his superior clout, especially to Hennessey. It also became painfully evident that there was absolutely no reason for them to be there—they were just having their chains yanked.

Some new satellite photos were displayed, which would have meant nothing to Betsy in and of themselves. But the DIA representative led them patiently through an elaborate chain of analysis and deduction to demonstrate the true import of these photographs: namely, that the Iraqis had adapted their South African G-5 missiles to carry chemical and bacteriological payloads. This was not unexpected; no one had shown a greater willingness to use such weapons in the past than Saddam. However, two weeks after the invasion the thought that Americans might be the target—not Kurds or Vakhan Turks—lent a special and ominous urgency to the information.

After that they flew back to D.C., and each went his or her separate way in his or her separate bureaucracy. Betsy went back to her job, and, she assumed, so did the other members of the task force. The only difference was that they had to meet once a week, on the tenth floor of the New Executive Office Building, to discuss their progress, in a living reenactment of the old Indian tale of the blind men and the elephant. All of the members had been terribly busy even before they'd been named to the task force, and the weekly two-hour meeting was a huge bite out of their time budgets. Since everybody could simply read everybody else's stuff, Betsy didn't understand, at first, why they had to go through the formal oral presentations every Monday.

Each member of the task force had his or her weekly presentation ready and weekly paper turned in on time, with the exception of Hennessey, who played mum. The first time this happened, Betsy assumed that it was an oversight. The second time she realized it was a pattern, and all her good-girl instincts were appalled. What would the taxpayers say? When Hennessey showed up for the third meeting with nothing to say and nothing to hand out, a subtle change came over the task force. Simply by not having said anything, Hennessey had taken on a certain air of authority. Millikan, of course, did not preside over the meetings—his assistant, Dellinger, did. Since Dellinger's only role seemed to be to remind the group over and over that anything of substance had to go through Millikan, the members of the task force rapidly stopped paying attention to him. An unspoken competition arose. When people took their seats around the table, they turned toward Hennessey. When they gave their presentations, they faced Hennessey. When one of them handed out a newly minted classified document, the author would watch Hennessey's face as he scanned through the pages; and if Hennessey didn't bother even to leaf through it, the author would be humiliated and defensive for the rest of the meeting. In this way, simply by doing nothing—by withholding information—Hennessey took on a certain gravity that made him into the éminence grise, the undisputed defacto leader of Millikan's task force.

The NSF guys believed that the Iraqis had been carrying out some advanced research in DNA technology, to develop a means to alter their forces' genetic codes in such a way so that when they attacked with their chemical/biological agents (the distinction between chemical and biological was blurry in this case) only those with the genetic protection would survive. This had the advantage that changes in wind would not alter the weapons' usefulness, and conquered territory could be occupied without delay. They had some substantial evidence that the Iraqis had tried to work with such techniques in experiments with animals, and Betsy was able to bolster that theory with the information she had developed about the distribution of Iraqi student visas to schools with advanced veterinary-medicine programs.

The Army knew gas. Had worked with gas since World War I. Was afraid of germs. Knew little about them. The military guys came in with their flip charts and meteorological charts to explain how and why the Iraqis would use gas. They were not stupid. As the group that had to actually put the rubber to the road, they had to deal with the situation with the tools they had at hand.

The people at NSA always prided themselves on knowing things—which they did. But they weren't good at organizing their knowledge into a decent presentation. They were like people who owned a large furniture store but had no idea about how to arrange things. They had incredible infrared satellite imagery, they could spot small buildings that might be rather large biological warfare sites, they had phone intercepts, they had every Iraqi checking account under surveillance. But they had no overall notion of what Saddam was up to in this area.

A couple of treasury types sat in and had interesting ideas on the flow of cash to and from Iraq, as well as a complete guide to the financial structure of the European chemical industry as it had evolved since the days of I. G. Farben. But nothing came together.

The State observer updated the group on his department's current policy: a psychological attack on all fronts to convince people of the Hitlerian tendencies of Saddam, the beginnings of the drive through Mubarak to isolate Saddam within the Arab community, the freezing of all Iraqi assets, and the use of the UN as a rallying point for the coming counterattack. Domestically, the spin doctors were trying to figure out the best way to justify the sending of American people out to a vast and foreboding desert to face unknown threats.

Spector and Betsy represented the Agency, and they split the work. Spector reviewed everything the Agency had done on the subject, from all aspects of the vast resources available to Langley, with no firm conclusion except that Saddam was probably up to something. Betsy pulled together all her records since 1989, and all the little think pieces she had written to herself, together with what she had learned, and what she suspected, about what was going on in the domain of Professor Larsen—and all the other Larsens at the other universities.

The night that Kevin and Margaret were attacked in Adams-Morgan was the one, ghastly interruption in the cobwebbed life that Betsy led in the weeks following her trip to Kennebunkport. On that Friday night, she had come home late from work, where she'd been trying to pull her report together in preparation for the Monday meeting. The streets of Rosslyn had been crowded with foreign students and officials in town for the NAISS convention, which had only reminded her of the futility of her quest.

When she got back to her apartment, she smelled vomit in the hallway, not quite masked by the sharp scent of ammonia floor cleaner. She knew that it must be connected to Kevin somehow.

She opened her door and found Kevin sprawled across the living-room sofa, looking sick unto death, and Cassie in the kitchen talking on the telephone in low tones. Cassie was wearing a T-shirt. On top of that she wore a shoulder holster with a large gun in it.

Cassie interrupted whoever was on the other end of the line. "Can I call you back?" she asked in a hoarse voice, and then hung up without waiting for an answer. She turned and leveled her gaze at Betsy. Her eyes were red. "Found him passed out in front of our door with a bottle of gin in his lap," she said. "There was quite a mess."

"I'm so sorry, Cassie. You shouldn't have to put up with his behavior."

"Skip it. You want to know why he was there, in that condition?"

"Because he's an alcoholic?"

"He and a friend got mugged."

"Mugged! Where?"

"Adams-Morgan. Two young Hispanic males approached them while they were sitting in their car. Pulled guns. Demanded their money. Something went wrong. Or maybe they just got jumpy. Shots were fired. Couple of them went right by your brother's head. Few more went into his friend's body."

"He's hurt?"

"She."

"Who was he with?"

"Our neighbor."

"Margaret's hurt?"

"Margaret," Cassie said, "is dead."

Kevin had got up the next morning, declined to talk about anything, declined to eat, refused to accept a ride to the airport.

Had told a vague rendition of the story more or less like Cassie's. He had flown back to Wapsipinicon and stopped answering his telephone. But he continued to change the message on his answering machine several times a day, just to let people know he was still there.

So if someone had been trying to shut Kevin up, they had succeeded.

Margaret's body had been flown back to Oakland, California, her parents' hometown, for a closed-casket funeral.

The *Post* and the *Times* had run their boilerplate, fill-in-the-blank crime stories about the assault, which had competed for space against stories of the five other murders that had taken place in D.C. and Prince George's County on the same night. These had been followed the next day by boilerplate analysis of how the incredibly high murder rate on the east side of the District rarely leaked over into the west side, and when it did, people were always more shocked than they should be. Police were still on the lookout for a pair of Hispanic males who had been seen tampering with a nearby streetlight shortly before the attack.

After that the assault on Betsy's brother's life, and the death of Margaret Park-O'Neil, had been forgotten entirely by the news media, which seemed to be preoccupied with events in Kuwait, and with newer and fresher murders.

The executive summary of Betsy's fifty-page report was clear and to the point, and even Hennessey read it:

—Baghdad has for years been coordinating a high-tech, high-science effort among like-minded Arab states using the resources and expertise of the American academic community.

—During the last two years major land-grant universities across the United States have been targeted by Baghdad for major research efforts to perfect a bacteriological-warfare agent that is simple, effective, and transportable.

—There have been substantial movements within the scientific faculties of Iraq, the gaps filled by adjunct professors brought in at short notice, and high pay, from across the Arab world.

—USIA student/research visas show a three-hundred-percent increase in the number of students coming from the region to study at eight major land-grant universities in the United States. We have reason to believe that many of these students are traveling under cover.

—The Iraqis are carrying out substantial bacteriological-warfare investigation using U.S. facilities and personnel in order to assure that even if there were preemptive strikes on their known installations, their efforts could continue.

In comparison with the other reports, the thoroughness of Betsy's report was overwhelming, so much so that there was a respectful silence across the room. As had become the norm, everyone turned to look at Hennessey, who made an "I'm impressed" face and paged slowly through the document.

Dellinger didn't even read it. He closed the meeting by saying, "The National Security Council has seen all of these reports and recommends going full speed ahead on all inquiries, *except* Ms. Vandeventer's." With quiet scorn in his voice he said, "You evidently did not see the special-committee report—the Universities' Report of March 1988—that concluded that there was absolutely no threat to the national security of the United States in the full and open exchange of scientific and technical work."

Hennessey caught Betsy's eye and shook his head, telling her to keep quiet. But she did not. The thought of bullets whizzing past her brother's head had made her feel somehow reckless. "Yes, I know that report. It was written by a bunch of self-interested university presidents who needed foreign-student funding and brains to keep their own research efforts going. It was supported by a number of international research organizations that needed USG funds to carry their work now that their capital has dwindled. It was written by a bunch of ivory-tower researchers to whom the entire world is as interchangeable as airports. I know that report."

Dellinger listened to this with a brittle and condescending smile, then turned to Spector and said, "I'm sure that Mr. Spector can continue to supply Agency input into this process. Ms. Vandeventer's contributions have been duly noted, and her participation will no longer be needed. This meeting is concluded. I'll see the rest of you next week, same time, same place."

After the meeting in March with the agricultural attaché, in which Betsy had spilled the beans about her extracurricular research, Howard King had grabbed Betsy's breast and then shoved her into a filing cabinet. She had, by dint of a tremendous effort of will, made it through that entire experience without crying.

Now it was Millikan's turn to punish her for the same infraction. He had tried to do it in the meeting at Langley back in April and been stymied by the tactic that Spector had suggested. But he hadn't forgotten. He'd been watching and waiting for the opportunity to shove in the knife. And now he had done it.

A year ago she might have burst out crying on the spot. A week ago she would have gone home and done her crying in her bedroom, which was private except insofar as it was bugged.

She walked calmly to the elevator and checked out at the security post downstairs. Spector left her alone. She caught the tube, got off at Rosslyn. Walked up the hill. Got to the apartment. Closed and locked the door behind her. Put her stuff down and took a seat on the living-room sofa.

But she didn't even think about crying. A strange kind of anesthetic calm had settled over her. She picked up the remote control, turned on CNN to watch the latest news from the Gulf, and wondered, idly, whether this was the last phase in her slow metamorphosis into an iguana.

thirty-two

WHILE THE disassembled corpses of ten or a dozen chickens wrestled in a turbulent pot of boiling lard on Mrs. Dhont's smelter-grade stove, Clyde and the Dhonts and various shirttail relatives and neighbors played football in the recently harvested cornfield. The corn stubble had mostly been plowed under, but much of it still projected from the ground at crazy angles like pungi stakes. Despite these and other hazards, Clyde acquitted himself honorably, considering that several members of the opposing team had won Olympic wrestling medals. Clyde had developed survival strategies over the years: for example, rather than trying to block a Dhont, he would simply dive to the ground in the youth's path, like an exposed farmer crouching down before the onslaught of a funnel cloud, and often as not the attacker would crash into him, jackknife forward, and plant his face securely in the earth.

Mrs. Dhont rang the dinner bell, which according to Dhont rules meant that the game had entered its last series of downs. Clyde was beginning to entertain the notion that he might escape from this game with no broken bones, just a few lacerations and widespread bruising. Then, while out on the left wing trying to block one of the older and smaller Dhonts, he heard Dan, Jr., the quarterback of his team, yelling at him, and turned around. There was the ball, no more than a yard away from him, boring in like a dirty artillery shell. He caught it on impulse. Given more time to think about the implications, he might have dropped it. A general cry of approval and bloodlust rose from the defense, which was now scattered over approximately a square mile of churned black ground. The barbed-wire fence that marked the goal line was at the other end of this expanse, though Clyde's view of it was partly obscured by the curvature of the earth. He tucked the ball into the pit of his stomach and crossed both arms over it, which was an ungainly way to run, but de rigueur when playing against massed Dhonts. Then he began to run. One side of his pelvis had been staved in by the knee of Dylan Dhont when he'd blocked him on the previous play, and so he moved in a nearly sideways, crablike stutter.

A bulky mass materialized in his peripheral vision: Hal Dhont, one of the cousins, a three-hundred-pounder who was on Clyde's team. Hal churned forward, tearing across the soil like a rogue combine, and they gained a quarter mile of yardage before encountering any organized opposition. Hal converged on DeWayne Dhont, who tried to evade him; but at the last moment Hal stuck one arm out sideways and clotheslined DeWayne. Hal then slammed his body into another Dhont and came almost to a stop. Clyde rear-ended him, spun around his back, and broke into the open. He was unsure of his bearings; the size of the playing field almost forced the players to carry compasses and sextants. When he finally identified the goal line, he was dismayed to see that no fewer than three Dhonts were guarding it. One of them was Desmond—currently a first-string Twisters wrestler, who, as all local police officers knew, went out with his teammates and hunted football players for sport.

It would be several minutes before he reached them, and there was no point in trying his courage with it just yet. He jogged for a while, attempting to catch his breath and to get his mind on other things. He put some more thought into the recent murder of Dr. Kevin Vandeventer.

Clyde came into the sheriff's department at four in the afternoon and saw the report coming in on the wire. He tore it off and read through it three times carefully. It had originated from a South Dakota Highway Patrol base in the western part of that state. Last night a trooper, westbound on I-90, had pulled through a rest area at four in the morning and noticed a car with Idaho plates stopped in the parking lot, one occupant asleep in the passenger seat, which had been reclined. This was technically illegal, but the highway patrol was in the habit of looking the other way; in that part of the country, where towns and motels were few and far between, it was a common practice for long-haul truckers to park their rigs in the rest areas of the interstate at night and to sleep there.

Several hours later another trooper had noticed the same car in the same place with the same person in it. It was midmorning, the outside temperature was already eighty-five, the sun was blasting in through the windows of the car, yet this motorist was still sound asleep with a blanket over him. He did not respond to knocking on the window. The trooper Slim Jimmed the door open. Although this was not explicitly stated in the report, Clyde knew that when the trooper had opened the door of that car, he had taken a deep breath and held it, and perhaps stepped back away from the vehicle for a few moments to let the first roiling wave of stench dissipate. If Clyde had been there, he would have opened both doors of Kevin Vandeventer's car so that the South Dakota wind could blow through it.

Vandeventer had been dead since about three in the morning. The local coroner's report stated that his neck had been broken by someone who had done a very neat job of it. There was no physical evidence anywhere—and if it had been done in the men's room, there never would be, because it had been thoroughly scrubbed and sterilized by the custodial service at eight in the morning.

The state patrol kept records of which trucks passed through its weigh stations at which times. From these it was possible to draw some inferences about which trucks had been in the vicinity of that rest area at the time of the murder. They were still trying to track down the truckers in question by telephone and radio, interviewing them when they stopped at other weigh stations along I-90 in Wyoming and Montana. So far none of them had seen anything, except for one insomniac who had seen headlight beams sweep across the walls of his sleeper cab at about three in the morning. He had looked out the window to see a car in the final stages of making an illegal U-turn in the median strip of the interstate. He could not remember any details about the car, which had taken off eastbound. Headed for Iowa.

The troopers had found tracks in the grass of the median strip that corresponded to this report. But the ground was hard and dry, and no useful impressions had been made in the dirt. A couple of speeding tickets had been issued to eastbound vehicles on I-90 during the wee hours of the morning, and these drivers were being interviewed. But Clyde knew that these leads would not amount to anything. If he were an Iraqi secret agent on hostile territory during wartime, and he had just broken a man's neck with his bare hands out in the middle of nowhere and was driving back to his safe house 650 miles away, he would be sure to observe posted speed limits.

It was a thirteen-hour drive from there to Wapsipinicon if you drove at exactly the speed limit and never stopped at all, which was impossible. Clyde figured that fifteen or sixteen hours was more realistic. They would come east on I-80 from Des Moines, head northeast on I-45 for a short distance, and then, most likely, take the University Avenue exit, which would bring them due north into the center of Wapsipinicon.

At six o'clock in the evening Clyde drove into Wapsipinicon and headed south of town on University Avenue, then took that several miles down to the cloverleaf where it intersected I-45. The geometry of the intersection was such that northbound traffic on I-45 had to make a 315-degree right turn, nearly a complete circle, in order to head north on University. People ran off the road there all the time, especially during the winter; before Twisters games a few RVs always rolled over into the ditch as they tried to negotiate the turn in too much of a hurry. It was posted at twenty miles per hour and festooned with signs prophesying doom to speeders.

Clyde knew it well. He parked his unit where he would have a clear view of all traffic on the ramp. Then he made himself comfortable and waited. A car or truck swung round the ramp every few minutes and headed north into town.

At 6:47 by his dashboard clock one such car happened to catch his eye. It was a maroon Bronco, a couple of years old. It had dark-tinted windows, which was a bit out of the ordinary, but still common around the university, being apparently some kind of status symbol among hot-rodders and party animals. But what really caught Clyde's eye was that the front of the Bronco—its bumper, grille, hood, and windshield—were encrusted with the smashed and dried remains of insects. This was obvious and incontrovertible proof that this vehicle had just been driven for several hundreds of miles at high speed across the plains.

Clyde zapped it with his radar gun and noted that it was taking the ramp at an even nineteen miles an hour. He waited for another car to go by him, then pulled onto University and discreetly followed the Bronco north into the city of Wapsipinicon. It was the sort of vehicle that rode high on its suspension, which made it easy to track from a distance.

A few blocks short of Lincoln Way, the Bronco turned right onto a gravel alleyway that ran along the backs of several commercial buildings that were part of the old business district. Clyde gunned his unit forward, fearing that the vehicle might lose him back there. He turned into the alley and did not see it anywhere ahead of him. He ran the unit forward to the end of the block, pulled out across the sidewalk, and looked both directions up and down the street but did not see the Bronco in either direction. He threw the unit into reverse and backed down the way he had just come, looking for possible turns that his quarry might have taken.

He found the Bronco parked in the lot behind Stohlman's Stationers, next to a steel door in the back of the building, which had been propped open. The rear doors of the Bronco were likewise open, and Roger Ossian, three-time winner of the North Central Regional Stationery and Office Supply Retailers Association Salesman of the Year Award, was unloading some boxed photocopying machines that he had apparently just picked up from a distributor in Des Moines or Omaha. Seeing Clyde Banks staring at him glumly through the window of a sheriff's car, he set his load down on the rear shelf of the Bronco and threw Clyde a friendly wave. He was a thoroughgoing Republican.

Clyde gave him a friendly tap on the horn, shifted the unit into drive, and idled up the alley to the street. Three right turns in a row got him northbound on University once again. Three blocks later he pulled in at McDonald's for some drive-through. But the lane was filled with waiting students as usual, so he parked in the parking lot and went inside to place his order.

As he emerged from the McDonald's with his Quarter-Pounder and fries, he heard a wet hissing sound from the next lot and glanced over to see a car emerging from Nor-Kay's Car Wash.

He plucked out three french fries to tide him over, then set his dinner on the hood of his unit, which would act as a hot plate, walked across the lot, and onto the property of Norman and Kay Duvall, monarchs of the Forks County car-washing industry. A solitary employee was holding down the fort this evening—an earnest fellow of maybe sixteen years.

"Hullo, Deputy Banks. Come campaigning?"

"Nope. Not on company time," Clyde said. "I was just wondering if you'd washed any cars in the last couple of hours that had a lot of bugs on 'em. I mean a *lot* of bugs." But the boy was already nodding vigorously.

"You wouldn't believe this car I did just a little while ago," he blurted, as if the mess had left him so traumatized he couldn't wait to share his feelings. "It was covered with an *encrustation,*" he said. "Came in from out west."

"How do you know that?"

"You learn," the boy said. "Bugs are different out there—when you see a lot of big old fat grasshoppers stuck in the grille, that tells you they came in from the west."

"What kind of car was it?"

"A light-blue Escort. Couple of years old."

Clyde winced. The Escort was a ubiquitous car. "Anything special about it? Any accident damage, any aftermarket add-ons?"

"Except for tinted windows, it was just a plain old stock Escort."

"Can you describe the driver?"

"Nope. Tinted windows."

"But didn't he at least roll the window down?"

"Just about an inch. Stuck a ten-dollar bill out through the crack. Didn't want any change. Didn't say a word."

"Well, did you at least see his hands?"

"He had big old hands. A couple of rings on 'em."

"Class rings? Wedding rings?"

The boy scrunched up his face, at a loss for words. "Not really either one, come to think of it. Just sort of nice-looking rings."

"Expensive?"

"Yeah. Kind of flashy. Gold."

"Thanks," Clyde said. "Give me a call down at the sheriff's department if you see him come through here again."

"Will do."

But Clyde knew, as he walked back to his car, that the man in the light-blue Escort would never come back to the same place again. A big old crow was flapping around Clyde's unit with an eye on the sack of food; Clyde ran forward and shooed it away, surprising himself with how angry he was.

Someone approached him from behind, and he turned to see twenty-one-year-old Del Dhont, who was on his team.

"Clyde!" he gasped.

Clyde sped up as fast as he could.

"Clyde!" Del said again, sounding a bit wounded. They were some thirty yards from the goal line now, and the defenders had begun to run toward Clyde, building up speed for an apocalyptic collision.

"Clyde!" Del shouted, outraged by Clyde's pigheadedness. "Slow down for half a sec and I'll block 'em!"

Clyde pounded forward another ten paces, then turned back and lateraled the ball toward Del, whose finely honed Dhont reflexes took over; he caught the ball and tucked it expertly beneath one arm before his brain had worked out the implications. One of the defenders—not Desmond—smacked into Clyde and knocked him on his backside. Desmond and the third defender plowed into Del at warp speed, sending him flying backward through the air for some distance before he even hit the ground. The ball bounced loose; the defender who'd bumped into Clyde scooped it up and started running the other way. Clyde stuck around long enough to check Del's vital signs, then trudged back toward the house. The dinner bell was ringing.

Fried chicken came out borne on an oval platter the size of a stretcher; Mrs. Dhont and one of her daughters-in-law each had to take an end of it as they maneuvered through the doorway from the kitchen. Mr. Dhont had fashioned a table from a single four-by-eight-foot sheet of inch-thick plywood, which was suitable for intimate dinners but nowhere near big enough for these larger family feeds. At such times he had a couple of his sons go down to the rec room, fold up the five-by-ten-foot Ping-Pong table, wrestle it up the stairs, and graft it onto the old four-by-eight-footer. This provided a total of some fifty feet of linear seating space, plus generous acreage in the center for stockpiling of strategic food reserves.

As a rule of thumb Mrs. Dhont liked to slaughter and cook one chicken per guest, and the heap of grayish, blood-flecked feathers in the side yard testified that she had done her best this morning; but there had still been a shortfall, and so she had also heated up some selections that had been mellowing in one of her deepfreezes: a side of roast beef, and a ham the size of a short-block Chevy V8, which continuously orbited the fifty-foot circumference of the makeshift table on their own platters. Clyde was hardly able to eat for all of his platter-passing obligations.

He snapped out of a reverie. Someone had just asked him something, and everyone was watching him and waiting for an answer. They all seemed to have vaguely malicious looks on their faces.

"Beg pardon?" he said.

"I said," Darius said, "Princess cooked up real good, didn't she?" He nodded at the big haunch of meat on the platter.

Princess was Desiree's horse. She'd been presented to Desiree as a Christmas present when Desiree was twelve. She must be twenty-five years old by now; Desiree still came out to fuss over her every week or two. She had not been ridden, nor done any productive work, in a decade. The Dhonts, who liked their humor predictable, could scarcely make it through a dinner without speculating as to Princess's possible merits as a source of nutrition.

Clyde was obligated to play along. "Finally retired her, huh?"

Much smirking around the table. "No kidding this time," Darius said. "Go and have a look."

They wouldn't leave him alone until he looked. So he excused himself and went over to a window from which he could see the stable that had been Princess's home.

The stable was gone. A new concrete slab had been poured in its place, bolts and pipes sticking up out of it.

Everyone laughed at the surprise on Clyde's face.

He returned to the table, eyeing the big piece of meat. "Princess must've spent too much time hanging out with the cattle," he said, " 'cause she sure tastes like beef to me."

More laughter. Clyde continued, "I'll tell Desiree next time she calls."

This forced them to own up. "We're just pulling your leg, Clyde," Dick said. "We took her over to the vet lab. She's fine."

"What are they going to do to Princess over at the vet lab?"

No one was exactly sure. Finally Mr. Dhont spoke up. "She's doing her patriotic duty. Just like Desiree."

"What's that mean in the case of an old horse?"

Mr. Dhont shook his head. "Don't really know. We weren't encouraged to ask," he said significantly.

"They put out a call for old horses," Dick said. "If you had a horse who was about to end up in a hopper at Byproducts Unlimited, you could just call the vet lab and they'd come around and take it off your hands for free."

"You were going to knacker Princess?"

"Of course not, honey," Mrs. Dhont said, "we'd never do that. But the man from the vet lab said that all these horses had to do was give blood every so often."

"What're they doing with horse blood?"

"They won't divulge that," Mr. Dhont said bluntly. He looked a little miffed at Clyde's prying.

"We felt that since all Princess ever did was mow the lawn anyway, she might as well do it for a good cause."

"How many horses they have over there now?" Clyde asked, trying to sound offhanded about it.

No one was sure; all the Dhonts looked back and forth at each other. "Bunch of people have participated in the program," Dick finally said.

"When did the program start?" Clyde said.

"Lot of questions," Mr. Dhont grunted.

"Desiree's going to ask me all this when I tell her about Princess," Clyde explained, "so we might as well get it over with."

Dan Dhont, Jr., finished chewing something big and said, "The first time I heard about it was a month ago."

"Middle or late August?" Clyde said.

"Yup," Dan, Jr., said.

That put an end to the conversation; Dan had as much as admitted that the mysterious horse program had something to do with Saddam Hussein, and Saddam was a forbidden subject at that table ever since Desiree had been called up.

thirty-three

THE SECURE phone in the closet began to ring just after lunch one Saturday afternoon. Betsy's first thought was that it must be Kevin calling from the road to give her an update. He'd left a message yesterday morning announcing that he was bailing out of his life: he'd resigned from his job with the Rainmaker, packed some stuff into his Camry, and was about to hit the road, westbound. He wasn't going to stop until he reached Nampa, or perhaps even the West Coast. The funny thing was that he didn't sound drunk at all. He sounded more sober than he had in months.

But it was irrational for her to think that Kevin could reach her on the secure phone. Only a few people seemed to have access to that. She picked it up and heard the familiar voice of Edward Seamus Hennessey: "Nice afternoon—the temperature's not more than a hundred, the humidity's not more than ninety-five percent, the ozone count is setting records. Meet you at Iwo Jima in fifteen minutes."

It was a five-minute walk for Betsy to the Iwo Jima memorial. During the summer she went there on occasional Tuesday evenings to watch the Marine Corps color guard do their precision drill—she especially liked the "silent drill" in which, for a full twenty minutes, the beautifully schooled Marines performed with better than clockwork precision while the sunset turned the buildings along the Mall and the Capitol into infinite shades of pink and orange.

Today was not a day to be out at the monument. As Hennessey had pointed out, the weather was typically appalling. But Betsy had been indoors since yesterday afternoon, doing laundry and cleaning house, and she needed to get out even if the day was miserable. She walked around the base of the statue and read the names of all the battles the Marines had fought. She stopped at the south end of the statue, looked up the flagpole, and saw the hands reaching to plant it in the forbidding soil of Mount Suribachi.

At times like this, or when she walked the Vietnam Wall searching for the name of her cousin who had died there, or went to the Lincoln and read the walls, she loved her country. And when she loved her country, she could actually wax indignant about what she'd been going through. She should have felt that way all the time, of course, but nowadays it took a trip to a major national monument to get her into the right perspective.

She knew that to be seen having a private tête-à-tête with Hennessey was a career-ender, but that hardly mattered at this point. It was time to get out of D.C. Time to bail, just as Kevin had bailed.

She didn't know what she would do in Nampa. But as she read the names of the battles and thought of the young people who had died, sometimes wastefully, for the U.S., she began to understand. Wars were more than battles between declared enemies; they went on at all levels at all times, and sometimes the innocent got killed. She had given her best, she had taken it in the neck, but she was still alive, and there was a whole world outside the beltway where her name had not yet been sullied and where her career prospects ought to be fine. She turned to look through the ozone and pollen and humidity across the Potomac, across the Roosevelt Bridge, and saw the different shades of gray on Lincoln, Washington, and the Dome, the beautiful Dome, and then on to her right at the rolling waves of white headstones at Arlington. The thought that others may have died in these wars, some needlessly and stupidly, didn't make her feel justified—merely not alone.

She kept walking around the Iwo Jima reading the battles, and she ran into Hennessey, who did not see her.

"Nice day," Betsy said, aiming for a certain sense of irony.

Hennessey didn't answer. He was smoking a cigarette, looking nowhere in particular, and then he said, "My brother's up here." He motioned at a name. "He would have ended up drunk and in jail if he hadn't gone into the Marines and become a national hero. My family drinks too much. Always has. But we do interesting things, too. I'll never get my name carved in stone, of course."

He still hadn't looked at Betsy, and she moved over to lean against the rail around the monument. They were both exhausted, pained, frustrated. "Why do you stay?"

"I don't know. I guess I'm one of the few people around here who remembers what it was like to be proud to work for the government." Hennessey paused a bit. "You're a good kid. I wish you could have experienced this town during Truman—when I came onboard—or even under Kennedy." He paused again. "But that's not what I wanted to talk about. I brought you here so you could have some privacy."

"Privacy?" Betsy grinned and looked over at the line of idling tour buses in the parking area, the gangs of American and European tourists going to and fro.

"You know what I mean," Hennessey said.

"Isn't the phone in my closet good enough?"

"The enchanted telephone isn't appropriate for what I'm about to tell you," Hennessey said. He threw away his cigarette, turned to face Betsy, and drew himself erect, suddenly looking very much the government official.

Betsy remembered getting a tooth pulled once when she was a girl. Once the decision had been made and the go-ahead had been given, the dentist and his assistant had suddenly shifted into a higher gear and got the job done with startling speed. Ruthless, practiced efficiency. In a way, it seemed cold. But it was better that way.

Hennessey was operating in that mode right now, doing

something he had obviously done many times before. He'd made the decision and nothing could stop him. He took a step closer to Betsy, reached out, and grasped her upper arm firmly, looked her straight in the eye. Then he spoke some words to her that she didn't hear. But that didn't matter, because at some level she already knew, had known the moment Hennessey had reached her on the enchanted telephone.

The sweating, tired tourists circling dutifully around the Iwo Jima memorial were distracted, for a moment, by a woman's scream. It was a cry of anguish, not of fear. A heavyset female had collapsed to her knees and thrown both arms over her head and was clenching her thin auburn hair with both hands, as if she wanted to rip it all out. An older gentleman was bent over her with one hand on her shoulder, talking to her quietly. Some of the older tourists, who included many Marine veterans, felt a strange sensation of jumping back in time to the late 1940's, when the young widows of America's war dead had gone to the dedications of monuments such as this one and suddenly been overcome by grief.

This woman was far too young to have known anyone who had died in the war. The milling tourists could only speculate. But the older ones knew what they were seeing.

thirty-four

OCTOBER

COLUMBUS DAY weekend was nearly over, and Tab Templeton still had not shown up for work. Clyde had arranged with him last week to help out with some demolition in the basement of the apartment building. Demolition always went quickly when Tab was involved.

Clyde had encountered Tab at Hardware Hank a couple of weeks ago, pushing a cart loaded with PVC pipe. Rumor had it that Tab had been working regularly, doing odd jobs for someone or other, and Clyde had learned that he could no longer simply cruise the streets, pick him up off a park bench, and put him to work; he had to have an appointment.

But for Tab to make an appointment and for him to remember it were two unrelated propositions. He'd apparently forgotten this one. Clyde had spent the weekend dithering. He would pound away with the sledgehammer for a while, grow tired, and remember that Tab could get this work done four times faster; so time spent searching for him should be time well spent. He would get in the car and cruise by Tab's usual park benches, vacant buildings, bars, and restaurant Dumpsters, then become despondent after an hour or two when he thought of all the time he had wasted. He would go back to the sledgehammer and repeat the cycle. Now twilight was approaching on the last day of the three-day weekend. He had an appreciable heap of debris in the back of his truck but nothing close to what he'd planned on. And he was due to pick up Maggie from one of the Dhonts in another hour or two.

He did something so unexpected that he surprised even himself: he went out for a beer. All weekend long he had been driving past the old Stonefield Brewery, a blazing red-sandstone building in downtown Nishnabotna that might have passed for a fortress if it hadn't been so ornate and Victorian. Jack Carlson, a descendant of one of the less august branches of the Stonefield family, had bought the place ten years ago after it had gone out of business trying to make the same sort of thin yellow swill that came out of the big Milwaukee breweries. All the old copper vessels were still intact. He had begun brewing darker, heavier stuff and had succeeded beyond anyone's wildest imagination.

Jack Carlson and Clyde Banks had known each other since they'd been kids, and Jack was always urging Clyde to stop by and have a beer. Clyde rarely did, but tonight he was tired and dirty and lonesome and thirsty and felt that he could consume a beer without being racked by guilt.

Besides, he could always claim it was a campaign appearance.

He sat at the bar, a nice mahogany one that Jack had scavenged from a failed tavern in Chicago, and ordered a pint of bitter.

After a few minutes Jack Carlson himself came out from the office in back and made a fuss over Clyde. He drew himself a beer, reasoning that this was a special occasion, and then the two went to a booth and sat down to catch up with each other. Clyde had to explain why he was covered with Sheetrock dust, and this led him to the subject of Tab Templeton.

"Saw him a couple of times last month," Jack said.

"He was *here*?"

"A few times," Jack said, savoring Clyde's astonishment.

"Heard he was working for someone. Wouldn't think he'd earn enough to drink *here*."

"He wasn't drinking," Jack said. Then, seeing the look on Clyde's face, he corrected himself. "Well, he was, of course, in the general sense. But he didn't come here to drink beer. He came to pick up yeast."

"He came to pick up yeast," Clyde repeated.

"Brewer's yeast," Jack said. "Forms quite a thick layer of sludge down there in the bottoms of our fermentation vessels. We clean it out and try to find something to do with it besides just throwing it away and polluting the water. Lot of times we sell it to health-food companies—it's full of vitamins. Last month we sold some to Tab."

"How much?"

Jack shrugged. "Maybe half a dozen steel drums full." Jack grinned at the memory. "You should see Tab sling a drum around. He's like a human forklift."

"Well, what the heck would Tab want with that much brewer's yeast?"

"Seemed clear from the way he was talking that he was moving the stuff for his employer."

"And who was that, do you suppose?"

Jack shrugged. "Someone who needed yeast and didn't have the muscle to hump the drums around town."

"Did they pay for it?"

"Yeah. We charge a nominal fee."

"Whose name was on the checks?"

"Tab paid cash."

Clyde slumped back in his seat and tried to imagine such a thing: someone entrusting Tab with a wad of bills.

"Maybe someone's doing an experiment with the stuff up at the university," Jack said, nodding toward the bluffs. "Or maybe some vegetarians up there are trying to start up their own health-food company."

"What was he driving?"

"A big old van."

"Can you describe the van to me?"

"Dark and old. Probably a Chevy."

"Could it have been a black van?"

"Could've. Why?"

"Just curious."

"Yeah," Jack Carlson said, "and I'm just brewing beer for a hobby."

Lots of mail came the next day, including a few letters from Desiree. They'd done a mass-casualty drill that weekend, so she hadn't been able to come home and Clyde hadn't been able to visit her. She was dealing with the guilt by writing every day and calling at bedtime to coo into Maggie's ear over the phone.

> Still sticking needles into butts like mad. Lots of nice diseases over there in the Gulf. Many of the reservists not up to snuff physically—can't believe some of them got into the service in the first place. Had a young man in here with a scar up his chest like a zipper—he'd had open-heart surgery as a boy and somehow got into the Army anyway.

> Getting geared up for the mass-casualty drill this weekend. Lots of triage tags floating around—one is enclosed.

She had enclosed a cardboard tag on a loop of string, apparently made to go around a patient's neck. The tag was about three by six inches and bore lines for the patient's name and notes on his condition. At the bottom were three colored strips attached by perforations, so that they could easily be torn off. The strip on the bottom was green and bore a cartoon of a tortoise.

> If we leave the bottom (green) strip attached, it means the patient is basically okay, there's no big rush. If we tear it off, what's left is the yellow strip with the picture of the hare on it—that means better hurry and get this one some attention. If we tear that off, what's left is the red strip with the picture of the speeding ambulance on it.

Tactfully, she didn't explain what Clyde could see with his own eyes: if the red strip was torn off, what remained was a black strip with a little icon that might have been a cross; but when he looked closer, he saw it was probably supposed to be a dagger.

> We know all about nasty old anthrax now and so they are training us in something more exotic: botulin toxin. They think Saddam may have some of that in his stockpile, too. I hope they're wrong, because though we have tons and tons of anthrax vaccine, the botulin serum is in very short supply. I suppose they are trying to make more, but it's a slow process. Apparently you can't just crank the stuff out like sausage. They gave us some handouts to read—mostly copies of research papers. Gave my little Iowan heart a thrill to see that a lot of this research comes from our very own hometown. Remember Dr. Folkes, the old man who rides his bicycle to work? Turns out what he's been doing all this time is studying botulin. So his name and the name of our fair city are all over this research.
>
> Give the little one a big hug and kiss for me. I've been thinking that when I get out of this in one piece, we should give her a new little brother or sister as a present for Christmas ninety-one. We've been holding off, I know, but now I want to do everything right away.

thirty-five

"DR. FOLKES? Clyde Banks. Sorry to disturb you in the evening like this, but as you may have heard, I'm running for Forks County sheriff, and I've made a personal commitment to knock on every door in the county before the election, and, well, your turn just came up."

Dr. Arthur Folkes had emerged onto the porch and now peered at his visitor through large glasses with lenses even thicker than Clyde's. Between the two of them they must be separated by a good inch of expensively ground glass. Rumor had it that he was in his mid-eighties. He certainly looked that way from the shoulders up; his blotched scalp was completely bald, and loose flesh sagged from his neck and jowls. But he moved like a sixty-year-old fencing master. For decades he had been making a spectacle of himself by riding his Raleigh to the university every day, snow or shine. Every few years, just to break the monotony, he got run off the road by a thoughtless student or careening school bus and racked up a few weeks in a body cast.

"That's okay. Haven't had any peace anyway," he said. "Door's open."

Clyde opened the screen door, wiped his feet carefully on the mat, and stepped in. Dr. Folkes had already retreated inside the house, so Clyde crossed the porch, made another show of wiping his feet on a second mat, and entered. It had the wet human smell that he had learned to associate with houses where people had grown old. There was another smell, too, a hospital smell, though Clyde didn't consciously recognize it for a while.

He had lost Dr. Folkes's trail and stood uncertainly in the foyer until he heard the old professor's voice from the kitchen. "Don't worry, I'm not going to trap you here for hours. You get a lot of old people doing that to you?"

"Some folks are quite pleased to receive a visitor," Clyde allowed.

"Got something going on the stove and want to keep an eye on it," Folkes said.

Clyde found his way into the kitchen and discovered Folkes frying up some Italian sausages. "I'd offer you some, but I know you probably want to exchange some pleasantries and move on."

Clyde said nothing to this remark, still trying to work out whether his host was trying to be polite or rude.

"Not much of a politician, are you?" Folkes said, eyeing him through a column of fennel-scented steam.

The telephone began ringing. Dr. Folkes ignored it. Clyde wondered whether he was hard of hearing; but he'd heard the doorbell.

"No, sir, I don't imagine that I am."

"I'm kind of a knee-jerk Democrat. Like most academics, I guess."

"That's a decision I respect, sir. But you may find that the traditional policy differences that separate the two parties don't have much relevance in the position of county sheriff."

"Ah. Well-oiled riposte."

The phone stopped ringing after nine or ten times, then immediately started ringing again. "Hate it when people call during dinnertime," Dr. Folkes said.

"I have a handout here with some drunk-driving statistics—comparing Iowa's ninety-nine counties." Clyde laid a sheet of paper on the spotless avocado Formica of Dr. Folkes's kitchen counter.

"Hell," said Dr. Folkes, squinting at it from across the room. "You handwrote it. Don't you have a computer or a typewriter or something?"

"Thought the numbers spoke for themselves."

"What do they say?"

"We have the lowest rate of drunk-driving arrests and the highest rate of drunk-driving fatalities in the state."

"Ah. And you're thinking that as a bicyclist, this one is near and dear to me."

Clyde said nothing.

"Well, I'll review your statistics and probably vote for you. Satisfied?"

"No, sir."

Dr. Folkes was in the midst of transferring the sausages onto a marred plastic dinner plate decorated with large daisies. He stopped and peered at Clyde. "How's that? I said I'd vote for you. What do you want me to do? Go out and distribute campaign literature for you? I've already spent enough time pulling your bumper stickers out of my chainwheel."

"When I knocked on your door, you told me that you never got any peace in the evening. That makes me wonder whether you are having any problems that might be of interest to the sheriff's department. So even if I have your vote, I can't honestly say I'm satisfied until I've—"

"Oh, shit, no, it's nothing like that," Dr. Folkes said. Laughing, he turned his back on Clyde and carried his plate into the dining room. Clyde followed him there. "It's the goddamn phone calls, Mr. Banks."

"Prank calls?"

"I wish they were. No, it's work related. And it's nothing that you can help with. But thank you for making the offer."

"What's your line of work there at the university?" Clyde said, trying to sound conversational.

"I'm a microbiologist," Dr. Folkes said through a mouthful of sausage. "I study things that are yucky."

"Yucky?"

"Most of the time when people ask what I do, they don't really want to know. They are just being polite. If I really tell them, they get uncomfortable. Since I suspect that all you really want is to extricate yourself from this conversation and move on to the next house, I'm giving you an easy out." He looked at Clyde expectantly.

"Cop work is like that," Clyde said after a thoughtful pause. "Lots of high-speed road accidents. Farmers caught in grain augers and such."

Dr. Folkes nodded enthusiastically, seeming to find this analogy insightful.

"So I wouldn't say that I am easily grossed out," Clyde continued.

"Well, then, what I do is study a particular genus of bacterium called *Clostridium,* of which the best known is *C. botulinum*—the manufacturer of botulin toxin."

"People ever bring you tainted soup?"

"All the time. Most of it isn't tainted at all—just old. And the tainted stuff isn't always tainted with *C. botulinum.* But I have acquired some interesting strains that way, yes."

"What do you do with them?"

"Mostly freeze 'em. But I grow some of it."

"Pardon?"

"I grow it," Dr. Folkes said, mildly irritated. "Come here." He wadded up his napkin and threw it onto the table, then jumped to his feet, wheeled, and strode back through the kitchen to a door. The door opened onto a narrow, steep stairway descending into a dark basement. Dr. Folkes stomped down into darkness, his hand flailing above his head until it caught a length of twine strung through a line of screw eyes. Bluish light flickered from down below and then exploded as several long fluorescent fixtures came to life. Clyde followed him down the nearly vertical steps, hunching to avoid banging his head on the ceiling. The hospital smell became much stronger.

The basement was perhaps half the size of the house. One wall was bulging inward as the foundation wall gave way to the pressure of the soil and was being held at bay by a few massive timbers propped against it and anchored to the floor. An antique toilet was fixed to another wall, a rust-streaked porcelain tank above it with a cobwebbed pull chain dangling. In one corner, next to an ancient, stained laundry tub, was a heavy workbench made from a particleboard door set up on four-by-four legs. The workbench held a plethora of laboratory glassware, some of which was upside down on a rack of dowels, drying out, the rest containing fluids that were either transparent or muddy brown. Larger jugs sat on the floor underneath, containing what Clyde took to be bulk raw materials.

The most prominent object was a five-gallon glass carboy in

the middle of the workbench, filled to the shoulder with brown fluid veiled with yellow foam. Dr. Folkes was already there, eyeing it carefully. He waited until Clyde was standing right in front of it and allowed him to have a gander.

"See, now, right there," he said, "is enough botulin toxin to kill everyone in the state of Iowa."

Clyde stepped back a pace. "Are you joking?"

"When I'm joking, Mr. Banks, I try to say things that are actually funny."

"Well, isn't it dangerous to have it here?"

"Let me put it this way," Dr. Folkes said in a tired tone of voice, as if he were running through this explanation for the thousandth time. He went over to a Peg-Board where numerous tools were hanging, neatly arranged, and selected a clawhammer. "This hammer right here could kill everyone in the state of Iowa–if you went around and bashed their heads in with it. True?"

"Theoretically."

"But no one thinks it's unsafe for me to have a hammer in the basement. Now, do you want me to carry through with the analogy, or are we clear?"

"I follow," Clyde said. "But why are you doing it here? Don't you have a lab at the university?"

"Yes. But this isn't university work that I'm doing here. This is private. You know how Professor Larsen has all those spin-off companies out at the technology park?"

"I've heard he has several companies going there."

"Well, this is my spin-off, and it's got a better profit margin than anything that son of a gun will ever do. No overhead–except for this door and these four-by-fours from Hardware Hank."

"You make money from this?"

"Yep. Not a fortune by any means, but enough to buy me some nice vacations."

"How?"

"You mean, where exactly is the market for botulin toxin?"

"Right."

"It's used in medical treatments. The toxin works by paralyzing muscles. So, for example, if you have a wandering eye because some of the eye muscles are out of whack, the doctor injects a tiny amount of this toxin into the muscles that are too strong, paralyzing them."

Clyde mulled this one over. "If this is enough to kill three million people, then isn't that overkill for a few people with wandering eyes?"

"Very good," Dr. Folkes said. "It's massive overkill. Most of this stuff goes to the military."

"For weapons?"

Dr. Folkes looked disappointed in Clyde. "Nah! This wouldn't be enough for weapons production. They'd build a gold-plated assembly line somewhere for that. My stuff is used in preparing the antidote."

"How's that work?"

"They inject botulin toxin into horses. Small amounts at first. As the horse builds up an immunity, they inject progressively higher doses, until the amount of toxin running through that horse's bloodstream is a thousand times what would kill a human. They draw blood from the horse and isolate the immune protein, then shoot it into soldiers."

"Does it work?"

"Who knows? No one's ever used botulin toxin on an actual battlefield. Saddam's working on it, though."

The phone upstairs was ringing again.

"And that," Folkes said, "is why I never get any peace these days. *Military.*" He shook his head and rolled his eyes as he uttered the word, as if words could never express the depth and complexity of his relationship with the military. "They must have my phone number posted above every urinal in the Pentagon. So it's nice of you to ask, Mr. Banks. But I'm afraid you can't help me with the kind of hassles I've been getting."

Dr. Folkes turned away and began stomping up the stairs. "Kill the lights when you're done. Just don't touch anything if you want to make it out of this basement alive."

Clyde came up a few minutes after and found Dr. Folkes polishing off the last of his dinner. "Saw you had some brewer's yeast down there on your workbench," he said.

"Bacteria food," Dr. Folkes said. "*C. botulinum* needs that and a few other goodies."

"Such as?"

"Why? Going to grow some of your own?"

"Just curious."

"Sugar and chicken soup."

Clyde pondered the matter of chicken soup at some length. "Would beef or pork work?"

Dr. Folkes grimaced. "Don't take me literally. It's not really chicken soup. It's a solution of various proteins. Remember, the stuff grows wild in all kinds of soup that's been canned wrong. And I won't tell you anything more, because you already know enough to grow these little bugs in your own basement and compete with me and my little spin-off."

"Dr. Folkes, I realize that that was a facetious comment. But is it really that easy to grow this stuff?"

"You saw my setup down there. That look like million-dollar technology to you?"

"Well, Dr. Folkes, it sure has been interesting getting to know you a bit and talk about your work."

"Well, I hope you go out and catch some drunk drivers."

"I'll be sure and do that, sir, and I appreciate your vote. I'll see myself out."

thirty-six

IT WAS two o'clock in the morning of Clyde's night off. But he was in uniform anyway and brandishing an unfamiliar weapon: a metal detector. He had borrowed the implement from the frugal Ebenezer, who occasionally used it to seek lost treasure in the mud-covered floodplains of the local rivers after seasonal floods. When he had explained the nature of the night's errand, Ebenezer had even offered to sleep over at his house and keep an eye on Maggie. As Clyde stalked up and down the warehouse floor of Byproducts Unlimited in a bobbing pool of yellow light, he could not help wondering whether Maggie was awake, and what she would think when the gaunt, spectral face of Ebenezer swam into view above her crib.

Clyde was accompanied by one Chris, an edgy, chain-smoking, thirtyish rent-a-cop who had been deputized to hold Clyde's big black cop flashlight. In more blessed circumstances Clyde might have been annoyed to find himself wrapped in a moving cloud of acrid tobacco smoke, but there he was glad of anything that might deaden his sense of smell.

The warehouse adjoined the rendering floor on one side and the loading dock on the other. It was divided into long aisles by stacks of wooden cargo pallets, each pallet occupied by bulging plastic sacks stenciled with the legend "MegaPro: Packed with Pride at Byproducts Unlimited." For as long as Clyde could remember, Byproducts Unlimited had been a part of the landscape, its fleet of ramshackle box trucks careening down gravel farm roads with the stiff legs of dead livestock poking out the top. The animals' fat ended up in drums, destined for restaurants, and their protein ended up as MegaPro powder, used to make dog food and other delicacies.

The rent-a-cop dropped Clyde's flashlight while trying to light another cigarette, his hands gone clumsy with the October chill. He cursed, picked it up, apologized. Clyde said nothing, just moved on to the next pallet and scanned each sack in turn with the big disk of the metal detector.

The rent-a-cop had reason to be jumpy. His company had been hired on short notice a few days ago, when Byproducts found evidence of a break-in at one of their back doors. It seemed that these break-ins might actually have been going on for as long as a few weeks. Nothing important had been stolen, though, despite the fact that tools and VCRs and TV sets were lying out in plain sight in the company's workshops and offices. Tire tracks were noted in the dirt behind the building.

In a seemingly unrelated development, early-morning fishermen noticed a large, persistent gasoline slick near the end of a public pier up at Lake Pla-Mor. A diver was sent down and came up with the news that a black van rested on the bottom, fifty feet beneath the surface. The van was hauled out and examined, not only by local detectives but by some FBI people who drove out from Chicago. It was suspiciously free of useful evidence. Some prints were lifted from the driver's-side door, which had been found hanging open; they matched the prints of the oft-arrested, oft-fingerprinted Tab Templeton, who was still missing.

The tires of the van were examined and found to match the tracks behind Byproducts Unlimited. They also matched the tracks that Clyde had discovered at the site of the mutilation of Sweet Corn, the government horse. Sheriff Mullowney was photographed and videotaped standing proudly by the dripping, sludge-filled hulk of the Satan Van. He had wasted no time declaring that the War on Satan was over and won.

Clyde had examined the van himself. He had opened the driver's-side door and put his hands in the places where Tab's handprints were found. He had leaned against it, as if trying to push it forward, and satisfied himself that Tab had made those prints while shoving the van down the pier. This all made sense to a point; if Clyde wanted a large vehicle moved without using its engine, Tab would be the first and last candidate for the job. Rumors continued to circulate that Tab's skeleton had been found near the scuttled van, picked to the bone by the walleyed pike with which Lake Pla-Mor was stocked. But Clyde knew that Tab had been hired to sink that van, and that, if he was dead, he was dead for some other reason.

A handyman had discovered a nest of empty Night Train Express bottles and Twinkies wrappers in an unused janitor's closet at Byproducts Unlimited. Tab's fingerprints were all over the place. Sheriff Mullowney, eager to wrap up this case with a ribbon and a bow before Election Day, had set up a crisis headquarters on the riverbank out back—a borrowed RV with a large coffeemaker and donated pastries, patched into Byproducts by long, thick extension cords—and begun dragging the river day and night, hoping to find Tab's corpse.

It was three-thirty in the morning before Clyde found anything. Chris the rent-a-cop, asleep on his feet, was startled once more by the squeal of the metal detector and swung the light around to see that Clyde had it pressed up against one of the MegaPro sacks.

"Just hold the light right where it is," Clyde whispered, too scared and excited to speak out loud. He shut off the metal detector and laid it gently on the floor. He took an old Boy Scout knife out of his pocket, opened up the long blade, and slit the bag from top to bottom. Reddish-brown powder hissed onto the floor, smelling like dog food.

Something glinted yellow in the midst of it. Clyde thrust his hand into the pile of MegaPro, groped around, and withdrew a long colored ribbon. Something heavy followed and swung back and forth in the light of the flashlight, glinting a rich yellow. Clyde held the mangled treasure up in the light and gazed at it for a long time, and it suddenly dawned on Chris that, like an archaeologist in a pharaoh's tomb, he was looking at the glint of gold. But this was less well preserved; it had been hacked and twisted almost to shreds by some kind of swinging industrial chopper.

"What is it?" Chris finally blurted.

"Olympic gold medal," Clyde said. "Montreal, 1976. Wrestling. Heavyweight."

"Oh, Jesus!" the rent-a-cop cried. He looked down at the pile of red powder in which Clyde stood ankle-deep. "Oh, holy Jesus!" Then he dropped the flashlight and ran for the open loading-dock door. He almost made it out to the back lot before losing his doughnuts.

"God have mercy on your soul, Tab," Clyde said. He laid the medal down where he'd found it, picked up the flashlight, shook the red dust from his feet, and struck out in search of a telephone.

thirty-seven

AS THEY stepped out of the station wagon onto the circular driveway of the big house, she came out to greet them, a rolling thunderhead of white satin preceded by a wall of dense, sweet perfume. Anita Stonefield was clutching a stick with a glittery five-pointed star on the end of it, both thickly coated with something like ground glass in an epoxy substrate, and as she threw her arms around Desiree and Maggie, the star sizzled through the air in a wide, cometlike arc, catching Clyde under the nose and leaving him incapacitated with pain.

Another car pulled into the drive and Anita broke away and wafted toward the new arrivals with the same level of intense niceness that always made the candidate for sheriff break into a cold sweat and want to run away. Desiree had surprised Clyde by showing up for the weekend; she'd wangled a couple of days' leave out of her commanding officer and hitched a ride home with two Chicago-bound nurses. Clyde took the commander's generosity as a sign that grim tidings were in store for everyone at Fort Riley. Desiree was certain that he was just doing it "to be nice."

But Desiree didn't watch CNN the way Clyde did. Just the day before, Clyde had seen Dick Cheney on the tube, announcing that many, many more troops were going to be needed in the Gulf. Clyde had already accepted an invitation to Anita Stonefield's annual UN Day picnic. He could not imagine a politic way to cancel, and Desiree seemed to like the idea of getting out and socializing. So here they were, making their way around the side of the Stonefield mansion, following the shrill sound of excited children's voices toward the vast backyard.

It had been a damp, gray autumn afternoon, and dusk seemed to be falling a few hours earlier than it had the day before. The Stonefields had set up a yellow-and-white tent and brought in some heavy barbecue capability. As Clyde surveyed the diverse cuts of meat sizzling on the massive grills, taken from several animal species, he found that he could not keep inappropriate memories of Byproducts out of his mind.

Anita threw one of these picnics every year, just prior to the UNICEF trick-or-treat night, of which she was the regional organizer. It was an afternoon affair—all the kids came in their costumes, were issued their little orange trick-or-treating boxes, and got the opportunity to gawk at actual foreign people brought in as part of the party's theme. With the assistance of Dean Knightly, Anita was able to pick out a guest list that covered as many as sixty different nations. Iraq had been dropped from the list this year; in its stead was a Kurdish family studying on a Syrian passport.

Clyde had been getting a lot of invitations lately to events where he was completely out of place, or at least irrelevant, probably out of sympathy. Dean Knightly called every so often to check in on him. And the Stonefields invited him to every social function they mounted. As the result of this series of engagements, Clyde had cemented his vote among the Republican upper crust even more firmly than ever; Dr. Jerry Tompkins said that in recent weeks his share of this sector of the vote had skyrocketed from ninety-six to ninety-nine percent, with an error margin of six percent.

Clyde was given the job of handing out the little orange boxes to the children and acquitted himself well enough that he probably raised his standings in the crucial too-young-to-vote segment of the electorate. Then he prowled around the Stonefields' one-acre yard with one of Jack Carlson's fancy beers in his hand, trying to settle his mind, and happened across several foreign students working around a portable gas grill. One of them was built asymmetrically and moved with a characteristic limp.

"Is this the *halal* section?" he inquired from a distance. He was afraid that he might defile something by coming too close with alcohol in his hand.

Fazoul was delighted and insisted he come closer. It had been much too long, they both agreed. Fazoul had been busy with his research, and because the absent Desiree handled all of the Bankses' social contacts, Clyde hadn't seen many of his friends, new or old.

Fazoul heaped a plate with kabobs and thrust it upon Clyde. Seeing that Clyde could not talk with his mouth full, Fazoul shouldered the burden of conversation. He always seemed to wander back to the subject of the Middle East, and the extreme perfidy and demonism of Saddam Hussein and, by extension, most Iraqis, and, to a lesser extent, a great many Arabs. It was clear that this subject obsessed him; when he really got rolling, he would become spitting mad, waving his hands around and quoting verses from the Koran in Arabic and then translating them into English in order to bolster his points; as if he feared Clyde might be a secret admirer of Saddam. Clyde chewed and nodded, thinking that a show of agreement might calm Fazoul down; but it only seemed to egg him on.

One of Anita's operatives soon drew Clyde away to shake hands and eat dinner. Much later Clyde realized he had lost track of his wife and daughter and learned thirdhand that they had gone home so that Maggie could get to bed. Anita Stonefield had arranged a ride home for Clyde so that he might stay late at the grown-up phase of the party.

John Stonefield had bought all of the land there, and built the country club and the neighborhoods surrounding it, during the fifties, handing over the choicest lots to his sons. Terry's interest in houses was limited to the purely financial dimension, and he did not care about their architectural style or interior decoration any more than he cared about what kind of paper his blue-chip stock certificates had been printed on. He ceded all control to Anita, who had designed, and caused to be built, an immense structure directly across the fairway from the clubhouse. She had been aiming for something out of *Gone with the Wind* but was forced to make some concessions to the Iowa weather: the spacious veranda was walled in behind thermal glass, and the widow's walk had been enclosed in an odd hybrid of gun turret and cupola. Banks of powerful searchlights had been planted around the place, set in massive subterranean footings, all aimed upward at the house and bouncing off its white aluminum siding so brightly that, according to local legend, it was used as a traffic cone by jumbo jets stuck in holding patterns for O'Hare.

That was the setting in which Clyde and various other Republican candidates, Fazoul and various other foreign students, and a couple of dozen local country-club members and other movers and shakers were now trapped for the next few hours.

At some point in the evening Clyde found himself wandering through the place with Fazoul in tow, trying to get away from the sound of Anita's stereo, which was piped into every room through speakers hidden in the ceilings. She had put on a two-CD set of recycled sock-hop favorites performed by an ersatz group called the Original Artists, and the place was jumping with drunken Republicans performing archaic dance steps.

They wandered, squinting, through an arctic brightness of snowy rugs and glass objets d'art pierced by powerful halogen spotlights, and into a simulation of a library. The walls were hung with paintings and photographs of scary Germans with giant mustaches, looking as if they were about to pop an aneurysm because of the music.

From this room a spiral staircase ascended to the second floor and from there continued up to the cupola, which, to judge from the drifts of cigar ashes in the giant ashtrays and the beer-bottle caps in the wastebaskets, Terry had installed as a refuge. It worked in that role for Clyde and Fazoul insofar as there were no speakers there, and no dancers either. A ring of windows provided a 360-degree view of Forks County: the golf course to the north, and, to the south, gently rolling farmland, with woods down in the folds of the earth, sloping imperceptibly toward the city of Wapsipinicon and the confluence of the rivers.

Close to the house they could clearly see Professor Arthur Larsen taking Anita behind the imported Irish gazebo and groping her ample breasts while she grabbed his head and pulled his lips down to hers. Clyde turned his back on this scene, worse than anything he had seen at Byproducts. Fazoul saw it but did not react visibly; for him it was apparently just part of the normal scenery of the modern United States. Clyde found this embarrassing, but there was nothing he could do about it.

"How may I help you, Clyde?" Fazoul said.

"Pardon?"

"You said you wanted to pick my brain. If I understand that idiom, then for you my brain is always ready to be picked."

"Well." Clyde thrust his hands into the pockets of his uniform's trousers and balled them into fists, then stared fixedly at

Terry Stonefield's telescope for a good minute or so. "Been noticing a few things, is all."

Fazoul raised an eyebrow. He had sized Clyde up in the months since they had met and had apparently realized that when Clyde took to noticing things, and bothered to mention those things to someone, a lengthy conversation might be in store. So he backed up a couple of paces and lowered himself gingerly to a window seat, made himself comfortable, and waited for Clyde to continue.

"I think something funny is going on in Forks County. I think it's serious. I think it has something to do with foreign students—probably ones from Iraq. And it has to do with botulin toxin."

Fazoul nodded at him reassuringly until Clyde spoke the final words. Then he did a double take, as if he could not believe Clyde had said what he'd said. He heaved a deep sigh and ran one hand across his gnarled scalp, pulling what was left of his hair back from his forehead. He shook his head and closed his eyes in deep thought. "Please continue," he said quietly.

"Well, a little earlier you were voicing some opinions about Saddam. And it so happens that I've been studying up on old Saddam ever since he started threatening to kill my wife. And I can't claim to be a big Saddam expert by any means, but I do know he's been working like mad on nukes and Superguns and missiles and biological and chemical warfare. To hear all the things he's been working on, you'd think Iraq must be just one big laboratory, and all the Iraqis must have Ph.D.'s. But I've seen Iraq on TV, and I know it's not a big laboratory. So where does he keep all his scientists? Well, when Dean Knightly told me that there were fifty-three Iraqis right here in Wapsipinicon, I started to put it together. EIU isn't even that big of a university. There are dozens like it. If Saddam has fifty-three propellerheads here... well, you can work out the math. I cruise through the university a couple times a night, because the campus cops are short-staffed and they've asked us to pick up some slack for them. And I've seen the foreign students through the windows of the academic computing center at three, four in the morning. I've heard they can use computers to exchange information with friends in other states or countries.

"So I got to thinking, just to be paranoid for a minute, what if all these Iraqi grad students were actually part of Saddam's big plan to kill my wife? When I started thinking of it in those terms, it got me kind of worked up emotionally."

"Of course it did," Fazoul said. Clyde thought Fazoul's eyes were glistening just a bit.

"So let's think it through. What would the Iraqis be up to here in Forks County? EIU's got a decent engineering school, or so they claim, but what it does better than anyone is veterinary medicine. Now, if I was Saddam, why would I send my propeller-heads to vet-med school? Well, the first thing that popped into my head was anthrax. That's a veterinary disease, but ever since August the media can't stop talking about how Saddam is going to use it as a biological weapon.

"You might have heard that at the beginning of August, almost on the same day as the invasion of Kuwait, we lost a deputy. He was running down a runaway horse from the vet-path lab that had been cut up by cattle mutilators. He died of a coronary. I tried giving him CPR but it didn't work. For some reason the FBI was real interested in this case.

"Then I heard through my in-laws that the government was recruiting old horses to bleed for their country at the vet-path lab. And I heard from Desiree that the Army had plenty of anthrax vaccine but was short on botulin antitoxin. And I talked to an old fellow who's a botulin expert, and he explained that the way they made that antitoxin was by injecting horses with botulin so that they built up a powerful immunity to it, then drawing their blood. I looked it up in the library and learned that botulin toxin kills by paralyzing muscles—especially the heart and breathing muscles.

"So putting two and two together, I figured that my friend the deputy didn't die of a coronary like we thought. That horse he was chasing was one of the Army's four-legged antitoxin factories, and its veins were full of enough toxin to kill a thousand men, and that toxic blood was streaming out of it because it had been mutilated. When Hal was chasing it around, he got some small cuts on his hands from vaulting over barbed-wire fences, and when he finally got that horse calmed down and was stroking its neck or whatever, he got some of the horse's blood into those cuts, and suddenly his heart and lungs became paralyzed. The coroner didn't think to do a test for botulin toxin and naturally assumed that it was a heart attack. When the government heard that one of its two botulin horses had been assaulted, it sent out the FBI to investigate. They must have known that Hal didn't really die of a coronary, but they aren't talking about it because it's a national-security thing.

"So that leaves us with the question of who mutilated that horse and why. We're supposed to think it was satanists. But I think that the whole spate of cattle mutilations was just a blind that someone dreamed up so that they could mutilate the botulin horse without drawing too much attention.

"Why would someone want to mutilate a botulin horse? Well, maybe they wanted to obtain a sample of that horse's blood. If they could do that, they'd have a sample of the antitoxin that the Army is going to use to protect Desiree and all the other soldiers if war actually breaks out. According to my professor friend, there are many different strains of *Clostridium botulinum*. So having a sample might enable this someone to pick out a strain that would produce a toxin against which the government serum was less effective. Then this someone could produce large amounts of the toxin in a fairly simple factory.

"Well, Fazoul, if that was all there was to it, I wouldn't have much more thinking to do. I would conclude that the samples had just been Federal Expressed to Baghdad and production was under way there. But there's more to the story."

Through most of this narration Fazoul had been staring out the window at the lights of Wapsipinicon, nodding frequently, as if he agreed with Clyde but did not find the information especially new or interesting. But at this moment he startled just a bit and turned to look Clyde in the eye. For the first time in the conversation, it seemed, he did not know what Clyde was going to say next.

Clyde continued. "I have this crazy idea that no one except me is ever going to believe. No one except me, and maybe you, because I just have the feeling you might be crazy enough."

"What is your idea?" Fazoul said, slightly provoked by Clyde's sudden reticence.

"That Saddam has a biological-weapons production facility under construction—maybe even up and running—right here in good old Forks County."

Fazoul did something surprising: he smiled. He tried not to, but he could not keep the smile from spreading onto his devastated face. "May I hear your thinking?"

"I don't have this one nailed down as well as the first part," Clyde said. "But, to begin with, it just makes sense. He's got his rocket scientists here. Why not make the stuff here? It's easy to get hardware in Iowa, and he doesn't have to worry about satellite photos, or getting bombed by the Israelis. Dr. Folkes says that the stuff is so potent, if you had, say, a truckload of it, you could change the direction of the war. And moving a truckload of stuff from Iowa to the Middle East isn't very difficult for a guy like Saddam."

"I agree with you that the idea is plausible," Fazoul said in a soft, reassuring tone. Then, more urgently: "What is your evidence?"

"The bacteria have to be fed certain things: brewer's yeast, sugar, and a protein solution," Clyde said. "Well, I heard from Jack Carlson that Tab Templeton bought a load of brewer's yeast around the first week of October and drove it away in a van matching the description of the van used by the supposed satanist cattle mutilators. And we know that in his final week or two Tab was living out of a closet at Byproducts, where they've got sacks of protein just sitting out on the warehouse floor for the taking. I went by Nishnabotna Corn Processors and talked to the fellows at the shipping department there and learned that Tab had purchased some drums of corn syrup just a week before his death. And I personally saw him down at Hardware Hank with a load of PVC pipe. In the last week I've been out at the Co-op and the other farm supply places around here, and I've learned that Tab also purchased a number of large fiberglass storage tanks of the type farmers use to store pesticides and other bulk liquids.

"I figure that if I was a pencil-neck Iraqi graduate student trying to build a botulin-toxin factory in an old barn or garage in the middle of Iowa, I'd have a couple of problems. For one thing, there'd be lots of heavy physical labor—moving drums and such. For another, I'd be certain to attract attention standing in the checkout line of Hardware Hank with a load of sewer pipe. So the smart thing would be to hire someone like Tab Templeton to do all that for me."

Fazoul said, "Do you really believe that someone as security conscious as Saddam would place a secret of such importance in the hands of an American drunk?"

This one stopped Clyde in his tracks, because it was an objection he had made to himself many times. He faltered, broke eye contact with Fazoul, stared out the window.

"You're right. It's impossible," Clyde said. "I'm just being paranoid." Then he remembered something. "The only thing is that Tab is dead. Which doesn't exactly come as a surprise, because we've all been waiting for him to die for a long time. But it's hard to believe that even someone as drunk and stupid as Tab would have just fallen into that hopper by accident. And it doesn't explain how he got access to that van, or why he shoved it off the pier into Lake Pla-Mor."

"It is a very interesting piece of thinking," Fazoul said after a lengthy silence. "With your permission I may take it up with some friends of mine who have some familiarity with the current state of affairs in the Gulf. Perhaps they might be able to supply some small additional clue that would prove or disprove your hypothesis."

"Well, that'd be real nice," blurted the astonished Clyde. He had merely wanted to use Fazoul as a sounding board and had hoped only that he wouldn't laugh in Clyde's face. He was startled and somewhat embarrassed to learn that Fazoul might actually repeat his wild-ass theories to personages even more exotic and sophisticated than himself.

Down below, a red Corvette backed out of a parking space on the sodden lawn, peeled out, shot halfway around the circular driveway, and screeched to a halt in front of the front door. The horn began honking. Voices drifted up the spiral stair from below, calling Clyde's name.

"I guess that's my ride. Hope I don't have to arrest him for DWI," Clyde said. "Stay in touch."

"Don't worry about that," Fazoul said.

Clyde made his way down to the first floor and out to the foyer, where he nodded good-bye to several guests. He exchanged an air kiss with Anita and walked out the door toward the Corvette, which was revving its big motor impatiently. Clyde opened the passenger door and leaned way down to look inside the low-slung vehicle. Behind the wheel, reeking of European cologne, was Buck Chandler.

"Let's blow this pop stand, Clyde boy!" he hollered, slapping the wheel.

"How drunk are you?" Clyde said.

"Hey!" Buck said, as if he were glad Clyde had been rude enough to ask. He shoved the 'vette into Park, threw the door open, and hopped out as lightly as a man his age could on football-battered knees. "Check this out," he said. He shrugged his shoulders and shot his cuffs theatrically, held his hands out to his sides, then closed his eyes and picked one foot off the ground. Standing on one leg like a flamingo, he began touching the tip of his nose with his index fingers, alternating between the two hands. "One hundred . . . ninety-three . . . eighty-six . . . seventy-nine . . . seventy-two . . . and so on and so forth," he said, finally opening his eyes and putting his foot down. He raised his eyebrows expectantly.

"Spent all your booze money on your car, huh?" Clyde said, climbing into the passenger seat. Buck laughed heartily and climbed in behind the wheel. Clyde fastened his belt and cracked the window a bit, hoping to get some fresh air.

"Been on the wagon for a couple of months, Clyde. Never felt better." Buck punched the gas, and the Corvette spun around the drive with shocking acceleration.

"Well, that's a good thing, because when I get elected, I'm going to be hell on drunk drivers."

Buck laughed again. "That's why I stopped boozing," he said. "I knew old Clyde wouldn't cut me any slack. That, and I knew I had to tend to my business if I was going to pay all the goddamn divorce lawyers."

"Well, normally I think it's a real tragedy when a divorce happens," Clyde said, "but it looks like it kind of suits you."

"Couldn't have said it better, Clyde," Buck said. The Corvette veered from Stonefield Drive out onto the River Road and screamed in toward the heart of Wapsipinicon like a descending Scud.

thirty-eight

COMPASSIONATE LEAVE lasted for a week, which didn't seem very generous to Betsy until she realized that, in those circumstances, a week lasts a year. Paul Moses came out to help with the details of transferring the body and dealing with the funeral directors. It did not occur to Betsy to wonder why an NSA cryptographer should pull that particular duty. Or, rather, it occurred to her and she decided not to think about it.

She didn't begin thinking about those things until her compassionate leave was all used up, Paul had gone back to Washington, and she had chewed through a few weeks of her vacation leave. She knew that Cassie would have some pungent observations to make about this: a woman who would use her vacation days only when an immediate family member had died, so that she could spend those days in abject misery.

She spent many days sitting at the kitchen table in the farmhouse in Nampa. Long breakfasts with Mom stretched into long lunches. They read every word of the local newspaper, watched a fair amount of daytime TV. It wasn't very productive, but that was okay.

She knew she'd gone a long way in her own recovery when she began to think about everything that had happened. And then she realized that she had figured out a lot of things subconsciously in the last few weeks.

For example, the mugging in Adams-Morgan hadn't been a mugging, it had been an attempt on Kevin's life concealed as a mugging. Margaret Park-O'Neil wasn't just a neighbor who happened to become Kevin's love interest; she had been planted in his path by someone who knew Kevin well enough to know that he had a weakness for Asian women. She was working for someone, for one of the "good" guys, and her job was, among other things, to act as Kevin's bodyguard. She had died in the line of duty.

What followed was a little more difficult to swallow.

If Margaret–Kevin's perfect love interest–had been planted in his path, what did that tell Betsy about her own perfect love interest, Paul Moses? What on earth was Paul doing in Nampa handling the funeral arrangements if he really worked for NSA?

How about Marcus Berry–Cassie's supposed love interest, who spent all his time in the Midwest? The President himself had told Betsy that Edward Seamus Hennessey had a man on the ground in Wapsipinicon, Iowa, looking after the Iraqis there.

Which meant that Cassie herself was part of the game. Betsy ran over the chronology in her mind: she had given the fateful briefing to the Ag attaché early in March. Two days later her previous roommate had suddenly been sent off to another post. Two days after that Cassie had shown up, the ideal roommate, and moved into the apartment.

She and Kevin were pawns, that was obvious. Like many pawns, Kevin had already been sacrificed. Cassie, Paul Moses, Marcus Berry, and Margaret were rooks and bishops and knights. Who was the king? Almost certainly Hennessey. But this wasn't a chess game with only two armies and two kings. The board stretched off in all directions, its boundaries lost in darkness and distance, and she sensed that other parts of it were crowded, and furiously active.

On Halloween evening Betsy was driving her mother back home from a trip to the Nampa shopping center, and as they passed through the streets of the town, they saw the trick-ortreaters making their way down the sidewalks in their flimsy store-bought disguises, carrying their bags of loot.

"Look at all the children in their costumes," Mrs. Vandeventer exclaimed. "Isn't that adorable?"

For the first time in about a month Betsy smiled. "We have the same thing in Washington, D.C., Mother."

Mom got a vaguely distressed look on her face. "Isn't it dangerous out there?"

"Yeah," Betsy said, "but some people like it that way."

thirty-nine

STANTON COURT had been a cornfield on the edge of Wapsipinicon until sometime during the War, when the university had annexed it and thrown up row after row of long, low, jerry-built barracks, sheathed in tar paper and roofed with corrugated metal. It was supposed to be a temporary measure, but the additional housing space had become indispensable, and the city had grown up around it in the years since then. Sometime during the sixties the barracks had been re-covered in aluminum siding, as a tacit admission that they were probably going to stand there as long as the university did. A few months later an enormous hailstorm had come through, pelting the south and west sides of the buildings with knobby fists of ice moving horizontally at sixty miles an hour.

The marks were still clearly visible a quarter of a century later as the high beams of the Murder Car swept across them. Clyde was using the country brights because it was Halloween night, and Stanton Court probably had the highest density of small children of any location in the state of Iowa. The university used these barracks as cut-rate married-student housing, and they were populated by members of ethnic groups who, unlike their American counterparts, had no hang-ups about having children.

By the standards of the average Iowan, it always looked like Halloween on these narrow streets, where saris and turbans were more common than T-shirts. But however determinedly the parents might cling to their cultures, their children were growing up American and were aware of the fact that on this one night of the year they could obtain virtually unlimited amounts of candy simply by knocking on doors and demanding it. They were all out in their Batman and Ninja Turtles gear, much of which was larded down with reflective tape that glared acid colors in Clyde's headlights. But some of the parents had ginned up homemade costumes that were invisible at night, so Clyde used the high beams.

He stopped in front of a barracks and put the station wagon in park. The tiny front yard lacked the usual assortment of plastic tricycles and sword-fighting equipment, but looking through the tiny kitchen window, which was wreathed in steam, Clyde could see baby bottles drying on a rack, and he could see the back of Farida's head as she labored over the stove.

Maggie was still asleep in the backseat, and Clyde knew she'd wake up if he tried to move her. Clyde got out of the car, pushed the door shut without latching it, and tripped down a short front walk that had been plowed up from underneath by the roots of a scrawny crabapple tree.

He was hoping they wouldn't make a big fuss over him, but they did; Farida had tea going and had baked some kind of little pastry, extremely sweet, and flavored like Earl Grey tea. When they realized that Clyde was reluctant to leave Maggie alone in the car, Farida made a brief phone call. Something like fifteen seconds later a teenaged Vakhan Turk girl arrived, a calculus textbook under her arm, and cheerfully agreed to sit in the car and look after Maggie for as long as might be necessary.

Clyde was directed to the best piece of furniture in the house, an overstuffed chair that had been draped with a heavy, colorful woolen fabric to hide the fact that all the stuffing was falling out of it. The fabric was rough and nubbly, with little designs woven into it, and Clyde figured that it was probably homemade. If this tapestry was replaced with a tatty afghan knitted of garish polyester yarn, the chair would be just like all the furniture that Clyde had grown up on, so he immediately felt right at home. A cup of tea and plate of pastries were set before him, Fazoul took a seat on an equally devastated hide-a-bed sofa, and they munched and sipped and discussed weather and football and infant rearing for some half an hour.

After Clyde had eaten enough of the pastry to satisfy Farida's ferocious and implacable hostessing instincts, he allowed himself to relax and sit back in the chair. He could see more of the tapestry when he did this, and as he listened to Fazoul going on about his son's latest round of ear infections, his eyes began to focus on it.

He slowly realized that it was not an abstract geometric design. The border of the fabric was a long train of green boxes on wheels with curlicues on them that Clyde took to be some kind of letters. The wheeled boxes had mustachioed heads popping out of the tops. The heads had green helmets on them. Others had black sticks poking out of them in various directions, and some of the black sticks had red dotted lines coming out of them. The red dotted lines converged on little brown huts that reminded Clyde of the tent that Fazoul and his cohorts had erected in Albertson Park. There were small human figures around these tents. Some were lying on the ground with red stuff coming out of them. Others were carrying little black sticks of their own. Spreading his legs apart and shifting back into the sunken recesses of the chair, Clyde could see that he had been sitting on top of an elaborate rendition of a helicopter with red lines radiating from it in all directions. Headed directly for Clyde's crotch, and for the helicopter's tailpipe, sitting on a rooster tail of yellow-and-orange flame, was a surface-to-air missile.

If Fazoul noticed that Clyde was noticing all these things, he didn't show any sign of it, just kept talking about normal parent things—now it was the relative merits of cloth versus disposable diapers. Farida kept jumping up to get candy for trick-or-treating children.

"Let's go for a drive," Fazoul said suddenly when the conversation had arrived at a natural stopping place.

"Mind if I use your washroom?" Clyde said. Here, if he'd been among fellow Americans, he would have made a lame crack about how the tea was getting to him.

"Not at all," Fazoul said.

On his way to the toilet Clyde happened to pass by the open door of the unit's single bedroom. He glimpsed a picture on the bedside table: a family portrait of a handsome young man, a beautiful young woman, and four children. While he was peeing, his mind was working on this image, and when he finished, he walked past the bedroom more slowly and took along, hard look at the photograph. The handsome young man, he realized, was Fazoul before whatever terrible thing had happened to him. The young woman was not Farida, however.

He was startled by a noise within the room. Fazoul emerged from the closet carrying a plastic grocery sack with something heavy in it and saw Clyde.

"My first wife," he explained, "and our children."

Clyde looked at Fazoul. He could not bear to ask the question.

"All dead," Fazoul said gently. "Saddam came to our village with gas."

Clyde's head swam and tears welled up in his eyes. He turned around in the doorway and staggered down the narrow hall and out into the cold night air, terrifying a solitary trick-or-treater dressed up as a commando. Fazoul gave him a few moments alone out there, then came out of the house quietly and clapped him on the shoulder. "Don't worry, Khalid," he said. "We will see to it that Desiree has nothing to fear from that man. I am personally committed to it."

Not until Fazoul spoke these words did Clyde understand that he was in the grip of two emotions: not just shock over what had happened to Fazoul, but fear for what might happen to himself and his family.

The teenaged girl jumped out of the car, exchanged pleasantries with Fazoul, and skipped off into the night.

"She watched her mother getting gang-raped by the Iranians when she was five years old," Fazoul said.

"Nice girl," Clyde said. It was all he could think of.

They climbed into the Murder Car and sat there for a few minutes while Clyde collected his wits. Then he started the engine, shifted it into drive, and let the idle pull them forward. Maggie stirred in her seat and said "bvab bvab bvab."

"Did you say 'Iranians'?" Clyde said a couple of minutes later, as they were pulling out of the maze of Stanton Court and onto a main street.

"We have bad luck with real estate," Fazoul said. "We have always been transhumant people, which means that we follow our flocks. We have a problem with fixed borders. So we are equally despised by the Iraqis, the Iranians, the Chinese, Russians, Kazakhs, Armenians, Azeris, and so on."

"That's a tough situation to be in," Clyde said.

"Not for long," Fazoul said.

"What do you mean?"

"Technology is making borders irrelevant. The governments who still value their borders refuse to understand this basic fact. We are way ahead of them. Of course," he added sheepishly after a brief pause, "governments and borders are still very important for the time being, as the Kuwaitis could testify."

"Did you want to drive any particular place?"

"The interstate would be good."

"North or south?"

"Doesn't matter."

Clyde headed south out of town, hooked up with New 30, and took it east to the interstate. He had got the clear impression that Fazoul wanted to get away from the city, so instead of heading north, which would have taken them through the outskirts of Nishnabotna, he turned south, following the signs for St. Louis.

Fazoul made himself comfortable and said nothing for several minutes. Every so often he would reach out and adjust the rearview mirror mounted on the outside of his door, apparently looking back at the lights of the twin cities. Clyde checked the mirror, too, trying to figure out what Fazoul was looking at. The only thing visible at this point were the blinking red lights on the water tower and the radio tower.

They drove for another ten minutes or so. Since Fazoul didn't seem to be in much of a talking mood, Clyde turned up the radio a few notches. He kept it tuned to an all-news clear-channel station out of Des Moines and reflexively reached for the volume knob whenever he heard the jingle that preceded a newscast.

The voice of George Bush came out of the dashboard. Clyde and Fazoul listened to him as they drove through the Iowa night. He was giving a speech somewhere, explaining the situation in Kuwait City right now, telling some awful stories about what was being done to the people there, saying how it was just like Nazi-occupied Europe under the heel of the SS. Clyde saw no reason to disagree with the comparison; but he resisted it anyway, because he knew where the President was going with it.

"That's a clear-channel station–it bounces off the ionosphere," Fazoul suddenly said. "But it is an exception. Most radio transmissions are line-of-sight affairs. Radio doesn't bend around corners very effectively."

Clyde turned down the volume. He checked the mirror again and saw that the red lights had dropped below the horizon.

Fazoul opened up his crinkly plastic grocery bag and pulled out a tangle of wires. Somewhere in the midst of it was an off-white plastic rectangle about the size of a business envelope, riddled with small holes in a grid pattern. Numerous electronic components were stuck into those holes and hooked together with a bird's nest of tiny colored wires. A long wire trailed out of the tangle with a plug on it; Fazoul shoved this into the Murder Car's cigarette-lighter socket. Red and green LEDs came to life on the circuit board. Fazoul pressed buttons and watched LED bar graphs surge up and down on the thing.

"Someone has bugged your car," Fazoul announced.

Clyde nearly drove off the road.

"But the bug does not include a tape recorder. Only a transmitter. They can't hear us now, unless they are trailing us with airplanes or helicopters." Fazoul looked up through the sun roof. Clyde resisted the temptation to do the same.

"Who would bug me? Sheriff Mullowney?" Clyde said. He was embarrassed by the stupidity of this question as soon as the words came out of his mouth. Fazoul chuckled quietly and did not make a big deal out of it.

"If we ripped the bug out of your car and examined it, I could tell you exactly. We have the fingerprints of all the local Iraqi agents on file. But it's safe to say that it was either the Iraqis, the Israelis, or FBI counterintelligence. Probably the FBI—we have no reason to think that the Iraqis or the Israelis are aware of your prowess as a counterspy."

"What the heck is going on?" Clyde said.

"You know as much about that as anyone, Khalid. All you lack is context."

"Context?"

"You have figured out some very interesting things about Iraqi activities in Forks County."

"But I never actually believed any of it was for real."

"Imagine that it is for real. Imagine that you are right. Then try to imagine all the ramifications."

"I've done nothing but, Fazoul. I have nightmares about Desiree."

"That's not precisely what I mean. Those are personal ramifications. I'm talking about the realm of politics. I'm talking about repercussions in places like Washington and Baghdad and Tel Aviv."

"I don't know anything about Washington and Baghdad and Tel Aviv."

"That," Fazoul said, "is your biggest problem at the moment."

They drove on in silence for a while. Clyde laughed hollowly as he worked something out in his head: "They didn't put a tape recorder in my car because they knew I was a local yokel who'd never, ever drive out of sight of home."

Fazoul did not contradict him.

They were driving down a long, straight stretch of interstate with nothing in the median strip except tall grass that had withered with the first hard frost. An oncoming semitrailer rig roared northward, doing a good eighty or ninety miles an hour, and its running lights receded into the darkness.

Clyde angled sharply across the passing lane and the shoulder. The big wagon rolled sharply to the left as the wheels plunged off the edge of the shoulder and into the median. "Clyde!" Fazoul blurted, reaching out with one of his mangled claws to brace himself against the dashboard. Clyde sent the wagon plunging down into the median like a diving B-52, braked hard, and swung the wheel around. The massive back end of the car swung around of its own momentum, neatly reversing their direction. Clyde punched the gas, and the mighty 460 hauled them up out of the ditch and onto the shoulder of the northbound lanes. The entire operation took just a few seconds, and then they were headed back into town again at a comfortable sixty miles per hour. Maggie murmured, shifted in her car seat, and went back to sleep.

"First in my class at the Iowa Law Enforcement Academy," Clyde said. "They taught us stuff like that."

"Very impressive," Fazoul said, sincerely enough.

"But the FBI, or whoever, is exactly right. I'm just a local yokel," Clyde continued. "Iowa Law Enforcement Academy didn't teach me anything about Baghdad."

"Well, would you take it the wrong way if I offered a suggestion?" Fazoul said gingerly.

" 'Course not."

"Come clean to the FBI. They probably know most of what you've learned anyway. If you didn't approach them with this, it just looks like you're hiding something."

"I sort of pride myself on doing good fundamental police work," Clyde said. "And I don't have what it takes right now. I don't have solid evidence. They'll laugh at me."

"They may laugh at you because that's part of the game they have to play," Fazoul said. "But everything you tell them is going to end up in Washington, on the desks of people who aren't laughing."

"Fazoul, who the heck are you?" Clyde said. It felt good finally to ask this question.

Fazoul said, "You saw the photograph. You have seen my new son. That's who I am."

"But beyond that—"

"I have friends with access to more information about this matter," Fazoul said. "Since our chat at the Stonefields' I have been in communication with these friends, over channels that neither the FBI nor the Iraqis nor anyone else can monitor. They tell me that your wild idea is quite plausible."

Another long silence. Clyde finally forced himself to say something. He spoke through clenched teeth. "The FBI fellow looked at my report on the horse mutilation and said it was very well done," he said. "I don't like to toot my own horn, but that's what he said. He told me that I should consider sending in an application to the FBI someday."

"Ah," Fazoul said very quietly.

"I'm going to lose the election, Fazoul. I'm just going to get my ass kicked."

"So they say."

"And it got me to thinking, well—"

"I see," Fazoul said. "The FBI thing is very important to you."

"Yeah," Clyde confessed, feeling kind of thick in the throat. "I didn't realize it until now. The idea of coming in with a half-assed report—something that would go into my file—"

"Would it help," Fazoul said, "if I told you that the local FBI man might not have been entirely sincere?"

"Well, that did occur to me," Clyde allowed. "All I'm saying is that it's a point of pride for me not to hand in a Mickey Mouse report."

Fazoul was silent for a minute. Then he said, "They tell me that, in the middle of July, three men carrying Jordanian passports came to Eastern Iowa University in the guise of graduate students. The late Dr. Vandeventer arranged the entire business. These men are not really Jordanians. They are Iraqis. One of them is a very highly placed member of Saddam's inner circle—a man who was involved with the Supergun program and other such adventures. One is a security man acting as bodyguard and muscle for the first. The third is a biological-weapons expert."

"You say they came in mid-July. Two weeks before the invasion."

"Saddam made the final decision to invade Kuwait in mid-July," Fazoul said. "At that moment any number of contingency plans went into effect. This was one of them."

"Why are you telling me this? To fill out my report?"

"Yes. You said you lacked hard evidence."

"But you said that the FBI already knows about all of this."

"Someone at the FBI probably does. Others do not—or perhaps they are unwilling to believe in it for reasons of their own."

"Are you talking about, like, internal politics?"

"Exactly."

"I've never been very good at playing politics. You can ask Mullowney."

"Think of it like football. You don't have to be the coach or even the quarterback. Those roles are being played by people you don't know, people in Washington. You are like a center. All you have to do is snap the ball on cue."

"And then get hammered into the ground by a three-hundred-pound defensive lineman."

"Something like that," Fazoul said. "I cannot promise an easy resolution, or even a safe one."

They came over a subtle rise, and suddenly the lights of Nishnabotna were laid out before them.

"The Velcro diaper covers are handy," Clyde said, "if you can afford them."

forty

NOVEMBER

IT WAS the second of November, the Friday before Election Day. At five o'clock in the morning Desiree had called from Fort Riley, wide-awake and very serious. Orders had been filtering down from on high, expanding and ramifying as they made their way through the chain of command, and last night she had got word from her commanding officer that her division, the Twenty-fourth Mechanized Infantry, was going to go over to Saudi Arabia to hammer Saddam's legions into dust. She had been trying to get through to Clyde all night to tell him the news, but all the long-distance lines out of Fort Riley had been busy.

Clyde had been light-headed and woozy all day long. Many

people were honking at him as he drove the Murder Car into Wapsipinicon; he couldn't figure out why until he chanced to look at the speedometer and realized he had been driving fifteen miles an hour. The ample flanks of the station wagon were adorned with "Vote Banks" signs, and he didn't think he was doing much for his already desperate standing in the polls by holding up traffic. So he pulled into a McDonald's, got a large coffee, and burned his mouth on it, trying to get himself snapped back to reality. He turned off the radio, which carried no news of the impending deployment anyway—just endless repetition of George Bush giving a speech the day before and fulminating about the Iraqi soldiers' "outrageous acts of barbarism." He took a few deep breaths, got Maggie's Binky back into her mouth, and then forced himself to drive into Wapsipinicon at a snappier pace. When he picked up speed, the wind flowing over the sides of the station wagon caused the campaign placards to flutter and buzz alarmingly.

They parked in the expansive lot of the University Methodist Church—a crucial repository of strategic espionage data. Clyde chose a space near the street, reckoning that it couldn't hurt for the official Banks campaign vehicle to be seen at a church, and on a Friday no less. One or two closet Republicans honked their horns at him and waved as he was disengaging Maggie from the automotive transport module and socketing her little fuzzy pink-clad body into the backpack system. He swung her around onto his back and walked into the side entrance of the church. It was a crisp fall morning, but he still felt as if he were wading through syrup. The thing he had feared most since the beginning of August was happening. Desiree was going to the Gulf.

The Howdy Brigade worked out of a spare office donated by University Methodist, which was a sprawling and mighty church with a great deal of office space to spare. The church's administrative wing had a particular churchy smell to it that took Clyde back to his boyhood; as if all churches, or at least all Protestant ones, used the same brand of disinfectant. Back in the sanctuary he could hear an organist practicing footwork, playing deep, rumbling scales on the pedals. He walked quickly by the pastoral offices, lest he cross paths with a minister and get caught up in endless socializing of the type he used to avoid but that was obligatory since he had become a candidate. Finally he came to a door festooned with snapshots of foreign students of all shapes and colors that had been laminated into a multiethnic collage and labeled "Howdy Brigade."

"Well, howdy, Clyde, aren't you the punctual one this morning," said Mrs. Carruthers. "What can the Howdy Brigade do for you today?"

"I understand you've got a deal worked out with Dean Knightly's wife where you get word of all the new international students coming into town."

"That's right. It's part of our mission to make sure that within twenty-four hours of their arrival in Wapsipinicon, each foreign visitor is greeted by a member of the Howdy Brigade with a food basket and a three-W packet."

"Three-W?"

"Welcome to Wonderful Wapsi. It's a package of maps, phone numbers, coupons, and so on that helps them ease the transition to their new home."

"Ma'am, do you keep records of which students arrived in town on which dates?"

Mrs. Carruthers considered it. "Well, we receive the notifications from Sonia Knightly—she usually faxes them to us or drops the list by in person. And I think we should have them filed away somewhere."

She opened up one drawer of a massive battleship-gray institutional surplus file cabinet and picked through it uncertainly for a while. Maggie was fussing to a point that inhibited further conversation, so Clyde hustled her down the hallway to the nursery and changed her diaper on the table there.

By the time he got back, Mrs. Carruthers had drawn out one file folder and was spreading a miscellany of curly faxes and hand-scrawled notes out on a table. "Was there any particular time period you were interested in?"

"Mid-July of this year."

"Oh. That would be an unusual time for new students to arrive—usually they come a week before the semester begins in August."

"I'm pretty certain about it, ma'am."

She picked up a note handwritten on EIU stationery. "This is Sonia's writing. It's not dated. But I haven't seen it before—Roger and I were on vacation in mid-July."

Clyde took the note from her hand and scanned it for a moment. "This is what I was looking for," he said. "May I take it with me?"

Mrs. Carruthers looked stricken and put one hand to her breastbone.

"What is it, ma'am?"

"Well, it's just that, as I said, I was out of town when these students arrived, and I'm afraid they must have slipped through the cracks."

"Cracks?"

"I have no recollection of assigning a host family to those poor fellows. I don't think they've been visited by the Howdy Brigade."

"Mrs. Carruthers, it's funny that this should happen."

"Funny in what way?"

"As you may know, I've made it a special part of my life in recent months to reach out to our Middle-Eastern visitors."

"Yes, Dean Knightly told me!" Mrs. Carruthers said, her face lighting up. Then a new realization flashed into her mind, and she became stricken all over again.

Clyde was having to run his stressed and preoccupied brain in overdrive to keep up with all the stray notions running through Mrs. Carruthers's head. He finally put it all together: not knowing the reason for Clyde's visit, she had put two and two together and got five: she thought he had come to upbraid her for not having sent the Howdy Brigade around to visit these characters in July.

Having worked all this out, and seeing signs of an approaching nervous breakdown on Mrs. Carruthers's face, there was only one option open to him. "Ma'am, I wonder if you might allow me to take these new arrivals under my wing a little bit, and serve as the Howdy Brigade's representative as far as they are concerned."

Mrs. Carruthers was so overwhelmed that she nearly blacked out and appeared to suffer from acute inner-ear malfunction for a few moments. "Would you and Desiree be so kind?" she whispered.

"Oh, I don't think of it as kindness, Mrs. Carruthers."

She remained skeptical that any human being could be capable of such generosity of spirit and required several minutes of additional convincing. In the end, though, she fell for it; rummaging through her purse for a key chain, she opened a storage closet in the back of the office and invested Clyde with the full insignia of Howdy Brigade authority: a food basket consisting largely of tiny wax-encased cubes of smoked cheese, and the all-important three-W packet. Clyde then had to wait for several minutes as she composed a handwritten letter of apology to the July arrivals for having neglected them for so long; while this was being accomplished, he took Maggie down to the nursery, changed her diaper again, and let her taste all of the toys.

"You have an address for these fellows by any chance?" he said offhandedly when he got back.

"I've just been on the phone to Mrs. Knightly about that," she said, and handed him a piece of scratch paper with the crucial data written out in flawless cursive. Clyde could already see the house in his mind's eye; he'd knocked on the door four months ago as part of his campaign and encountered a family of Indians waiting for the moving truck, milling around in the front hallway amid stacks of boxed VCRs and laundry machines.

It was a split-level house in a neighborhood of prosperous split-leveldom. Clyde made sure that all the car doors were locked and that Maggie was still sound asleep. Then he hung the food basket over his wrist and stuck the three-W packet under his arm and strode up the walk, trying to manage a welcoming, Howdy Brigade kind of smile.

He had made it only halfway up the walk before the front

door was opened; as he'd suspected, someone had been watching him through the pink gingham curtains in the upstairs bedroom windows. Clyde didn't want to stop in the middle of the yard, so he kept striding forward, focusing his attention on a squirrel that was bounding awkwardly across the brown grass carrying a hickory nut the size of its head.

"Yes? Sir? Hello?" said a voice from the door. Clyde covered another couple of strides as he was looking around for the source of these words. "Can I help you, sir?"

"Howdy!" Clyde finally said, bounding up onto the concrete front porch, which was as bare as it had been during his last visit there. "Mrs. Knightly says we owe you fellas one heck of a big apology! And I'm here to do the apologizing."

"Yes, sir, one moment please," said the man in the doorway, who then retreated inside, closed the door, and shot the dead bolt.

There followed several minutes of internal discussion, which Clyde could hear only dimly through the house's walls. During this time he stood there on the porch with a fixed smile that was beginning to wear out his facial muscles, which were rarely exercised so. He looked around and tried to gather useful data, but to all appearances the house might as well have been vacant. He supposed that if he'd been Sherlock, even this absence of data would have been a significant clue. But it didn't seem to be getting him anywhere at the moment. The tidiness was a positive detriment to clever detective work.

The door opened wide. "Please come in, sir," said the man he'd talked to earlier. "Come in."

The foyer was paved with bluish-green flagstones and contained no furniture of any kind. Dead ahead was a living room carpeted in sculpted ivory shag with little sparkly things woven into it. Two sofas, a coffee table, and a TV were neatly arranged there, looking as clean and unused as if they had just been delivered from the furniture-rental place. Sitting on one of the sofas was a man in a suit, twiddling the TV's remote control nervously in his hands, though he kept the channel fixed on CNN.

The first man was a wrestler; Clyde could tell because, like many Dhonts, he looked as if he had a nylon stocking over his face even when he didn't, and he had cauliflower ears. He seemed to be paying a lot of unwarranted attention to Clyde's armpit and waistband, and so, as a confidence-building gesture, Clyde set the food basket down on the floor and shrugged his jacket off. The man leaped forward and took it from him but, rather than turn his back on Clyde to hang it in the closet, simply draped it over one forearm while his eyes traveled over the lines of Clyde's neatly tucked-in flannel shirt, looking for untoward bulges. "Can't stay for long anyway," Clyde said. "My daughter's out in the station wagon."

There was an awkward moment of silence, as if this man couldn't believe the bit about the daughter.

"So," Clyde said, "what's your major?"

The man in the living room made a tiny little coughing noise.

"Please," said the wrestler, and backed a couple of paces onto the ivory shag, holding out one thick arm toward the living room. "Please." His hand was decorated with a couple of none too tasteful gold rings.

"Oh, do you mind?" Clyde said, and stepped forward into the living room. The second man hit the mute button on the remote control and stood up. With some effort this man caused a large, toothy expression to spread across his face, as if he were a thespian-in-training doing strange facial exercises. Clyde responded with a grin that probably looked about as lifelike.

"Well, howdy!" Clyde said, stepped forward, and extended his hand. "Clyde Banks."

"My name is Mohammed," said the man in the suit, shaking Clyde's hand. He was wearing a watch that looked to have been hewn from a solid brick of gold bullion.

"Mohammed. Is that a common name where you are from?" Clyde said, speaking very clearly and distinctly and not using contractions, the way Anita Stonefield always did when addressing foreign students.

"Yes. Very common," said the man.

"Well, Mohammed, I am sure that your studies here at Eastern Iowa University are keeping you very busy, and so I will not waste your time. I am from the Howdy Brigade. It is our duty to be ambassadors of goodwill to our foreign visitors. We would like you to have this food basket and this three-W packet, which contains much useful information about Wapsipinicon."

Clyde proffered the two items. Mohammed's eyes shifted in the direction of the wrestler, who stepped forward briskly, took the basket and the envelope from Clyde, and set them down on the coffee table.

"It is a great honor," Mohammed said through clenched, grinning teeth. "Mrs. Knightly is a fine woman, and any friend of hers is a friend of ours."

"How are your studies going so far?"

"Excellent, thank you," Mohammed said, exchanging a secret look with the wrestler, as if he had just uttered a witticism. Then, forcing the issue: "Can I get you tea? Coffee?"

"Oh, that is very kind of you, Mohammed, but there are other foreign guests still waiting for a visit from the Howdy Brigade."

"Then it would be a bad thing for me to keep you here one second longer," Mohammed said, taking a step toward Clyde, and more or less forcing Clyde to step back toward the exit.

"I hope you enjoy that cheese," Clyde said, reaching for his jacket. But the wrestler actually held it out for him. Clyde had helped many an old lady on with her coat and knew how the procedure was done on that end, but this was the first time anyone had performed the service for him, and he managed to get his arms all twisted around behind himself before the transaction was finished.

"Its smoky aroma is most enticing," Mohammed said flatly. "We will have a rare feast tonight."

"Please extend the Howdy Brigade's greetings to the other fella," Clyde said. "Is he off at the library studying now?"

"Yes," Mohammed said, clenching his fist and making a little punching motion. "Hitting the books."

The wrestler opened the door. "Well, it's been real nice

meeting you fellas, and keep in mind that my wife and I are your host family for as long as you are in Wapsipinicon. So if you ever have any questions or problems, give us a jingle."

"Your generosity would put a king to shame," Mohammed said. "Good-bye, my friend."

"'Bye now," Clyde said, stepping out onto the porch. He walked out into the yard, turned around, and looked back; Mohammed was gone, but the wrestler was still watching him through the open door. By the time he got back to the station wagon, the door had been closed; but he thought he could see the wrestler peering through a gap between the kitchen curtains. Clyde waved one more time and the gap disappeared.

forty-one

IT WAS 3:33 A.M. on Election Day, and Clyde was already up and alert, sitting in his living-room La-Z-Boy trimming his nose hairs and watching CNN with the sound turned off. Maggie had awakened him for a bottle and a diaper change, and now he could not get back to sleep; the slightest thing kept him awake these days. And wild nose hairs were hardly a slight thing. They had never troubled him until his early thirties, when his nostrils had begun to sprout a new type of hair with the consistency of baling wire. Whenever one of them got long enough to reach the other side of the nostril, paralyzing discomfort resulted. The only solution was to push a rapidly spinning motorized knife up into his nose.

The first time Clyde had done this, he'd considered it the bravest act he had ever performed. Now it had become almost routine but still gave him a mild thrill of danger. It always made him feel much better. But the freshly cut hairs were square and sharp on the end and would only send him into a worse fit in a few weeks when they got long enough. In that sense the nose-hair trimmer was as addictive as cocaine.

Clyde's insomnia had got pretty bad the last few months, for any number of reasons, including the fact that Sheriff Mullowney kept changing his schedule around, always giving him the most inconvenient and unpleasant shifts, never giving his biological clock a chance to settle down. This position—La-Z-Boy, muted CNN, nose-hair clipper—had become common. CNN seemed to show less nonsense at this time of day, concentrating on real news. This morning the news from the Gulf was dominated by images of Saudi women driving around in big Mercedes-Benzes and being arrested. Apparently it was illegal for women to drive there. Clyde shuddered to think of what would ensue if one of his Saudi Arabian counterparts tried to prevent Desiree from operating a motor vehicle. She would end up in the clink in Dhahran, no doubt, sentenced to amputation of her gas-pedal foot, plus twenty years' hard labor for putting the gendarme in a full nelson and teaching him some manners.

Clyde had only one thing left to endure before his political career came to a merciful end: the victory party that the Stonefields were throwing for all the county GOP candidates, out at the country club. He had spent enough time with the local Republicans to know their style and could hardly stand to imagine what it would be like this evening, once they all got into the Canadian Club and news began to flow in of how the people of Forks County had rejected their wisdom and leadership yet again. Clyde had tolerated them reasonably well until the UN Day party, when he and Fazoul had seen Anita Stonefield and Professor Larsen making out behind the gazebo. That image had impressed itself as deeply on Clyde's mind as anything he'd seen all year.

He stayed up long enough to catch the four A.M. newscast. CNN always made him want to stay in front of the tube for another twenty-five minutes, just to see if anything new had happened in the last half hour. The sparse, ominous drumbeat of the "Crisis in the Gulf" logo had worked its way into his subconscious and triggered as many emotions as the cry of his baby. He forced himself to switch it off.

The only light in the living room now came from the blinking LED on his answering machine. He turned the volume way down and listened. There was only one message, and it was from Jack Carlson: "Clyde, I'm trying to organize a Clyde Banks defeat celebration at the pub Tuesday night. Wouldn't be the same without you. Hope you can make it. 'Bye. Oh, and it's okay if you should happen to win."

This was not a difficult decision. None of the Republicans would have anything to do with him after today, anyway, so there was little harm in offending them by not going to the country club.

So that night, when Maggie's bedtime approached, he put her in her jammies, drove down to the old brewery with her, set up her Portacrib in Jack's office where it was dark and quiet, put her to bed, and then came out into the pub. He was received as a conquering hero by a very small audience: Jack Carlson, Ebenezer, Dean Knightly, a sprinkling of mature Dhonts, a few other old family friends from around town, and—to Clyde's surprise—Marcus Berry. Jack began the proceedings by confiscating Clyde's car keys. "If I let you have these, Clyde, you're going to end up being the only person the sheriff's department arrests for DWI this whole year." Then a large glass of something brown, bitter, and thick was in Clyde's hand, and it tasted good.

A few pints of that and other of Jack's creations, plus the good company, helped to put some distance between Clyde and the disastrous numbers that soon began rolling in from Dr. Jerry Tompkins's exit polls. It was almost as if he were not experiencing it in real time but remembering some tragically funny misadventure several years after it had happened. All of the Dhonts came by Clyde's table to pound him on the back, punch him in the deltoid, or give him crushing handshakes or bone-snapping high fives.

Marcus Berry didn't stay for long and didn't drink anything, but he managed to get Clyde alone in a corner for a few minutes. "Have you given any more thought to filling out one of these?" he said, taking some papers out of his breast pocket. Clyde uncreased them and held them up to the light. It was an FBI job application.

Clyde felt himself getting very excited and had to take an extra swallow of ale. "Well, I wasn't sure if you really meant it."

"Wouldn't have said it otherwise," Berry said.

"Kind of hard to imagine—me in the FBI," Clyde said.

Berry turned around and squinted at the chalkboard on the wall, which usually announced the night's specials but today held the numbers coming in from the polls. "With a third of the vote in, Mullowney has seventy-two percent, you have twenty-five. Have you given any thought to your future in the Forks County Sheriff's Department, Clyde?"

Clyde sucked his teeth. "Would working for the FBI require me to relocate?"

Berry grinned. "Do I look like a Nishnabotna native to you?"

"Hard to imagine—us living someplace else."

"C'mon, Clyde. I know you're more cosmopolitan than you let on. And when Desiree gets back from the Gulf, she'll be an experienced traveler, too. A little change of scenery never hurt anyone."

"Well, I don't see any reason not to fill this thing out," Clyde allowed. "It's just that—with the Gulf thing and all—"

"You can't make any decisions until things have settled. Of course, Clyde." Berry reached out and chucked Clyde on the shoulder. "That's understood. This isn't a job at McDonald's we're talking about here. You don't have to start tomorrow. It's a professional situation, and we are used to making accommodations for people we really want."

Berry excused himself and strolled out, leaving Clyde aglow with excitement. An hour later, when his standing in the polls surged to twenty-nine percent, he even experienced a momentary feeling of panic at the thought that he might inadvertently win the election and blow his chances with the FBI.

"Damn, I need a smoke," said a Texan at his elbow. "Care to keep me company out there?"

It was Dean Knightly. Clyde scooped up some chips in his free hand and followed Knightly out the side door into the alley, which was paved with old brick polished satin smooth by a century of traffic. It led straight back toward the grass-covered levee just a stone's throw away. Knightly stopped just outside the door to light a Camel, then began strolling toward the river. He and Clyde clambered up the steep slope of the levee and stopped at the top, looking down at the river. The black water flowed swiftly but silently, reflecting the lights of Wapsipinicon on the bluff. When the water caught the light this way, and when the surface of the river was not chopped up by wind, you could see all the patterns of turbulence in the flow: ephemeral whirlpools and sudden upwellings that combined with one another and transformed themselves into other shapes and patterns. It was as mesmerizing as staring into a bonfire. Both men watched the river in silence for several minutes.

"Kind of amazing," Knightly said, "that your whole life, every minute you've been alive, this has been going on. Hell, you could have come here anytime in the last ten thousand years and watched this river and never seen the same thing twice."

"Yeah," Clyde said. "Makes you wonder what all else you've been missing."

Knightly laughed and took a drag on his Camel. "Yeah," he said. Then, a minute later, he continued: "As a matter of fact, Clyde, I've been wondering the same sorts of things about some of my little foreign scholars right up there in Wapsipinicon."

"That so?"

"Oh, yes. I do think we have some crafty ragheads up there."

"Anything of interest to law enforcement?"

This question seemed to touch off a large internal debate in Knightly's mind, which necessitated the consumption of another cigarette. "I want to be clear," he said. "So listen up."

"I'm listening."

"My students come in for all kinds of crap from the people here. Not just from rednecks but from people who are supposed to be educated and enlightened."

"I know that." Fazoul was not the first foreign student Clyde had pulled out of a scrape.

"I know you know it. I'm just chalking it up on the blackboard, so to speak, as a thing to keep in mind."

"I'll keep it in mind."

"Good. So we're being real gentlemen about this so far. We are being politically correct academic leftists, fully aware of the extent of racism in our society. And that's good. But we also have to be very clear about something that is not very politically correct."

"And that is?"

"Wapsipinicon is crawling with foreign spooks. Always has been. Hell, during the heyday of the shah we had our own local office of SAVAK here—the shah's gestapo—and they would do surveillance on Iranian students and actually carry out wet ops on a small scale—like riddling some student's car with bullets in the middle of the night, just to intimidate him. Most of our foreign students come from developing countries, Clyde, where they don't have things like democracy and human rights, never have, and probably never will. They come here with a mind-set that is far more alien to our college-town openness than we can possibly imagine." Knightly shook his head and laughed darkly. "Those Howdy Brigade people just kill me."

"I know what you mean," Clyde said.

"In these countries sending a student overseas for several years is a big deal. It's not just a luxury for spoiled kids who haven't decided what they want to do for a living yet. It's dead serious. It's a large expenditure of money, made by a government—usually sort of a nasty government—that expects to get a healthy return on its investment. So when you look at the foreign students from countries in the Middle East, Africa, and Asia, there are few of these who haven't been thoroughly vetted by their country's equivalent of SAVAK. Many of them have actually signed up with such organizations. Many have had to leave wives and children behind, as hostages.

"The message being that there are all kinds of scary governments that have flung out tendrils of power into places where you'd never expect it. If you could do a thorough sweep on all the places frequented by my students—run-down houses in campustown, those tacky apartment complexes on University Boulevard, the offices and labs where they work—you'd find countless listening devices. You'd find bugs on top of bugs."

"Well, sir," Clyde said, "I know you're expecting that I'm not going to believe you. But I do believe you."

"Okay," Knightly said. "So what do we have on the chalkboard now?"

"Number one, there is racism and prejudice," Clyde said. "Number two, that doesn't mean that a lot of these foreign students aren't up to"—he groped for a word—"shenanigans."

Knightly laughed hollowly. "Shenanigans. I like that. That's Ebenezer's word, isn't it?"

"Yeah."

"Well, I've got used to the shenanigans. It's part of my job. These guys know the rules, they always stay within certain boundaries, and we rarely have serious trouble. Fazoul is a fine example. He's up to all kinds of shenanigans. But his behavior is flawless. If only they could all be like Fazoul."

"You having trouble now?"

Knightly sighed in exasperation. He started to speak two or three times and then stopped himself before a full word had escaped his lips. "It's not that there's trouble per se," he said. "Hell, maybe I'm just feeling a little jumpy because of the Gulf War."

"I know I sure am."

"Of course you are. But I can't escape the impression that we have some very naughty students in town nowadays. Students who are looking at some big-time detention if they ever get caught."

"Where are they from? What are they doing?" Clyde said.

"You realize that it's totally unethical for me to say anything," Knightly said, "because it looks like I'm feeding the racism and prejudice, which is a big no-no right now. And there's another reason that, if this gets out, I'm in deep shit. I'll get to that reason later."

"Okay."

"We seem to have some Jordanians in town right now who are not really Jordanians," Knightly said. "Which makes me wonder, what are they? I happen to think they are Iraqis."

"One of them is, at least," Clyde said. "One of them is Abdul al-Turki of Mosul, Iraq. Thirty-two years of age."

Knightly turned to look at Clyde to see whether he was joking. He was silent for a long time. "Now, how in the *fuck* did you know that?" he said.

"Noticed one of the Jordanians was a wrestler," Clyde said. "Went over to the EIU wrestling department and looked through all their old wrestling magazines, found pictures of him from some international meets back in the early eighties. He was on the Iraqi national team. He was disqualified for the eighty-four Olympics because of steroid use."

"Well, I'll be damned," Knightly said. "Hell, I'll bet the CIA doesn't even know what you know."

"CIA?"

"I mean the FBI," Knightly said, "they're the ones who do counterintelligence." He shook his head. "I'll be damned. So they are Iraqis."

"The one is, anyway."

"If one is, they all are."

"What kind of shenanigans are they up to?" Clyde said.

"I don't know," Knightly said. "I just know they're not doing what they said they were coming here to do."

"Which was?"

"One of Professor Larsen's goddamn things," Knightly said. "Supposedly these guys were coming to do some research sponsored by one of Larsen's little spin-off companies."

"Was it supposed to be an academic thing? Or a private-enterprise thing?"

"Hell, Clyde, there's no difference anymore," Knightly said. "The boundary has been erased, there are no rules. It's the most corrupt aspect of the United States right now."

A few beers plus getting hammered in the election had made Clyde a bit more inquisitorial than usual. "Tell me to shut up if you want to, but you did more than just teach people how to raise food when you traveled, didn't you?"

"I'm telling you the truth. That's all I did. Oh, I was on the edge of a bunch of things. And I knew a bunch of people. But I never did any kind of work like that—never. It would have been fatal for somebody like me. Where I worked, I was totally hanging out by myself. I was tolerated because I was useful for everybody. But I learned enough to know that what's going on with Larsen, here, is something different. Case in point: Kevin Vandeventer didn't get killed in a highway robbery. He was working visas for Larsen."

"You think he got killed over visas?"

"Visas are hot shit. Anyone can get in to do anything on a student visa."

"As long as someone like you is willing to vouch for them."

"Exactly. And I have no choice but to vouch when I'm told to vouch."

"Who's telling you to vouch?"

"My boss, the president of EIU," Knightly said, "who takes his marching orders from the board of regents, and they take their orders from whoever provides the funding–which used to be the State of Iowa and the alumni. But now these hybrid operations like Larsen's have become hugely important."

"Okay," Clyde said, "I see why this is off the record. Because if Larsen finds out that you're throwing a monkey wrench into his machine–"

"All fucking hell will break loose," Knightly said. "Come on, I'm freezing my ass off."

They sidestepped carefully down the levee and began strolling back up the alley toward the brewery. "Do you have any specific information about what these guys are up to?" Clyde said.

"Nah. I've heard from their neighbors. They keep their curtains drawn day and night. When they go out–which they usually do at odd hours–they use one of two vehicles, both of which have tinted windows, and they've got a garage-door opener, so they never have to show their faces out-of-doors. They seem to eat a lot of pizza and take-out food."

"Why'd you hear from the neighbors?" Clyde asked. "People just call you up to gossip?"

"They call me up to complain."

"What do they have to complain about? These guys aren't being friendly enough?"

"The radio transmissions," Knightly said.

"Radio?"

"None of their neighbors can watch TV, or listen to a message on their answering machine, or use their wireless phones or their baby monitors, without getting all kinds of strange radio noise."

"In Arabic?"

"It's not in any language," Knightly said. "I've listened to it—one irate citizen played her answering-machine tape for me. It's scrambled or something. They've played with the signals electronically so that not even an Arabic speaker can understand what they're saying." Knightly pulled the side door open and held it for Clyde. Clyde wanted to ask more questions, but he got the feeling that Knightly must have told him everything he knew by this point.

Much later he went out and transferred Maggie's car seat into Ebenezer's car, and his grandfather gave them a ride home. Maggie woke up during the transfer and spent most of the ride fussing and crying, so they didn't converse much. Clyde had Ebenezer swing by the sheriff's department, which was only a block out of their way, not far from the brewery. Ebenezer orbited the block, singing fragments of forgotten lullabies in his hoarse voice—worn to leather from eight decades of shouting hymns—while Clyde ran inside and borrowed a sheet of paper and a ballpoint pen from the duty officer. He scrawled out a two-sentence note to Kevin Mullowney, congratulating him on his victory, and giving him notice that Clyde would serve out the remainder of 1990, minus any accumulated vacation days, and then leave his job there for good. He folded it up and shoved it under Mullowney's door before he could think better of it, then ran outside and waited for Ebenezer to swing by again.

Clyde got Maggie into the house and settled back in her crib. He listened to the messages on the hated answering machine, mostly from reporters asking him to comment on his failed campaign. When he'd got to the end of the new messages, he unplugged the machine and put it on a high, dusty shelf in the back corner of the garage. Then he went into the house, locked the doors, turned on CNN, and settled back into the La-Z-Boy.

He had been awake for twenty-four hours and did not feel

sleepy. He should have been thinking about the things Knightly had told him. Instead, though, his mind was stuck on one comment he thought he had heard from Marcus Berry. If memory served, Berry had said something like, "Come on, we know you're more cosmopolitan than you let on."

"Cosmopolitan" was not an adjective commonly used to describe Clyde or any other lifelong Forks County resident. It must have been a reference to the fact that Clyde had done some traveling around the world as a younger man. Or perhaps Berry was talking about Clyde's relationship with Fazoul. Or even Desiree's mysterious ancestry.

In any case Berry must have been referring to something that Clyde had never mentioned to the FBI. Which meant that the FBI had been learning about Clyde independently. Someone, probably Marcus Berry, had been checking Clyde out.

Which was to be expected if Clyde had actually applied for a job with them. But he hadn't.

He remembered the job application in his pocket and took it out and tried to read it by the flickering light of the tube.

The next thing he knew, it was morning, and Maggie was crying upstairs in her crib. CNN was still running, going on and on about the Saudi women drivers, which meant nothing important had happened. The job application had fallen to the floor and remained there until Maggie went down for her nap, at which time Clyde sat down over it with a ballpoint pen and began to fill in the blanks with small, neat block letters. As he did, he could not help imagining that maybe, at this time next year, he'd be in Washington, D.C., where losers and incompetents like Mullowney were not tolerated, and where people really knew how to get things done.

forty-two

BETSY WAS not surprised when, a week after returning to work from her long absence in Nampa, she was called out to Langley for a polygraph. When she'd entered the Agency, they had done a test to establish a baseline against which all subsequent tests were compared. An emotional shock could change the baseline, making a new polygraph necessary.

She didn't care. She had come back to the Agency to discover that she was no longer interim branch chief—the position had been filled by one of her former officemates. This was not the career blow it might have seemed—she had given them notice that she was going to outprocess 12/31/90 in any event. In the meantime they had stripped her of virtually all access she'd once had, revoked her passwords and privileges and clearances. Now they assigned her meaningless scut work on a day-by-day basis and didn't raise any eyebrows when she failed to turn it in. Instead she worked in the third-floor library filling out applications to graduate school on the West Coast, hoping to get in under the deadline for the spring semester.

So when she presented herself at Langley's main entrance and went to the reception area staffed by the ever-so-nice-wives-of-spies, she was relaxed. The receptionist motioned for her to come inside to meet her polygraph operator. Kim McMurtry was fairly new in this position, but that didn't mean she was unknown in the rumor mills of the Agency. She had come out of Texas A&M, where she had been a cheerleader. But she was no airhead. She had served in the Agency as a summer intern after her freshman, sophomore, and junior years, specializing in what was euphemistically called personnel work. She was now the ace of the poly staff, a sweet little five-foot-three blond beauty with a nice Texas twang, a tight ass, and a mind like a steel trap. She believed in the poly, and she loved to crack people, especially people like Betsy who never fluttered. Betsy knew all of these things just from listening to office scuttlebutt. Poly operators loomed very large in the careers of Agency employees, and if Agency people were good at anything, it was gathering and exchanging intelligence.

They went across the hall in front of the security guards to the row of poly rooms, and Kim cheerily asked Betsy to sit in the cunningly uncomfortable straight-backed chair. "You know the drill, I'm sure. But before we hook you up, you'll have to sign this release."

"What kind of release?" Betsy asked. This was a new wrinkle.

"We have reason to believe that you have committed a felony while pursuing your work with the Agency."

"What?"

"This release waives your Fifth Amendment rights. You're welcome to read through it."

The tactic had already worked; Betsy's calm was thoroughly shattered. "This is bullshit! What kind of a setup is this?"

McMurtry smiled sweetly. "Could I just recommend that you take your seat again and lower your voice? As I said, you are under investigation for a felony."

"So I'm not allowed to get angry?"

"Please sit down, or I will summon a security guard."

"That's more bullshit."

"We have a signed and sworn statement from the DCI's executive secretary, Mrs. Margaret Hume, that you physically assaulted her, right here on these premises, in April. Given that, and your size advantage, I think I have every reason to fear for my safety."

Betsy fell back into the wooden chair and uttered the only sentence she could think of that wouldn't get her in deeper. "I want a lawyer."

"You don't get a lawyer. You signed away those rights when you came on board. Now, are you going to sign this release?"

Betsy considered her situation. She didn't believe for a moment that the Agency would ever charge her with a felony. She was being mind-fucked, pure and simple. She knew it. She didn't care anymore. She signed. What the hell.

Kim was happy. She already had Betsy on the defensive. She hummed a little tune to herself as she wrapped corrugated hoses around Betsy's torso above and below her breasts to track her respiration. She attached fingertip detectors to note changes in the galvanic skin response. And then she put on the blood-pressure cuff and pumped it up—tight, tight, tight. Betsy's arm felt like an iron pipe.

Kim McMurtry took on a stainless-steel sheen when she began to ask the control questions: Is the sky blue? Is your name

Betsy Wilson? Is this November? Did your brother commit treason . . . ?

Betsy felt her heart pound into high gear and knew that the needles must be bouncing all over the chart.

"No."

Kim said nothing, just began another round of questions, most of them of no consequence. Betsy tried to control her breathing, but she knew that for the first time in taking the poly she was shook. She had the feeling that, up on the seventh floor, where all of this was being monitored in real time, money was changing hands. Vandeventer had been rattled; McMurtry took the pool.

"Do you need to go to the toilet? You don't look well," Kim said.

"No."

"We want you to be relaxed."

"I'm dead," Betsy said. "Let's get this over with." A deep-red rash had spread down her arm. The petechiae—little vessels under the skin—had begun to burst from the pressure of the cuff. She knew that within a couple of hours the rash would spread down the full extent of her arm.

She had done nothing, but she was guilty. She had bought into a closed system. She had seen the inside of the inside, and as Hennessey had pointed out months and months ago, there was nothing there. She must now pay.

"What do you want?" Betsy asked Kim after she had returned from talking to somebody outside in the hallway.

"Nothing else," Kim said brightly. "Thank you for your cooperation." She took the sensors from Betsy's body and said with real sincerity, "Have a nice day now, ya hear?"

She got up and walked out through the check-in point, presumably for the last time. The job that had taken her two years in waiting and security checks and polys and interviews to get had come to this. She walked, as if in a dream, to the desk staffed by the nice-old-wives-of-spies, turned in her badge, and got her coat.

"Bye-bye, dear," one of the nice-old-wives-of-spies said. Betsy ignored her and, on her way out, stopped in the middle of the CIA seal set into the lobby floor and read the inscription on the wall: "You shall know the truth, and the truth shall set you free." She took one last look at the stars on the wall and went out into the chilly November afternoon.

As she walked out, dry-eyed and numb, she heard a familiar voice. "Good afternoon, madam, would you be needing a ride downtown?"

"Sure." She got into the cab and then noticed that Ed Hennessey was waiting for her in the backseat with two cups of coffee.

"Let's go. You're late for your welcome-back party."

forty-three

NISHNABOTNA'S COURTHOUSE Square was lined with hundred-year-old buildings of rough-hewn, flame-red sandstone. Local legend still spoke of the day, early in the century, when the skies had turned purple and a tornado had approached, as they always did, from the southwest. The people of Nishnabotna had gathered there in Courthouse Square, just a couple of blocks northeast of the Iowa River, and watched it churn its way across the small village of Wapsipinicon; everyone knew, in those days, that tornadoes could not cross rivers. Many had crowded onto the roofs of the sandstone buildings to get a better view. The death toll had been well into the double digits, and the facades of the buildings were still pocked with tiny craters made by riverbank pebbles that had been picked up by the whirlwind and snapped through the air like bullets. A sentimental memorial had been erected in Courthouse Square, balancing the Civil War memorial, and a commissioned statue depicting the brave men of Nishnabotna trying futilely to shield the women and children with their bodies.

Having survived that cataclysm, the red buildings had been immune to just about all other ravages except for the human failings of bad taste and cupidity. Some of the best ones had been torn down and replaced with modern boxes, sheathed in metal and glass and covered with flat, leaky roofs. The First National Bank of NishWap had established its Courthouse Square branch in one of these. The upper story contained a small office suite that was occupied primarily by buckets and plastic garbage cans positioned under the worst leaks. From time to time their custodians would swing through and empty out the buckets.

A few years ago they had found a more lucrative use for that top-floor suite: they had rented it to the federal government, which had sited the Forks County office of the FBI there.

And so it was that, two days after his crushing defeat in the 1990 election at the hands of longtime incumbent Kevin Mullowney, Clyde Banks angle-parked his big wagon in front of that glass-and-metal box in Courthouse Square and turned off its big 460.

He did not, however, turn off the radio, because an interesting item was running on the news. It was President Bush, explaining to the nation that he was going to send a whole lot more troops to the Gulf. A *whole* lot more. Clyde sat and listened to the President for a while, drumming on the steering wheel. This did not exactly come as news to him, because Desiree had told him last week that the Big Red One was deploying. Knowing this so far in advance of the President's speech gave him quite an unfamiliar sense of being a savvy insider. This, Clyde supposed, was probably how Terry Stonefield felt every day of his life.

Clyde did not listen to President Bush because the information was new to him. He listened because his heart fluttered and skipped beats all the time; because he could not sleep at night for thinking about Desiree; because he had lost his appetite and would only pick at his food; because a powerful urge to weep came over him at the oddest times. His courage needed bolstering. In some strange way the campaign had served this purpose for him until the day before yesterday.

Now there was nothing to occupy him except worry, and so he sat there in his station wagon for a few minutes, its woody sides all gummed up with duct-tape stickum from the recently stripped-off campaign signs, and listened to President Bush, hoping that he would hear something reassuring. He had inherited a skepticism of politicians from Ebenezer and was not in the habit of looking to Washington for comfort and spiritual guidance. But today he would take comfort wherever he could get it.

He did feel a little better by the time he switched off the radio and got out of the car. He wasn't sure why; the speech had been all about how hundreds of thousands of military personnel, including his wife, were going to Saudi to clobber Saddam. But it always helped a little when the President complained about what a son of a bitch Saddam was. And it helped more to know that Desiree would be accompanied by half a million other people. If the President sent half a million people off on a fool's errand, it would hardly be the first time. But half a million people possessed a good deal of common sense among them; if they were sent off on a fool's errand, there would be repercussions. Half a million good people with tanks and helicopter gunships and telephone charge cards ought to be able to take care of themselves to some degree.

It was late afternoon and dusk already. Heavy November clouds had sealed off the sky like steel plates. Light shone from the windows on the top floor. Clyde entered the door in the corner of the building and ascended a long, narrow flight of stairs. Numerous empty buckets and garbage cans were stacked on the landing at the top; weather had been dry recently. Clyde rapped on the door and then pushed it open.

Marcus Berry had the whole office to himself. He'd spread out some papers on a big old folding table and draped his jacket over the back of a chair as he worked. When Clyde came in, he thrust his arms into the sleeves of the jacket and shrugged it on and stood up all in the same motion, then crossed the room to shake hands.

"It was nice to see you at Jack's place the other night," Clyde said.

"Hey, when Jack Carlson invites me to a defeat party for Clyde Banks, who am I to turn it down?" Berry said. "Have a seat, Clyde."

"Can't stay. Left my baby with the neighbors."

"Well, I hope you're here to drop off the job application," Berry said brightly.

Clyde felt himself blushing. He handed over the completed form. "Excellent," Berry said.

"Well, you might change your mind after you read this," Clyde said. He was about to lose his nerve, so he took a sheaf of handwritten notes out of his back pocket and threw it into the middle of the table, like a desperate riverboat gambler laying down a pair of sixes.

"Typewriters all busted down there at the sheriff's department?" Berry said.

"This ain't an official report," Clyde said. "It's a tip from a concerned citizen."

Berry pondered this as he walked slowly up and down the length of the room, stretching his muscles.

"Not to bring up a sore subject," Berry said, "but have you raised this with your boss?"

"I think it's more of a federal issue," Clyde said.

"Some bad guys crossed a state line, huh?"

"I think these bad guys have crossed some national borders," Clyde said.

"Ah. You think we should send a copy to the DEA?"

"It's not a drug thing," Clyde said.

"Not a drug thing," Berry repeated.

Clyde was getting less and less sure of himself and felt his face getting very hot. The report looked foolish resting there on the table, handwritten on lined paper like a child's homework assignment. "If I tell you straight out, you'll laugh," he said.

"I doubt it."

"But if you read that," Clyde said, nodding at his report, "I've got it all explained from start to finish, and maybe it won't seem so foolish."

"Well, I'll be certain and have a good look at it, then," Berry said. "Is there anything else I can do for you, Clyde?"

"You already did it," Clyde said. "I'll see you around, Marcus."

"Watch your step," Berry said, "those stairs are not for the faint of heart."

Clyde considered these words as he walked down the steps, wondering whether he was faint of heart. Sometimes he sure felt that way.

forty-four

"JUST TO expedite this," Hennessey said as the cab pulled away from Langley, "let's just stipulate that I'm an amoral, manipulative son of a bitch and that what I did was unforgivable."

The man did have an infuriating talent for taking the wind out of Betsy's sails. She heaved a big sigh and looked away from him, staring out the window at the wooded parkland surrounding the G.W. Parkway.

"If you needed a Trojan horse into the Agency," she finally said, "why didn't you just ask? Why go to the trouble to set me up with a fake life and fake friends?"

"The first thing that ought to be said," Hennessey said, "is that although those people have gotten to know you for professional reasons that are sort of nasty and sneaky, some of them have come to love, or at least like, you for personal reasons that are perfectly sincere, and you should not make the mistake of rejecting them."

"I appreciate your saying that," Betsy said. "But I know that I'll never forgive you."

Hennessey sipped his coffee and thought about that one for a while, tilting his head back and forth as he worked through some kind of internal debate. "No," he finally said, gently and almost reluctantly. "No. That's not acceptable."

"What do you mean, it's not acceptable? What you did sucks and I'll never forgive you. Accept that!"

Hennessey held up one hand. "Oh, by all means. I'll stipulate from the very beginning that I suck. A lot of my associates suck, too—or else I wouldn't bother to hire them. We all suck for a living. But what's not acceptable is for you to be high-handed and condemnatory."

"What's wrong with condemning it?"

Hennessey sat up straight and became coolly angry. "What the fuck do you think you've been doing the last five years, sitting at that workstation? You type in requests for information, and the information appears, as if by magic. Where the fuck do you think that information comes from? You think it's all from the Encyclopedia Britannica?"

"Of course not!"

"Of course not. It comes from the world, Betsy. It comes from sources who are really out there embroiled in the fly-blown streets of shitty Third World cities all over the globe. And I'm not talking about noble James Bond types, either. I'm not romanticizing this. That information is gathered in any way possible. Any way. Up to and including killing people, or sending them to their deaths. Blackmailing them. Threatening them. Buying them off. Stealing from them. Defrauding them. Preying on their weaknesses for cute boys or cute girls. You ever seen war, Betsy? I have, and I can tell you it is like a fucking universe of total moral degradation. That's the kind of environment that the information comes out of. And you sit there at the Castleman Building and pull it up on your screen like some kind of a fucking librarian and have no concept of how it got to be there. So don't get high-handed and condemnatory with me. You wanted to work for the CIA. You got what you wanted. And whatever naughty things I've done to you don't even register on my moral Richter scale."

Betsy could find nothing to say to Hennessey. But she knew better than to challenge him. He could blend into the background when it suited his purposes. But when he wanted to command a room—or the backseat of a taxicab—he could do that, too.

They rode in silence for a few minutes. Finally she said, "Just tell me that it was worth it. Tell me that something good has come out of all this."

Hennessey smirked. "Good?"

"Useful, then. Is anyone paying attention to the problems I was talking about?"

"We've been working on it," Hennessey said. "Expanding on your ideas."

"Expanding how?"

"Well, you assumed, and we agreed, that the Iraqis are using university classrooms to train their people. University lab facilities to do their research. University computers to store their data and send their E-mail. And all that is true." Hennessey took another gulp of coffee and sat up straight, warming to the subject. "But you didn't go far enough, and neither did we. Until now. And now it's probably too goddamn late to do anything about it."

Betsy was still nonplussed. She shrugged, waiting for the rest. Hennessey stared out the window at the Potomac for a minute and then continued. "Production. The sons of bitches may have set up a biological-weapons production facility somewhere in this country. Probably Forks County, Iowa."

"Anthrax?"

"Botulin."

"Figures. That would be easier to grow," Betsy said. "You know, it makes sense in a way." She thought about it for a while, then shook her head. "But I don't buy it. Why would they do it on foreign ground?"

"Millikan and the task force agree with you. They refuse to believe the story. Millikan won't go to Bush with this information." Hennessey nodded at the notes. "Not unless we can back it up with something respectable. And I have to admit that what we've got is pretty tenuous. I believe it on even days and don't believe it on odd days."

"What do you have?"

"At this moment, Betsy, the linchpin of our national security vis-à-vis biological weapons is the random observations of a big, dumb-looking deputy county sheriff who just got the shit beat out of him in a local election and whose wife is a nurse going off to the Gulf."

"Isn't Marcus there? Can't he dig anything up?"

"What's to dig up? This whole operation is so far under the

radar that there simply isn't any objective evidence to support it. Oh, yeah, I almost forgot: the deputy county sheriff has a sidekick. A Vakhan Turk nationalist and suspected terrorist who has been personally running a mole at Langley for the last three years. I almost have enough evidence to arrest this character, and I definitely have enough to arrest his goddamn mole. But instead I've got to play hands-off because I don't want to blow the botulin thing." Hennessey shook his head sourly. "Life is fucking crazy sometimes."

"So what do we do?"

Hennessey threw up his hands. "I don't know. If Millikan hadn't cobwebbed me with this goddamn task force, I'd move our whole office out to Nishnabotna. But the fact is I am cobwebbed. The only person who has any freedom of action is this poor son of a bitch in Iowa."

The cabbie took them to Arlington and dropped them off in front of a barbecue restaurant. Hennessey got out and said, "Thanks, Hank, good job."

From the Bangladeshi came a Mississippi accent so thick that Betsy couldn't understand it. Hank looked around, enjoying the surprise on her face, and said, "I was a theater major at Ole Miss. Couldn't make it on the stage. Ended up joining Hennessey's li'l group." He waved his hand dismissively. "Heck, Renaissance Man, I guess I'll tell you my life story some other time."

Paul Moses had emerged from the restaurant and was standing there looking sheepishly at Betsy. He and Hennessey exchanged nods, and then Hennessey got back into the cab with Hank and drove away, leaving the two of them standing on the sidewalk staring awkwardly at their shoes.

Paul had handled all of the details after Kevin's death, even flying out to Idaho with the body. He had presumed nothing, had given Betsy plenty of space, and had been flawlessly polite and professional from start to finish. He had stayed at the Days Inn in Nampa and dedicated one day to driving up to the Palouse to visit his parents, then, after making sure that Betsy needed nothing more, had flown back to D.C. Betsy had been back for almost a week now but hadn't seen him yet. For that matter, she hadn't seen any of the other members of the gang—not even Cassie, who had been out of town on TDY.

"Welcome back," Paul said. "We put together a little shindig for you, if you're not too alienated to come in and say hi."

She could not keep from feeling a wave of affection for him. What had happened that night in Wildwood said everything about his character. He had been hard as a lead pipe for two hours while they'd necked on the couch, but when the time had come to actually do it, he had lost his erection and been unable to get it back. Betsy understood that there were many factors that could cause male impotence. But she liked to think that in Paul's case, on that night in Wildwood, it had been caused by his own feelings of shame—shame over the deception that he and Hennessey's other people were practicing on Betsy. Paul had talked in Wildwood about how much he looked forward to escaping from D.C., and while that might have been part of the deception—a way of getting Betsy to drop her guard—she was convinced that he had been sincere.

"I might as well at least poke my head in," she said.

Paul led Betsy into the restaurant and straight back to a private function room, where several people jumped up and shouted, "Surprise!" Cassie was there, and Marcus Berry, and so were their friends Jeff and Christine who had been on the Wildwood trip. They'd hung up a banner: WELCOME BACK IDAHO!

Hennessey had chosen his words carefully in the cab: he had allowed that *some* of these people genuinely liked Betsy and hadn't been faking it the whole time. Looking around at their faces, Betsy could rapidly tell who really cared for her (Paul and Cassie) and who had just shown up to be social (everyone else). And, indeed, most of them drifted away after having a drink and shaking her hand, and the party dwindled to Paul and Cassie and Betsy. After an hour or two Paul gave the women a ride back to the Bellevue, and finally Betsy and Cassie were left to themselves, sprawled out on the furniture, staring across the living room at each other.

"Sorry," Cassie said after several long minutes had gone by.

"Cassie," Betsy said, "it doesn't even register on my emotional Richter scale."

They talked for an hour or so, about nothing in particular, and both were reassured to see that the friendship was much the same as it had been before. Cassie had gone through a striking change in demeanor: cooler, more sober, much less the party girl, but still with a perverse sense of humor.

"How about you and Marcus? Is that for real? I can't resist asking you," Betsy said.

Cassie got a hint of a smile on her face. "Marcus is gay. So am I. We're probably the only two gay black agents in the whole damn Bureau. So it's a natural we'd end up in Hennessey's shop."

"Why? Is Hennessey black and gay?"

Cassie laughed. But she didn't throw back her head and scream with laughter as the old Cassie would have. "Straight and Irish," she said. "But he hires unconventionally."

"Why'd he pick me as his Trojan horse? Because I'm single and alone and a Mormon from Idaho?"

"Partly that," Cassie said without hesitation. "Partly because you had already been working on the Iraqi thing. But when he found out that you had a brother working in Larsen's shop, that was it." Cassie winced. "Sorry. Sore subject."

"I'm over it, Cassie," Betsy said. "As much as I'll ever be."

forty-five

"CLYDE, THANKS a lot for calling in to Washington today," said the voice of Marcus Berry, sounding hollow and distant. Clyde pressed the phone against his ear a little harder. He was standing in the Hy-Vee grocery store in north Nishnabotna, right next to the little snack bar where all the oldsters gathered each morning for the ninety-nine-cent breakfast special. They had interrupted their socializing and political discourse when Clyde had pulled up in his unit, come in from the cold in his deputy-sheriff uniform, ordered a cup of coffee, planted himself by the phone, and, at six-thirty A.M. on the dot, punched in the collect call to Washington.

Now they were getting back into it, and Clyde was having a difficult time hearing the person or persons on the other end of the line. He pushed the stainless-steel button on the front of the phone that made it louder—a popular feature here. Now he could hear chairs creaking and papers shuffling at the other end of the line.

"Sorry to put you on the box," Berry said.

"Box?"

"Got you on a speakerphone."

Clyde said, "I've heard of those."

"Is this a good time for you? Or—"

"Good as any," Clyde said. "Just got done working the night shift. So I'm well rested."

"Okay, well, just wanted to go over some things with you," Berry said, shuffling papers and not even noticing that Clyde had made a joke. Clyde was crestfallen and a little bit irritated. But he could hear dim chortling way in the background, and a muffled voice interrupting Berry and pointing something out to him.

"Oh, sorry, that one went right by me!" Berry said. "Yes, well, hopefully we can find you some work that's not so relaxing. By the way, I passed your application on through the proper channels, so you may be hearing from the regional office soon."

"Appreciate it," Clyde said. So the purpose of this call was not to discuss his job application, but his report. That was a surprise.

"You dug up some really interesting stuff here, Clyde," Berry said. He spoke slowly, with long pauses, shuffling the papers again and again. "Your ID of Abdul al-Turki is the talk of the counterintelligence division. Quite a victory. Congratulations."

"Well, thanks," Clyde said. "It was the cauliflower ears that did it. Uh, I don't know much about immigration law—that's why I came to you guys. Can we arrest this guy?"

"Pardon?" Berry said after a long pause.

"We can prove he's Iraqi. But he's here on a Jordanian passport, under a different name. So can we arrest him for an immigration violation?"

Berry seemed stunned and uncertain. The muffled voice in the background surfaced again for a short exchange. "That's a good question, Clyde," Berry said, sounding like a teacher complimenting a second-grader. "I can't say I know that much about immigration law."

That seemed to close the issue as far as Berry was concerned.

"Been doing some extracurricular work," Clyde said. "The people who live across the street from these three fellas are the brother and sister-in-law of some friends of my sister's neighbor. So I got their permission to sit in their spare room and keep an eye on the house for a day." Clyde left out the fact that he'd had Maggie with him the whole time. "Got the license plates of their two vehicles—the ones with the tinted windows—and ran the plates. One of them is registered to one of the local Iraqi graduate students who has been here for a couple of years. The Escort was bought from a used-car lot in Davenport in late July. The salesman there says customer paid cash. Windows were not tinted at that time—the tinting appears to be an aftermarket product applied recently. We may be able to get them on a minor violation there—there are limits on how dark the windows are allowed to be."

Another muffled conference in Washington. "Excuse me, Clyde, I'm not sure if we understand the part about the windows," Berry said. "You are accusing these guys of running a biological-weapons production facility, correct?"

"Not accusing. Suspecting," Clyde said.

"So why would you want to hassle them about their windows being too dark?"

Clyde was startled that Berry needed to ask this question. "If you can stop them for a minor, legitimate violation, you may have probable cause to search the vehicle and uncover evidence of larger crimes—say, a weapons violation, or something."

"And then what?" Berry said, playing dumb.

"Well, then you can arrest them for the weapons violation, maybe get them kicked out of the country."

"Ah, I see," Berry said, apparently finding this a novel and interesting thought. He mulled it over for a minute. "But what do we learn from something like that?"

"Pardon?" said Clyde, shoving his finger into his free ear and leaning so far forward that his forehead pressed against the cold steel of the pay phone.

"What do we learn? We already know they're traveling under fake IDs. And we can be damn certain they've got weapons, probably unlicensed. If we arrest them for those things and kick them out of the country, we don't learn anything new."

Clyde was at a loss for words. He had never heard police work characterized as an educational process before. But maybe the FBI was different. He decided to try another tack. "What about the FCC?" he said.

"You mean, as in Federal Communications Commission?"

"Yeah."

"What about them?"

"Well, the radio transmissions from this house are coming in over people's toasters," Clyde said. "That's clearly in violation of FCC regulations."

The muffled voice said something to Berry; Clyde could just make out the words "Iraqi military frequencies."

"They know their phone lines aren't secure," Berry said, "and they're not stupid, so they're using, uh, some frequencies they shouldn't be using in this country."

"Now, I don't know anything about that kind of law," Clyde said, "but someone there in Washington must. They must be violating a law somewhere. We ought to be able to turn that into a warrant that would get us inside the house."

"I have to say your strategy escapes me, Clyde," Berry said. "These all seem like really minor violations. We could give these guys traffic tickets, too, right?"

Clyde couldn't believe that Berry didn't understand this. It was just basic police work. You used minor violations to work your way up to the big stuff.

Something Berry had said to him earlier finally went off in his head, like a firecracker with a slow fuse. "You said that they know their phone lines aren't secure?"

"Yeah."

"Well, are they secure, or aren't they?"

"What do you mean?"

"Do you guys already have a tap on their phone?"

"Clyde, I'd be reluctant to get into specifics about that over the phone."

That sounded like a yes to Clyde. "That's great," he said. "How'd you get the warrant?"

"Pardon?"

"In order for you guys to get the warrant for the phone tap, you must have had some evidence on these guys! What have you got on them?"

"What we've got on them is that they stink to high heaven," Berry said, laughing. "Listen, Clyde, we're operating under a time constraint here, and we need to jump ahead real quick."

"Ahead?"

"What can you tell us about your friend Fazoul?"

Clyde was taken aback and stumbled around for a minute. "Oh, well, I don't know. He's not an Arab. Doesn't care much for the Arabs."

"We know that."

"Seems to be real smart with technology. Stays in touch with the other members of his ethnic group."

For some reason these observations caused Berry and the other man in the room to laugh giddily.

"You participated in a ceremony with Fazoul and some of his buddies in the park a few months ago," Berry said when he'd calmed himself down. "What was the deal with that?"

"Oh, some kind of traditional shindig they do with their infant sons," Clyde said. "He named his son after me and some other fellows."

"He named his son," Berry said, apparently writing the words down, "after more than one person?"

"Well, for starters, they're all named after Mohammed," Clyde said. "And then the boy got some other names, I suppose to tell him apart from all the other Mohammeds."

"What were those names?"

Clyde was at a loss to understand what this had to do with Iraqi biological-weapons production. But he answered the question. "Khalid, which is how they pronounce my name."

More muffled conversation. "Clyde, not to burst your bubble or anything, but Khalid is a very common name among Muslims. Khalid was a great Islamic general—they call him the Sword of the Faith. So lots of Muslims—especially ones with revolutionary leanings—name their sons Khalid."

Clyde didn't say anything, but he resented this. He knew all about this Sword of the Faith stuff. The fact that there had been a real Khalid didn't mean that Fazoul might not have chosen that name because it was similar to Clyde's.

"Any other names?" Berry said.

"Yeah. The name of some other fella. I-you something."

"Clyde, is there any possibility that that name might have been Ayubanov?"

"Yeah. That's it."

"That's it?"

"Yeah."

"You're positive?"

"Yeah. But this Ayubanov character wasn't there."

More giddy laughter from Berry and his anonymous cohort. They laughed at the strangest times.

"So they just used a picture of him as kind of a stand-in," Clyde said.

The laughter stopped instantly and was replaced by a long silence. "You saw it?"

"Yeah."

"You said picture—you mean photograph, I hope?"

"Yeah. It was a color snapshot."

"You've personally seen a photograph of Mohammed Ayubanov?" Berry said.

"I guess so."

"Okay, we'll get a sketch artist out from Chicago sometime

soon," Berry said after conferring with his friend again. "In the meantime, can you give us a description of the man? Any identifying marks, any remarkable physical characteristics?"

"Well, tall and dark and sort of Middle-Eastern looking," Clyde began.

"What color are Ayubanov's eyes?" Berry said.

" 'Scuse me," Clyde said, "I got a call coming through from the dispatcher."

"What color are Ayubanov's eyes?" Berry said again.

"Sorry, fellas, but duty calls. Talk to you again soon," Clyde said, and hung up the phone.

Everyone in the snack bar was staring at him interestedly. As soon as he turned around, twenty sets of dentures bit into as many ninety-nine-cent breakfast specials, and conversation resumed. Clyde walked slowly out to his unit and sat there behind the wheel for ten minutes or so, staring off across the cornfields, covered with frozen stubble.

There were so many strange things about this conversation, he hardly knew where to begin.

They were trying to send him a message. They couldn't just come out and say it, for some reason, and so they were saying it in other ways.

He had expected that either they would believe him, in which case reinforcements would arrive shortly, or else they'd think he was full of shit, in which case they would ignore him. But instead the message seemed to be, *We believe you and you're on your own.*

And there was another thing, too. Something about the way their minds operated.

"Those guys aren't cops," he said to no one in particular.

Out on the highway someone stretched a yellow light into red. Clyde pulled out of the Hy-Vee, chased them down, and wrote them a ticket. Which is what real cops did.

What we've got on them is that they stink to high heaven.

What was that supposed to mean? You couldn't get a warrant with some vague nonsense like that. Any evidence they were getting from their phone tap was useless in court. A complete waste of time.

Except that they didn't seem to care about what would or wouldn't stand up in court. These guys acted as if the judicial system didn't exist.

They acted as if they'd never stepped into a courtroom their whole lives. By cop standards they were clowns. Amateurs who never could have graduated from the Iowa Law Enforcement Academy, who would have been drummed out of even Sheriff Mullowney's department.

So who the hell were they, and what were they doing pretending to be FBI agents?

forty-six

I'm writing this about six hours into our luxury charter flight to the Gulf. They picked us up in a big, nice new 747. Strange to see all these folks in Army green, piling their duffel bags on the edge of the runway and climbing up onto this nice plane. We have stewardesses and everything. For once everyone sat up straight and paid attention when they showed how to use the oxygen masks. We've also got our gas masks in the overhead luggage bins in case a Scud hits the airport in Dhahran.

They served us a meal—not too bad, but nothing like the hot dishes you are probably getting from the Dhonts. Doused the lights a few minutes ago and I tried to sleep but can't. Walked back to the rest room and looked at the faces of all the people in their green camo (Army doesn't have enough desert camo to go around yet!). All these regular-looking folks just listening to their Walkmans, or leaning back trying to sleep, or sitting in pools of light like I am right now writing to loved ones. Not a single G.I. Joe among them. Just plain old people like you see on the street, except we all wear the same clothes and call ourselves soldiers. I hope when the time comes we will be.

Clyde read the letter several times over as he sat there in the station wagon in the parking lot of Wapsipinicon Senior High School. Directly in front of him was the breezeway where, long ago, he had watched Desiree handle that Nishnabotna boy and decided that he had to marry her.

Maggie woke up and needed to be changed and fed, which occupied body and mind for a few minutes; a good thing, since the sight of the breezeway had led his thoughts down a sentimental and dangerous path.

Another letter was resting on the front seat of the Murder Car. This one had been postmarked in Washington, D.C., and bore no return address. It was addressed to Clyde in care of the Forks County Sheriff's Department. It contained a single sheet of paper that had come out of a laser printer or something. It said:

> The man with the cauliflower ears murdered my brother. Regardless of what the Bureau does or doesn't do, you must stop him.
>
> You must not rely on the United States government to do anything worth doing. You must get it through your head that you are totally on your own.
>
> Believe me, it's better that way.

Clyde heard a rapping on the window and wiped fog away with one hand to reveal the face of Jonathan Town, steaming like a locomotive as he breathed into his clenched fists. Clyde beckoned him in. Town pulled at a door handle and was startled to find that it was locked. Clyde was a little bit startled himself and reached across the car with one arm to unlock the door while holding Maggie's bottle steady with the other. He snatched up the mystery letter from D.C. and stuffed it into his coat pocket as Town climbed into the car.

"Sorry," he said as Town came in from the wind.

"That's okay," Town said quickly. "Can't be too careful here.

Someone might force their way in and try to sell you some band candy."

Jonathan Town had got a journalism degree at Iowa State and done time on some newspapers in Minneapolis and Chicago. He had come back from this sojourn with a quick, sarcastic wit that eternally set him apart from most of Forks County. Clyde always had to remind himself not to be offended by it; in a way, Town was giving him some credit, assuming Clyde was smart enough to get the joke. It was just a difference in style, nothing more.

Clyde reached up above the sun visor with his free hand and took out a scrap of paper on which he had written the words, *Car is bugged—just small talk for now, please*. He handed it to Town, who pulled a face and looked askance at him. "Soon as Maggie finishes her bottle," Clyde said, "I can take you out and show you that property."

"Okay, whatever," Town said, and settled back into his seat, prepared for a long spell of boredom. But this was nothing new for Town, who always acted bored.

"How's things at the school newspaper?"

"The usual. My football reporter forgot to mention some third-stringer in his story about the Waterloo game, and I heard about it from the parents. Someone's been sneaking into the darkroom to smoke pot. And the yearbook is already in crisis."

Maggie pushed the bottle away. Clyde shifted the wagon into drive and pulled out of the parking lot, glad to be out of sight of that breezeway. They made small talk. A few miles out of town, the road plunged into the Wapsipinicon Valley. For the most part it was thickly forested, with big old hardwood trees that had lost most of their autumn color several weeks back; most of them were just naked black sticks now, though the oak trees held on to their dead brown leaves tenaciously. The road became rather steep and then broke from its ruler-straight trajectory and began to wind. Outcroppings of shale and sandstone, poking out through the thick carpet of fallen leaves, could be seen among the trunks of the big trees. Down below them in the river bottom, the Wapsipinicon had carved a meandering path deep into the sandstone.

"I guess we can talk now," Clyde said. "They say the radio can't make it out of the valley."

"Well, that's a relief," Town said. In the corner of his eye Clyde could see his passenger giving him a searching look.

"I suppose you think I'm a paranoid maniac now," Clyde said.

"Crossed my mind," Town said. "What makes you think Mullowney is bugging you?"

Clyde laughed out loud for the first time in a few weeks and whacked the steering wheel with the flat of his hand. In the backseat Maggie echoed him, greatly relieved to see her saturnine father behaving so. Clyde turned around and smiled at Maggie, then returned his gaze to the winding road. "It's not Mullowney," he said. "Actually, I'm not sure who it is. First, I figured it was some foreign students down at the university."

"Ah," Town said, seeming to find this slightly less implausible. "Well, I'd believe it. But you'll have to make your case to my readers." He shifted position for the first time since he'd got into the car, rummaging in the breast pocket of his blazer for a reporter's notebook and a ballpoint pen. "Why would some foreign students want to do that?"

"Well, but then I decided it was the FBI, because they knew more about me than they ought to," Clyde said. "And then I decided it was some other folks just pretending to be FBI agents."

"Uh-huh," Town said quietly. "I hate it when that happens."

Clyde downshifted the big wagon and let its weight pull them down into the valley at not much more than a jogging pace. He told Jonathan Town an edited version of the story, leaving Fazoul out of it.

This shifted attention away from the truly wild part about fake FBI agents and toward more down-to-earth elements of the story, such as Tab, who had been a tried-and-true news item for decades—ever since he'd become the heaviest ninth-grader in the history of Iowa. Town wrote it all down and asked the inevitable question: "You told your boss about this?"

"FBI handles anything that crosses state lines. They also handle counterespionage. So I told them about it a couple of weeks ago, right after the election."

"How do you think Mullowney would feel about your going over his head?" Town asked, smiling at the thought of it.

Clyde cracked a smile, too. "It don't much matter what he thinks," he said. "He couldn't like me any less than he already does."

"How can you stand to work for him?"

"I can't. Went ahead and handed in my resignation. But that's another story."

"When's your last day as a deputy sheriff, then?"

"End of the year. But I got some vacation days stored up, so it'll really be sometime around Christmas."

"What's that going to do for the family finances?"

Clyde heaved a big sigh and ground his teeth. "Desiree's getting special combat pay," he said. "When she gets back, if things get bad, she can always go back to nursing full-time."

"Well, back to the main story," Town said, sensing he was wandering into a minefield. "How'd the FBI react to the news that Saddam Hussein is building a biological-weapons production facility in Forks County, Iowa?"

Clyde winced. "Well, they haven't done anything dramatic, if that's what you mean."

"Anything dramatic?"

"Anything that would be obvious."

"In other words, as far as you know, they haven't done diddly."

"Yeah."

Clyde saw Town writing this response down in his notebook and thought about how lame it would look in a *Des Moines Register* story. "The local agent went to D.C. just to show this report to his higher-ups," Clyde said. "I know they're real interested."

"But that's not news. At least it's not Iowa news. Iowa news is lots of new FBI agents coming into Nishnabotna and fanning out across the city, or something like that."

"Well, I'm not sure if that's the tack they want to take with the investigation," Clyde said.

"What tack do they want to take, then?"

"Sort of a wait-and-see approach, I guess. They seem to agree that these guys are shady characters, but they don't just want to swoop down and make arrests and file any charges—the way a cop would."

"But FBI agents are cops."

Clyde sighed again.

"Oh, yeah," Town said. "You said something about their not really being FBI."

"I don't know how the G-men operate," Clyde said, "but a cop is very organized and disciplined about gathering solid evidence that will stand up in court, and then filing charges and securing convictions. No one seems to have explained that to these guys."

"Well," Town said, sitting up in his seat and flipping way back to the very beginning of his notes, "the thing about the horses producing botulin antidote for the Army is definitely story material. The fact that the military only had two horses in the whole country for this purpose seems like a lack of preparedness on their part and would make a nice little exposé. And the fact that one of them got mutilated—by *someone*—makes the story even better because it dramatizes the vulnerability of the program." Town stared out the windshield for a minute, chewing thoughtfully on his lip. "Would the *Register* run it? Well, I don't know, I'm only a stringer. But I'm inclined to think they might spike the story, or at least put it on ice until the crisis in the Gulf has resolved, so it doesn't look like they're undermining the military effort. Of course, you're going way, way, way beyond that story and into an incredible, amazing espionage thing. Which isn't bad in and of itself, because amazing espionage stories really happen sometimes. But all you're giving me in the way of evidence is the Tab Templeton story—which was already covered to death on the sports page—and a memo from the internal files of the Howdy Brigade, and this little black-and-white photo from an old wrestling magazine. Is that right?"

Clyde ground his teeth. "Yeah, that's right."

"And on top of that already amazing story, you have a whole 'nother story brewing about something fishy happening with the FBI. And the only evidence you have for that is that you talked to some FBI guys on the phone and ended up with a gut feeling that their heads were not where a cop's head should be."

Town said nothing for a while, letting all of this speak for itself. Clyde ground his teeth some more. "Okay, okay," he said, "separately, each one of those sounds like a wild story. But together they reinforce each other."

"Could you explain that?"

"The idea that Iraqis are up to some shenanigans here might sound pretty wild. But if they were, you'd hope that someone in the government would be worried about it. Like the CIA or something. And that might explain why the folks in Washington have been acting kind of funny."

"From my point of view that makes it a worse story, not a better story," Town said, "because I can't break it down into bite-sized chunks. I've got to explain this huge tapestry of events. I've got to write a damn book."

"I'm not used to dealings with the media," Clyde finally said, "so I don't know the drill. But isn't it the case that sometimes a paper will send out an investigative reporter to dig for more information?"

Town drew a deep breath and let it out, and Clyde got the impression that, out of politeness and respect for Clyde, he was making an effort not to break out laughing. "The investigative-reporter thing is largely a Hollywood myth," he said. "No one really does that. No one has the attention span. No one has the budget. Not that many people have the talent."

"Okay. Well, that clears up a lot of misconceptions for me," Clyde said.

"Basically you need to give the *Register,* or the *Trib* or whomever, this story on a platter."

"No one's going to investigate this thing except for me," Clyde said.

"You got it."

"Okay, well, let's get out of this dang valley, and I'll buy you a cup of coffee for your time," Clyde said.

"Nah, you don't have to do that," Town said. But a few minutes later, as they were winding their way back up, he said, "I tell you what. I'm going to bounce this off my editor at the *Register.*

Like I said, based on what you've told me, there's no story here. But it would be such a big deal if something was going on—I'd hate to miss it."

"Whatever you think is best," Clyde said.

"But even if they like it, they won't move unless you can give them a smoking gun. Something they can take a picture of."

"Like what?"

"Come on, Clyde," Town said, finally sounding a little impatient. "You're claiming that Tab Templeton constructed a botulin factory for these guys. Where the hell is the factory?"

"Could be anywhere," Clyde said. "In a house or an old barn or garage. None of the neighbors saw Tab or the van at the house where the Iraqis live, so it's not there."

"Show me the goddamn factory. That's what it comes down to, Clyde."

"I'll see what I can do," Clyde said.

forty-seven

DECEMBER

GEORGE BUSH had always got a bad cold around the beginning of December, and he had one now on the morning before Pearl Harbor Day as James Gabor Millikan gave him his early-morning national-security briefing. Millikan, on the other hand, was exultant. He had retrieved himself from the ruin that he had almost suffered from being too pro-Saddam. Through his Iraq task force he had blocked both Hennessey and that bottom fish in the Agency whose name he had forgotten, but who had been sternly dealt with and who would soon be cast back into the outer darkness. He had had a triumphant time organizing the United Nations effort, for which he had received so much approval from the President and from the press. All was going well—except that the President had that look on his face.

George Bush, underneath all the stiffness and Yaliness and

malapropisms, had one big problem for James Gabor Millikan. He was a softy. He really liked people. He worried about people. He worried himself sick about gas attacks and chemical warfare and his precious Americans dying in the sands of the desert. This irritated Millikan.

"So what about the biological and chemical developments?" the President asked as he turned to his military adviser.

"Nothing new. If they launch anything, it will be out of those South African weapons, and it will be nothing that we can't control."

"Are you sure? Are you really sure?"

Millikan interjected. "If I could, sir, you were unduly upset by the reports written by that analyst who has been mustered out of the service after miserably failing a routine polygraph examination."

Bush had a way of looking through people, and at this point he began doing it to Millikan. Bush said nothing, which made it even worse. Millikan at times like this could not stand the silence. "Our task force, which you yourself said was blue-ribbon all the way, is on top of this."

"What about Hennessey?"

"He's on board, sir."

"Who's he working for now? I can never remember."

"The Bureau, Mr. President."

"Oh, good! So he can do domestic stuff without kicking up a fuss in the press."

"If need be, Mr. President. But we don't see domestic as being a major concern."

When Millikan left the meeting, his assistant, Dellinger, was waiting for him, looking troubled. "Out with it!" Millikan said as they walked down the corridor together.

"The *Des Moines Register* has got wind of a wild story again and, once again, is asking some funny questions," Dellinger said, and went on to tell a bizarre little tale about a backwater university town in Iowa.

"Jesus Christ," Millikan said, "do whatever it takes to kill that story. That's just what we need! For the President to get wind of something like that."

"Yes, sir. I anticipated that you'd feel that way and already set some things in motion."

"Is there anything else?"

"Yes. You should know that Hennessey has had a couple of meetings with Vandeventer—the CIA person. None too discreetly, I might add."

"I am getting so tired of that woman," Millikan said, and heaved a deep sigh. "What access does she have? Weren't all her clearances removed?"

"Affirmative, as per your orders."

"Then I would like for you to investigate the possibility," Millikan said, "of making Hennessey's life very complicated and unpleasant for a while—using Vandeventer as the smoking gun. This pretense of working for the FBI is a paper-thin charade. Anyone with an IQ out of the single digits knows he's really CIA. And I didn't care as long as he was chasing Turks around, or whatever he was doing."

"Yes, sir. Chasing Vakhan Turks."

"But now he's stepped into this other business. And I think he's got rather careless by dealing so openly with a woman who is only a few hours out of the Agency. Really, what is the point of having a law against the Agency operating within the United States if this kind of leakage is tolerated? I think that Hennessey's actions in this case raise deeply troubling ethical issues that would make a much better newspaper scoop than any of this nonsense about Iraqis and botulism."

"I know of some editors who are highly sensitive to issues of government ethics," Dellinger said, "and who have no love for Republican administrations in general. If you don't mind, I will pass your insight on to them—anonymously, of course."

But Millikan was just warming to the task. The more he thought about it, the broader the horizons that seemed to open before him. A wonderful idea came to him, and he toyed with it for a few moments before voicing it. "In fact, I think that this is just the sort of thing that we have inspectors general for." He raised an eyebrow at Dellinger, who looked stunned at the audacity of this notion.

But Dellinger's astonishment rapidly developed into a sort of mischievous excitement. "That's rather heavy artillery," he said.

"We're at war," Millikan said. "That ups all antes."

"Then I will look into the idea," Dellinger said, and threw his boss a crisp salute. He exited the White House and headed for his car at a run, off in search of inspectors general.

forty-eight

> We are all miffed at our Saudi hosts. They invited us here to protect their country, but they don't want us to mingle with their people and so they have put us on sort of a reservation—an old cement factory on the edge of Dhahran. We are in long rows of tents living on this great big slab of dust while we wait for the Big Green Machine to get us sorted out and sent off to the desert. Was sitting in the mess tent yesterday waving both hands over my plate trying to shoo all the flies away. Then the wind shifted and I smelled something foul and saw the latrines only a few yards away, with the same flies swarming around them. Pointed this out to my commanding officer (not that I was the only nurse or doctor who had noticed it!), and now the whole Medical Corps is in an uproar over what some people are calling "Civil War Hygiene." But that's not entirely the Saudis' fault. It's pure Army.

Clyde had arrived at the Happy Chef a few minutes early, and read this and two other letters from Desiree as he sat on the bench just inside the entrance, waiting for his breakfast date to arrive.

Happy Chefs always had to be close to the highway, because each one was marked by a giant fiberglass effigy of an ebullient, potbellied chef in a big white hat, holding a huge wooden spoon over his head, much like a Civil War colonel brandishing his cavalry saber. This one looked pretty big as Happy Chefs went; it had to be, in order not to be dwarfed by the Wal-Mart behind it, which looked like something out of Abu Simbel.

It was the first week in December, and the Happy Chef (both the fiberglass statue and the restaurant itself) had been adorned with garlands of emerald-green tinsel and blinking lights. Christmas advertising supplements to the *Des Moines Register* and the local paper were strewn like red-and-green chaff all over the bench and the lunch counter, reminding Clyde of the ill-fated business with Jonathan Town. Town had called him a few days ago, sounding irritated. “Thanks for nearly getting me fired,” he had said.

“You in trouble at school?”

“No, no, I’m talking about my stringer job.”

“The *Register*?”

“Yeah. I talked to my editor in Des Moines about your Iraqi thing. He said he’d take it the next level up. Four days later I hear from my boss’s boss’s boss directly—he calls me on a damn cell phone from Washington. He reads me the riot act, tells me that if I breathe a word about the story to anyone, they will disavow any knowledge of my actions, fire me instantly, and let it be known that I’m some sort of a crackpot who has no connection with the *Des Moines Register* whatsoever.”

Clyde had mulled this over. “I suppose this isn’t a normal way for them to reject a story idea.”

“Let me put it this way. When one of my kids comes to me with a lousy story idea for the school paper, I usually break the news personally—I don’t have the secretary of education call him from Washington and yell at him for fifteen minutes.”

“Why do you suppose they did it that way?”

“Your guess is as good as mine. The guy who bawled me out lives in Washington, if that tells you anything.”

“I’m not sure it does,” Clyde had said, remembering his and Fazoul’s conversation about how clueless Clyde was when it came to the big bad world.

“Look, all I’m saying is that this guy sounded scared,” Town had said.

And then Clyde had had an insight: Town was talking about how this big *Register* honcho was scared. And that might very well have been true; but what he really meant was that he, Jonathan Town, was scared. And when Clyde had understood that the big *Register* honcho and Jonathan Town were both scared, he had begun to feel scared himself. Not that he didn't already have plenty to be scared about. But it was all local stuff, personal stuff, and the news that people who lived in Washington were scared threw a whole new layer of generalized dread onto the thing.

The area in front of Happy Chef's cash register had two benches facing each other about six feet apart, and for several minutes an older fellow had been sitting across from Clyde, reading the newspaper and chewing on a mint toothpick that he had plucked from the cup next to the till. Clyde had glanced up at this gentleman when he'd come in. Not recognizing him, he had turned back to his intensive study of all items from all newspapers pertaining to Desert Shield. Someone had left a *Chicago Tribune* on the bench, and this provided a lode of data that Clyde wouldn't otherwise have seen.

"Hell, I don't know," the older fellow said, tossing a newspaper onto the bench. "My niece says it's all about oil."

"Beg pardon?" Clyde said.

"My niece. Nice girl. College student—you know how they are."

"I suppose." Clyde hadn't been a college student himself, but he had arrested enough of them to know their patterns.

"So last week I'm trying to carve the goddamn turkey, and all she wants to do is talk about how the Gulf thing is just a grubby squabble over oil."

"What do you think?" Clyde said. He had participated in enough lunch-counter discussions to know that this was always a sure-fire comeback.

"Well, I suppose she's got a point, in her self-righteous college-student way. I don't imagine we'd have half a million people over there if it was some shitty little country in Africa. So maybe it is about oil."

"I suppose you're right," Clyde said.

"So should we be over there like we are, just to keep dibs on a shitload of oil?"

"Yep," Clyde said. "We should."

"But all we hear about from Bush is that Saddam is like Hitler. It's always gestapo this and Hitler that, and how we're going to uphold democracy in Kuwait—which is a feudal aristocracy, for Christ's sake."

Clyde put his *Trib* in his lap and nodded out the window. The man turned round to see what Clyde was nodding at. The only thing in that direction was a First National Bank of NishWap; beyond that the barren cornfields stretched away to infinity. "What you looking at?" he inquired.

"The electric sign," Clyde said.

The sign on the bank said 8:37, and then it said 6°F and then the equivalent in centigrade.

"Six degrees," Clyde said. "Pretty damn cold. And I don't see many trees out there that we could use for firewood. So. We get oil, we live. We don't get oil, we die."

The man turned back around and looked at Clyde. "Simple as that," he said.

"Oh, there's probably a lot more to it that I don't know about," Clyde said, "but that's how I look at it."

"Six degrees," the man repeated. He picked up a *USA Today* and looked at the weather map on the back page. "That's forty degrees cooler than Washington. Big difference. Forty degrees clarifies a lot of issues, doesn't it?"

"I don't know," Clyde said, "I've never been to Washington."

"Well, you haven't missed anything," the man said. "You can take my word for it."

Something finally occurred to Clyde. He looked out into the parking lot and saw a couple of large navy-blue cars sitting in the lot with great clouds of steam coming from their tailpipes. Young men in suits and sunglasses sat in the cars talking into cellular telephones. He looked back at the other man, who had a slightly sheepish look on his face.

"You the guy?" Clyde said, rising to his feet.

"I'm the guy. Ed Hennessey," the man said, rising and extending his hand. "Shit, you're a big guy. But you weren't a heavyweight?"

"Nah," Clyde said. "One weight class below heavyweight. I'm not that big by local standards."

"Well, certainly not compared to this Tab Templeton. He was a fucking behemoth," Hennessey said. "I remember watching him years ago in the Olympics with this kind of morbid fascination. So when the file came across my desk, it was a real blast from the past. That poor son of a bitch."

Hennessey beckoned Clyde forward and into the restaurant. Clyde felt a little edgy walking past the "Please Wait to Be Seated" sign so cavalierly. But Hennessey, as if he owned the place, led him straight back to a large booth in the corner, which could have seated the whole Dhont family. They drew a few stares as they sat down—not because Clyde was semifamous as a wrestling and political failure, and not because Hennessey was a stranger wearing a suit, but because only two of them were taking up a whole booth. Hennessey folded up his long overcoat and laid it out on the orange vinyl seat, and Clyde, knowing that the corner of the restaurant would be cold, just kept his parka on. Hennessey corralled the table's ashtray and set up a pack of cigarettes and a silver lighter in front of him, as if this fuel would keep him from freezing in the chill draft pouring down off the big picture windows. "I like this place," he said, looking around. "Everyone is a real human being here."

Clyde did not really understand what Hennessey was talking about; it seemed like an odd thing to say. "They are pretty good with hash browns here," he said.

"Good! I'll keep that in mind," Hennessey said. He seemed sincerely pleased, as if this were the best news he'd heard all year. "Anyone can flip a burger, but hash browns are a black art," he said.

"I've fried up a few potatoes down at the jail," Clyde said, "and always found it hard to achieve the right balance."

"I'm shanty Irish. A south Boston boy—you'll hear the accent when I get excited or drunk," Hennessey said. "We know potatoes. But most of us still can't make a decent slab of hash browns to save our lives. We can boil stuff like nobody's business, but frying is too exotic."

The waitress came around with an insulated pitcher of coffee. Hennessey thanked her warmly and poured mugs full for both Clyde and himself. Both men reached for the mugs as if they were life preservers in the wintry North Atlantic. "Didn't realize your duties extended to cooking," Hennessey said.

"It's a long story," Clyde said.

"Anyway, you'll be out of the deputy business—when?"

"Christmas Day at four in the afternoon."

"Shit. That bastard stuck you with the Christmas Day shift?"

"I volunteered," Clyde said, "since my wife isn't home anyway."

"So that the others could spend it with their families. What a mensch," Hennessey said. "What happens for you after Christmas?"

"Try to live on Desiree's combat pay. I've got some real-estate things going. We'll find a way," Clyde said.

"You know, I'm tremendously impressed that I wasn't able to sucker you with the prospect of an FBI job," Hennessey said. "I did sucker you for a couple of weeks there, didn't I? But not for long—which makes it all the more impressive."

"I guess you did have me going for a while," Clyde said, taken aback by Hennessey's frankness. The man used speech in a completely different way from anyone Clyde had ever known. People around here spoke like the Nishnabotna in February, when it was all jammed up with ice, and the movement of water underneath was only suggested by occasional groans and pops. Hennessey spoke like a free-running stream. Like a man whose speech was a tool of his trade, a tool he'd spent many decades perfecting.

"Thought I was playing you like a fish," Hennessey said, "and then I get this." He reached into his breast pocket and took out a sheet of lined paper covered with Clyde's neat handwriting. He pulled a pair of half glasses out of his other pocket and slipped them on. "I am withdrawing my application to the Federal Bureau of Investigation," he read, "as I do not think it would advance my personal goals at this time." He looked up over the glasses into Clyde's eyes. Hennessey had emerald-green eyes in an otherwise colorless and withered face. They could be very cold and penetrating eyes, Clyde realized. "Now, that's an interesting sentence. 'Advance my personal goals.' What does that mean, Clyde? Other than the obvious stuff like raising your kid."

Clyde's heart jumped to a higher gear. He said nothing.

"Does it have anything to do with Fazoul and the Iraqis? I need to know."

Clyde felt his chest getting all tight. He took a couple of deep breaths, trying to calm down.

"Clyde, you're scaring me," Hennessey said. "Cool it with the emotions for a second. I want to know what are your intentions regarding those fucking ragheads and their botulin factory."

Clyde looked out the window and started grinding his teeth.

"Yesterday," Hennessey said, "you spent an hour and a half on the telephone with a JAG lawyer at Fort Riley, drawing up a last will and testament. True? You don't have to speak. Just nod."

Clyde nodded.

"Clyde, I'm a three-pack-a-day smoker with four kids and three ex-wives, and I didn't draw up a will until a couple of years ago. What's going on with you?"

"Bullshit," Clyde said. "That's bullshit."

"Pardon me?"

"You're CIA," Clyde said. "I don't think they'd let you out of the country without a will."

Hennessey raised his eyebrows and whistled. "Okay. Let me rephrase. I know some heavy smokers with kids and ex-wives who don't work for the CIA, and who didn't get around to thinking about their wills until they were twice as old as you, and a whole lot closer to the end of their life expectancy."

"What's the CIA doing inside the United States?" Clyde said. "That's unconstitutional."

"Oh, nice change of subject, Clyde. Don't think I won't come back to this. By the way, it isn't unconstitutional. It's just illegal as hell," Hennessey said.

"What are you doing illegally, then?"

"Promise not to tell?"

"Yup."

"Cross your heart and all that shit?"

"I either promise or I don't."

"Okay. Clyde, I shouldn't tell you any of this, but I know my secrets are safe with you. None of the people who want to know this stuff will take you seriously—which is their fault, not yours. But that doesn't matter. You'll never tell because you promised you wouldn't. You'll never reveal what I'm going to tell you here at the Happy Chef, any more than you'll describe to me the face of Mohammed Ayubanov. Just as Fazoul entrusted you with the face of Mo, as we affectionately call Mr. Ayubanov in certain precincts of northern Virginia, I'm entrusting you with the Tale of Ed."

The waitress came by. Hennessey ordered the number five, with extra hash browns on the side, and Clyde ordered the same thing; he reckoned that Hennessey would probably pay the tab, and so the extra potatoes did not seem extravagant.

"Okay, Sherlock. As you have correctly deduced, I really work, and have always worked, for the CIA, which happens to be a dangerously screwed-up and mole-ridden organization. We recruit the most wonderful youngsters from places like Wapsipinicon and send them off to exotic lands and they never come back. Someone is selling them out—perhaps several someones are. We call these someones moles. Now, if you were running such an organization, how would you find the moles, Clyde?"

"I guess I'd try to hire better people."

Hennessey threw his head back and laughed delightedly. When he'd got calmed down, he said, "But it's the fucking federal government, Clyde. That's not an option. We take what they send us. Now, in all seriousness, if you knew that moles existed, and you were pretty certain that they were posted here in CONUS, what would you do?"

In the last couple of months Clyde had seen enough military paperwork to know that CONUS meant "continental United States." "Well," he said, "it's illegal for you to actually do anything here."

"Right."

"Doesn't the FBI handle counterintelligence?"

"Yes. They keep saying so, anyway."

"Wouldn't that extend to mole hunting?"

"So far you are one hundred percent right, Clyde. It's just that, at this point, there is a little hitch. See, catching foreign agents is one thing. Usually they are posted at foreign embassies, or at places like Eastern Iowa University. They are on alien soil. They are more vulnerable. They are easier targets for the FBI's counterintel people. But a mole is a different thing. A mole is an American, hence operating on his own home territory, which makes everything a hundred times easier for him. And rather than having to penetrate our institutions from outside, he's already ensconced in the holy of holies—the CIA. Do you have any idea how hard it is for the FBI to tackle a problem like that?"

"Pretty hard, I guess."

"It's a fucking nightmare. They can't possibly make any headway without extensive cooperation from the CIA itself. And when we start down that road, we run into legality problems in no time flat. The lines are terribly ambiguous. If we sit down in a conference room with the FBI guys and tell them about someone we think is a little suspicious, are we violating the law against operating in the U.S.? Who the fuck knows? The way things are in Washington now, almost anything we do could be exposed and picked apart in some congressional hearing.

"Besides, Clyde, if you think about it, we've got something of a catch-twenty-two here anyway. If the CIA is compromised by moles, then any efforts the CIA makes to find the moles, or to help the FBI find them, are also compromised. Makes you tear your hair out," he said, running one hand back over his scalp, thinly veiled with steel-wool-colored hair. "So a few years ago, this one tired old war-weary son of a bitch came up with an idea. He was going to deal with this mole problem once and for all. He officially resigned from the CIA. He spent a year doing basically nothing—supposedly he was teaching on a part-time basis at Boston College, but that was bullshit. Then he came back down to Washington and began a new career—working for the FBI, in the counterintelligence office. And he brought a few handpicked people along with him from the Agency—some of those better people we should have hired to begin with, as you said. And he set about trying to root out moles from the CIA. For all intents and purposes, he was a CIA man. But he was operating under an FBI flag of convenience, which did two things for him: one, made the whole thing legal, and two, created a firewall between him and the mole-ridden Agency, so that his efforts would not be compromised before they could come to fruition."

"So how has your plan been working so far, Mr. Hennessey?"

Hennessey grimaced and shrugged. "It was okay for a while," he said. "We made some headway. But last week the shit really hit the fan. There are some people out there in Washington who don't like me very much, and all of a sudden they are shocked, shocked to find that I'm doing what amounts to CIA work inside the U.S. They have managed to launch an investigation of yours truly by an inspector general, which, in D.C., is very scary and serious business."

"You going to prison?"

"Oh, hell no. I'm much too careful. I'll be back in a nice office at Langley within a month. But it does cramp my style pretty badly."

"What have you been doing in Forks County? The Iraqi thing doesn't have anything to do with moles, does it?"

"No, it doesn't. We've been here keeping an eye on your friend Fazoul."

"Why?"

"We found a CIA person at Langley who was doing the wrong things—had too much money in his bank account, didn't do so hot on the polygraph, etcetera. We put him under surveillance. We found that he was being run by a foreign agent based in Wapsipinicon, Iowa, of all places—obviously a graduate student at your fine university. This person turned out to be very hard to pin down—he was very good. We put Marcus out here with the task of finding which foreign graduate student was running the mole. And although we never found a smoking gun, we did build up some circumstantial evidence that the culprit was none other than your friend Fazoul. Which was a big surprise, because Fazoul is a Vakhan Turk—a man without a country. Your average dispossessed, landless ethnic group doesn't have its act together well enough to place and run moles at the CIA, so I took an interest in Fazoul and his boss, Mohammed Ayubanov. The Vakhan Turks have become sort of like my hobby.

"Then this goddamn horse-mutilation thing happened. Then I find myself in a turf battle. Marcus is my guy, remember, and he's in Nishnabotna for one thing and one thing only, and that is to keep tabs on Fazoul and his merry men and wait for them to get in touch with their supposed mole at Langley. But all of a sudden the FBI is saying, 'Hey, we've got a man stationed there, let's get him working on the horsies.' So Marcus, who as you noticed is not a cop and never will be, suddenly has to pretend to be a cop in order to preserve the fucking cover story about why he's there, and instead of chasing Fazoul he's running around after a bunch of goddamn horses." Hennessey rolled his eyes. "Jesus. Never work for the government, Clyde."

"Doesn't seem likely that I ever will."

"That's good. People go into the government thing with these romantic ideas—just like you, a few weeks ago, when you filled out the job application. Then they encounter the reality and become cynical and jaded. Most of them quit at that point, which is the rational thing to do. But some of us stay on. Why would anyone stay on even after he had become cynical and jaded?"

"I can't guess. Maybe to pay the mortgage?"

"That's part of it," Hennessey said. "But the real reason is character defects."

Hennessey let that one hang in the air for a while as the waitress showed up with the two number fives. She feigned surprise at their nearly empty coffee thermos, filled both their mugs, and replaced the thermos with a fresh one.

Both men went for the hash browns first: disks of golden brown, the outer shell as crisp as ice on a puddle, the center moist and soft but still chewable. Their eyes locked across the table. Hennessey sighed and looked as if he were about to weep. "Oh, yeah," he said through his food. "Oh, yeah."

"What's yours?" Clyde said after they had been eating for a minute or two.

"Pardon?"

"What's your character defect?"

"Exactly!" Hennessey said, stabbing his fork at Clyde. He spoke the word so loudly that heads turned around the room. Then he quieted down. "That's exactly how you have to think in D.C. If you're dealing with anyone who's been there for more than five years, you have to ask yourself, 'Okay, what's this guy's character flaw?' After a while you develop a taxonomy. A classification system. So you have your people-on-a-power-trip. Your self-deluded types. The occasional fanatic, though the system tends to weed those out." Hennessey paused long enough to pop another bite into his mouth. "Me? I like to win."

"That's your flaw?"

"It is when you like it as much as I do. It's kind of a sick thing, the pleasure of winning."

"I wouldn't know," Clyde said.

Hennessey laughed ruefully. "Your problem with this Iraq thing is that you've got tangled up, unwittingly, with people who long ago decided it wasn't sophisticated to be sincere, that sincerity was for fools, that sincere people were put on earth to be manipulated and exploited by people like them—for the greater good, of course. This is currently the most common character flaw in the Washington establishment—attempts to be Machiavellian by people who lack the talent, the panache, to pull it off. So here you are, good old Clyde Banks, desperately trying to deal with this very real problem here on the ground, and it's as if you're in a nightmare where these fucking bush-league Machiavellis listen to what you're saying but don't really understand."

"That's pretty much what it feels like," Clyde said, frowning at his corned-beef hash and nodding his head.

"You and I know that something is going on in Forks County, and we would like to do something about it," Hennessey said, "but between the two of us are about ten thousand of these people who are too busy looking down their noses at us to actually grasp the problem and take action. You must know that taking action is looked down upon, Clyde. This is the postmodern era. When events come to a cusp, we're supposed to screw our courage to the sticking place and launch a reanalysis of the eleventh draft of the working document. Actually going out and doing stuff in the physical world is simply beyond the comprehension of these people. They're never going to do anything about the Iraqis in Forks. Never."

"That sort of confirms what I was thinking," Clyde said.

"Which brings us back, unless I'm mistaken, to your sudden desire for a last will and testament."

Clyde nodded and ate for a while. Hennessey did the same, both men gathering strength for the next round.

" 'Course," Clyde said, "Army wants you to have a will anyway, when one of you goes overseas on a combat mission."

"Of course," Hennessey said.

"But you're right in what you're thinking," Clyde said. He swallowed hard and turned his head to look out the window. His rib cage shuddered like an old truck engine trying to start up, and hot tears suddenly sprouted from his eyes and ran down his cheeks. He shifted his body toward the window, rested his head on one hand, and let the tears run for a minute or so, knowing that no one but Hennessey could see him.

Hennessey sipped coffee and looked out the window, too. "Sheriff Mullowney won't help. FBI won't help. CIA can't help," Hennessey said after a while. "Old Clyde is on his own, and this time he's not going to lose, is he?"

Clyde shook his head and tried to say "Nope," but his voice didn't work.

"That's the spirit," Hennessey said. "You've got to love to win. Should we go out and win one, Clyde?"

"We?"

"I'm not going to sit here and bullshit you. In a little while I'm going to fly back to D.C., and I probably won't leave until this thing is over. I won't be here with you on the front line, I won't be risking my life. Currently my stock is very low with both the CIA and the FBI, because I haven't been winning recently. I've been getting my ass kicked, frankly, which really pisses me off—but that's neither here nor there. The point is that I cannot arrange for planeloads of heavily armed federal agents to descend from the skies. Or anything like that. But I may be able to make myself useful in smaller ways."

forty-nine

BETSY THOUGHT it was appropriate that she would have her session with the inspector general on the winter solstice, the darkest day of the year. As long as she had been in government work, the two most awesome words in tandem were "inspector" and "general." These people had, depending on one's point of view, the power of God at the minimum, or, at the maximum, of the IRS. IGs could be Torquemadas—who delighted in giving pain—or Thomases—who falsely embodied tiresome principles—or, perhaps worst, Siricas, who would nibble you to death. They wrote their own charges, and it was alleged that in the Agency there were no procedural niceties like habeas corpus to get in their way.

Betsy had hardly been surprised when her supervisors at the Agency had informed her that her polygraph with the redoubtable Kim McMurtry hadn't gone very well. It had, in fact, gone so badly that it had set into motion a new investigation of which little was revealed to her. But from its very slowness she inferred that it must be a gigantic, multiagency engine of destruction. Now, a month and a half later, it had come to this: be in such-and-such an office on the tenth floor of the New Executive Office Building at nine-thirty A.M. on 21 December, to have a little chat with the inspector general.

No formal statement of the charges against her had been made. She knew she was in trouble, but she could not tell how serious it might be. She knew only that there was one way out of Washington, and it passed through a certain doorway in the NEOB.

She took the metro over to Farragut West and checked

through security at nine-fifteen. She took the elevator to the tenth floor and went to the ladies' room to wash her face and get ready for what was to come.

She was shocked by the face in the mirror. In the last year new lines had creased her forehead. The beginnings of a permanent frown could be seen. She had never been the kind of girl who dotted her *i*'s with smiley faces. But she didn't think of herself as a sad or tragic person and was disturbed to see that she now wore the mask of a victim, of one who had undergone great pain.

The door was a solid unmarked slab of wood that could have led to a janitor's closet. There was no answer to her knock, so she tried the knob and found that it was unlocked. She entered a dimly lit anteroom with a desk, a chair, no telephone, and the standard picture of George Bush on the wall. She thought back to that day in August when he'd taken her out on his Cigarette boat and told her to hang in there. She could take some satisfaction in knowing that she'd done that.

It was nine thirty-three and no one seemed to be around, so she went to the next door and knocked. A thin, rather high-pitched voice said, "Come in, please."

She opened the door and entered a conference room, much more brightly lit. One person was in there, seated at the end of a table that could have handled twelve people. She was struck by how large he was, for a man with a high-pitched voice. He had a high forehead, emphasized by advanced baldness, and wore rimless glasses. On the table in front of him was a blotter with a yellow legal pad on it, three government-issue Skilcraft pens, and an archaic reel-to-reel tape recorder.

Betsy looked around reflexively. He said, "There are no cameras, no one-way mirrors, none of that. You'll be dealing with just me. And our government in its wisdom appointed me to find the truth, which is a pretty simple job description by local standards." He stopped for a moment, then mused, "Probably the next generation will have no need for human beings in this job—just chemical tests and voice-stress analysis. Hmm, hmm." Then he stood up. He must have been six-seven or six-eight. "My name is Richard Holmes. I always tell people that's no relation to

Sherlock. I'm actually a shirttail descendant of Oliver Wendell. He used up six or seven generations' worth of brains, so the rest of us have labored in obscurity as bureaucrats or tax lawyers. Though I do have a granddaughter who shows promise."

Betsy shook his hand and said, "Pleased to meet you. Betsy Vandeventer." She'd been around long enough not to fall too quickly for this kind of folksy, self-deprecating chatter. But Holmes did not seem blatantly insincere.

"That's a relief," Holmes joked. "Well, shall we get on with this?"

He sat down and motioned for Betsy to sit to his left, near the tape recorder. "You'll like the view," he said, and she did. A little snow squall was coming down, and it looked glorious—for those who weren't driving. "Before I get started asking questions of you, do you have any for me?"

"Is this it? Just you and me?"

"Yes." And then, leaning toward her, sotto voce: "I hope people won't talk." He delivered his jokes ponderously and almost apologetically, like a professor.

Betsy smiled politely. "One more. Am I in trouble? Are there charges against me?"

"That was two. The answer to the first question is yes. Dr. Millikan feels that you have committed security violations—passing information around to those with no need to know, or, to be specific, to Mr. Hennessey. That's a hard one to make stick. You are very conscientious about basic security procedures. As to the second question, no. There are no charges against you. You never handled budget, which is where most of the problems come from. You never hired or fired anyone, which is another common source of trouble. You were never in Operations, so you didn't kill the wrong people or overthrow the wrong government." He paused, reached under the table, and brought up a thermos and two cups. "You're going to be talking a lot, so I brought something to wet your whistle. I hope you like hot chocolate."

"That would be lovely."

"Now I'm turning on the tape recorder. This should be the only recording of this conversation, because this is supposed to be one of the designated secure rooms in this building." He cleared his throat and turned on the machine; the reels spun smoothly and silently, exerting a sort of hypnotic effect on Betsy. He spoke for a few moments, rattling off the who-what-where-when-why of the interview. Then he turned off the machine and stared directly into her eyes for the first time since she'd entered the room.

"You know we're quite close to war in the Gulf. You also know that you were largely on the mark with your views. Based upon your unofficial consultation work with Mr. Hennessey, I think you think that some elements of this crisis are to be found in the middle part of this country. I will ask you to tell me your views on this. You have total immunity on this subject. You must trust me when I tell you that."

Even after all she'd gone through, Betsy believed the words of this strange, tall old man. She wanted to ask many questions about where this report would go after he'd finished it. It was strange that the interview was happening in the NEOB and not at Langley.

He reached for the switch on the tape recorder. She held up one hand to stop him and said, "What's the downside for me?"

"If your hypothesis is wrong, you will be scapegoated, for internal USG consumption. It is almost inconceivable that any actual penalties will be levied against you. You'll never work for government again."

"Sounds like a good deal to me," Betsy said. "Roll that sucker."

He started the machine again. "Ms. Vandeventer, I understand from your file that you will be leaving your current position at the end of the year."

"That is correct."

"What were your duties?"

Betsy recapitulated her five years at the Agency, out of practice describing her work only in the most general terms.

"Ms. Vandeventer, I should have reminded you that this interview is classified at the very highest level, so feel free to go into detail, complete with any discussion of sources and methods that may be relevant, and any commentary you may wish to make, pro or con, on Agency personnel and practices."

Twenty minutes later she was still talking. Holmes refilled her hot chocolate and gently reminded her to move on to the fateful briefing with the Agricultural attaché.

Betsy burned her lips on the chocolate, fresh and boiling hot from the thermos, and forged on. With the exception of a time-out to turn the tape over, Holmes did not interrupt her. He simply looked at her through the scratched and smudged lenses of his glasses and made incredibly intricate doodles on his tablet. Finally she told the tale of her final polygraph test and summarized the ensuing several weeks of meaningless make-work.

"Is that all?"

"I believe so."

"Then one last question. During your time at the Agency you were strongly enjoined from doing forward-leaning analysis. When you broke this rule, you were severely reprimanded. Now I would like you to do some forward-leaning analysis for me. Based on everything you've seen and experienced in the last year, what is your analysis of our current situation vis-à-vis Saddam?"

It was a very strange request from an inspector general, but Betsy saw no harm in playing along—they had only ten more days in which to persecute her. She cleared her throat, drained the last of the hot chocolate, sat up straight, and composed her thoughts for a moment before answering. "Saddam has shown a baffling level of stubbornness in Kuwait. It's crazy for him to keep his forces there in the face of such enormous odds. No one can figure out why he hasn't backed down—most people just shrug their shoulders and say he must be a madman.

"But I don't think he's a madman. I think that his strategy relies on the assumption that he's holding a weapon of mass destruction in his hands. When we get down to crunch time, he can lob biological-warfare agents into Israel and force the Israelis to attack him. This will destroy the coalition that Messrs. Bush and Baker have worked so hard to build. The anti-Saddam forces will fall into disarray, and there's a good chance he'll be able to remain in Kuwait with no repercussions other than some economic sanctions."

"And you think that the weapon in question is now within our borders."

"I think that some very bad men were dispatched from Baghdad and inserted into this country shortly before Saddam's invasion of Kuwait. They must have been sent to do something extremely important. They killed my brother, and Margaret Park-O'Neil, to cover their tracks. I think it is not unreasonable to suspect that these men may be producing biological weapons within our borders even as we speak, most likely somewhere in the vicinity of Forks County, Iowa."

That was as simply and clearly as she could put it. Holmes seemed satisfied; he nodded deeply and turned off the tape machine with a satisfying *clunk*. He stood up and looked out the window—the snow was already melting under a bright winter sun. "You know," he said, "at moments like this I always like to recall Bismarck's statement that God protects drunks and the United States of America."

Betsy felt invigorated and renewed. Holmes looked drained and exhausted, as if she had passed her burden of knowledge onto him and it was already weighing him down. He looked at her somberly and said, "I understand why you're leaving government service. But it's a shame. We need people like you." He unplugged the tape recorder and began neatly coiling up its power cord. When this was finished, he put his pens and papers away into a big lawyer's briefcase. Then, as if suddenly struck by a thought, he took off his glasses and looked at her with the nicest, deepest blue eyes she'd ever seen. "Please believe me when I tell you I'm so sorry about your brother."

"Thank you," Betsy said, and then, to her own surprise, dissolved into tears. She pulled a new packet of Kleenexes from her purse, put one to her face, and began to sob out loud. It was a strange combination of sadness over Kevin combined with relief that she wouldn't be thrown into jail, that she could get out of town and begin her life again, that she'd told someone who had listened.

Holmes sat down. He didn't know what to do. He patted her on the shoulder once or twice and waited.

"Boy oh boy," Betsy finally said when it was over. "Sorry about that."

"Quite all right."

"I hope I've been of some help."

Holmes winked at her. "It's safe to say that you have," he said. He opened the door and held it for her. Betsy walked into the darkness of the anteroom and nearly tripped over Ed Hennessey, drinking coffee from a Styrofoam cup the size of a paint bucket.

"What are you doing here?" she blurted.

"Christmas shopping," Hennessey shot back, "which is what you should be doing."

"I can take a hint. I'll get lost," Betsy said. She walked out through the slablike door, and as it closed behind her, she could hear Hennessey greeting Holmes and chaffing him mercilessly about his baldness.

fifty

MOST OF Eastern Iowa University's seniors wanted to graduate in spring, when they could do their walk in front of the regents and the president of the university, and some worthy speaker such as Dan Quayle or Mike Ditka would be there to talk and receive an honorary doctorate. Besides, the campus would look pretty and there would be plenty of parties.

The December ceremony, on the other hand, had the ambience of an Organization of Asian and African States meeting. The foreign graduate students had to go through the ceremony for the pictures to take back home, not only for their families but for their governments as well—a photograph of a scholar standing in his robes and hood next to his graduate adviser seemed a more tangible proof of completion than a faked-up piece of sheepskin. Most of them had to be out of the country within a week after finishing their degrees, so the winter ceremony also had an air of finality about it.

On the morning of Saturday, the twenty-second of December, Clyde and Maggie were in the TV room. Maggie was pulling herself up on things, clearly intending to be an early walker. Clyde was watching Iraqi schoolchildren running air-raid drills on CNN, and going through a week's worth of mail. He found a cream-colored envelope made of nice heavy paper and opened it, expecting another wedding invitation from some shirttail Dhont six times removed. Instead it was an invitation from Fazoul to attend his graduation ceremony. As part of a package deal the Twister Bookstore had thrown in ten personalized invites to people renting robes and hoods from them, and Fazoul had been nice enough to put Clyde on his list.

It was a nice little bright spot in a bad month. And the business with the Iraqis was putting him through an emotional mangle. Part of the time he was anxious that he would never figure out where the Iraqis had built their facility. When he was chasing down a promising lead and began to convince himself that he had almost found them, he came face-to-face with the realization that he was very likely to die soon. He'd already made up his mind, in an abstract and theoretical way, that he would settle for that.

The notion of never seeing Maggie again was impossible to entertain when he was in the same room with her. When he was out in the station wagon by himself with a pump shotgun and a high-powered rifle resting on the seat under an old blanket, following a suspected Iraqi agent and beginning to think that he might be close, then the possibility seemed very real, and his heart pounded so hard, it almost knocked him over, and he wondered whether he would be any use when it came down to actually doing something.

In the midst of all this the notion of going to see Fazoul receive his international-business MBA lifted his spirit. Even that was bittersweet, for he knew that Fazoul's visa ran out immediately after graduation, and that he would never see the family again after today unless they all lived through the next couple of months and then made a trip to wherever the Vakhan Turks were currently encamped.

He wrested the remote control from Maggie's grasp, sending her into a tantrum, and switched over to the Weather Channel just in time for the Gulf weather report, which was his favorite part of the television coverage. It made him feel somehow closer to his wife. It was somehow reassuring to see the familiar high- and low-pressure symbols advancing across the Tigris-and-Euphrates region.

The phone rang, and he knew that it was Desiree. Her unit held a drawing to see who and in what order people would be able to make phone calls. "Hi, darling," she said, and Clyde knew something was wrong. The voice had lost its snap, its confidence.

"You okay?"

"Yeah. Better let me talk to my baby."

"She's sleeping on top of me here."

"Let me hear her breathe."

He put the mouthpiece as close to Maggie's mouth as he could without waking her up. On the other end of the line he could hear Desiree beginning to come apart.

"Nice to hear from you, babe," he said. He knew they had only three minutes.

"Honey," her choked voice came through the ether. "Always remember, I love you."

In the upper Midwest people generally didn't say they loved each other unless one of them was on his or her deathbed. Television provided the bizarre, alien spectacle of actors kissing total strangers as they strode onto the sets of talk and award shows. People hugging while they extended the "peace of the Lord" to each other in church drew sharp frowns. People loved each other. That was enough; it wasn't necessary to talk about it. Desiree loved Clyde; she knew it, he knew it. They didn't talk about it. They lived it. Clyde knew something was terribly wrong, that Desiree had learned something. That she was scared to death.

He went to the kitchen, carrying the baby on his hip, mixed

up some formula, and then went back to the recliner to feed the baby and watch CNN. He almost fell asleep again and was awakened by a grumpy noise from the baby when the bottle fell from her grasp. He felt too drained to go through the motions anymore. He changed her diaper, got her stuff together, and left for the graduation ceremony, leaving her with the Dhonts.

At one fifty-five he pulled into the vast, mostly empty parking lot of the Flanagan Multipurpose Arena, which they used to call the armory until they had put a new high-tech roof on it and painted over the cinder blocks. As he approached the entrance, he spotted Ken Knightly standing there, smoking his Camel in a most serious way.

"How's it goin', Dean?"

"Hey, Clyde. Big day. Our buddy Fazoul is heading back to Vakhan land. Hold this for me, would you?" He handed Clyde a half-smoked Camel while he reached in a backpack for his robes and hood, which had evidently been tightly wadded together and stored in a damp location since the spring ceremony. "Don't want to immolate myself," he explained, nodding at the cigarette. "These robes are made out of frozen gasoline, you know." The robe was already zipped up, so he threw it on over his head like a T-shirt. Then he pulled out something floppy and violet: a gaudy, oversize beret. "Got this as a freebie with an honorary doctorate at the University of Dubai. Doesn't blow off in the wind as easy as the goddamned mortarboard, which is an important consideration out here on the prairie. We'd better go in. Thanks." He took the cigarette back, smoked it down to a butt in several long draws, and stamped it out at the threshold of the Flanagan's main entrance.

The gym was about one-quarter full. Knightly led Clyde down onto the maple floor of the basketball court and pointed out some empty seats close to the dais where he and other university dignitaries would be seated. "If you would do me a little favor and sit there, Clyde. We've gotta talk after this is done."

The Twisters' pep band, dressed in their blazers and gray flannels, began to play "Pomp and Circumstance."

Clyde was a softie for ceremonies—even the flag ceremonies at

Cub Scout meetings. He looked around the half-filled gym and saw a few parents, but mostly wives and children, all dressed in their best. He saw one of the Iraqis he'd been following and wasn't sure whether to be glad that the man was getting out of Dodge, or frustrated by his inability to catch the guy red-handed.

The degree candidates were led in by the president of the university, his administration, and then the faculty in their robes and hoods. Then came the students themselves with their different specialities represented by different series of colors on the hoods. By the time they were all in, the pep band played with a bit less flair. Then the "Star-Spangled Banner" was played, and then a suitably neutral prayer ("O Creator of the Universe") was uttered by the local Unitarian pastor.

Clyde sat down and stood up on command, like a twelfth-century newly converted peasant at his first Mass, but his mind was elsewhere. He didn't even realize the ceremony was over until he felt a gentle squeeze on his left arm, and there was Farida. "We're so happy you could come." She extended her baby son over to Clyde. "Could you hold him while we take pictures?"

The baby was sound asleep, an angelic, honey-skinned creature with astonishingly long and thick eyelashes. Clyde watched as Fazoul stood bedecked in his M.S. hood next to his adviser, Chung-Shin Kim, and then with Dean Knightly, who seemed blinded by all the mini-strobes and badly in need of a smoke. Then Fazoul motioned for Clyde to come up. Clyde was surprised when he was dragged in with the entire family.

"This is good-bye, my friend," Fazoul said as he held Clyde's hand in a long handshake. Then he hugged him. "Don't forget me."

Farida came up, tears in her eyes, and said, "Know that we are praying for your wife. We are all in the same struggle here."

Fazoul said something sharply to her, and she responded in English, "We are together. That's all."

Knightly stepped in and said, "We'd better get you folks down to the train station. The Amtrak's showing up in about forty-five minutes. I'll give you a ride. You want to come along, Clyde?"

"Got space?"

"Got a Suburban."

"Sure. My shift doesn't start for a couple of hours."

When they arrived at the station, it became clear that the next train to Chicago was going to be filled with newly minted Ph.D.'s and M.S. students going to Union Station, then catching the El to O'Hare for flights back to their various homes around the globe. It was an incredible multiethnic crowd in a decidedly mixed set of moods—many didn't want to go back to their homelands, while others couldn't wait to be free of what they saw as the cultural barbarism of America in general and the Midwest in particular. But all of them seemed to agree that Dean Knightly was the best thing about this place, and so Clyde enjoyed standing there, leaning back against the wall of the station, watching the graduates and their families line up to shake his hand, hug him, kiss him, press small gifts into his hands. By the time the train pulled into the station, tears were running freely down Knightly's face.

Clyde and Knightly stood together as the train pulled away, and Knightly said, "You know, it rips me apart every time we send a bunch of them on. They have to go back. They can't stay. It's better that they go. But working with these people is the best job any man can have in this business."

"You've got some bad ones, too."

"Sure, but at least they're smart and motivated bad ones. I hate to say this, but I have real contempt"—he caught himself—"I have a strong feeling of disappointment about most of our American kids. They don't know why they're here." Knightly heaved a big sigh, stretched, then turned his back on the receding train, putting that particular batch of students out of his life. "Okay, Clyde. Let's go get a beer."

"Can't do that. Got to go to work."

"How about tonight, after you get off work?"

"Ken, I don't get off until midnight."

"That's okay."

"Then I have to go collect Maggie and get in bed."

Knightly appeared not to hear any of this. "Come to my place,

Clyde. Go ahead and bring that darn baby. My wife will look after her. We've got some talking to do."

There was black ice on the roads that day, the shortest day of the year, and as soon as dusk fell, the cars started going into the ditches, and Clyde and the other deputies on duty began to litter the highways of rural Forks County with road flares and to jam the airwaves with requests for tow trucks. This was all good for Clyde, because he needed something to make the time go by faster. He had finally got it through his skull that Knightly had something important to say to him, and the end of his shift could not come soon enough. He watched the tow-truck drivers carefully, wondering just how a fellow went about getting a job like that, and what the pay was like. Certainly you could make a lot of money at it on a day like today.

Then he remembered his larger mission and reminded himself that he had other concerns for the time being.

He went back to the department and dropped his unit off for the second-to-last time; his next and last shift as a sheriff's deputy would begin fifty-six hours from now, Christmas Day, from eight in the morning to four in the afternoon. He fired up the Murder Car and went out to Dick Dhont's to pick up Maggie. By now he had perfected the trick of easing her from crib into car seat, and of spiriting her out into the station wagon, without waking her up. Dick Dhont handed off the baby-supply bag, and Clyde judged that it had sufficient provisions to keep Maggie alive for another few hours. He tossed it onto the passenger seat, on top of the blanket that concealed the two long guns, said good night to Dick, and then drove straight to Knightly's house.

Ken Knightly did not seem to care for the company of professors or for the architecture of the yuppie/academic suburbs that had grown up to the north and west of Wapsipinicon. Rather, he lived in a part of Nishnabotna that many locals referred to simply as "Nigger Town" in recognition of the fact that something like twenty percent of the residents were black. Knightly had bought the mansion constructed by Reinhold Richter, the town's first and last lumber king (he had cut down all the trees), back in the 1870s. He went in and ripped out all the stuff he didn't like and all the wires and pipes that didn't work anymore, then got it declared a historic-preservation site for the tax advantages, then put in state-of-the-art infrastructure. All told, there were nineteen rooms in the Richter mansion, and Knightly and his wife were going to fill all of them with the assembled evidence of their twenty years of living abroad.

The yard was still torn up from construction, a sea of churned black mud frozen into a hard and brittle moonscape. Clearly it didn't matter where Clyde parked, so he parked close to the door and carried Maggie gingerly up the steps onto the veranda, which was wide enough to race horses four abreast. Clyde looked for the doorbell and couldn't find it. But a hand-lettered sign had been tacked up where you might expect to find a doorbell, reading "Pull the Rope." An arrow directed his attention upward to a brass handle projecting from the door frame. It required a hefty yank. Some eighteen inches of frayed nineteenth-century rope eventually came out. As soon as he let it go, an internal mechanism began to reel it slowly back in, and a box of chimes rang out "Sleepers Awake." Maggie startled and began to shriek. The door opened, five feet wide and three inches thick, and there was Knightly.

"Got to muffle those goddamned chimes, Sonia," Knightly barked. His wife shouted something equally strong back, Clyde thought, but not in English.

Sonia came down the giant stairway. She was brilliant and tiny, with olive skin and a lovely smile framed in perfectly applied red lipstick, as if it were not one o'clock in the morning. "Nice to meet you, Clyde. Ken has said good things about you." She said this as if it were all that she demanded in the way of a character reference. Then she turned the full powers of her charm and energy on Maggie, who was anxious for a few moments, then fell silent, fascinated by the sounds and fragrances emanating from Sonia, and consented to be taken away somewhere and rocked back to sleep.

Clyde followed Knightly through the living room, the library, and finally to the back porch, where his host yanked a flashlight off a wall bracket and aimed its powerful halogen beam at his feet. "Watch your step," Knightly instructed, "we haven't fixed the stairs yet." Indeed, they were rotten, buttressed by concrete blocks. He picked his way over the treacherous, ankle-breaking tire ruts frozen into the mud of the side yard and entered the garage, a three-car model with a high roof. Clyde knew better than to ask, and simply followed.

The garage was completely filled with dusty junk, except for a narrow winding passageway between sofas, filing cabinets, shipping crates, and old foreign motorcycles, which led to a crude ladder made of two-by-fours and nailed to a wall. It led to a trapdoor in the ceiling. Knightly climbed up a few rungs and knocked on it with the butt of his big black cop flashlight—three longs and two shorts.

The trapdoor opened. Knightly shone the light up, piercing the square of blackness, and illuminated a ghastly face that would have sent Clyde running all the way to the Illinois border if he hadn't recognized it.

"Fazoul!" Clyde said. "I'll be darn."

They clambered up the ladder and into the attic. Clyde was surprised to find a warm, well-furnished, windowless space. There was a desk, a wet bar, and the smell of Knightly's Camels, a small but good home entertainment center, a urinal plumbed into one wall, a pool table, but no telephone.

"We've all got to have a hidey-hole," Knightly said. "Someplace where nobody can find us and we can do what we want to do."

"How many people know about this?" Clyde said.

"Sonia, Fazoul, and now you."

Fazoul threw his good arm around Clyde's shoulders and said, "We have to talk."

Clyde said, "I figured you were halfway over the polar ice cap to wherever."

"Ah that, that was easy. I have a brother who works at O'Hare. He has access to the international-departures area."

Knightly turned to Clyde and drawled, "Ain't that convenient?

You would be surprised, Clyde, if you knew how often convenient things happened to Fazoul and his thousands and thousands of brothers."

"Well," Fazoul admitted, "I am using the word 'brother' in an extended sense. He is a compatriot. When I went into the men's room, he happened to be there, working on a defective air-drying machine. He is now over the ice cap somewhere with my wife and little Khalid."

"How did you get back here?" Clyde asked.

"In his car. After I had fixed the drying machine."

"I suppose I ought to check your driver's license," Clyde said, "but I have the feeling you got one that looks pretty good."

"Anyone who can fix a drying machine," Fazoul said, "can forge a driver's license."

"So," Knightly said, "I'm going to get the coffee machine fired up, because if I break into the bourbon collection now, I'll fall asleep, and Fazoul wouldn't approve anyway. And you can help yourself to those." He nodded at a Dunkin' Donuts box on the top of the bar.

"Some coffee would be not bad at all," Clyde said.

"I called this meeting because I'm getting tired of waiting for something to happen," Knightly said. "I keep waiting for the C-130's to descend on Forks full of SWAT teams in protective moon suits, and it never seems to happen, and I'm getting the idea that it never will."

Clyde looked questioningly at Fazoul. Fazoul said, "Dr. Knightly knows quite a few things. We consider him one of us."

"Sonia is half Kurd and a quarter Azerbaijani and a quarter Russian," Knightly said, "and when she became the center of my life, well, my life got even more complicated than it was to begin with, which is really saying something. It's a very, very long story, but suffice it to say that I'm on Fazoul's side—whether or not I want to be. But I do want to be."

Knightly finished prepping the coffeemaker and fired it up. "We have to compare notes on this Iraqi thing. I have to tell you that I just got fed up with these SOBs after about mid-November and told them that they had to clean up their act. Even doing that was a hassle and a half because they refused to come in and see me, or to answer my phone calls. But when I did get through to them, they were insolent, and I got really pissed. So I went to the feds to see about getting them kicked out of the country, and I got cobwebbed. And when I complained about that, I was finally told, confidentially, some shit about how there might be difficulties for our students abroad if we got tough here. And that's about all I know of my own knowledge, though Fazoul here has filled me in on the botulin thing."

"I've been following them around town," Clyde said. "Sometimes I do it on my days off, and sometimes I do it when I'm on shift, if there's nothing else going on. But I just keep coming up dry. None of them ever changes his movements. They get up, they go to the university or the vet-path lab, they come home at the end of the day."

"What do they do during the day?" Knightly said.

"All of them work in buildings that have key-card entry systems," Clyde said, "because of the animal-rights protesters. So I can't follow them in. But I don't imagine they've got their factory built inside one of the campus buildings. So I can't figure out who's tending the factory, wherever it may be."

An inspiration came to Knightly. "They're using the goddamn steam tunnels! All of those buildings are connected by steam tunnels. Those boys must know you're tailing them. When one of them wants to go to the factory, he goes to work like it's a normal day, then slips down into the steam tunnels and emerges half a mile away, hops on a bicycle or something, and goes wherever."

"That sounds believable," Clyde said. "But if that's true—if the students we've been watching are the ones doing the work—then they have to shut down the operation soon. Because I just watched most of them graduate. They have to be out of the country within seventy-two hours."

"I agree," Knightly said. "So the question is, are they going to release the toxin here in the States, as a terrorist operation—or threaten to do so—or ship it back to Iraq somehow?"

"We think they are going to ship it," Fazoul said. "They have been making transport arrangements within the last few days.

One of those who received his Ph.D. today went directly to Ryder after the ceremony and rented a flatbed semitrailer rig. The Iraqis and their various front organizations have leased several shipping containers designed for transporting bulk fluids."

"I'll bet it's a shell game," Knightly said. "They're all decoys. They're not going to ship the stuff out of the States."

Clyde found Knightly's theory perversely encouraging, because it suggested that Desiree would be safe. "Why do you say that?"

"It just doesn't make sense," Knightly said, pouring out mugs of coffee. "Why would they make it here and then ship it to Iraq? Why not just make it in Iraq? The technology is nothing special."

Fazoul shook his head no. He seemed very sure of himself. "It was out of the question for them to build it in Iraq. If they did, word would get out to the Israelis, who would bomb the facility and send tons of botulin toxin into the air."

"But it's a tiny thing! Couldn't they just hide it under a gas station or something?"

This seemed logical to Clyde. It had occurred to him before, in fact. Knightly wouldn't stop pressing Fazoul until he answered: "The Iraqi ministry responsible for this research has been penetrated and compromised by a hostile organization. No matter where in Iraq they concealed the facility, word would be sure to leak out–Israeli and American military planners would soon have the precise coordinates."

Knightly laughed. "A hostile organization. The Vakhan Turks, maybe?"

Fazoul wouldn't say. Knightly laughed again. "Did it ever occur to Ayubanov that if he weren't so goddamned good, he wouldn't force people like the Iraqis to hide their bioweapons facilities among innocent bystanders out in the middle of fucking Iowa?"

Fazoul cringed at Knightly's mention of the name Ayubanov. He did not laugh at Knightly's good-natured but sharply pointed heckling. Finally Knightly gave up. "Shit," he said, "Mo Ayubanov. What a guy I picked to owe favors to."

They sat and sipped coffee and ate doughnuts for a while.

"That's a very important piece of information—what you just told us about the 'hostile organization,'" Knightly said. "Has Mo considered passing that along to someone in Washington?"

Fazoul blanched at this suggestion.

"Because the people in Washington are probably in the same boat that I was until you enlightened me just now," Knightly continued. "They see no reason to believe the Iraqis would build such a thing in Iowa. If Mo made one phone call and set them straight, maybe they'd take some goddamn action!"

"I doubt it," Clyde said. He sketched out the vague understanding of the Washington situation that he'd got from Hennessey. When Clyde mentioned the interagency task force, Knightly rolled his eyes and moaned. When he mentioned the inspector general, Knightly set his coffee down, put his face in his hands, and remained in that position until Clyde was finished.

"Jesus," he said, "I know how those Washington people operate. We're really fucked now."

fifty-one

WHEN CLYDE was on duty, he usually did his dining at places like the drive-through window at Wendy's. No shift was complete without running a Dustbuster over the driver's seat of his unit to pick up all the spilled salt, french-fry ends, and straggly bits of lettuce he had left behind.

But this was his last shift, possibly the last time he would ever wear a law-enforcement uniform, and it was Christmas Day, and nothing was going on. There weren't enough cars on the road to make the necessary quorum for a road accident. And he had spent the last two days chasing Iraqis on numerous different modes of transport, at all hours of the night and day. So he decided to take his breakfast in sit-down luxury at Metzger's Family Style Buffet in downtown Nishnabotna, which could be relied upon to have a fine spread laid out along its mighty banks of steam tables.

As he came down the street, he saw a red Corvette with vanity license plates reading BUCK in front of the restaurant. His first impulse was to gun the motor and get out of there; he'd almost rather park in a frozen barnyard and eat french fries behind the wheel than share Christmas dinner with Buck Chandler. But he mastered this urge to flee and parked next to the Corvette. Buck had parked it badly, angling across two parking spaces, and one corner of the bumper was actually rammed up against the high curb.

Metzger's, Where Iowa Meets and Eats, had a big neon sign to that effect on its facade. After Clyde clambered up the high and precipitous stone curb, he involuntarily turned and looked up into the west, which is what most people around there did several times a day in lieu of tuning in a weather forecast. The sky in that direction consisted of a mass of dense and featureless gray extending hundreds of miles from south to north. A gauzy veil of high ice crystals had already drawn itself across the face of the sun, smudging it into a bright soft-focus splotch in the southern sky, within which the disk of the sun could be crisply resolved. The empty streets of Nishnabotna were illuminated by bright but bluish light that cast no shadows.

The big picture windows of Metzger's Buffet were framed in synthetic green garlands and plastic holly, and thickly fogged by the vapor escaping from the steam tables. Clyde hauled the massive door open, jangling innumerable sleigh bells and detonating a cacophony of synthesized electronic carols from various motion-sensitive gewgaws that had been hung from the doorknob. The "Please Seat Yourself" sign was up; Metzger's was running on a skeleton crew.

Clyde was pleased to find himself there. He had eaten so many meals and attended so many banquets and rehearsal dinners in this place that it made him feel more at home than he would have felt in his own house without Desiree.

It had been an active couple of days. Fazoul had told him, during their late-Saturday-night conference in Knightly's hidey-hole, that the Iraqis had rented a truck, so Clyde had done a routine records search and discovered that one of the newly arrived "Jordanian" Ph.D. candidates had, in the last few months, somehow found the time to obtain a truck driver's license. This person was none other than Abdul al-Turki, the wrestler with the cauliflower ears.

On Sunday, Clyde had taken it upon himself to follow al-Turki around town—not very difficult, given the size of his rig. He had to admit that the Iraqi handled it as if his postgraduate studies had been not in the field of chemical engineering but rather in advanced theoretical truck driving. Clearly the years since his ejection from international wrestling had been put to good use learning an honest trade.

But the chase had been short-lived. Al-Turki had driven the rig down to the Matheson Works on Sunday afternoon and swung it expertly through an arrow gate in the high brick wall that surrounded that vast property. The gate was promptly closed and locked behind him.

There were three possible exits from the Matheson Works. Clyde had slept in the station wagon near one of them, Fazoul in the Knightlys' Mazda near another, and Knightly himself, in his capacious four-wheel-drive Suburban, near the third.

On Monday morning—yesterday—the truck had emerged from Clyde's gate with a reconditioned shipping container on its back and made the short trip down to the barge terminal, where the container had been loaded on a barge bound for New Orleans, which departed immediately. Clyde drove down the river a few miles, hiked out onto a sandbar he knew, and checked it out as it went by, using a big pair of binoculars he'd borrowed from Ebenezer; "Aqaba," its port of destination, had been freshly stenciled onto it. Clyde had called Hennessey, who had called some of his friends in the brown-water division of the Coast Guard, who had done an investigation of the container at Lock and Dam Number Thirty-one, where the Iowa River joined the Mississippi. The container was found to be full of corn oil, and nothing else.

Almost immediately after dropping off the container at the barge terminal, the Ryder semi had returned to the Matheson Works, followed closely by Knightly, vanished through the now-familiar gate, and emerged an hour later with a new container loaded on its back. Al-Turki proceeded to head east on U.S. 30. Fazoul chased him, just to make sure he didn't double back, and Clyde, when he returned from his excursion to the sandbar, called Hennessey again. Hennessey pulled some strings at the Illinois Highway Patrol. They pulled the truck over on the pretext of searching for drugs. Once again, nothing but corn oil.

Then, late in the afternoon yesterday, a freight train had pulled out of the Denver-Platte-Des Moines yards adjacent to the Matheson Works, headed west, carrying several hundred shipping containers, several hoboes, and—by the time it had cleared the metropolitan area—three Ph.D. candidates belonging to the Vakhan Turk ethnic group, all dressed in the same gear they would have used for riding ponies over Central Asian mountain passes in the dead of winter. As the big freight had lumbered across the state of Iowa, these three had crawled up and down its length, one car at a time, checking the serial numbers and destinations of the shipping containers, and relaying them via citizens-band radio to none other than Ken and Sonia Knightly, who were shadowing the train in the four-wheel-drive Suburban. Ken did the driving, and Sonia wrote down the numbers and the destinations. Ken pulled in at every pay phone he saw so that Sonia could relay the information back to Fazoul, who typed it into his laptop, encrypted the data, and E-mailed it God knows where to be checked over by whatever intelligence apparatus Fazoul's people were running.

By the time Clyde had got back from the Christmas Eve Mass late last night, they had identified one suspicious container, leased by a Jordanian company that was thought to be a front organization for Iraqi interests, and bound for Aqaba by way of Tacoma—an odd bit of routing that was suspicious in and of itself. While the Vakhans on the train could not get the container open to inspect its contents (and dared not, lest they spill botulin toxin along hundreds of miles of track), they did notice some suspicious welds and fittings along the bottom, which looked as if they might have been added recently. Perhaps it was a tank within a tank, the outer one containing corn oil to deceive any customs inspectors, the inner one full of toxin.

"Third time's a charm," Hennessey had said, and had proceeded to ruin the holidays of many FBI agents by mobilizing a C-130 and vectoring it westward. Notwithstanding his pessimistic statements in the Happy Chef, he seemed, within the last day or two, to have suddenly amassed tremendous power and resources.

As Clyde entered Metzger's diner, Hennessey was probably passing overhead, making ready to intercept the train in a little crossroads town in western Nebraska where not too many people would be killed if it turned out to be booby-trapped. The rendezvous was going to happen in about four hours. Until then Clyde had nothing to do but be nervous, and to try to keep himself from foolishly hoping for too much. He had just talked to Ken and Sonia Knightly, who had encountered heavy snow on their way back across the state and had checked into a Best Western on the northern outskirts of Des Moines to wait the storm out.

"Morning, Clyde. Merry Christmas," said a man's voice, a polished and fine voice. Clyde looked to the end of the smorgasbord and saw Arnie Schneider sitting there before a bloody mastodon roast, gripping a giant two-pronged fork and a knife or short sword, using them to tap out a metallic rhythm on the edge of the butcher block. He was listening to a Walkman, probably to drown out the sound of the Christmas-music tape on the overhead speakers. He was eerily lit from below by the red glow of a powerful battery of heat lamps, and his bifocals, flecked with tiny droplets of juice and blood, reflected the meat table, upside down and miniaturized, a carnal microcosm. Clyde nodded at the mighty roast, eschewing the almost equally stupendous turkey. Arnie slid his weapon through the meat, cutting off an inch-thick slab, and the newly exposed face sighed out a glittering sheer waterfall of juices.

The first room had eight or ten circular tables, each capable of seating a dozen people. Solitary male diners were scattered across the room, one per table, listening to the fuzzy, rasping, oddly distorted Christmas music and having at their meat and potatoes. One of them was Buck Chandler. He had his back turned to the room, facing the corner, and sat hunched over, chewing his food very slowly and staring fixedly at a waterfowl mural that had gone all brown with cigarette smoke.

Buck hadn't seen him yet, and so, in the short term, Clyde could get away with choosing another table. But Buck would probably see him eventually and then be offended. So Clyde shuffled forward awkwardly, bumping into an empty chair in an effort to make some noise so that Buck would notice him. But Buck kept staring at those ducks on the wall. As Clyde came around the table, he was shocked by Buck's appearance: his eyes were red and bleary, and he had not shaved, or even combed his hair, in a couple of days. Buck inhaled convulsively through a mouthful of beef and then uncorked a slow, gassy belch that inflated his cheeks and eventually escaped through his nostrils, suffusing the corner of the room with a strong chemical vapor that reminded Clyde of his soon-to-be-ex-boss.

"Buck," Clyde said, "you mind?"

Buck swiveled his eyes toward Clyde, then dropped them toward his plate and bowed his head. Clyde took a seat.

"Merry Christmas," Clyde said. It might have been a cruel thing to say. But Clyde reminded himself that his life situation was, if anything, worse than Buck's, and he was keeping his chin up.

Buck Chandler did not respond to this salutation for several minutes, and when he did, it was with the words, "Fucking camel jockeys."

Clyde had grown up listening to Buck Chandler's voice announcing Twisters football games from the press box at the stadium, the roar of the crowd in the background, and he could never get over hearing that voice saying such words.

He didn't know what to say in response to "Fucking camel jockeys" and so he kept eating. After some minutes he noticed that Buck was staring at him disgustedly.

"Oh, I know you're buddies with those kinds of people."

"Would you like me to leave you alone?" Clyde said.

"That's real nice of you, Clyde, to be buddies with our foreign guests. But you keep in mind something." Buck set his steak knife down with exaggerated caution and began shaking his finger at Clyde, gripping the edge of the table with his other hand to steady himself. "Don't trust 'em, Clyde. 'Cause they got no principles."

Since Buck Chandler was not being too coherent, Clyde brought his Sherlockian capabilities to bear on the problem. One good hypothesis was that Buck had got involved in a real-estate transaction with some foreign students, which had ended badly.

"Shit," Buck said, "you might have thought they'd at least wait until after Christmas to burst my goddamn bubble. But no. Hell, they don't even *have* Christmas. Why would they?"

"Don't know," Clyde said.

A new, and apparently terrifying, thought occurred to Buck. "My 'vette," he blurted. "You came to repo my 'vette, didn't you, Clyde?"

"Sheriffs don't do repo work, Buck. You can rest easy about that darn Corvette."

"Oh, yeah. Thank God."

Clyde chewed and pondered. When he'd dropped off the divorce summons at Tick Henry's house, it had been sometime in midsummer. Buck had been homeless and living in squalor. After that he hadn't seen Buck until around Halloween, when he was on the wagon, well dressed, and driving a new Corvette.

He didn't know much about the real-estate business, except that it worked on a commission basis—a large number of small transactions, the income accumulating slowly and steadily over time. It did seem remarkable, now that he thought about it, that Buck had turned his business around dramatically enough to buy a Corvette—in no more than three months' time.

On the other hand, if he had made one very large sale, he could have got the whole bundle at once. But sales that large were unusual in this area.

"You got into a business deal with some Arabs?" Clyde said.

Buck scoffed and shook his head in disgust. "Deal? Swindle is more like it."

"How much do you figure you got swindled out of?"

Buck lowered his head and stared into his food again. The

look on his face told Clyde that Buck Chandler hadn't been swindled out of anything. "They just pulled out on me, that's all. Cut and run."

"I never heard about this deal of yours, Buck."

"Well, course not! That's 'cause it was a secret deal from the word go."

"Is it still secret?"

"Hell no. Fuck no," Buck said. He took a big breath and his eyes blazed up as he realized something: "I don't have to keep any secrets no more! To hell with 'em! What're they gonna do, sue me?"

"I'd like to see 'em try," Clyde scoffed, getting into the spirit of the thing. "What kind of a deal did you put together, Buck?"

"With the Kuwaitis," Buck said.

"Are you pulling my leg?"

"As God is my witness," Buck said. "Round the middle of August, a couple weeks after that invasion of Kuwait, this fella comes to my office. Arab fella. Spoke real good English. Told me that he was representing a sheikh from Kuwait. Said they'd just got out of Kuwait City by the skin of their teeth. Brought a bunch of their money out with 'em."

"And came out here to Forks County, Iowa?"

"That's what I asked him!" Buck said, a little too insistently. "Why the hell would they come here? Well, turns out that the nephew of this sheikh was a student here at EIU and had a nice big house rented for himself—you know how these Arabs throw money around—and so when they escaped from the Iraqis, this was as good a place as any for them to go to ground."

"Did you meet these people?"

"I wouldn't believe a word of it until I saw the sheikh personally," Buck insisted. "So this fella took me to the house and I met the guy. He was the real thing, boy, all dressed up in the robes, with the towel on his head and the whole bit, sitting there watching CNN twenty-four hours a day. He shows me a carry-on bag full of cash—must have been hundreds of thousands of bucks in it.

"Well," Buck continued, fortifying himself with a swig of coffee that had a strong odor of schnapps rising from it, "this sheikh is a real operator. He was looking for someplace to put his money. And I'm sure he put a lot of it into stocks and other investments, like any sane person would. But he wanted to launch a little venture right here in Forks, too, and that's why they needed yours truly."

"What kind of venture?" Clyde asked.

Buck frowned and leaned his head toward Clyde's, still reluctant to blurt out the secret he had held for the remarkable span of three months. "A high-tech thing. I told you his nephew was at EIU, right?"

"Right."

"Guess what he's studying there."

"I can't imagine."

"Chemical engineering. And what's the most important chemical in the world, Clyde?"

Looking at Buck, Clyde was tempted to answer that it was ethanol. But he shook his head and shrugged in mystification.

"Water. They don't have enough fresh water in that part of the world. So this nephew was working on desalination technology. And he came up with an invention, Clyde. A new technology that could take the salt out of seawater much cheaper than the way they do it now. He made it work at the test-tube level, but in order to test whether it would work commercially, they had to build a pilot facility. I'm just telling you what they told me, Clyde."

"So the sheikh needed you to sell him a building that was suitable for housing a small chemical plant."

"Just for starters, Clyde. Any real-estate agent could do that. But they needed more. They needed a full-fledged partner. That's why they came to me."

"You lost me there, Buck," Clyde confessed. "Why didn't they just buy the building and send you on your way?"

"Because of the need for absolute secrecy and discretion. If word got out about this invention, the big boys would be all over them in no time—Du Pont, Monsanto, all those guys. They'd reverse-engineer the process and steal it."

Clyde said, "I still don't follow."

"Aw, come on, Clyde. You know what kind of town this is. If some raghead with a twenty-thousand-dollar Rolex comes waltzing in and plunks down a sack of C-notes to buy an abandoned building, you don't think word's gonna get out? Hell, they might as well just broadcast it over the tornado sirens."

"I see," Clyde said. "They needed you to front for them."

Buck was offended. "Well, there's a little more to it than that, Clyde, or else they wouldn't have cut me in for such a nice chunk of the deal. I was the local partner, the man on the ground, on the scene. You know what I mean."

"Sure," Clyde said.

"So I was the one who bought the building, and I was the one who hired the laborers and so on and so forth."

"Laborers?"

"Yeah. The building was a disaster area, so I hired Tab to clean it out. And when they started building the pilot plant, I made the arrangements with Tab to go out and pick up the materials and deliver them. The grad students took care of actually putting it together."

"But they never showed their faces outside."

"Now you're getting it, Clyde. We had to arrange this whole thing so that not a single raghead face ever showed itself to the outside world, not a single raghead voice was ever heard on the phone. Instead, it was yours truly who handled all interface functions."

"Did they get their equipment all put together, Buck?"

Buck shrugged and copped a "Who, me?" look. "I don't know, Clyde, I guess so. They wouldn't let me inside the place—didn't want me to see any of their trade secrets."

"You got orders on the phone from the sheikh," Clyde said, "and you went out and spent money and gave orders to Tab, but you never saw anything."

"Right. Except it wasn't on the phone, it was on this radio thing that they gave me. These guys were so paranoid, they wouldn't even use the phone."

"Did Tab see anything?"

Buck looked nonplussed. "I don't know. I guess if he was helping them put the rig together, he must have got inside and seen something, at least, before he went off and killed himself." Buck's voice trailed off uncertainly as he spoke this last sentence, and he suddenly got a woozy look about him.

"What happened yesterday?" Clyde asked. He had dropped the conversational front now and was interrogating Buck Chandler like a suspect.

"They pulled out," Buck said. "I went by their house. But they're gone. And then I went by the barn, too, and they're not there either."

"Barn?"

"Yeah."

Clyde's heart started to beat a little faster. He carefully sipped some ice water. "This place that you bought for them. The place where they built their pilot plant. For some reason I was picturing it in one of the old buildings on the grounds of the Matheson Works. That's where I figured it would be. It'd be perfect—it's empty, the whole thing is surrounded by a high wall. But you say it was a barn?"

"They also leased a space at the Matheson Works," Buck admitted. "They stored some shipping containers there. But the facility itself was at a barn."

"Buck," Clyde said, "where is that barn?"

The silverware began to hum, then to buzz, then to rattle. A deep rumbling noise came down from the sky, up through the ground, in through the walls. The gadgets hanging from the doorknob began to play their tinny Christmas carols.

"It's out by the airport," Buck said. "It's that old dairy farm that went out of business a couple of years back. Just a stone's throw from the runway."

Clyde slapped his napkin down on the table and ran out into the middle of River Street and looked up into the sky, which had gone solid gray. Half of the firmament was blotted out by an immense shape passing low overhead, in the direction of the Forks County Regional Airport. Rows and rows of massive wheels trundled out of giant bomb-bay openings in the underside of the Antonov freighter, so close, Clyde could see that the tires were bald and threadbare. Then it was gone, and a fine mist of kerosene descended on the street, and the rumbling gradually died away to be replaced by the sound of distant tornado sirens and car alarms that had been set off by the disturbance. Finally there was nothing left except a fine rain that was beginning to fall out of the clouds, coating Clyde and everything in the street with a thin lacquer of ice.

fifty-two

CLYDE RAN toward his unit, tried to stop too late, and found no traction. He skated the last few feet, slamming heavily into the side of the car. For a moment he thought that he was glad his career was over so that he wouldn't have to go out and haul people out of ditches during what promised to be a day of nasty weather. Then he remembered that what he would actually be doing would probably be much worse than that.

He got in his car and drove the half mile to Knightly's place, ignoring the radio calls coming in from the dispatcher: a car in the ditch here, a Mexican in need of a jump start there. He was tempted just to switch the radio off but left it running in case something of interest came in.

Fazoul had heard him pulling into the Knightlys' side yard and was already on his way down the ladder, wearing his Twisters sweatsuit with its hooded sweatshirt pursed tightly around his face. "The airplane," he said.

"I know where they did it," Clyde said. "Right next to the airport."

Fazoul rolled his eyes and shook his head. He led Clyde across the yard to the Knightlys' back door, no longer caring whether the neighbors noticed, retrieved a hidden key, and opened up the house.

For the dozenth time in the last couple of days, Clyde fished a scrap of paper out of his pocket bearing ten or eleven different Hennessey-related phone numbers and started dialing them. At some length he got through to someone who was actually working on Christmas Day, and who forwarded his call to what sounded like a skyphone on an airplane somewhere. "Yello!" Hennessey barked over the engine noise.

"Merry Christmas," Clyde said.

"Yes, Clyde. Merry Christmas! We just flew over you about half an hour ago."

"Got to talk to you about those Iraqis."

"Did they build a pipeline?"

Hennessey sounded ebullient, almost giddy. Clyde wondered if he himself had been so overconfident an hour ago when he'd walked into Metzger's.

"Nope. They landed an Antonov."

"Jesus fucking Christ!" Hennessey said. Then he said it a couple of more times, his voice trailing off with each repetition.

"What do we do?" Clyde asked. On the other end he could hear Hennessey yelling to someone: "Get me all the statistics on the Antonov transport ship and have them ready. It's a big Soviet plane." Then: "Clyde, I'm still here. I'm thinking." Then he said nothing for thirty seconds. Then he said to someone else, "Tell the pilot to plot a hypothetical great circle route from Nishnabotna to Baghdad. It's got to refuel somewhere. Move!"

"Could you shoot them down over the ocean somewhere?" Clyde asked. Then he bit his tongue, remembering the Russian crew he had helped out of the cornfield last spring.

"If the President ordered it," Hennessey said. "But I don't imagine our Soviet allies would be too keen."

Clyde said, "Don't you need some sort of passport check and export permit on international flights?"

"I'll check on that." Hennessey shouted more orders at someone; Clyde got the impression that there was an endless queue of FBI agents in the aisle of the plane, standing there waiting for their turn to be barked at. Hennessey continued: "I'm looking out the window at your weather, or rather the weather that's going to be hitting you in a few hours, and looks to me like it sucks. Am I right?"

"It's been icing down for about an hour. Temperature is dropping like a stone. Now it's turning to snow."

"So if they were stalled long enough by the local red tape, they might get snowed in."

"If it comes down to that," Clyde said, "I can just pull my car across the runway and stop them from taking off."

Hennessey pondered that one for a while. Fazoul didn't have to ponder it for very long; he was already shaking his head no.

"Clyde," Hennessey said, "I think that making these guys feel trapped is not what we want to do. See, something kind of funny has happened in the last twenty-four hours."

"Funny?"

"Yeah, if you like sick humor. Suddenly everyone woke up. People in D.C. are actually taking this botulin thing seriously all of a sudden. Otherwise I wouldn't have been able to requisition this damn plane. But now it's too late."

"What do you mean, too late?"

"Clyde, they already made the damn toxin. And it's sitting there on the edge of fucking Iowa, practically in the suburbs of Chicago, directly upwind of the Loop, if you know what I mean. Let me put it this way: if they had made the stuff in Iraq and were trying to ship it into the U.S., we would do anything to stop them, right?"

"Yeah, I suppose we would."

"Well, it's already here. We would like nothing better than to get the shit out of our country. And that's what they want, too. My girl Betsy figured it all out."

"Betsy?"

"One of my people here. She finally put it all together. The Iraqis want to lob this shit into Israel."

"How do you figure?"

"If they use it on us, Bush will go nuts and just kick the shit out of them. On the other hand, if they use it on the Israelis, then the Israelis go nuts and bomb Baghdad and bring down our whole coalition—the Arab countries pull out and line up on Baghdad's side. So your Iraqis, as it turns out, are currently engaged in trying to do exactly what most people in our government would like them to do."

"You want to let them go?" Clyde exclaimed. Fazoul stiffened and went into the next room to listen in on another extension.

"As far as I personally am concerned," Hennessey said. "If they get snowed in by natural causes, we can get some G-men on the ground there and deal with the situation in a calm and controlled fashion. That might work. But kamikaze sheriffs pulling station wagons across runways is bad. It'll get them excited, and for all we know, they've got that container packed in a blanket of high explosive that'll send it right up into the prevailing winds of this big goddamn storm, which is headed straight for Chicago.

"But that's just my opinion," Hennessey continued after pausing for a moment to let Clyde savor that last image. "As far as a lot of other people are concerned, it would be a fine thing if those Iraqis got out of Dodge with their Antonov and relieved us of a great threat—and a greater embarrassment." Hennessey's voice became muffled for a few minutes as he conferred with one of his agents. Clyde thought about what Hennessey had just said and realized for the first time that this entire situation might never be brought to light—that Jonathan Town might never get to write his scoop for the *Des Moines Register*, and that the people responsible for this mess in Washington might get out of it with absolutely no damage to their careers.

"Good news, Clyde, and whoever's listening on the other extension," Hennessey finally said. "The pilot worked out some course calculations for that Antonov. We know the approximate range of the plane. So we can say with certainty that if he's going to get that sucker to Baghdad by the great circle route, he's got to refuel somewhere in the North Atlantic, most likely in Iceland. So there's a solution that works for everyone. They fly the shit out of the country. They run low on fuel, and we wait for them to land in some godforsaken place rather than shooting them down, which would blow our alliance with the Soviets to little bits. And we nail them there."

"So you want me to do nothing," Clyde said.

"Hell, Clyde, you've already done a hell of a lot. You broke the goddamn case. It's just that Washington took too long to wake up. If you do anything now, you're putting half the Midwest at risk."

"I understand."

"Over and out, Clyde. I'll talk to you later." And the connection went dead.

Fazoul came in from the other room. "I would like to be on that airplane," he said, "so that I can personally ensure that I do not lose another family in the way I lost my first one. Will you give me a ride to the airport?"

"Hell," Clyde said, "if all Saddam wanted to do was rile up the Israelis, he wouldn't have had to make such a large amount of the stuff. So I was just thinking I owe it to my wife to go to the airport myself and see what's what."

The ice was now covered with a thin but growing layer of dry, floury snow that made it even slicker, like dancing powder on a polished ballroom floor. Clyde put the chains on the unit's rear tires and set out for the airport with Fazoul riding shotgun.

Conditions were terrible, and Clyde spent most of the time steering into whatever direction he happened to be skidding. He hit two different parked cars in the space of as many blocks but kept going, reasoning that if he was still alive tomorrow, filling out the accident reports would be a pleasure to be savored.

Interstate 45 had been closed. Semitrailer rigs had begun to stack up in the vast parking lots of the Star-Spangled Truck Stop, engines idling, lights and TV sets glowing inside their cabs. The enterprise was made up of several modules: a motel, a restaurant, a filling station, a truck wash, a convenience store. Clyde pulled up in front of the convenience store, set the parking brake, and went inside.

"Merry Christmas, Clyde," said Marie, the cashier, who, like Clyde, always seemed to pull the worst shifts.

"Merry Christmas, Marie," Clyde said. He pulled out his credit card and slapped it down on the counter.

"What can I get for you?"

"Cigarettes."

Marie frowned. "I didn't think you smoked."

"Don't."

"Well, how many cigarettes you want?"

"All of 'em," Clyde said.

He followed the section-line roads down to the airport. Visibility was poor, but when they got to within half a mile of the airport, they could dimly make out *Perestroika*'s fuselage, which created a hump in the skyline like a distant bluff, its tail thrusting to a height that exceeded most of the buildings in the twin cities.

"What are you thinking?" Clyde said.

"With all due respect to you and your fine country," Fazoul said, "your government's performance in this affair has not been such as to command my respect. There are many things that could prevent Hennessey's plan from working. What if the Iraqis claim they have hidden a container of the toxin somewhere in a major city and threaten to blow it up, or dump it into the water supply? The President will let them have all the fuel they want in Iceland. He will give them an *escort* to Baghdad."

Clyde said nothing. He was not entirely sure that Bush was as lily-livered as Fazoul made him out to be. But he had to agree that healthy skepticism was probably a good policy.

Rather than zeroing in directly on the airport, Clyde orbited halfway around it and came at it from the south, passing directly in front of the bankrupt dairy farm that Buck had mentioned. The detour was not made strictly out of curiosity; it would also enable them to approach the Antonov from an unexpected direction and reduce the chance that they would be noticed.

The farm was separated from airport property by a tall chain-link fence, and even from the road Clyde could see that a section of it had been cut down and flopped onto the ground, and a pair of fat tire tracks, rapidly filling up with snow, ran through the gap, leading from the barn directly to the apron of one of the shorter runways.

From there they could look directly across the airport and get a view of *Perestroika*. The blowing snow made it into a dark-gray silhouette in the midst of a universe of white. They could see that its nose had been tilted back to expose its cargo bay, making it look like a giant aluminum crocodile that had opened its mouth wide to swallow something: a big red capsule that sat on the apron, ready to be towed on board by a small tractor.

He kept on driving a quarter of a mile past the farm, in case any Iraqis were there acting as lookouts, and finally eased the unit down into a ditch. It could not be seen there, and even if it was noticed, it would simply appear to have slid off the road. As a sheriff's deputy on duty, he could easily have come up with a plausible excuse to drive right onto the tarmac and start poking around, but it had occurred to him that the Iraqis must be in an extremely nervous frame of mind about now, and a sheriff's car, or even a sheriff's uniform, might get them dangerously excited.

The unit was well stocked with cold-weather gear; sheriffs were supposed to help people during blizzards, not get frostbite and end up needing help themselves. Clyde and Fazoul helped themselves to hats and mittens and even ski masks, which, in this part of the country at this time of year, were actually worn by people who were not bank robbers or terrorists. Clyde checked himself carefully to make sure he wasn't wearing anything that would identify him as law enforcement.

They got out of the car and unloaded four cases of cigarettes from the trunk and backseat. These were awkward to carry, so Clyde unrolled a sleeping bag that was stashed in the trunk. They loaded the boxes into the sleeping bag and then began making their way down the ditch in the direction of the airport, climbing up onto the shoulder from time to time to survey the scene. They traded off dragging the sleeping bag behind them like Santa Claus's giant sack of goodies. The snow was coming down heavier now, and it seemed as if the sun had set half an hour ago, even though it was really high noon.

Two cars were parked near the Antonov, illuminated from within by their dome lights. It was too cold for anyone to stand outside. Clyde immediately recognized one of the cars as part of the Iraqis' fleet of tinted-window specials. The other was a big navy-blue Caprice sedan.

"That blue car is government-issue if I ever saw one," Clyde said. "Probably the INS guy, or Commerce."

Headlights flashed in the distance as a new vehicle appeared on the driveway that connected the airport's main parking lot with the highway. The parking lot was empty and trackless except for some forlorn rental cars that would have to be chiseled loose from their sarcophagi of ice tomorrow morning. The front doors of the terminal building were locked, the building itself completely dark. The new arrival was a four-wheel-drive Blazer moving along crisply on its big, fat tires, chains making a distant ticking noise as they whacked against the insides of its fenders.

"Mark Lutsky," Clyde said, "the airport manager. Bet he's happy to be called in on Christmas."

Lutsky swung around into his private parking space and clambered out of the Blazer, all bundled up and hunched against the driving snow. He scrambled to a side entrance, windmilling his arms to keep his balance on the ice, and keyed his way into the terminal building. Lights began to come on inside. A minute later doors popped open on the cars sitting on the apron, and men began to scramble and skate into the building, as did some figures from the Antonov. Even the Iraqis, and the continent-hopping crew of *Perestroika,* had to bow to the supreme power of the world: filling out forms, presenting documents, getting papers stamped.

Visibility kept dropping. Clyde and Fazoul made their way down the shoulder at a jog, no longer particularly worried about being seen. Clyde couldn't take his eyes off the red container. It was a cylindrical tank with some plumbing and valves underneath it, the whole thing contained within a rectangular-space frame the exact size and shape of a normal shipping container, so that it could be moved and stacked like any other cargo.

Despite Hennessey's observations about the desirability of getting the toxin out of the country, Clyde kind of hated to see it go. He couldn't help but share Fazoul's concerns about where it would end up if they let it leave Nishnabotna. So he was disappointed to see that the runways were still dark and mostly snow free, skeins and whorls of snow skimming across the pavement in the wind, but none of it sticking. A few low dunes of snow had begun to march across the long runway, but they looked insignificant compared to the bulk of the Antonov.

Fazoul wasn't talking any more than Clyde was. But he had other things on his mind. "What is wrong with this picture, Khalid?" he said, pointing to the Antonov.

"I wouldn't know," Clyde said after examining it for a minute. "I don't know much about planes."

"But you do know that they need fuel."

"Yeah."

"And as Hennessey pointed out, fuel is critical to the Iraqis' mission–if their mission is to get the toxin all the way to Baghdad."

"Yeah." Clyde finally figured it out. "But they aren't refueling the Antonov." He pondered it. "Maybe it's because the airport is shut down for Christmas."

"This operation must have been planned for months in advance," Fazoul said. "They could not have been so stupid as to forget about getting the plane fueled."

"So what do you think is going on?"

"I fear that the Iraqis intend to crash the plane into Chicago."

They slogged on for another minute. Clyde tried to get his heartbeat under control.

"I don't think so," Clyde said. "First of all, if they wanted to nail Chicago, they would have just towed the container into the city, which takes all of an hour and a half, and blown it up."

"True," Fazoul said.

"Secondly, I know the crew of this plane, and they may not be what you call upstanding citizens, but they are not kamikazes for Saddam Hussein either."

"Then explain to me the mystery," Fazoul said. And he did sound genuinely mystified, which was something new. Clyde had got used to Fazoul knowing everything he didn't.

"How do you know the crew?" Fazoul asked.

Clyde told him the story about how they had driven off the road in May. "So they owe me a favor," he said in conclusion.

Fazoul shook his head and laughed.

They walked straight across the tarmac as if they belonged there. They walked past the red container, trying not to stare at it; but Clyde could see work had been done on it recently, the torch burning away its red paint to expose dull steel underneath, laying down new silver welds where rectangular containers about the size of cigar boxes had been attached to the outside of the tank. There were at least a dozen of these. They were wired together with armored cable of exactly the same type Clyde had seen Tab Templeton buying at Hardware Hank back in September. Clyde could not see inside these boxes, but he assumed they were packed with explosives.

It was incredible that the tank was just sitting there unguarded. But the Iraqis' car was idling not far away. Clyde assumed that the defogger was running full blast, and that on the other side of the tinted windshield someone was watching him and Fazoul as they approached, and that this person was ready to detonate the explosives on the toxin container by remote control.

Fazoul was dragging the cigarettes. As they approached the Antonov, Clyde began waving his arms over his head and hollering, "Tovarisch! Tovarisch! Vitaly! Vitaly!"

One of the Russians came cautiously down the cargo ramp, wearing a fur hat that looked like a yearling bear cub curled up on his head. Clyde recognized him; it was the guy who had suffered a broken arm back in May, the beneficiary of the Big Boss's inflatable splint. Clyde saw no Iraqis inside the Antonov, so he turned his back on the car, hooked a thumb under the bottom of his ski mask, and peeled it back to expose his face for a moment. Then he pulled it back down; but the Russian had recognized him and looked delighted. "Sheriff!" he said.

Clyde winced and glanced in the direction of the car. This could not have been very obvious to the Russian, given that Clyde was standing twenty feet away and wearing a ski mask; but something about growing up in a totalitarian state had made him exquisitely sensitive to this kind of body language. *"Moi drug,"* he corrected himself. He held up his formerly broken arm and slapped it heartily, demonstrating its soundness. Then he looked at Fazoul quizzically.

Fazoul stopped at the base of the ramp, unzipped the sleeping bag, hauled out one of the cases, and ripped the lid open to expose the familiar Marlboro logo—making sure that all of this was clearly visible to whatever Iraqis might be watching from the car.

"Oy," said the Russian, and glanced nervously toward the terminal building. "In, in." He beckoned them up the cargo ramp with movements of his big furry head.

The interior of the Antonov was like the vault of a cathedral. But most of it was full this time. It was stacked three high and five wide with shipping containers. Like the one resting out on the apron, they were tank containers for carrying bulk liquids. The resemblance ended there; these did not appear to be wired with gobs of plastic explosive, and Clyde did not imagine that they were full of biological-warfare agents. They were plumbed together with a jury-rigged network of wrist-thick hoses. The plane was redolent of kerosene.

"It is jet fuel," Fazoul muttered, "the whole plane is full of jet fuel."

fifty-three

CLYDE AND Fazoul and the Russian had an awkward several minutes sitting around in the back of the plane's cargo hold, in a narrow space aft of the enormous jungle gym of fuel tanks. From time to time they would make a foray into sign language, which never led anywhere. Fazoul seemed to know one or two words of Russian but was in a reticent mood.

Clyde's head was spinning, trying to figure the angles.

The government was going to let the Antonov leave the country and wait for it to land in Iceland. But it would just keep going. By the time NATO, or whoever, figured out that it was carrying an extra fuel supply, it would be over Europe. Was NATO going to shoot down a Soviet plane full of botulin toxin over Europe? Clyde didn't think so.

Fazoul pulled a walkie-talkie out of his pocket, turned it on, and spoke into it a few times, until he got a response from some other Vakhan Turk–speaking scholar in the area. Then he spoke rapidly for half a minute or so.

In the middle of this Vitaly the pilot showed up, fresh from having his passport stamped. He was startled to see Clyde sitting in his airplane with a disfigured Turk and a large cache of cigarettes. Then he warmed to the occasion and gave Clyde a hearty greeting dripping with fake sentiment. Fazoul turned off his walkie-talkie and put it back in his pocket.

"I guess you won't be able to take off in this weather," Clyde said hopefully.

"Oh, no. This is nothing. You forget, we are from Russia."

"But don't they have rules?"

"If we were at one of your big airports, they wouldn't let us out, but Mr. Lutsky is our droog, he likes us, he likes Black Sea caviar, he likes Stoli. He will let us do this trip, no problem."

"But there's no deicing equipment here."

"Do you think there's deicing equipment at Magadan?" The thought of modern equipment at Magadan made him laugh so hard, he almost had to sit down. "No, Sheriff. This is nothing. This plane is a Russian plane. A Siberia plane. Nothing can stop it."

"What are the Iraqis doing in there?" Clyde said, nodding toward the airport.

Vitaly did not miss a beat. "The Jordanians are turning in their visas. They have special visas for students. Much paperwork." He rolled his eyes.

"Who's paying you?" Clyde said.

Vitaly blinked in surprise, then held his mittens out, palms up, and shrugged, as if this were the first time payment had occurred to him. "Clyde, *moi drug.* If we have legal problems here, we can certainly make some arrangement. You want me to buy your cigarettes? I am delighted to buy them. Cash on the barrelhead."

"You can have the cigarettes," Clyde said. "Here is what I want. My friend and I want to exchange our coats and hats with two members of your crew. They will go out of the plane carrying this sleeping bag, empty, wearing the ski masks over their faces, and they will go in that direction." Clyde pointed toward Nishnabotna. "And they will keep walking until they find a church or a convenience store or something and then they will wait."

"Khalid—" Fazoul began, but Clyde held out one hand to silence him.

"Wait for what?" Vitaly said.

"For the plane to take off."

Vitaly was stunned. "Clyde. You want to travel to Azerbaijan with us?"

Clyde was tempted to tell Vitaly that they probably weren't going to stop at Azerbaijan. But it would do for now. "Yes," Clyde said, "I have always wanted to see Azerbaijan."

"But my crew. I need my crew."

"You need the money that the Jordanians are paying you for this very special trip," Clyde said. "And if you do not do this thing for me, I will arrest all of you now. I have more sheriffs waiting outside the airport to back me up."

Vitaly pondered it for a very few moments. "Clyde," he said brightly, "you will love Azerbaijan. I am sorry to say that it is much more beautiful than Iowa."

Vitaly summoned the least important two members of his crew and explained matters to them. Their faces betrayed only the merest traces of surprise; clearly, flying Antonovs around the globe was not a job for the faint of heart or rigid of mind. The exchange of clothing went quickly, the Russians remarking about how much better the American stuff was. One of them jokingly offered to give Clyde a fistful of rubles. Vitaly was unnerved by

Fazoul, his Turkic DNA and ghastly war injuries so clearly evident, but he averted his gaze from the Vakhan with a conscious effort and smiled charmingly at Clyde.

Basically, Clyde realized, Vitaly was in the middle of the biggest deal of his life and had dollar signs in his eyeballs even as he was shitting his pants with anxiety. Clyde's presence on the plane was a problem; if he could make the problem go away by jettisoning two of his crew members, so be it.

The stack of fuel tanks made a sort of jungle gym within which it was possible for Clyde and Fazoul to move around to whatever vantage point they wanted and get a clear view down the fuselage toward the open nose of the aircraft. They climbed up to near the top of the stack and watched the conclusion of the regulatory ballet down on the tarmac.

The federal official who had shown up in the big government sedan came out of the terminal building with a sheaf of papers and did a slow walk around the red tank, then waved his clipboard at it dismissively and began to scrawl on some forms.

"You must get out of the plane now, Khalid," Fazoul said. "After this there is no other chance."

"And leave you here all by yourself?"

"Yes."

"What are you going to do then?"

Fazoul didn't answer.

The Commerce official finished writing on his clipboard, handed the yellow copy to Vitaly and the pink copy to one of the Iraqis, and then got back into his car and drove away, hoping he could return to what was left of his Christmas before the roads got totally snowed in. While this was happening, the two crew members wearing Clyde's and Fazoul's clothes went down the ramp with the empty sleeping bag and vanished into the blizzard.

"What did you say on the walkie-talkie, Fazoul?"

"In order to reach Baghdad, this plane will have to fly over the Caucasus, and then over some parts of Turkey and northern Iraq where my people are. My people have ways of making airplanes crash."

"You're going to make the plane crash on your own territory? How's that any better than letting Saddam drop the stuff on you later?"

A blast of wind, ice, and snow hit the Antonov broadside, rocking it on its suspension. The Iraqis—three of them—ran onto the plane to get away from the weather, laughing and joking at the viciousness of the storm, snowflakes caught in their lacquered black hair. Clyde recognized the important one, Mohammed, whom he had given the Welcome to Wonderful Wapsipinicon package. One of Vitaly's crew had started up the little tractor and was driving it up the loading ramp, towing the red tank behind it.

"You're going to sabotage this plane somehow—blow it up over the North Atlantic and kill everyone on board. Aren't you?" Clyde said. "That's the only thing you can do. Because there's only one of you, and there are three Iraqis."

"Four," Fazoul said, and nodded toward the ramp. A fourth Iraqi came running in from the car with the tinted windows, carrying a small black box with an antenna sticking out of it—the radio detonator, presumably. Clyde was only half-surprised to see that this person was none other than al-Turki, whom he had last seen driving a Ryder truck loaded with corn oil toward Chicago. Al-Turki must have ditched it there and made his way back last night.

"But if there's two of us on the plane, and we have the advantage of surprise," Clyde said, "we can wait until we're someplace safe, like over Greenland, and we can subdue the Iraqis, and Vitaly can land it safely somewhere. You don't have to die, and the Russians don't have to either."

Fazoul glared at him. "Get off the plane, Khalid. You should not be worrying about what happens to these Russians. They are cockroaches."

"Too late," Clyde said. "The Iraqis think I'm a crew member. If I leave, they'll know something's up."

"They probably know something's up already," Fazoul said, "but they know they will have plenty of time to kill us in the air."

The whine of a hydraulic pump could be felt through the

structure of the plane and the stack of fuel containers. The cargo door was closing, even as the crew members were securing the tank and the tractor in place. Either they had brought the little tractor with them, or else they were simply ripping it off from the Forks County Regional Airport.

One by one, they heard the engines start up. The crescent of blue light coming in from outside grew narrower and narrower, like a moon in eclipse, and finally vanished, leaving nothing but yellow indoor light. The cargo door was sealed.

"I am angry with you, Khalid," Fazoul said. "The correct thing would be for me to kill you. Because your plan is much less certain to work."

Now that the nose of the plane was horizontal again, there was space up there for the passengers—padded seats in a partially noise-proofed compartment sandwiched between the cockpit and the cargo hold. Three of the Iraqis went there immediately. Al-Turki stayed behind for a minute, fiddling with some connections on the outside of the tank. Clyde and Fazoul clambered to a slightly different position so that they could see what he was doing. Al-Turki began to back away from the red tank, paying out wire from a reel, wrapping it around the occasional fixed object. He backed all the way into the passenger compartment and then shut the door.

Clyde looked questioningly at Fazoul, who shrugged. "Maybe they are afraid that if they continue to rely on the radio detonator, perhaps your clever electronic-warfare specialists will figure out how to trigger the bomb in midair by beaming a signal into the plane. This is what I would be afraid of. So they turn off the radio and hook up a hardwired detonator instead."

Sheets of something cold and wind driven were flailing against the metal skin of the Antonov, sounding like wet concrete sprayed out of a pressure hose. The engines throttled up, but the plane didn't move; the wheels were iced up. Up in the cockpit Vitaly began to alternate the thrusts on the engines violently. Finally the wheels cracked loose and the ship jerked forward. Tons of fuel sloshed back and forth in all of the tank containers, causing the whole jungle gym to strain against its moorings, and yanking the Antonov back and forth on its suspension in a slow oscillation that took a minute or two to die away. But the plane was moving—plowing and skidding to the southeastern extreme of the airport, where the twelve-thousand-foot runway began.

Vitaly turned the plane around very, very slowly, trying not to get that fuel sloshing. When he had it aimed in the right direction, he sat for a minute or two, perhaps running through a checklist, perhaps just screwing up his courage. Clyde hoped foolishly that they would call the whole thing off and that he would get to stay home today.

Then Vitaly released the brakes and racked the engines up as high as they would go. The combination of the engine noise, which must have been breaking windows in town, and the wind and ice and sleet sliding off the skin of the plane overwhelmed Clyde's hearing and made it impossible to think.

The Antonov accelerated weakly but steadily, its tires pounding through snowdrifts. The takeoff run lasted forever; Clyde could not believe that they were still in the airport. The runway could not possibly be long enough for this. But then the noise of the tires diminished and went away entirely. The ride was still rough, but now it was the roughness of an airplane in turbulence, no longer that of a four-wheel-drive vehicle speeding across rough ground. Hydraulics whined and the doors over the landing gear slammed shut like the gates of hell. The Antonov hit an air pocket the size of a city block and seemed to lose about half its altitude; tremendous sloshing noises came from all the fuel tanks, and the whole jungle gym began to creak and pop and bend out of shape. Clyde could not see outside, but he knew the territory and calculated that they must be about to crash headlong into the bluffs of University Heights.

The right wing dipped as Vitaly banked the ship northward, which would be necessary to avoid the bluffs. Clyde counted to ten, then twenty, then a hundred. They didn't hit anything. The ride got smoother. Clyde's ears popped, then popped again.

They had cleared the twin cities.

Maggie wasn't going to die today.

And Clyde was going far, far away from home.

Clyde checked his watch. It was just past one in the afternoon. "How far to Iceland?" he said to Fazoul.

Fazoul had wedged himself underneath one of the fuel tanks and was busy working on something. Clyde clambered down for a better look. "How far to Iceland? You have any idea?"

Fazoul rolled his eyes. "It is not a place frequently visited by Vakhan Turks." He had taken some items from a belt pack that he had been wearing under his Twisters sweatshirt and was deeply involved in a project of some sort.

"Just off the top of my head," Clyde said, "I figure that by the time we've gone a thousand miles, we've cleared most of the parts of Canada where people are living. Two thousand probably gets us way up into the Arctic. Three thousand, and we're over the ocean. Four thousand is too late—getting close to Europe. Does that sound good to you?"

"Yes," Fazoul said absently, snipping a couple of small wires.

"How fast you figure this crate flies? Five hundred?"

"Something like that."

"So in six hours we jump the Iraqis, and if we screw it up, the only thing that dies is a lot of fish."

"Fine," Fazoul said. He began pushing buttons on a small electronic box he had just lashed to the fuel tank with some black electrician's tape. "And in seven hours this brick of plastique explodes." He pointed to a lump of translucent clay jammed between a fuel tank and a reinforcing gusset. "Unless one of us lives long enough to disconnect it."

"And how is that done?"

"By cutting these wires. Or jerking them out, if you are in a hurry. And if you want to detonate it immediately, just turn on this red switch." He gently fingered a small red toggle switch wired into the circuit.

Clyde sat there for a minute or so, looking at the timer,

counting down the digits from 07:00:00. The sight of it filled him with a strange feeling of peace. Maggie had not died, and because of this device, Desiree wouldn't die either. At least not from botulin poisoning.

The climb to cruising altitude seemed to last about an hour. Then the engines throttled back and the plane settled into a steady attitude. The skies must be clear up there, Clyde thought, because the flight was smooth, and when the door leading to the passenger deck was opened, he was startled and disoriented to see bright sunlight shining down the stairway from the windows above.

Al-Turki came down with one of the crew members and walked around the red tank a couple of times, checking its moorings, his breath steaming out of his mouth as he asked questions. Then he retreated to the warmth and quiet of the passenger compartment.

About an hour later a crew member came back into the main cargo area carrying a stainless-steel thermos and staring up into the jungle gym, trying to catch sight of them. Finally Clyde stuck one hand out and waved to him.

The crew member climbed to their level and handed off the thermos, threw them a mock salute, and then climbed back down. Clyde opened it up and gave it a sniff; it was hot tea, and no beverage was ever more welcome.

There seemed to be no more point in hiding high up in the reeking stack of fuel tanks, so they climbed down to the deck and retreated toward the tail section of the plane, where they could not be observed, and sat down on some duffel bags. Clyde poured some tea into the lid of the thermos, and he and Fazoul passed it back and forth for a while. It was made in the Russian style, almost too bitter to drink. But the trudge through the blizzard, and two hours in the cargo hold of the Antonov, had left them dehydrated and chilled to the bone. This was perfect.

Which made it all the more disappointing when Fazoul dropped the last third of it, a full cup, onto the floor. The steel lid bounced down the tread plates for some distance, and Clyde had to run it down. When he came back, Fazoul was leaning against a duffel bag, breathing raggedly. Clyde aimed his flashlight at Fazoul's face and saw that his lips had gone purple.

"We have always avoided religious discussions," Fazoul said in a thick, slurred voice. "Now, at the risk of being rude, I would like to recommend that you accept Islam here and now. We have only a few minutes to live. It is unfortunate. But our wives and children are safe."

"What's going on?" Clyde said. He was afraid Fazoul was having a heart attack or something.

"The tea," Fazoul said, now stopping after almost every word to fight for breath. "Iraqis—know that—we are here. Russians told. Cockroaches.Couldn't shoot us—because of fuel tanks—so—the tea—with botulin."

Clyde knew that Fazoul was right. He recognized the symptoms now; Fazoul's eyelids were drooping just as Hal Karst's had done.

"Red switch. Now! You—have—poison—too," Fazoul said.

"Fazoul," Clyde said, "you can count on me to blow this plane up if that's what it takes. And if I ever see Farida and little Khalid, I'll tell them you went straight to heaven like a jihad man, and that you were thinking of them the whole way."

"Red—switch," Fazoul said. His body went into convulsions, racked by oxygen deficiency, and Clyde threw his arms around him and held him so he wouldn't batter himself against the cold metal of the deckplates. The convulsions grew weaker over a minute or so, and then Fazoul's body went entirely limp.

Clyde arranged Fazoul on the deckplates and closed his eyes. He said a prayer over him, trying to make it something ecumenical that would not offend the dead Vakhan. Then he took a few deep breaths, stretched his arms, and wiggled his fingers, checking for any signs of numbness. His fingers felt a little stiff, but that could have been due to the bitter cold.

Dr. Folkes had been taken aback when Clyde had shown up on his doorstep a couple of weeks before Thanksgiving and started asking a lot of pointed questions about botulin immunization. The torrent of phone calls coming into the old professor's kitchen from the Pentagon had, if anything, only increased during the weeks since his first encounter with Clyde, and he knew that Clyde's interest in the subject must have some kind of deep significance. At some length he had dragged the whole story out of Clyde.

"So you're afraid of being exposed to the stuff right here in Nishnabotna?" Dr. Folkes had said. "I see. That's remarkable."

"And normal civilians can't get their hands on the vaccine—even during peacetime," Clyde had said. "But I know you and all your lab workers are immunized. So. How about it?"

Folkes had given him the first shot then and there and had been building up his resistance with twice-weekly injections ever since. Last week he had proclaimed Clyde Banks to be the most botulin-resistant human being on the face of the earth, unless the Iraqis were up to similar tricks.

The incredible noise of the engines and the wind and the creaking and sloshing jungle gym of fuel overwhelmed all other sounds. Clyde did not realize until almost too late that someone was approaching, picking his way between the fuel containers and the inside curve of the fuselage with a flashlight. The Iraqis had sent someone back to make sure they were dead.

Clyde had almost no time. He didn't know how many of them were coming. And he was trapped in the tail of the aircraft. So he did the only thing he could think of. He rolled Fazoul's body over on its side and pushed its arms and legs this way and that, so that the body no longer looked composed, and then flung himself facedown on a duffel bag next to the empty thermos and played dead. He had barely come to rest when the insides of his eyelids glowed red in the beam of the flashlight.

He could almost feel the light traveling up and down his body, like a groping hand looking for signs of life.

The ambient noise was his enemy now. He had not heard the man, or men, with the flashlight approach. He could not now hear whether he, or they, had departed. He counted to a thousand and then allowed one of his eyelids to come open just a crack. Dim light was scattering back into this space from some lamps hanging near the toxin tank, and by that light he could not see anyone. He opened his eyes all the way and tried to count to a thousand. But the cold was too much for him in his thin clothes, and he had to move. So he moved decisively, rolling to his feet as rapidly as his frozen joints and muscles would allow, and looking all around for anyone who might have been lurking. But there was no one there.

He turned once more and looked at Fazoul's body. His friend's death was just beginning to hit him. He tried not to think about it; it would just make him scared and despondent, which he could not afford right now.

He had no training for this, no real idea what to do. For some reason he remembered his survival training from Boy Scouts. *When you realize you are lost in the wilderness, STOP: Sit, Think, Organize, Plan*. So he sat down in a position where he could not see Fazoul and moved on to the Thinking. Clyde did a lot of thinking; he reckoned he could handle this part.

It was a terrible situation. But he shouldn't get emotional about it. It had been a stupid and crazy chance to begin with, climbing on board this plane, and he had no right to expect better. It would be childish to whine about the way things had turned out. Ebenezer would be disgusted with him: *You made your bed, you have to lie in it.*

It was best to think of it like a cop, he finally decided. He was in a plane with a bunch of perpetrators. He just had to make the proper arrests and bring the situation in hand. They were a couple of thousand miles out of his jurisdiction at the moment, but these men had, after all, stolen a tractor from the Forks County Airport, and he felt a certain justification in playing the role of Long Arm of the Law.

He had faced much worse odds at the Barge On Inn, against men who were in some respects more formidable than these, and had prevailed just by the force of his uniform and badge.

Clyde Banks stood up and stretched, which felt good. He did some toe-touches and windmills, getting the blood flowing, the internal furnace fired up. Then he began to make his way forward between the tanks and the fuselage, following the gentle curve of the Antonov's body.

The stack of fuel containers ended ten or fifteen yards aft of the bulkhead that walled off the insulated, heated passenger compartments in the nose. The toxin tank rested in the middle of this space, strapped and chained to floor rings. The stolen tractor was still hitched to it, pointed aft, its Iowa license plates now looking bizarrely out of place. As out of place as Clyde.

A tremendous weight knocked Clyde forward. Someone had tackled him; but the tackler had failed to wrap his arms firmly around Clyde's body. Clyde came close to falling down face first on the cold, steel floor plates. But a reflex took over. As he had been trained by various wrestling coaches starting in elementary school, he took the weight on his upper right arm and rolled through to a standing position. He turned and found himself looking at al-Turki from a distance of perhaps six feet.

Al-Turki had not been fooled by Clyde's playing possum in the back of the plane. Judging from the look on his mashed-in wrestler's face, he was surprised by the way Clyde had rolled through his attack. And it was not an entirely unpleasant surprise. He advanced, and Clyde instinctively fell into the traditional match opening position, then dropped his right leg back half a step and went into the stutter-step stance, extending his baseline for the charge he knew al-Turki would make.

Al-Turki grinned. He squared off and bent his knees, patiently regarding his prey, readying an attack. He started talking to Clyde about something. Clyde couldn't hear him. It was probably some kind of chatter about wrestling.

Clyde knew he would have to move quickly and decisively. His opponent probably outweighed him by a few pounds and was a late-model hard body. In wrestling, weight and strength were the ultimate trump cards and would eventually win out, even over the vastly superior wrestling skills that Clyde had learned from wrestling against Dhonts his whole life. Time was on al-Turki's side. Even if it wasn't, he presumably had a gun, and though Clyde hoped the man would not be stupid enough to fire it in a cargo hold full of jet fuel and botulin toxin, he did not want to tempt him.

Clyde launched his attack first, wanting desperately to look like a blur, but knowing that, suffering from the combined effects of age and cold, he moved at freeze-frame speed. He feinted toward al-Turki's right and then ducked under the Iraqi's left arm, spun behind him, and, with his right leg, kicked the inside of the man's left knee. His momentum combined with al-Turki's surprise at the move allowed him to complete the motion and take the other down. Clyde, no featherweight, fell fully and hard on top of al-Turki, but feeling the muscles underneath his opponent's suit, he instantly sensed that he would have little chance of holding him down. He thought about trying a judo chop—he had practiced them once—but he had as much chance of penetrating the muscles of al-Turki's neck as he did of biting through the airplane's deckplates with his incisors.

Al-Turki tried to reestablish his base on hands and knees, but Clyde kicked out his right leg. Then al-Turki executed an escape maneuver called a Granby roll, which worked more or less perfectly; he was almost out of Clyde's control when Clyde, in desperation, laid a cross face on the Iraqi, putting his full weight behind the blow, slamming the bone of his forearm across the Iraqi's nose and shattering it. Blood spurted out. Al-Turki's lips moved, and Clyde could barely hear him uttering some kind of exclamation of pain and surprise in Arabic. While the Iraqi was in shock, Clyde reached around his body and jerked the gun out of his shoulder holster, then flung it back into the darkness of the cargo hold; it spun off into the jungle gym and disappeared. One less thing to worry about.

Al-Turki inhaled deeply and shouted for help as loudly as he could. Both he and Clyde knew that this was hopeless, but only al-Turki knew that the shouting was just a cover for another maneuver: with his free hand he reached around and got a grip on Clyde's testicles. Clyde felt it coming at the last moment and twisted away, losing his grip on al-Turki, who was quick to capitalize on the situation with a chicken wing on Clyde's left arm. Clyde hollered. The pain from the testicles was bad enough. Al-Turki twisted, trying to wrench Clyde's arm out of his socket.

But here al-Turki's tremendous strength and Clyde's slight weight disadvantage led to an outcome neither man expected: Clyde was lifted completely off his feet. This reminded him of a trick maneuver that Dhonts liked to execute when they were showing off: kicking against al-Turki's legs and midsection for traction, he did a somersault and straightened out his arm. Al-Turki still held the left, but Clyde's right was free, and so he returned the favor, reaching out to grab al-Turki's balls. Al-Turki let go. Clyde got away from him.

Al-Turki was still shaking his head in annoyance and, Clyde thought, genuine fear. *You should have anticipated this, you son of a bitch,* Clyde felt like saying. *Of all the hick towns in the world, you picked the wrestling capital of the universe.... You made your bed, you have to lie in it.*

Clyde kept his eyes fixed on his opponent's—rule number one. As the two men circled each other, al-Turki was looking around for a weapon, or something. Clyde didn't dare take his eyes off the Iraqi to see what he was looking at.

Almost too late Clyde figured it out. Al-Turki had maneuvered around to the point where he had a clear path to the door in the bulkhead. Clyde saw him gather his feet beneath him and make a run for it. Clyde ran him down just short of the door and tackled him around the legs, sending al-Turki face first into the steel deckplates. They skidded for a couple of feet and thumped into the bulkhead; Clyde prayed the impact hadn't been loud enough to alert the other Iraqis.

Clyde jumped on al-Turki's back and established control, but not before the Iraqi had struggled to his hands and knees. Al-Turki paused for a moment to gather his strength, then exploded off the floor in another well-executed escape maneuver. If they had been of equal size and strength, Clyde might have dragged him back down, but al-Turki was simply too strong; Clyde ended up on his knees behind the standing Iraqi, his arms wrapped tightly around the other's waist.

Al-Turki lunged for the door handle. Clyde managed to drag him back half a step, just out of reach. Al-Turki reached down, grabbed one of Clyde's pinkies, and wrenched it back.

Clyde knew he couldn't hold on to the Iraqi for more than another three seconds.

He remembered a bridging maneuver that Dick Dhont had used to pin him once.

He got his feet underneath him and thrust upward, lifting the Iraqi straight up in the air with Clyde's face buried between his shoulder blades. At the same time, Clyde arched his spine as far backward as it would go, bending his body back into a horseshoe. This sent al-Turki's head plunging down toward the deck like a spiked football, even as his legs flew up into the air.

The imbalance sent them both falling backward, adding the weight of both men to the force with which al-Turki's head smashed into the deckplates.

For a moment they formed an arch: Clyde's feet firmly planted at one end, al-Turki's head at the other. Every muscle in al-Turki's body suddenly went limp, and the arch collapsed. Clyde ended up lying on his back with al-Turki's body on top of him.

Clyde rolled him onto his stomach and zipped al-Turki's wrists together behind his back with some plastic handcuffs he had stuffed into his pocket when he'd abandoned his unit. Then he did the ankles. He dragged al-Turki back among the fuel tanks where he could not be seen from the door in the bulkhead, zipped the wrists and ankles together, and then, just for good measure, zipped the whole mess to a heavy iron loop recessed into the floor. He didn't really expect al-Turki to wake up, but there was no point in taking half measures. He went through the Iraqi's pockets and found a number of passports and other miscellanea, but no knives he might use to cut himself loose.

His balls hurt so badly he felt he might throw up, and at least two fingers were broken. Clyde thought of the time Dan Dhont had jogged six miles to the emergency room after an especially perverse chain-saw accident and found the strength to ignore it. He was half-numb from cold anyway.

The wire running from the passenger compartment to the explosives on the tank container was a simple two-strand lamp cord. Clyde wrapped it around his hand a couple of times and then ripped it off.

There were five Russians and three Iraqis left on the plane.

The Russians were bad guys, but Clyde knew they weren't willing to die. On the other hand, some of the Iraqis might be willing to give their lives for this project. The only thing he knew was that he couldn't walk into the passenger compartment and assault all of them at one time.

Sooner or later someone else was going to come out of that door. Just in case it was a Russian, Clyde dug a Forks County traffic-citation form out of his pocket, stole a pen from al-Turki's breast pocket, and drew a cartoon of a bomb—a bundle of dynamite sticks hooked up to an alarm clock. And just in case it was an Iraqi, Clyde did some rooting around in the crates and lockers where the crew stored their spare parts and eventually dug up a chunk of iron pipe about two feet long. It wasn't Excalibur, but it would probably obviate any more wrestling matches.

As it happened, the first person to emerge from the door, some twenty minutes later, was a Russian. Clyde kicked the door shut behind the man and blocked his retreat, then hefted the pipe as a warning. The Russian was suitably shocked to see Clyde alive, then deeply impressed.

Clyde held up the bomb cartoon. The man raised his eyebrows.

Then, realizing a carrot-and-stick approach might be even better, Clyde took out the pen and added something new: a large dollar sign. He handed it to the Russian and said, "Vitaly."

By way of response, the man pushed up his sleeve a few inches to expose his wrist. It had a red welt around it, obviously from a handcuff that had been recently removed.

So all the Russians were handcuffed up there, except when they were sent back on errands.

"Clyde," Clyde shouted, pointing to himself.

"Boris," the crewman shouted.

Clyde beckoned Boris back to the locker where he had found the pipe, and dug out another. He tossed it to Boris, who was so surprised he nearly dropped it. He looked quizzically at Clyde.

"Tovarisch?" Clyde shouted.

"Da," Boris said.

"Let's boogie," Clyde said, and pointed Boris forward, still not trusting him enough to go in front.

Boris flagged him down and pointed at the pen. Clyde handed it to him, and Boris proceeded to draw a little floor plan of the passenger compartment, with little boxes representing the inhabitants. "Rooski, rooski, rooski, Iraqi, rooski, Iraqi, Iraqi," he said. Then he pointed to the last of these Iraqis and made his hand into a pistol.

"Okay, he's mine," Clyde said, pointing to himself. "You get these other two."

The door in the bulkhead led to a steep metal staircase. The brilliant light of the sun filtered down from the windows of the passenger compartment above. Boris went first, creeping to the bottom of the stairway with his pipe hidden in his sleeve, and looked up. Then he beckoned Clyde forward; none of the Iraqis had heard them coming through the door.

Clyde couldn't stand waiting anymore, so he jumped through the doorway, ran up the stairs three at a time, and burst into the passenger compartment. The leader of the Iraqis was seated farthest forward, closest to the cockpit door, so that he could keep tabs on Vitaly. He was about four strides away from Clyde, and Clyde had covered half of that distance before he had even looked up.

Clyde had spent enough time in the Barge On Inn, hitting dangerous people with nightsticks, to know that if he wound up and swung the pipe like a baseball bat, the man would see it coming and dodge it or block it. So he lunged forward, thrusting the end of the pipe at the Iraqi's face like the point of a sword, and caught him in the temple hard enough to snap his head back against the bulkhead. That didn't knock him out, but it did leave him stunned long enough for Clyde to go upside his head with the pipe one more time.

He turned around to see one of the Iraqi Ph.D.'s laid out in the aisle, and the other one curled up in a fetal position in his seat as Boris rained blows on him. It appeared that Boris was in a rather vindictive mood; or maybe he had decided it would be useful to demonstrate his commitment to Clyde's side of the dispute.

Clyde confiscated the Iraqi leader's gun and handcuffed him, then cuffed the mauled Ph.D.'s as well and let Boris worry about freeing his comrades. He opened the cockpit door and was almost knocked flat by the intensity of the sunlight coming in over Vitaly's shoulders.

"Clyde, my good droog!" Vitaly said. "I am so happy to see you well. And I am sorry that my crew members did not keep your secret very well. But the Iraqis were suspicious about these two mysterious cigarette smugglers who came out of the blizzard, and they were very persuasive."

Clyde knew all about people like Vitaly; he arrested them all the time, and he knew that there was no point in trying to pin him down and prove his guilt. Vitaly would have plausible excuses stacked up like jumbo jets above O'Hare Airport on a foggy Thanksgiving. "Speaking of persuasive," Clyde said, "you can either keep flying this crate and get blown to bits pretty soon, or land it and get lots of money from my government. It's up to you."

Vitaly throttled the engines down and banked the Antonov into a turn. "There is a Canadian Air Force base not far away, with a beautiful runway," he said. "Did you get all four of the Iraqis?"

"All four."

"Good," Vitaly said. "Let's crank some tunes." He reached over his head and punched a button on a car stereo that had been jury-rigged into the Antonov. It was a Jane's Addiction CD—"Been Caught Stealing." It came through magnificently, even over the engine noise—the Russians had converted the Antonov into the world's largest ghetto blaster. "Have you ever tried Crimean brandy?" Vitaly shouted.

It was late afternoon now, and the sun plummeted below the horizon in the space of a few seconds as the Antonov lost altitude. Ghostly blue lights appeared in the sky around them; Vitaly identified them as the exhausts of fighter jets, which had been sent up to escort them in.

Fifteen minutes later the big runway at the Canadian base could be seen, like a string of diamonds against black velvet, and Vitaly brought the Antonov down onto it, occasionally glancing away from the landing lights to fire up another cigarette or to reach for his QuikTrip plastic insulated go-cup of Crimean brandy. The Antonov landed much more gently than it had taken off. But when Vitaly put the brakes on, the sloshing in the fuel containers was much worse and jerked the plane violently backward and forward a dozen times before it gradually died down; tremendous wrenching and popping noises could be heard even through the two bulkheads between the cockpit and the hold.

They were directed onto an apron. Powerful lights were pointed at them, and they were told to remain in the plane. They did, for about three minutes; then one of the crew members came forward and announced that some of the plumbing in the hold had ruptured, and that the plane was rapidly filling up with jet fuel. So they took the party out onto the runway.

Clyde checked his watch. Several hours were left before Fazoul's time bomb exploded. When all of the Russians, with their lighted cigarettes, had cleared away from the plane, he climbed up into the twisted and partially collapsed jungle gym, avoiding the rivers of jet fuel that were coursing down all around, and had a look at the bomb. He saw the wires that Fazoul had told him to cut. He put the jaws of the wire cutter around them, then stopped himself. Sometimes wires sparked when they were cut, and a spark would be a bad thing in these circumstances.

So he pulled the wad of plastique out of the cranny where Fazoul had wedged it, and stripped off the electrician's tape holding the timer in place, then simply took the entire bomb with him, being careful not to bump the red switch. He climbed down carefully through the jungle gym, not wanting to lose his footing on the fuel-slickened bars, and walked out of the plane.

It was unbelievably cold out there. The Russians were nowhere to be seen; Canadians had apparently come around and picked them up, and Clyde was strangely alone.

A small jet plane landed on the adjacent runway, bearing the insignia of the United States government. Looking up into the clear night sky, Clyde could see the landing lights of more planes, coming down behind it in the same pattern.

The Gulfstream taxied onto the apron, keeping a respectful distance from the Antonov. Clyde ran toward it; it must be warm in there. By the time he reached it, its door had been opened and its stairway deployed, and a familiar figure was standing on the ground, trying to get a cigarette lit, cursing the cold.

"Deputy," Hennessey said, "you're out of your jurisdiction. But I promise not to tell on you."

"Got any bomb experts?" Clyde said, holding out the plastique.

Hennessey looked at it and raised his eyebrows. "We got every kind of expert known to the United States and Canadian governments," he said, pointing to the train of jets stacked up into the stars. An Air Force C-130 touched down, and they watched it roar to a near halt and taxi onto the apron. "See, Clyde, it is amazing what feats of organization our government can accomplish—if you don't mind waiting until it's too late."

fifty-four

JAMES GABOR Millikan was not entirely unhappy on the morning of Boxing Day, 1990. He still had his job at the National Security Council. Moreover, he had managed to position himself in such a way that the pivotal role he had played in turning Iraq into a major military power would end up as a scholarly footnote, while his strenuous exertions on behalf of peace and freedom and democracy would appear in headlines and newscasts the world over.

Despite all that, it had been a terrible year. While he had been pursuing the pure science of diplomacy, he had been deceived by his diplomatic colleague of decades, Tariq Aziz, one of the few people with the wit to appreciate what he was doing. As a result, he had had to scramble to maintain his position. He had been forced to do some undignified and injudicious things. He still didn't know exactly what costs and damages he had racked up in the process; the accounting would take a decade to sort out. He had inflicted some grievous blows on his rival, Hennessey, but Hennessey had shown more than his usual resourcefulness and had managed to emerge from the thing as a hero. Millikan could only thank God that Hennessey's exploits would remain unknown outside a small circle of high government and military officials.

Millikan stood outside a discreet side entrance to the Hotel Crillon with his assistant, Richard Dellinger, waiting for the Iraqi limousine to pull up for a final meeting with Aziz—one last attempt to avoid war.

Iraq was going to be ground to pieces by the twenty-three-nation coalition that Bush and Baker had assembled. Millikan and Aziz, great respecters of each other's skills, were no longer allies working to bridge the gulf between the massive and unfocused power of the United States and the quixotic vision of Saddam Hussein. Events had passed them by, and they now had to wait for events to conclude so that they could come back on the stage and try to keep the world together.

The Iraqi stretch Mercedes pulled up to the door, preceded and pursued by a motorcycle guard from the French Foreign Ministry. Once again Aziz was accompanied by Gérard Touvain, the French Foreign Ministry liaison. Millikan strode forward to be presented by Touvain to Aziz. After a perfunctory handshake with the Frenchman, Millikan gave his best warm, two-handed grasp to his old colleague.

"Mne ochen' zhal'," Millikan said to Aziz. I'm terribly sorry.

"We did our best, *mon vieux,*" Aziz responded, and the two entered the Crillon arm in arm. Touvain tagged behind, pointing out for whoever would listen the *"belle lumière"* of the hotel. They soon came to the same small, exquisite dining room where they had lunched in March. Millikan introduced Richard Dellinger. Aziz introduced his chief assistant—a new man, coarser and meaner looking than the one Millikan had seen in March. Touvain was politely told to buzz off.

On the small table was a tray with a bottle of iced Stoli, beluga caviar, and plates of black bread, butter, onions, chopped hard-boiled eggs. "It looks as though it will be some time before we will meet this way again," Millikan said with honest regret in his voice.

"Unfortunately, you couldn't be more correct, Jim," Aziz responded.

"A toast," Millikan said when the shot glasses were filled with the now syrupy Stoli. "To diplomacy, when you and I will work to bring Iraq back into the community of nations after Saddam's inevitable defeat."

"I'm afraid that I will not be able to drink to that," Aziz responded, setting his glass on the table untouched. "I do not share your opinion of the military situation in Kuwait, *mon vieux*. Before your leader launches a foolhardy assault on the new Iraqi province of Kuwait, he should understand that we have developed a new weapon. If we are forced to use this weapon by the aggressive behavior of other nations, it will cause such terrible casualties in the heart of the illegal Zionist entity that the Jews will have no choice but to enter the war—which will destroy your coalition and bring the Arabs into a unified front led by my nation. And it will cause such terrible casualties among your forces that Americans, who do not have the stomach for brave enterprises, will demand an end to this stupid and thoughtless aggression."

Millikan, holding his shot glass full of icy, syrupy Stoli, listened calmly to his peroration, thought for a moment, and then downed it anyway—a breach of etiquette that startled Aziz. "Mr. Dellinger?"

Dellinger stepped forward and pulled a piece of fax paper from his pocket. It was a brief typewritten document written on the stationery of the Royal Canadian Air Force.

"Would you care to share the latest intelligence with His Excellency?" Millikan continued.

Richard Dellinger read the document, refolded the paper, and put it back in his pocket. Aziz slumped against the back of his Louis XV chair. He looked first at Dellinger and then at Millikan.

"Hennessey?"

"Please, Tariq. You offend me."

"Then who? You blocked any action in Washington with your task force. You caused the analyst who understood what was happening to be isolated. Who?"

Dellinger stepped forward and said, "We are not at liberty to divulge that. You understand—sources and methods."

Aziz sat there with hands folded for a moment and blinked. Then he stood, filled the four glasses, and said, "A toast—to my colleague Jim Millikan, who proved to be more resourceful than I had thought."

Millikan did not raise his glass. He considered this for a moment.

What the hell. In the past he had not received due credit for some of his finer accomplishments. And in the game that he and Aziz were playing, it was useful for Aziz to think that this was all Millikan's doing. He raised his glass and drained it.

They carefully prepared and savored their slices of black bread with butter, onions, pieces of egg, and caviar. Millikan proposed a toast. "To our continued association, Tariq, despite this unfortunate problem between our two countries."

A half hour later the caviar was gone, the vodka drained, and lunch well under way. Millikan had ordered the same menu as he had in March, as an unspoken symbol of the underlying continuity in the relationship between him and Aziz. He could not help noticing that Aziz ate quickly and seemed impatient for each course to arrive. In light of the new information, he had much work ahead of him.

"Something has come up," Millikan announced, "and I am afraid that I must rudely cut this meeting short."

Aziz was visibly relieved and wasted no time getting up. In almost no time they were standing by the side entrance waiting for the Iraqi limousine to pull up.

"There is truly nothing we can do, is there?" Millikan asked, looking at Aziz.

"No, my friend, and I do regard you as my friend. As we have both discovered in the past year, we diplomats really have little control over events." He paused and mused, "You know, when I was young I always thought that being able to define events meant that you had gained partial control. But I think that maybe Tolstoy had it right. That the Napoleons and great men are no more important in determining history than the most humble soldier in the front lines."

"I refuse to believe that," Millikan shot back.

"Yes, *mon vieux,* I know. And that is why I'm going home to put on a military uniform and you are going—as I hear it—back to the university."

"You and I both know that we will be back. We will have another day."

Tariq Aziz leaned back, looked at Millikan, and chuckled. "Of course we will."

Within moments he was gone, talking on his cell phone. Dellinger fell in beside Millikan as he strolled out into the Place de la Concorde.

"She was right," Millikan said.

"Pardon me?"

"Betsy Vandeventer. She had it exactly right: the Iraqi strategy was to use biological weapons to force Israel into the war, thus destroying the coalition. Very clever strategy. Very nice analysis on Ms. Vandeventer's part."

Dellinger seemed stunned and confused. "Would you like me to put a commendation in her file?"

"I'd like you to hire her," Millikan said.

"Hire her?"

"Yes. Now that she has a clearer understanding of how the chain of command works, she'll be an excellent addition to my staff."

Dellinger grinned. "I'll get right on it, sir."

"She despises me," Millikan said, "but she's human. So figure out what she wants, and make her an offer she can't refuse."

fifty-five

JANUARY 1991

JUST GETTING on I-66 and heading west seemed too easy, and Betsy had forgotten how to do anything easy and straightforward. So she took to smaller streets and wandered, keeping the sun generally on her left. She drove through Arlington National Cemetery, got caught in the swirl of traffic around the Pentagon, and ended up blundering southward into the city of Alexandria: first a dangerous-looking border neighborhood, but then into Alexandria proper, with its beautiful curving streets of lovely southern mansions, well-endowed churches, and private schools, all surrounded by nicely tended azaleas and dogwoods that would explode into bloom sometime later, after she had left the city behind.

"You want me to get out the map?" said the man in the passenger seat, a big man in jeans and a flannel shirt, who had been shifting uncomfortably and biting his tongue as Betsy wandered aimlessly around northern Virginia. "We're never going to see Steptoe Butte at this rate."

"What's your hurry?" she said. Both of them had two months' severance pay coming in, and Betsy had just got her security deposit back in full.

Paul Moses leaned his seat back in resignation, reached out with one long arm, and turned on the radio. He began punching the scan button and soon found a news station, which was doing a live phone interview with a reporter in Baghdad. The bombing was going to start any day now.

"What do you think?" he said. "Where should we stay tonight? I was thinking maybe Colonial Williamsburg."

"There's only one landmark I want to reach today," Betsy said, "and there it is."

They were headed west on Duke Street, which turned into the Little River Turnpike. Up ahead of them a tangle of ramps surrounded the approaches to a massive, ten-lane overpass, the beltway that ringed the city and marked—in some sense—the town limits of Washington, D.C. All ten lanes, in both directions, were filled with traffic, and traffic was stalled. Betsy accelerated above twenty miles an hour for the first time all day—although the rented car, burdened with much luggage and pulling a U-Haul trailer, didn't have much zip. As they passed through the shadow of the overpass, she suddenly let out a most un-Betsy-like Indian war whoop. And then they emerged into the bleak January sunlight again.

Stalled motorists on the outer ring of the beltway had the monotony of their morning commute broken by an unusual sight: a westbound car and trailer pulling onto the shoulder of Little River Turnpike just below them, and a couple of heavyset people in comfortable, rumpled clothing jumping out, throwing their arms around each other, and exchanging a long kiss. After a few moments the novelty of this sight wore off, and they turned up their radios to hear the latest report from the Gulf.

fifty-six

FEBRUARY

IT WAS three thirty-seven A.M., and for once Maggie was asleep. She had got to be a pretty good sleeper in the last few months. Clyde was prouder of this fact than anything. Out of all the hundreds of baby books, Clyde, through lengthy reading and scrutiny, had picked out the one that worked.

Clyde was not sleeping. He had hardly slept in three days, since the ground war had been launched and Desiree's unit had gone thundering forward into Iraq. Casualties were light. But earlier today he had seen a report that several members of Desiree's division had been killed when they had hit a mine in their Humvee. They were medics who had been coming to the aid of an armored personnel carrier that had been struck by friendly fire. At least two of the dead medics were female.

As soon as Clyde had heard this report, he had known in his heart that Desiree had been in that Humvee—probably driving it. That would be just like her. He had called the Pentagon hot line for families of servicepeople over and over, but it was always busy. Right now at least a couple of dozen Dhonts were awake around Forks County, hitting the auto redial buttons on their telephones, trying to get through. Clyde had given up and settled into his La-Z-Boy in front of the television, waiting for details to come through on CNN.

So far the Iraqis had not used any nonconventional weapons. Though that shouldn't have surprised Clyde, of all people. They'd been raining Scuds on Israel, but it seemed that Scuds weren't accurate enough to do much damage unless they had chemical or biological warheads. The Israelis were controlling themselves, just barely.

His nose had been itching for two days, and he had just become conscious of it. One of those big baling-wire nose hairs had made contact with the opposite side of his nostril. He went to the bathroom, groping his way in the dim light scattered off the TV tube, and got his rotary nose-hair clipper, then settled down in front of the TV again, turned it on, and began to nuzzle the clipper around, waiting for the satisfying click that it would make when it severed the offending hair.

The buzzing of the trimmer almost drowned out the sound of the telephone. He snatched it up, afraid that it might have been ringing for some time as he'd sat there grinding away. "Hello?"

There was a long pause, during which he could hear only static. Then some sound broke through: a deep, rhythmic whumping that got suddenly loud and then quickly died away. The sound, Clyde realized, of a helicopter passing by at high speed.

"Hello?" he said again.

"Hi, it's me," Desiree said. "Talk loud, baby. My Humvee hit a mine. My ears are still ringing."

"Where are you, honey?" Clyde blurted out before he had time to get choked up.

"Phone booth," Desiree said. "Oh, wow!"

A loud whining and roaring sound came through for a few

moments, then died away. Clyde could hear a lot of people whooping and cheering at the other end. "That was an M-one tank going by!" Desiree said.

"Where's that phone booth, sweetie?"

"Some little crossroads in Iraq."

"You're in Iraq?"

"Yeah. But I gotta go—lots of people are waiting. I just wanted to remind you to take the meat out of the freezer—some of it's about to expire."

"I'll take care of it," Clyde said. "You hurry home now, okay?"

"That's the plan, Clyde," she said. "That's the whole idea."

about the authors

Neal Stephenson is the author of THE SYSTEM OF THE WORLD, THE CONFUSION, QUICKSILVER, CRYPTONOMICON, THE DIAMOND AGE, SNOW CRASH, and other books and articles.

J. Frederick George is a historian and writer living in Paris.

Read on for a preview of

Interface

by

Neal Stephenson

and

J. Frederick George

NEW YORK TIMES BESTSELLING AUTHOR OF *QUICKSILVER*

NEAL STEPHENSON

AND

J. FREDERICK GEORGE

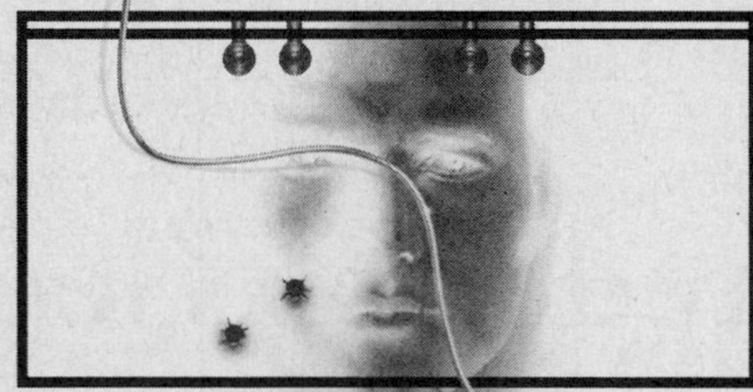

INTERFACE

"A *MANCHURIAN CANDIDATE* FOR THE COMPUTER AGE."
—*SEATTLE WEEKLY*

INTERFACE

On sale now

Springfield Central had started out as your basic Big Old Brick Hospital with a central tower flanked symmetrically by two slightly shorter wings. Half a dozen newer wings, pavilions, sky bridges, and parking ramps had been plugged into it since then, so that looking at it from the window of the chopper, Mary Catherine could see it was the kind of hospital where you spent all your time wandering around lost. The roofs were mostly flat tar and pea-gravel, totally dark at this time of night, though in areas that were perpetually shaded, patches of snow glowed faintly blue under the starlight. But the roof of one of the old, original wings was a patch of high noon in the sea of midnight. It bore a red square with a white Swiss cross, a red letter *H* in the center of the cross, and some white block numerals up in one corner. Well off to the side, new doors—electrically powered slabs of glass—had been cut into the side of the old building's central tower.

It made her uneasy. This wasn't Dad's style. As the governor of one of the biggest states in the union, William A. Cozzano could have lived like a sultan. But he didn't. He drove his own car and he did his own oil changes, lying flat on his back in the driveway of their house in Tuscola in the middle of the winter while frostbitten media crews photographed him in the act.

Zooming around in choppers gave him no thrill. It just reminded him of Vietnam.

He took this to the point where he probably wouldn't have known how to get a chopper if he had needed one.

Which is why he had to have people like Mel, people who knew the extent of his power and how to use it.

"We have limited information," Mel said, on the way down. "He suffered an episode of some kind in his office, shortly after eight o'clock. He is fine and his vital signs are totally stable. They managed to extract him from the statehouse without drawing a whole lot of attention, so if we play this thing right we may be able to get through it without any leaks to the media."

In other circumstances, Mary Catherine might have resented Mel's talk of media leaks at a time like this. But that was his job. And this kind of thing was important to Dad. It was probably the same thing that Dad was worrying about, right now.

If he was awake. If he was still capable of worrying.

"I can't figure out what the problem would be," Mary Catherine said.

"They're thinking stroke," Mel said.

"He's not old enough. He's not fat. Not diabetic. Doesn't smoke. His cholesterol level is through the floor. There's no reason he should have a stroke." Just when she had herself reassured, she remembered the tail end of the message she'd heard on her answering machine, the one that mentioned Sipes. The neurologist. For the first time it occurred to her that the message might have been about her father. She felt a sick panicky impulse, a claustrophobic urge to throw the helicopter door open and jump out.

Mel shrugged. "We could burn up the phone lines getting more info. But it wouldn't help him. And it would just create more potential leaks. So just try to take it easy, because in a few minutes we'll know for sure."

The chopper made an annoyingly gradual soft descent onto the hospital roof. Mary Catherine had a nice view of the capitol dome out her window, but tonight it just looked malevolent, like a sinister antenna rising out of the prairie to pick up emanations from distant sources of power. It was a tall capitol but not a big one. Its smallness always emphasized, to Mary Catherine, its unnatural concentration of influence.

Springfield liked to bill itself as "The City Lincoln Loved." Mel always referred to it as "The City Lincoln Left."

Mel and Mary Catherine had to sit inside for a moment and let the momentum of the rotor spin down a little. When she got the thumbs-up from the pilot, Mary Catherine put her hand on her hair and rolled out onto the white cross in her running shoes. She had thrown a trench coat on over her sweatshirt and jeans, and the buckle whipped back and forth on the end of its belt; the wintry air, traveling at hurricane speed under the rotor blades, had a windchill factor somewhere down around absolute zero. She didn't stop running until she had passed through the wide automatic glass doors and into the quiet warmth of the corridor that led to the central elevator shafts.

Mel was right behind her. An elevator was already up and waiting for them, doors open. It was a wide-mouth, industrial-strength lift big enough to take a gurney and a whole posse of medical personnel. A man was waiting inside, middle-aged, dressed in a white coat thrown over a Bears sweatshirt. This implied that he had been called into the hospital on short notice. It was Dr. Sipes, the neurologist.

She was used to being in hospitals. But suddenly the reality hit her. "Oh, god," she said, and slumped against the elevator's pitiless stainless steel wall.

"What's going on?" Mel said, watching Mary Catherine's reaction, looking at Dr. Sipes through slitted eyes.

"Dr. Sipes," Sipes said.

"Mel Meyer. What's going on?"

"I'm a neurologist," Sipes explained.

Mel looked searchingly at Mary Catherine's face for a moment and figured it out. "Oh. Gotcha."

Sipes's key chain was dangling from a key switch on the control panel. Sipes reached for it.

"Hang on a sec," Mel said. Since he had emerged from the chopper his head had been swinging back and forth like that of a Secret Service agent, checking out the surroundings. "Let's just have a chat before we go down to some lower floor where I assume that things will be in a state of hysteria."

Sipes blinked and smiled thinly, more out of surprise than amusement; he wasn't expecting folksy humor at this stage in the proceedings. "Fair enough. The Governor said that I should be expecting you."

"Oh. So he is talking?"

This was a simple enough question, and the fact that Sipes hesitated before answering told Mary Catherine as much as a CAT scan.

"He's not aphasic, is he?" she asked.

"He is aphasic," Sipes said.

"And in English this means?" Mel said.

"He has some problems speaking."

Mary Catherine put one hand over her face, as if she had a terrible headache, which she didn't. This kept getting worse. Dad really had suffered a stroke. A bad one.

Mel just processed the information unemotionally. "Are these problems things that would be obviously noticeable to a layman?"

"I would say so, yes. He has trouble finding the right words, and sometimes makes words up that don't exist."

"A common phenomenon among politicians," Mel said, "but not for Willy. So he's not going to be doing any interviews anytime soon."

"He's intellectually coherent. He just has trouble putting ideas into words."

"But he told you to expect me."

"He said that a back would be coming."

"A back?"

"Word substitution. Common among aphasics." Sipes looked at Mary Catherine. "I assume that he doesn't have a living grandmother?"

"His grandmothers are dead. Why?"

"He said that his grandmother would be coming too, and that she was a scooter from Daley. Which means Chicago."

"So 'grandmother' means 'daughter' and 'scooter—' "

"He refers to me and all the other physicians as scooters," Sipes said.

"Oy, fuck me," Mel said. "This is gonna be a problem."

Mary Catherine had a certain skill for putting bad things out of her mind so that they would not cloud her judgment. She had been trained that way by her father and had gotten a brutal refresher course during high school, when her mother had fallen ill and died of leukemia. She stood up straight, squared her shoulders, blinked her eyes. "I want to know everything," she said. "This Chinese water torture stuff is going to kill me."

"Very well," Sipes said, and reached for his key chain. The elevator fell.

All that Mary Catherine was doing, really, was coming to the hospital to visit a sick relative. The chairman of the neurology department did not have to guide her personally through the hospital. She was getting this treatment, she knew, because she was the Governor's daughter.

It was one of those weird things that happened to you all the time when you were the daughter of William A. Cozzano. The important thing was not to get used to this kind of treatment, not to expect it. To remember that it could be taken away at any time. If she could make it all the way through her father's political career without ever forgetting this, she'd be okay.

Dad had a private room, on a quiet floor full of private rooms, with an Illinois State Patrolman stationed outside it.

"Frank," Mel said, "how's the knee?"

"Hey, Mel," the trooper said, reached around his body, and shoved the door open.

"Change into civvies, will ya?" Mel said.

When Sipes led Mel and Mary Catherine inside, Dad was

asleep. He looked normal, if somewhat deflated. Sipes had already warned them that the left side of his face was paralyzed, but it did not show any visible sagging, yet.

"Oh, Dad," she said quietly, and her face scrunched up and tears started pouring down her face. Mel turned toward her, as if he'd been expecting this, and opened his arms wide. He was two inches shorter than Mary Catherine. She put her face down into the epaulet of his trench coat and cried. Sipes stood uncertainly, awkwardly, checking his wristwatch once or twice.

She let it go on for a couple of minutes. Then she made it stop. "So much for getting that out of the way," she said, trying to make it into a joke. Mel was gentlemanly enough to grin and chuckle halfheartedly. Sipes kept his face turned away from her.

Mary Catherine was one of those people that everyone naturally liked. People who knew her in med school had tended to assume that she would go into a more touchy-feely specialty like family practice or pediatrics. She had surprised them all by picking neurology instead. Mary Catherine liked to surprise people; it was another habit she had picked up congenitally.

Neurology was a funny specialty. Unlike neurosurgery, which was all drills and saws and bloody knives, neurology was pure detective work. Neurologists learned to observe funny little tics in patients' behavior—things that laymen might never notice—and mentally trace the faulty connections back to the brain. They were good at figuring out what was wrong with people. But usually it was little more than a theoretical exercise, because there was no cure for most neurological problems. Consequently, neurologists tended to be cynical, sardonic, remote, with a penchant for dark humor. Sipes was a classic example, except that he appeared to have no sense of humor at all.

Mary Catherine was trying to make a personal crusade of

bringing more humanity to the profession. But standing by her stricken father's bedside crying her eyes out was not what she'd had in mind.

"Why is he so out of it?" Mel said.

"Stroke is a major shock to the system. His body isn't used to this. Plus, we put him on a number of medications that, taken together, slow him down, make him drowsy. It's good for him to sleep right now."

"Mary Catherine told me that guys of his age, in good shape, shouldn't have strokes."

"That's correct," Sipes said.

"So why did he have one?"

"Usually stroke happens when you are old and the arteries to your brain are narrowed by deposits. This patient's arteries are in good shape. But a big blood clot got loose in his system."

"Damn," Mary Catherine said, "it was the mitral valve prolapse, wasn't it?"

"Probably," Sipes said.

"Whoa, whoa!" Mel said. "What is this? I never heard about this."

"You never heard about it because it's a trivial problem. Most people don't know they have it and don't care."

"What is it?"

Mary Catherine said, "It's a defect in the valve between the atrium and the ventricle on the left side of your heart. Makes a whooshing noise. But it has no effect on performance, which is why Dad was able to join the Marines and play football."

"Okay," Mel said.

"The reason it makes a whooshing noise is that it creates a pattern of turbulent flow inside the heart," Sipes said. "In some cases, this turbulent flow can develop into a sort of stagnant backwater. It's possible for blood clots to form there. That's probably what happened. A clot formed inside the heart, eventually got large enough to be caught up in the normal flow of blood, and shot up his carotid artery into his brain."

"Jesus," Mel said. He sounded almost disgusted that something so prosaic could fell the Governor. "Why didn't this happen to him twenty years ago?"

"Could have," Sipes said. "It's purely a chance thing. A bolt from the blue."

"Could it happen again?"

"Sure. But we're keeping him on blood thinners at the moment, so it can't happen right now."

Mel stood there nodding at Sipes while he said this. Then Mel kept nodding for a minute or so, just staring off into space.

"I have eight hundred million phone calls to make," Mel said. "Let's get down to business. List for me all of the other human beings in the world who know the information that you just gave me. And I don't want him being wheeled around this hospital for everyone to look at. He stays in this room until we make further arrangements. Okay?"

"Okay, I'll pass that along to the others—"

"Don't bother, I'll do it," Mel said.

It was like the old days in Tuscola, when a hot, portentous afternoon would suddenly turn dark and purple and the air would be torn by tornado sirens and the police cars would cruise up and down the streets warning everyone to take cover. Dad was always there, guiding the kids and the dogs down into the tornado cellar, checking to see that the barbecue and lawn chairs and garbage can lids were stowed away, telling them funny stories while the cellar door above their heads pocked from the impacts of baseball-sized hailstones. Now, something even worse was happening. And Dad was sleeping through it.

And Mom wasn't around anymore. And there was her

brother James. But he was just her brother. James wasn't any stronger than she was. Probably less so. Mary Catherine was in charge of the Cozzano family.

Sipes and Mary Catherine ended up in a dark, quiet room in front of a high-powered Calyx computer system with two huge monitors, one color and one black-and-white. It was a system for viewing medical imagery of all kinds—X-rays, CAT scans, and everything else. This hospital had had them for several years already. The hospital where Mary Catherine worked probably wouldn't get one until sometime in the next decade. Mary Catherine had used them before, so as soon as Dr. Sipes set her up with access privileges, she was able to get started.

After a while, Mel somehow tracked her down and sat next to her without saying anything. Something about the darkness of the room made people hush.

Mary Catherine used a trackball and a set of menus and control windows to open up a large color window on the screen. "They put his head in a magnet and baloney-sliced his brain," she said.

"Come again?" Mel said. It was funny to see him nonplussed.

"Did a series of CAT scans. Had the computer integrate them into a three-dimensional model of Dad's melon, which makes it a lot easier to visualize which parts of his brain got gorked out."

A brain materialized in the window on the computer screen, three-dimensional, rendered in shades of gray.

"Is this the way doctors talk?" Mel said, fascinated.

"Yes," Mary Catherine said, "when lawyers aren't around, that is. Let me change the palette; we can use a false-color scheme to highlight the bad parts," she said, whipping down another menu.

The brain suddenly bloomed with color. Most of it was

now in shades of red and pink, fading down toward white, but small portions of it showed up blue. “When lawyers and family members are present,” Mary Catherine said, “we say that the blue parts were damaged by the stroke and have a slim chance of ever recovering their normal function.”

“And amongst medical colleagues?”

“We say that those parts of the brain are toast. Croaked. Kaput. Not coming back.”

“I see,” Mel said.

“Been taking a stroll down memory lane,” Mary Catherine said. “Check this out.” She played with the menus for a moment and another window opened up, a huge one filling most of the black-and-white screen. It was a chest X-ray. “See that?” she said, tracing a crooked rib with her fingertip.

“Bears-Packers, 1972,” Mel said. “I remember when they carried him off the field. I lost a thousand bucks on that fucking game.”

Mary Catherine laughed. “Serves you right,” she said. She closed the window with the chest X-ray. Then she used the trackball to rotate the image of the brain back and forth in different ways to reveal selected areas. “This stroked area accounts for the paralysis and this small one here is responsible for his aphasia. In the old days we had to figure this stuff out just by talking to the patient and watching the way he moved.”

“I detect from your tone of voice that you think this is all basically superficial crap,” Mel said.

Mary Catherine just turned toward him and smiled a little bit.

“I like video games too,” Mel said, “but let’s talk seriously for a moment here.”

“Dad’s mixed dominant, which is good,” Mary Catherine said.

“Meaning?”

"He does some things with his right hand and others with his left. Neither side of the brain predominates. People like that recover better from strokes."

Mel raised his eyebrows. "That's good news."

"Recovery from this kind of insult is extremely hard to predict. Most people hardly get better at all. Some recover quite well. We may see changes over the course of the next couple of weeks that will tell us which way he's going to go."

"A couple of weeks," Mel said. He was clearly relieved to have a specific number, a time frame to deal with. "You got it."

"Guess what?" Mel said to the Cozzanos the morning after the stroke. It was six A.M. None of them had slept except for the Governor, who was under the influence of various drugs. James Cozzano had arrived shortly after midnight, driving his Miata in from South Bend, Indiana, where he was a graduate student in the political science department. He and Mary Catherine had spent the whole night sitting around in the Executive Mansion, which was nice, but not exactly home. Mary Catherine had tried to sleep in bed and been unable to. She had put on her clothes, sat down in a chair to talk to James, and fallen dead asleep for four hours. James just watched TV. Mel had spent the same time elsewhere, on the telephone, waking people up.

Now they were all together in the same room. The Governor's eyes were open, but he wasn't saying much. When he tried to talk, the wrong words came out, and he got angry.

"What?" Mary Catherine finally said.

Mel looked William A. Cozzano in the eye. "You're running for president."

Cozzano rolled his eyes. "You swebber putter," he said.

Mary Catherine gave Mel a wary, knowing look, and waited for an explanation.

James got flustered. "Are you crazy? This is no time for him to be launching a campaign. Why haven't I heard about this?"

His father was watching him out of the corner of his eye. "Don't squelch," he said, "it's a million fudd. Goddamn it!"

"I spent the whole night putting together a campaign committee," Mel said.

"You lie," Cozzano said.

"Okay," Mel admitted, "I put together a campaign committee a long time ago, just in case you changed your mind and decided to run. All I did last night was wake them up and piss them off."

"What's the scam here?" Mary Catherine said.

Mel sucked his teeth and looked at Mary Catherine indulgently. "You know, 'scam' is just a Yiddishized pronunciation of 'scheme'—a much nobler word meaning 'plan.' So let's not be invidious. Let's call it a plan instead."

"Mel," Mary Catherine said, "what's the scam?"

Cozzano and Mel looked soberly at each other and then cracked up.

"If you turn on that TV in a couple of hours," Mel said, "you will see the Governor's press secretary releasing a statement, which I wrote on my laptop in the lobby of this hospital and faxed to him an hour ago. In a nutshell, what it says is this: in the light of the extremely serious and, in the Governor's view, irresponsible statements made by the President last night, the Governor has decided to take another look at the idea of running for president—because clearly the country has gone adrift and needs new leadership. So he has cleared his appointment calendar for the next two weeks and is going to closet himself in Tuscola, with his advisers, and formulate a plan to throw his hat into the ring."

"So all the media will go to Tuscola," James said.

"I would guess so," Mel said.

"But Dad's not in Tuscola."

Mel shrugged as if this were a minor annoyance. "Sipes

says he's transportable. We'll use the chopper. More private and presidential as hell."

Cozzano chuckled. "Good backing," he said. "We'll go to the buckyball."

"What's the point?" James said. He actually shouted it. Suddenly he had become upset. "Dad's had a stroke. Can't you see that? He's sick. How long do you think you can hide it?"

"A couple of weeks," Mel said.

"Why bother?" James said. "Is there any reason for all this subterfuge? Or are you just doing it for the thrill of playing the game?"

"People my age get their thrills by having good bowel movements, not by playing games," Mel said. "I'm doing it because we don't yet know the full extent of the damage. We don't know how much Willy is going to recover in the next couple of weeks."

"But sooner or later..."

"Sooner or later, we'll have to come out and say he's had a stroke," Mel said, "and then the presidential bid is stillborn. But it's better to have a nice little planned stroke at home, while trying to lead the country, than a big ugly surprising one while you're picking your nose in the statehouse, don't you think?"

"I don't know," James said, shrugging. "Is it?"

Mel swiveled his head around to look directly at James. His face bore an expression of surprise. He was able to mask his emotions before they developed into disappointment or contempt.

Everyone had always assumed that James would one day develop from a bright boy into a wise man, but it hadn't happened yet. Like many sons of great and powerful men, he was still trapped in a larval stage. If he hadn't been the son of the Governor, he probably would have developed into one of those small-town letter-of-the-law types that Mel found so tiresome.

But he was the son of the Governor. Mel accepted that. He didn't say what was on his mind: *James, don't be a sap.*

"James," Mary Catherine said, speaking so quietly that she could barely be heard across the room, "don't be a sap."

James turned and gave Mary Catherine the helpless, angry look of a little brother who has just had his cowlick pulled by his big sister.

Mel and the Governor locked eyes across the bedspread.

"Hut one!" Cozzano said.